F
C
T
1

The Bellerose
Bargain

By Robyn Carr

Chelynne
The Blue Falcon
The Bellerose Bargain

ROBYN CARR

The Bellerose Bargain

Little, Brown and Company
Boston   Toronto

FIRST EDITION

Library of Congress Cataloging in Publication Data

Carr, Robyn.
　The Bellerose bargain.

　I. Title.
PS3553.A76334B4　　813'.54　　82–145
ISBN 0–316–12973–9　　　　　AACR2

*For Mary Tondorf-Dick, editor and friend, who makes
writing more than a craft.*

BP
Designed by Dale Cotton

*Published simultaneously in Canada
by Little, Brown & Company (Canada) Limited*

PRINTED IN THE UNITED STATES OF AMERICA

The Bellerose
Bargain

one

She did not actually stand taller than other women, but her bearing made her seem of larger stature. Her rich brown hair flounced around her shoulders, and one stray curl teased her cheek. Her eyes were a gray blue. The looks that generally drew the eyes of men were of another style — blue-eyed blonds with full, round figures. This maid was slender of form and had long, delicate fingers. She could not have exceeded seventeen years, yet she held her chin high and her eyes were as self-possessed as those of a woman with power.

Rodney Prentiss cast his eyes back into his tankard of ale and commanded his thoughts to cease. He had stopped at the inn for food and drink. Wenching was for the young bucks, and only old men who were soured with drink chased the maids.

He was traveling on business that had gone badly, and he was plagued with worrying about how he would explain his failure to the young lord who had commissioned him. On such a night he would have chosen a quiet country inn, and when he rode upon this one it looked to be such a place, but when he entered the common room he found he was mistaken. The seamen from a ship recently put in to Southampton were crowding the room, and locals eager for a raucous evening formed a quick but temporary camaraderie with those sailors. Ale was gulped, prostitutes were plentiful, and those who weren't singing were fighting.

He turned his head in search of the maid he had been watching. Not far behind him she leaned against the stone wall near the hearth, listening to a young minstrel sing. The young man's song was directed toward a harlot, who was attempting to prevent another man from nibbling her neck. Eyes half closed, the maid moved her head with the beat of the tune. It was plain her mind was miles away, her world being only the song and not the sights, sounds, and smells of this bawdy room. Rodney noted that a large, swollen bruise marred her upper arm, and with a frown he wondered if its cause could be the reason she allowed her thoughts to wander.

The innkeeper, a squat and balding man of over fifty years, walked through the crowd as far as Rodney's table. He was red in the face and was wiping his hands on a towel. He paused there for a moment and scowled at the serving maid. "Alice!" he barked.

Rodney saw the lass flinch at the sound of her name. She looked at the angry keeper, but did not cower in fear. She seemed to gather some internal mettle as she walked calmly over to him. They moved toward each other in the direction of the kegs and kitchen. As he scolded her for laziness, she did not change her manner. Rodney watched, fascinated. She moved through the room with an easy pace and a somewhat regal demeanor. Her clothes were merely poorly fitted rags, obviously worse in quality than those the other wenches wore, and her hands were rough and red, yet she held herself proudly. She did not seem right in the role of tavern wench. But then, he could not think what her role should be. She did not seem the wifely sort, he thought, for there seemed nothing soft and compliant about her. Were she a lad she would make a good seaman or guard. Something of determination was settled over her features. He noted strength and, strangely, an isolation. Though she was surrounded by people, she seemed all alone within herself.

He shrugged and drank deeply. A plate was virtually dropped before him, the gravy from the stew slopping over the sides and onto the table. A few greasy drips fell to the leg of his breeches and he scowled at the serving maid. It was the best pair of pants he owned.

"Ye'll pay the keeper, sir," the maid who served him said. "There ain't no rooms, but yer horse is stabled. Arman' says ye can bed with 'im if ye've a mind to."

Rodney nodded absently but looked at the wench closely. This copper-haired lass seemed to fit the tavern scene. She was not what one would call pretty except after too much ale, but neither was she hard to look at. She was short and full-breasted and her curls bounced around her face. Her lips were red and her smile quick and eager. He had observed her earlier and found that she did not put any unnecessary distance between herself and the patrons.

" 'At's a fine coat, milord," she said, her voice something of a whine.

"A gift from a beautiful woman," Rodney confided.

"Ye're from London, milord?" she asked. He nodded once and waited for her next question. "King's messenger?"

Rodney shook his head. "Not exactly, mistress."

" 'Ave you seen 'im, then? The king? I seen 'im. It weren't close, but . . ."

"You've been to London?"

"For the coronation. I was a bit young then, but me pop was sellin' 'is pots an' bowls. Mostly to the nobles, ye see. Me pop's pots an' bowls is the best in the south of England."

Rodney smiled at the maid and wondered about her age.

She was probably not over seventeen years either, but seemed older. Perhaps it was the atmosphere in the inn that aged her.

"Ye're noble, milord?"

He smiled at her. The question was strange only in that it hadn't come sooner. If one's clothing was substantial, one's hat plumed, and one's horse decent, there was always that possibility. Children and young women questioned men who traveled, and tried to find a way to determine their wealth. Many would trade the country life for the excitement of the city. And this lively lass would gladly trade what she had for a pocketful of lies.

"Gert!" the innkeeper shouted from behind her.

"I 'ear ye," she bellowed back, turning away from Rodney.

It was then that he was clear on the difference between the maids. This one called Gert was tough, at least as tough and quick with her retort as her employer. In this setting the lass who poured and served the ale had to be tolerant of the smells and foul language. The other maid, Alice, seemed to detest her chore. She had not smiled or tried to talk to the patrons. And a serving wench had to be resistant to the groping hands — or even appreciative of them. The bouncy little tart called Gert seemed to consider the grabbing and fondling a compliment of sorts.

He realized that he was musing about these maids because it was easier than thinking of the business that had failed. Charlotte Bellamy had failed him, when all should have gone well.

Fergus Bellamy had not been a rich man, but he had possessed a large estate west of London. He was baron to fertile lands and hard-working people. When his daughter, Charlotte, was born, his wife died. For a while, Fergus could manage with a wet nurse and a small staff of servants within the manor to care for the child. But then Cromwell had usurped all of England, sending nobles fleeing in every direction. Fergus went where one might expect a loyal Royalist to go, in the same direction that Charles, then the Prince of Wales, had gone. Charlotte was sent to Fergus's sister, a woman much older and not as well-to-do as Fergus, while Fergus fought by the side of young Charles throughout the years preceding the Restoration.

After eleven years of exile, Charles returned to England to claim the throne. Fergus did not immediately rush to his daughter's side, though he saw her once or twice after the coronation. He had petitioned the king to restore his family lands, but Charles was so besieged with petitions that he had not acted on Fergus's quickly. It was not a question of Lord Bellamy's loyalty, but rather a question of how much a king could do to restore the country to what it once was. Fergus Bellamy died before he could see his lands restored or take his daughter there to live.

There was another young man who had fought loyally beside Charles for many years, as had his family. He, like Lord Bellamy, had not come from much wealth, but his family had been loyal to the king's cause throughout years of exile. Geoffrey Seavers fled with his family into exile and was his family's only survivor after years of bleak living conditions and war. He should be granted some reward for his great sacrifices, but again, King Charles could only do so much. The offer of land in Virginia was common and easily made by the king. Seavers, like many other young men, found that offer desirable, but insufficient.

"I should like to travel to the Colonies and set up a post of sorts," he told the king. "But my dream is to serve Your Majesty on the sea, privateering and trading. I've proven myself capable."

Unfortunately, if that was truly his desire, he would have to wait, for with no lands in England, Seavers could hardly buy ships or pay ship hands.

Charles was not a man to be unappreciative of Seavers's skills. Seavers had a reputation for being an outstanding warrior and, since returning to England, had a captaincy under

Prince Rupert, who reported him to be an exceptional navigator. Certainly with the right financing the young noble could earn money for the crown, not to mention further protection for the English government. This time Charles's work was made simpler. When Charlotte Bellamy was left as the heiress to her father's lands, which were finally ready to be returned to the family, Seavers had one ship and was eager to be financed for more: a fleet. Charlotte would be a ward of the king; Seavers would be returning regularly to ask for money. A man as quick and logical as King Charles saw the answer clearly. He offered Seavers a bride, one Charlotte Bellamy, complete with estate and considerably more money than Seavers had asked for.

Rodney, a family friend for many years, had been Geoffrey's manservant and adviser since the Restoration. He had been sent to the manor where Charlotte had been raised to take her to London for her wedding. He sent word ahead and then rode quickly to the place. When Rodney arrived she was gone; she had fled from her marriage proposal.

The manor where she had been raised was in poor repair. The nearest village was not much to speak of either. When Rodney questioned the villagers on the whereabouts of Lady Charlotte, they first looked at him queerly and then repeated the title uncertainly. "Lady?" they questioned. And the only information they had was that she had left the country with a man who claimed to be a noble from London. The nobleman, of course, had not given his name. If he were truly of noble class, Rodney would be surprised. And the description the aunt and village people had given of the lass could fit any country maid within miles. No one else but Fergus Bellamy could be expected to recognize her — and he was dead.

As Rodney looked around the common room of the Ivy Vine, he could well imagine the fate of Charlotte Bellamy. Tavern wenches, farm girls, and maids, from every conceivable country station, would have illusions of dukes and earls riding through their villages, being stung by the pure loveliness of the country lasses, and taking them out of their humdrum lives to an existence of wealth and leisure in the fabulous London. But in the city they would be abandoned and left to find their way home — if they lived that long. Home for Charlotte would be uncertain, should the debonair man she fled with turn out to be a liar. Her ancient aunt was near death and lay uncaring in her dilapidated manor house. There were no servants to tend her save a washwoman, who visited only weekly, and the money they lived on must have been nearly nothing.

Rodney stuffed the last of his stew into his mouth, and it was in his mind to find a soft pile of hay in the stable for the night. Geoffrey was a good man, and it pained Rodney greatly to think of yet another disappointment for the lad. He had lost not only his mother and father, but three brothers and a sister as well, some from the wars, some from the chaos of the Restoration. To lose this fortune might tip the cart, and cause the young man to despair.

He stood wearily, shaking his head at his own thoughts. As he moved in the direction of the keeper, the lass called Alice bumped into him as she rushed by.

"Your pardon, sir," she said quietly, moving past him.

He watched her take her tray filled with pitchers of ale and mugs through the room. She was a pleasant change from the typical country girl, and he momentarily wished he were a younger man.

Rodney stood before the keeper and shook a few coins from his purse into his hand. At the sound of bellowing and laughing in the rear of the room, he turned to see a man, sodden with liquor, holding the struggling Alice clear of the floor. She kicked and squealed, her actions anything but playful. One pitcher of ale was rescued by a companion of her attacker, but the other fell from her tray and soaked her skirt and the floor.

"Will you be stopping that?" Rodney asked the keeper.

"Let 'em ruffle her feathers a mite," he returned bitterly. "Miss High and Mighty."

Rodney returned the coins to his leather purse and fastened it again to his belt. His eyes narrowed and crinkled at the corners as he fit the innkeeper with a glare. He turned and slowly threaded his way through the men, harlots, and wenches to get to the rear of the room. Alice's furious struggle seemed only to heighten the men's enjoyment of holding her.

By the time Rodney reached the scene, Alice was being held firmly on a seated man's lap, one of his arms holding her firmly and the other arm lifting a tankard of ale to his lips. Alice let her elbow fly, taking the man who held her in the chin, upsetting his ale, and blasting his head backward. He half rose with an angry growl and stood face-to-face with Rodney.

Rodney was not young, but he was large and could cast an angry stare that had frozen opponents earlier in his life. He shifted and raised his shoulders slightly, drawing his hands together as if he were more than ready for a fight. He lowered his voice and looked directly into the man's eyes. "Let the lass go," he said evenly. The table became silent for a moment. "Now," he advised.

Rodney was prepared to follow his words with action, for that was the way of such a place. But the man who held Alice shrugged and unlocked his hold. The maid straightened herself, brushed at her wet skirt, and walked rather casually away from the scene, never looking back or around. Rodney followed her with his gaze. Even under these conditions she seemed not to be stressed. It was a trait that he had admired in many men but had seen in very few women.

The evening had cooled and the sky was clear. Alicia stood near the corner of the inn and took a deep breath, trying silently to count the stars. She knew she would be allowed a few moments to collect herself, but no more. And she would not press the issue. It was easier to return to the common room on her own mettle than to have Armand come to the door and shout for her. It would be "Alice." He refused to use her real name, as did the other tavern wenches. "Alicia," she would correct them, but it had a lilt to it that these folk and others before them could not adjust themselves to.

She thought of the young minstrel's song, the words having long ago fled her mind, but the melody with her still. She plucked at the leaves of a bush and hummed softly. For a moment there was no loud inn, no groping hands, and no dismal future. Alicia had the night, the cool, fresh air, and a simple tune.

A low chuckle behind her caused her to turn abruptly. In the dimness of the night she could not see his face clearly, but she knew the man who stood there. She felt immediately safe in his company, for it had been only moments since he had come to her aid.

"I followed you here to help you dry your tears," he said with some mirth in his voice.

"And why would I cry?" she asked.

"Many a maid would be reduced to tears by such careless handling," he said.

She laughed at his concern. "Here? Do you think that is the first time?"

"My name is Rodney Prentiss, miss. I watched you in the common room."

"I am Alicia, sir. And I thank you for your help."

"Alicia?" he asked, puzzled. "That is not what the innkeeper called you."

"Of course not. Armand does not use my given name."

"And why?"

"Because it would please me," she said with a shrug. "I can recall few who would use it. Alice is more common."

"But it is important to you . . ."

"Aye."

He cocked a brow and looked at her closely. Her depth immediately intrigued him. "Tell me why it matters so much, fair Alicia."

"It is the only thing my parents gave me that I still possess. I was separated from them early in my youth and have no memory of either father or mother. But the woman who cared for me, God rest her, gave only my name to the family who took me in. I choose to keep it for that reason."

"And your family?"

"I assume they are dead."

"A sad assumption. Whom, then, do you call family? The innkeeper?"

"Armand?" she laughed. "Oh, no, the family I live with only sends me to him in the summer. I serve the food and ale and do other chores. The money is badly needed. Every summer since I was twelve."

"The family you live with?"

"It is the fourth family I have lived with. Or, fifth, perhaps, since certainly I lived with my parents for a time. I find it hard to call anyone family. . . ."

"You don't belong here," he said flatly.

She laughed lightly. "I have never belonged anywhere. But someday I will find my place. There must be a place right for me."

"I have been looking for such a place myself," Rodney said, laughing also. "Have you been to London?"

Her face seemed to close at the question. A frown replaced the prettiness of her smile. It was as if the question had been taken as an insult rather than common curiosity. "That is not the place," she said.

Rodney wondered at her reaction and then reached up to scratch the back of his neck. Just the thought of the periwig that was the fashion now made his skin itch all the more. "A wise decision, lass. I am loath to return myself."

"You live there?" she asked.

"At the moment. I don't imagine I'll stay."

"You are a nobleman?"

"I?" he laughed. "Sailor, soldier, friend, servant. Aye, I am more servant and friend now, since fighting is over for me. Servant to a young noble without enough money." He shook his head. "But he's a good lad and strong. It's only that things don't go his way."

"Well, my sympathy to you and your young lord, sir," she said primly. "For myself, I'm due in the common room before Armand comes for me with a stick."

"You can't possibly want to go back in there."

"And where, then?"

"You aren't frightened?"

"Of them?" she laughed. "Armand won't let them hurt me. A broken wench does not serve well and ofttimes flees with the first man asking."

"You speak so well," he told her. "For a country lass who was raised with simple folk, you speak as one educated."

"I can read," she boasted. "Though there is little to read," she added with a shrug. "And I can cipher a bit. The first family to house me were educated. He was a teacher once. But I was not to stay with them long. They had too many to feed." She seemed to be saddened for a moment and then brightened again as she looked at him. "I thank you. I've worked hard to remember."

"It shows that you're bright."

Her smile was sweet and genuine. It occurred to Rodney that she had not smiled inside the inn. That missing softness had made her seem somewhat plain, but when she smiled she was lovely and fresh looking, the only real country beauty he had seen.

"Thank you again, sir," she said, lifting her skirts and moving past him to the doors of the inn.

Rodney sighed his pleasure. Meeting Alicia was the one happy part of his discouraging journey. He found her unexpectedly refreshing, and so capable of managing her life.

When he found his stabled horse, he fondly stroked the

animal's neck and thought of the women whose paths he had briefly crossed. There was Charlotte, whose flight indicated she did not want a husband selected by the king. And the aging aunt, whose barely audible words from her bed drew pain in Rodney's heart. She spoke of years of imprisonment with a spoiled and ungrateful child. And there was Alicia, a bright and commanding lass of fair looks, whose lot it would be to live out her years in a simple cottage with nothing out of the ordinary taking place in her life.

When his head finally rested on the soft hay, the weariness from his traveling and his disappointments seemed to hit him all at once and even sleep came with difficulty. Just before his eyes closed he had a peculiar sensation. The women he had encountered, even though he never actually met Charlotte at all, were miles removed from one another. Yet in his mind their lives seemed to touch in a strange and unsettling way.

In a room that had been converted from a loft, there were two straw pallets, one small window, a coffer, and some scattered bundles of clothing. A dried bunch of mayflowers with ribbon streamers hung from a nail on a high beam; they had died as rapidly as the dream they came with.

Four serving girls lay on the two mattresses, their bodies in neat parallel lines to conserve the tiny space. The night was done; dawn was just breaking. The noises in the common room below them were low and infrequent, and the four maids lay exhausted in this insignificant room.

Alicia's eyes were not closed. She looked upward at the weathered beams. A squeaking she had heard before caused her eyes to shift and she saw the long, tubular tail of a rodent as he skittered across a beam. Life was predictable here. There were mice in the attic, chores in the morning, and little to look forward to.

There was a memory that was vague enough to be a dream, something stuck away in the back of her mind, that had given her comfort in the moments before sleep since she was a very little girl. It had to do with a red cloak. She remembered the fabric as being smooth and delicate, and the inside was deliciously warm. And when wearing the cloak she was always happy because she was always going someplace.

Associated with this wrap was a woman's face. She was ivory-skinned and gentle, with tender eyes and fair hair. The eyes were troubled and tinged with tears. She wore a velvet dress that was so soft that Alicia could almost feel the fabric against her cheek when she thought about it. And with the feeling against her cheek, she could remember gentle stroking of her hair and the sound of the woman's voice, and her words singed her memory. *"You will be so beautiful. I can barely wait to see . . ."*

"But I am not beautiful," Alicia thought with a sense of guilt and betrayal. "She would have been very disappointed."

Alicia liked to imagine that this woman was her mother, but reality insisted that it might not be so. Other women had cared for her during her early years and had been kind and dear, though there was no kinship.

She remembered stone walls, high and gray, and floors the same color. There were trees, but she was not sure if she ran among them and hid behind them or simply viewed them from a coach or window. Nothing she had seen since resembled this memory.

The clearest image was of a boy. Freckles spotted his nose and cheeks, and his eyes were the same pale blue as the woman's. He wore a white linen shirt and a brown wool jacket that was richly sewn, but he took care of it poorly — she could remember extra stitches and patches. And his hands were clumsy. He, too, was associated with the red cloak because he often buttoned it around her neck as he scolded her. "Now, be still, you mouse. Be still or I'll swat you good." Even now the remembrance gave her chills because there was love in his scolding, laughter in his voice.

She had not played with him, or if she had, she had no memory of it. Once, he had clutched her fiercely, let her go abruptly, and, in his laughing, scolding voice, pushed her away. "Now, get where you're going, and be good or else."

And that was all there was. Next was the Thatchers' farm. He was a teacher and his wife had babies and did laundry for the lady in the manor house. They told her what little she knew about herself. She had been found near their humble home with a woman who told them only Alicia's name; no family name or location of her birth. The woman had suffered through some dreadful accident and was injured. Her head was cut and her arm broken. Days must have preceded the Thatchers' discovering this poor woman and her young charge, for not long after they were taken in and cared for, the woman died. All Alicia had to remind her of that day was the dress she had been wearing; a white slip made from fine linen and sewn with some lace. It must have been the finest thing she owned, but it was soiled and torn badly from some unexplained journey and accident. There was no red cloak.

The Thatchers were good to her and adopted her as their own. Mr. Thatcher taught her to read and cipher when she was just a tot and encouraged her to call him Papa. But the children became too many and the cost of feeding them too much. Alicia was sent to friends in another shire who promised to care for her.

Her stay there was short since the cost of caring for her soon stretched their compassion to its limits. They passed her along to a couple traveling through their shire who had lost their daughter and yearned for a replacement. For two years Alicia struggled to fill that empty space for them, but their constant criticisms proved she had failed.

Osmond and Mae, the fourth couple she came to live with, were at least honest about their needs. The miller and his wife had four sons. The sons would work the mill and fields, but alas there was no one to help poor Mae with the household. And so they took Alicia in. And while Mae was kind enough, it was clear Alicia's position was to work for her food and lodging.

Osmond's brother, Armand, owned the Ivy Vine and needed help during the demanding summer months. Alicia was sent, and the money she earned helped Osmond manage his mill and feed his sons. She would return one more summer, and then would be either married to a local or told to leave and make her own way.

Marriage to a country farmer did not frighten her, for she thought she needed little to be content in life. Just once she would like to be chosen rather than thrust on someone who had to take care of her, but there was little chance of that, especially in marriage. With no family, no dowry, and, from her point of view, nothing much in the way of looks, she imagined it would not be easy to find herself a husband. And he, whoever this husband would be, would likely beat her soundly when he discovered she was not a virgin.

She had learned her lesson painfully and would never again wager any dreams on the lust of a man. It was the summer before that she learned love could be quick and ruinous. Young Lord Perry, a nobleman recently returned to England, rode through their village on his way to London. His rich clothes, fine horse, and full purse had the immediate attention of all the maids, but his eyes were turned toward Alicia.

"Do the young men tell you that you're beautiful?" he asked her.

She was taken aback by his question. He had only just arrived at the inn and the other maids were angry that Armand selected Alicia to serve his drinks and food. "No," she answered truthfully, her voice soft and surprised.

He caught her hand and his eyes were laughing. "They've missed you altogether then," he said. "They must fear marriage or love. You are beautiful."

His words lunged at her heart, for not only had she never

been considered pretty, she was not well liked. Minor kindnesses shown to her were rare, and the people she lived and worked with scorned her, calling her prideful and smug. She had very little to boast — clothes that were worn and did not fit, no time to primp, and no possessions to enhance her appearance — so this man's flirtations sent her fleeing him without even a thank you.

She was forced to return to bring his food and keep his mug filled, and in a very short time he learned her name and she his; and something that caused her heart to flutter and her mind almost to disfunction had happened between them.

When his meal was finished he caught her hand again. "Will you sit with me for a minute?" he asked her.

"Armand will beat me if I sit," she confided. "I am here to work, not to talk to our patrons."

"Beat you?" Lord Perry shuddered. "God's bones, I'd kill any man that laid a hand to you. You're too beautiful to strike."

Alicia only shrugged. Everyone was beaten for unfinished tasks and laziness, not to mention stealing or defiling a person or property.

"When will you talk to me?" he asked her. "I'd like to walk with you and know you better."

"I cannot leave,"she insisted. "I told you, I'm here to work."

"Tomorrow, then?"

"In the morning after the cleaning I have my own time, but not much."

"It's settled then," he announced. "I'll stay an extra night, and in the morning you can show me the country."

She remembered this stroll down country roads and through the woods as being an enchanted time, and remembered only recently that they had talked only about him. She did not blame him for that, since what could interest him about a country girl? When he told her he intended to stay yet another night so that he could be with her again, she was frozen with joy and lost a second night's sleep.

Visions of passion and love consumed her. She hurried through her morning chores and stole away from the inn before anyone had time to ask her where she was bound. She worried only briefly about being caught and punished. This once, lolling about the countryside with Lord Perry was more important than fearing Armand's beatings.

"Will you stay in the country and raise up a band of brats for a farmer?" he asked.

"I imagine I will — when you've gone."

"Ah." He laughed. "Then you think I'll leave you? You're so foolish, Alicia, if you can't see that I love you. You've hurt me badly now."

She stopped abruptly and looked up at him. "You love me?"

"I think I knew at once that I loved you. And what am I to do now that you don't believe me?"

"Good Lord, I can't imagine," she returned in absolute seriousness.

He laughed at her and bent to kiss her forehead. "I shall have to take you to London with me and make you my mistress."

"London, now!" she shrieked. "And to be your whore?"

His eyes were serious and his smile had faded. "Perhaps you'd be little else in all reality — but you don't know the city, love. Whores have come to a place of distinction there. The king's mistress all but rules the country."

"Culver Perry," she said in an admonishing tone, "if you love me so much, why would you wish for me to be a mistress to any man? I'm good enough to be a wife."

"It's truth, Alicia, you are indeed. But I am not able to marry whom I please. I must marry a nobleman's daughter for lands to add to my family's estate; otherwise they would disown me and not give me so much as an acre to farm. But they would not keep me from having you. I could dress you in silk, give you a fine home and all my love. Your comforts would be many."

"I would be alone. What comfort is that?"

"Refuse if you must, but whatever your answer, I have pledged to marry the earl's daughter and there's no help for it. I'll leave you without a fight. But I'd rather take you with me and find some joy in my life. . . ."

Rich clothes and a fine home intrigued her, and being chosen, regardless of what she was chosen to be, made her heart leap with joy. She had a sense of belonging, rather than feeling thrust on a man and left as his burden for a lifetime.

She answered his pleading on a summer afternoon. On a bed of grass near a stream, the promise was sealed with her virtue and he gave his word to take her away in the morning. He seemed well pleased to discover her virginity; it did not occur to her that he was surprised. She was advised to carry on with her chores as if nothing out of the ordinary had happened, and before the breakfast meal was served they would be on their way. She had followed his instructions carefully.

Alicia did not bemoan her lost virtue at first, because it had in fact been the first time she had been held and loved. There had not been so much as a kiss from a farmer's son in her life. And Culver Perry's strong, lean body against her own sent her common sense sailing off on a breeze. Then there was the pain of the consummation and it was over. He did not hold her once the thing was done but quickly donned his breeches and barked at her to get on her feet.

"Up, wench, we can't be in the woods all day."

Alicia had obeyed instantly, something she had been carefully taught to do since early childhood. Though she was longing for him to touch her again, she bit back her request and sought to charm him with her obedience. "Do you love me, Lord Perry?" she asked him.

He covered her breast with his hand, and his bewitching

blue eyes glittered. "You're a good wench," he replied. For at least a day she thought her question had been answered.

At morning's first light she awoke and gathered her clothing. She dressed quickly and crept quietly to his room, but heard no answer to her light tapping. Inside she found his empty bed and no evidence that he had ever been there. She went to the common room but there was no one about. With a sickening pain growing in her stomach, she sought out the stable. She found only the stable boy doing his early morning chores.

"Has Lord Perry taken his horse out on some errand?" she asked in a stunned but controlled voice.

"Ay, 'e 'as at that," the boy replied. "An' 'is things with 'im. Without a shilling for Armand. Bloke's run out on the fare," he said. He continued to rake hay into one of the stalls.

"Perhaps he'll return to pay."

The boy laughed heartily at that. "It's never a poor man what robs Armand, but those what says they're rich. Bloody nobles."

Alicia felt her heart plummet every time she remembered that morning. For a time she actually believed he would return for her and that some noble duty she could not understand had forced him to leave her against his will. But the truth was clear to her before she could delude herself for very long. He had lied so that he could lay with her, and had never intended to fulfill his oaths and promises. She, thankfully, had not confided her troubles to anyone and had not conceived. But something dear had been lost — and it was a great deal more than her maidenhead. She had felt something special and strong; she had trusted and been betrayed. The hope that he would return and attempt to repair the damage done was hard to dispel. But then seldom does a thief return to a debt. More than one debt waited at the Ivy Vine.

Looking back on all this as she waited for sleep to come,

Alicia wondered, despairingly, if there would ever be so much as one person in her lifetime who would not use her to his own end.

She turned toward the attic wall and tried to command her thoughts to return to the freckled boy and red cloak. A tear clung to her dark lashes. She strained to think of the gray stone walls and the woman with the pale eyes. Where are they? she wondered. Who are they, and why can't I remember them — find them? Was it something lived in another life, another time? Her concentration broke, and in the dark, swirling corners of her mind, she could feel and see the walls of the room, and the man's touch was real, the coarseness of his black hair and the finely honed muscles of his back and arms . . . his lips and hot breath . . . the love words and promises that filled her ears and soul as she was brought to exhilarating heights of passion. . . .

And in her sleep she released a jagged sob.

two

*T*he morning was good to Alicia. She found the sight of the late morning sun enlivening, and though the mess in the common room from the night before did not please her, it did please her to be the one to clear away the remains and spread fresh herbs over the floor. By the time she had been awake for an hour, she had done more than her share of chores and could wrest away free time to be alone.

Those who stayed the night in the inn did not usually rise with the sun. When Alicia entered the common room again later and saw Rodney sitting alone at one of the long tables, she smiled to herself. He was almost grotesquely large and his face was square and stern. His hair, a combination of thinning rust and gray, was pulled back and caught with a ribbon at the nape of his neck. She had seen the night before that when he stood and cast his grimmest look on other men, they were cowed by his size and expression. But she had already found that in this hulking man's heart there was a generous softness.

"Good morning, sir," she said brightly.

His head came up and he looked across the table at her.

His kindly eyes glowed as he looked at her. "A good morning to you, Alicia. I confess I did not allow you would rise so early, what with the lateness of the hour when you are finally given rest."

"I like the morning," she told him. "And you would like food; am I right?"

"In large supply, if you please. And milk, if there is any."

She returned to him only moments later with a porridge of eggs and pork and set the steaming plate before him. Bread and honey already sat on the table, and Rodney tore off a piece of bread to aid his knife in getting the food to his mouth.

"I'll bring your milk," she promised, turning from him.

"And bring yourself. I should dearly like to look at you while I eat."

"But sir . . ." she protested.

"Come now, Alicia, I've paid more than a fair price for my lodging here, and a pile of hay at that. Surely you'll be excused from your chores to sit with me for a while."

She thought for a moment and realized quickly that she'd like that. When she returned to his table, she brought two cups of milk and took a place across from him.

"Do you return to London now?" she asked.

"That was my plan when I went to sleep last night, but I've risen with a new one. My mission was to deliver a bride to my young lordly friend, but when I went to her home, she had fled. No one can clearly say why, only that she is gone and chooses something other than the king's marriage plans for her.

"I hate to bring the disappointing news to Lord Seavers, and so I've chosen to go back to the village where she lived and see if I can uncover tracks that will lead me to her."

"How sad. Did Lord Seavers love her very much?"

"He loved her not at all," Rodney said, shoveling more food into his mouth. He chewed and swallowed quickly. "The woman, Charlotte Bellamy, was left behind in England when her father followed Charles into exile. She'd been all but ignored ever since. About a year ago, her father died in London just before his family estate was restored to his name. Since that time Charlotte Bellamy has been pursued by every poor but able-bodied man at court, and she's not had a chance to look over the lot."

"And your master? He's poor?"

"In a manner. He's rich in name and achievements for the crown, but all that his family held claim to was lost in the wars. He was the lucky man to win the hand of the lady."

Alicia sighed and sipped from her cup. Oh, to be she! Sought after by one and all. No matter that it was her money they all wanted: she was part of the bargain too.

"Could she be in love with another?"

"That's possible, but not likely," he laughed. "Those I spoke with while I was looking for her said she was quite round, mean as a wild boar, and cruel to everyone who crossed her path. I think Charles heard the same tales and was grateful that her dowager aunt would not allow her to take up residence in Whitehall while the king chose her husband for her."

"The palace. Gor, I'd love to see it."

"You'd have to go to London for that," Rodney teased, remembering her displeasure with that idea from the night before.

"Maybe I shall, sir. When it suits me."

"Who allows you such freedom, lass?"

"Nary a soul, milord. But for chores I have to do, I'm let clean alone." She shrugged, feigning lack of concern for something she actually worried over a great deal. "I'm to be given my own life shortly. I will either marry some poor begging farmer or be cast off to make my own way."

"How is that?"

"I've no dowry and no family. No one will ask for me, and Osmond, the miller who's given me a place to sleep for the last few years, won't support a grown woman much longer."

"Grown woman," Rodney sighed. "You're barely weaned."

Alicia straightened her back indignantly. "I've reached seventeen since this summer, I'll have you know."

"Aye, I would've guessed. Still a child. What would you do on your own?"

"A hundred things, if I can find honest work. I'm good with money, sir, and it don't cost me much to keep alive."

Rodney scooped up the last of his porridge and downed the cup of milk.

"I'll be looking for honest labor if I don't hasten to my task and find the bride."

"Why doesn't he fetch his own bride, your young lord? Could be she thinks he can't care much and is hiding till he comes after her himself."

Rodney chuckled at her idea. "First, lass, there's another love that needs his time. His most recent acquisition, a ship, bought on a borrowed dowry, is being completed. Second, it wouldn't do for the groom to fetch the bride. It's not proper. And last, I feel sure that young Geoffrey is more frightened of what he might have doomed himself to than Charlotte Bellamy is."

Alicia rose and shook her apron. "Well, I wish you luck, sir, but if she's mean and ugly as you say, your master may be pleased you couldn't find her."

"He won't be pleased if he has to sell his ship."

Alicia turned suddenly back. A thought struck her. "First I thought how grand to have all the men want to marry her. Now I think how sad for her. She's got a problem black as mine. No one will choose her, only use her."

Rodney nodded his head in silent agreement. "The court's a lonely place, lass. There's not an honest drop of love to be found there."

"Then that makes me the lucky one, eh, sir? No chance that should happen to me."

Rodney dug into the purse that hung at his belt. He pulled out a gold coin and tossed it to her. "There," he said, as she caught it. "For listening to my troubles."

She smiled brightly and clutched at the coin. "But sir, I don't deserve . . ."

"It's not for your poor farmer, should you choose that course. Buy something special for yourself, Alicia." He walked past her toward the door. "I wager you deserved it long ago."

Holding fast to her gold piece, she watched Rodney leave from the door of the inn. He turned once to wave in her direction. It lifted her heart considerably to hold the coin. She had sacrificed nothing and was generously rewarded for being herself. A simple treasure turned rich.

It was Monday morning, Alicia's favorite time of the week, when the maids could take their baths after the laundry was done. This was the only time the girls could spend selfishly without repercussions. If one of them stole away for an afternoon walk, to be alone away from the others or to be with some lover just passing through, Armand would scream until he was blue. The innkeeper, it seemed, needed to know their whereabouts every minute of every day — except for that short time when they bathed.

Alicia was the last to bathe. This was decided by a conspiracy of the other girls to remind her of her place as a person unattached to any other by family or any other bond. She was detached from the other maids because she was reluctant to share secrets. And her manner of behaving as though she were unaffected by the way they ostracized her led them to accuse her of being haughty and conceited.

Finally her turn came in the tub, and though the water was cooled and soiled from the clothes and other bodies, she lowered herself into it gratefully. At least at Osmond's mill she was allowed to bathe more often than here at the inn.

Now Alicia rested the back of her head on the rim of the tub and closed her eyes. Behind her eyes there was much to behold, as visions of suitors, gowns, and riches danced around in her head. It was not noise, but rather silence that caused her eyes to open.

All three maids stood a fair distance from the tub with their hands behind their backs, smiling devilishly. She frowned and looked around the stable further. Though she had done her part to hold a linen towel and fresh clothing for each previous bather, her towel and clothes were draped over a stall a great distance from the tub.

"Gert!" she snapped. "I'll freeze to ice getting my clothes."

Gert simply smiled and walked out the stable door with an air of superiority. Mary and Sarah, less nonchalant, quickly dashed out, covering their mouths as they giggled.

"Mary! Sarah!" Alicia shouted. "My clothes!" But the stable door banged shut and only a horse turned to look in her direction. "Ooooo you sneaky sluts," Alicia hissed, picking up the soap and sponge and scrubbing her arms and shoulders almost violently.

Outside, the threesome stood with their ears to the door, gaining much amusement from Alicia's muffled curses and the sound of splashing water. "She'll 'ave 'erself a proper stroll to 'er shift," Gert said, hands on hips and backside swinging to imitate a sashay.

"Beg pardon, ladies," a man's voice said from behind.

All three turned as one to behold a hulking man who held his hat in his hand over his chest.

"I'm looking about for a serving maid named Alicia. Have any of you seen her?"

Gert's eyes twinkled. "As luck'd 'ave it, gov'na, she's just inside." She indicated the stable with her hand and then, picking up her skirt, dashed toward the inn, two giggling maids close on her heels.

Rodney watched them flee and then, with a shrug, turned and opened the stable door. He stared for a moment at the shimmering nakedness of Alicia as she stood in the tub, just preparing to step out. Her scream was loud and piercing and her arms flailed as she attempted to cover herself.

Rodney slammed the door the moment he realized his error. He glared in the direction of the inn where the silly maids peeked out around the corner of the building. He turned back to the door and spoke to the furious girl within.

"Alicia, forgive me. I had no idea . . ." He stopped and tried to stifle a chuckle. Girls' games were things he could barely remember from his youth. "Beg pardon, Alicia. I was cruelly misled."

He thought briefly of confiding to the lass behind the door that he'd seen a naked woman or two in his time and she was certainly the most beautiful, but he discarded that idea immediately. He scratched his chin at the thought, though, and knew that it was true. Ah, Alicia had a most alluring form. Geoffrey's anger with him would likely be short-lived.

"Alicia, dear child, I've come to see you and I am indeed chagrined that I have so rudely . . ."

The door snapped open and in the doorway stood Alicia, her hair dripping and her feet bare. She had hastily donned her blouse and skirt over a wet body and the fire in her eyes caused Rodney to step back a pace and give her a moment to cool her ire. Alicia looked past him to see if she could spot the culprits who had caused her embarrassment. Rodney caught the action.

"Aye, they are responsible," he confirmed.

"I'll find a way to reckon with them," Alicia muttered savagely.

Rodney bowed elaborately before her. "I can offer you a chance. If you'll hear my story."

Alicia folded her arms over her chest and leaned back on the stable door to listen. Her lips were formed into a pout and her eyes were narrow. She did not seem open to his proposition, so intense was her anger and mortification.

"Do you recall my chore of finding and delivering Lord Seavers's bride?" Alicia nodded. "Upon my return to her aunt's humble manor I found that the old woman had died. 'Twas no surprise to me, for I found her quite near her final breath the last time I saw her. But she is in fact gone, and Charlotte, blast the wench, is certainly gone too. No one could say whom she fled with or how she left. I've done my work, lass. I searched every small village near her home in the last month and not a soul saw her pass."

Alicia sighed and kicked a bare foot in the dirt. "How does this have anything to do with me?"

"A moment, maid Alicia. Charlotte Bellamy came from noble stock, that is true. And her inheritance is not rich by some standards, but to those of us who are not accustomed to wealth, it is enough to untangle the heaviest debts. Her upbringing, however, was far different from that of most courtly dames. Her aunt, a pinched and angry spinster living on a modest pension from her father, raised the girl without a thought to what would be acceptable behavior for a noblewoman. I doubt she could read or cipher as well as you."

"And how are you sure I can?" she asked him. "No one else believes I'm able."

Rodney chuckled tolerantly, for it was obvious that Alicia did not assume any connection between herself and this ghostly Charlotte. But the connection came clear to Rodney when he declared, in total frustration at the thought of delivering yet another disappointment to Geoffrey, that he wished he could take a lass as lovely and eager as Alicia to him instead.

And why not?

"What I propose, Alicia, is that you return to London with me under the name of Charlotte Bellamy."

Alicia's eyes grew round and disbelieving. "Are you mad? I don't even know the wench."

"Nor does anyone else," Rodney explained. "No one in London has ever seen her. There are those villagers who could describe her, but they would not venture to London — and for that matter would not be taken seriously if they did. There is no way to prove you are *not* Charlotte Bellamy."

"I should ride from here with you, using a name not even my own, to marry some jackanape young nobleman, who's spoiled and hungering for more money? On my death, sir, and no sooner. Let the brat find his own bride. I'll not be tossed about another time."

"The *brat* is a man of over thirty years and has fought in His Majesty's service for twelve years. He has good reputation and a name that opens many doors. And Alicia, he is most handsome."

"Then it'll trouble him little to find a willing wench."

Rodney released the purse at his belt and shook some coins into his hand. He counted them and returned most of them to the pouch. He stretched the purse out to her. "For a hundred pounds?"

"A hundred pounds?" she returned. It was more money than she'd earn in her lifetime. Indeed, it was a lifetime's worth of working hanging before her eyes. "A hundred pounds to marry the man? He must be a terrible wretch."

"A hundred pounds to come with me to London. I won't deceive his lordship. We'll tell him forthrightly that Charlotte is gone and can't be found, but you can stand in her stead without a soul noticing the exchange." He shrugged. "As I see it, the two of you can come up with a plan for Charlotte to die eventually, thus freeing Geoffrey to play with his fortune and ladies. That leaves you to do as you

please, as long as you're willing to do it out of England —
or at least out of London. Once dead, you can't be seen
strolling about the 'Change."

"And if your young lord will have none of this?" she
asked.

"Then take your gold and start afresh anywhere you
please."

"I thought you were poor? If the man has a hundred
pounds to throw away he can't be suffering much."

"Poverty is relative to the spender, lass. Geoffrey is too
poor to buy a fleet of ships, but not too poor to dress finely
and gamble large sums. He's too poor to buy a country estate
that encompasses villages, but rich enough to own a house
in town and land in the Colonies. He could keep you well
and comfortable if he goes along with my plan. Indeed, with
Charlotte's inheritance, he'll have his boats, and you'll have
some nice trinkets to wear to the Duke's Theatre."

Alicia mulled over what he had said. She looked at the
bag of gold, shook it a little, and looked up at him with suspicious eyes.

"And this young lord," she started: "is he very mean?"

"He is stubborn, but his lack of fortune indicates that
he's generous to a fault. And the ladies that have wanted
him have been many."

She pursed her lips and the petulance was evident again.
Rodney liked looking at the play of emotions on her face.
He appreciated her natural beauty more every time he saw
her, though her clothing and hairstyle did little to enhance
her. The freckles of youth were fading and a freshly scrubbed
ivory with a light blush was quickly replacing them. With
the proper clothing and hairstyle she could easily be the
toast of London. "You'll find that Geoffrey is desirable and
honest, and I doubt he would ever hurt a woman. I will be
near at hand to make sure he does not harm you in any
way."

"If we're found out in this, could we be imprisoned?" she asked.

"At the very least," Rodney answered with a smile. He guessed that he might succeed in appealing directly to her adventurous heart. The predictability of life here in the country, marriage to a poor farmer or life as a scullery, held nothing for Alicia's spirit. And London as a place to be abandoned or discarded did not appeal to her, but London with a hundred pounds, a title, and a rich man to look after her for a time was not a bad bargain for a tavern wench.

She calculated quickly in her mind: if she was careful with her spending, the money would last a considerable length of time; time enough at least, if she was clever, to eventually marry a man of means and secure a decent life for herself. A life that promised more than endless hardship and struggle.

She smiled wryly. "And what do I say to Armand?"

"Tell him you're going to London to dance with the king."

"And if he is angry?"

"Shake your gold in his face and laugh. You have the power now, lass. Not he."

The trust she was tempted to feel for him was now complete. When she was prepared to run away with Culver Perry he had cautioned her to silence. It was later that she realized it was not Armand's anger he worried over, but the fact that he intended to sneak away from his boarding debt and could not do so in the light of day. If he was truly going to take her away, what difference if Armand was angry? Who would follow Lord Perry to claim her back? She belonged to no one but herself and had, for so many years, been unwanted baggage everywhere she went.

"When do you choose to leave?" she asked.

"Two horses stand ready now. We won't ride through the night, but I reason we should choose another inn." He coughed and cleared his throat, trying to keep the corners of his mouth straight. "We may not be welcomed here."

Alicia's smile was bright and the excitement glittered in her eyes. She held up the bag again. "Mine to keep, no matter what? You swear?"

"On my word. Gather your things quickly. Lord Seavers will be more than a little anxious."

Alicia retrieved her shoes from the stable and then dashed toward the inn, her bare feet padding quickly and her bag of coin clutched tightly in her fist. She disappeared into the inn and Rodney walked leisurely to where the horses waited. He was standing there when the door to the inn opened and Alicia reappeared. Just behind her was the red-faced innkeeper, and behind him Rodney could partially make out the printed skirts and curls of the three maids with whom Alicia served. Rodney's round belly shook lightly as he tried to control an outright laugh. Certainly they had run straightaway to Armand when they noticed Alicia making her bundle of belongings to cart away.

"Ungrateful wench," Armand blustered. "I told meself this haughty wench'd be the first t'run. Aye, ye'll fly away on the high road wit' the first willin' man."

The corners of Alicia's mouth were turned up slightly as she struggled to keep up a serene front. She met eyes with Rodney and found some of her gaiety reflected there, and that was her permission to smile. Her eyes danced in delight and her face virtually sparkled. She handed the small bundle to Rodney and he worked at fastening it on the back of the horse that would carry her.

"Did ye consider that ye'll get nothin' of what's been promised, girl?" Armand questioned. "Here at least ye earn a civil wage and have a decent place t'lay yer head."

Alicia turned to him. Her eyes were cool and distant as she considered the squat, gluttonous man. "A pile of hay with the rats?" she asked him. "And wage? That sum you send to your brother, Osmond — I earn nothing here. That generous man doesn't yield me enough from what I've earned to buy a bolt of cloth. If not for Mae and her old clothes, I'd be naked."

"It costs t'feed a houseful such as Osmond's got hisself, but he at least cares fer what he's got. Ye'll find no strong arm on the road t'London, miss. Ye'll be back and ye won't find me a forgivin' man."

At this, Rodney turned toward Armand and his eyes were angry. "I've seen the protection offered this lass under your care. You'd happily see her mauled and used to sell one more cup of ale. Aye, she'd fare better in the hands of thieves."

Armand's face got redder and he was about to shout something more to Rodney, but the latter turned to help Alicia mount the horse. Behind Armand he could hear Gert's shrill whine. "Cartin' 'er proper arse off t'court, says she." Her cackle was piercingly clear. "An' goin' 't snatch 'erself a foin laird . . ."

Armand turned abruptly and slapped the wench, turning her cackle into a squeal, but shutting her mouth quickly thereafter.

"Ye've a debt t'me, Miss Queenie. I was t'have a wench to'serve through the harvest time. Don't show yer face here fer honest work when he's used ye and tossed ye aside fer the next. Aye, I knew ye'd run with the first more'n a year ago when that noble bastard played his way with ye and left without even payin' his lodgin'."

Alicia had barely settled herself on the saddle when that statement came, and her eyes shot to Armand's face. Her mouth formed a thin, furious line as she glared at him, and from behind him she could hear the smothered giggles of the other maids.

"Ye thought I didn't see what ye were thinkin'?" He let go a loud and sarcastic laugh. "I saw the way ye flaunted yerself under his nose and reckon ye hoped he'd take ye out of the shire. Mark me, lass, nobles don't give a tavern wench

35

more time than it takes t'spoil 'em and leave 'em by the roadside."

Alicia's eyes bore down on him and she instinctively refused to show how it hurt to have her foolishness thrown in her face. She had had years of practice in pretending not to feel the insensitive jeers thrown at her. The remark seemed not to penetrate Rodney's tough hide, for he turned to Armand calmly but sternly.

"Aye, there's a debt, man, and I trust it's to this one who's served so well through the summer. What do you owe her for her work?"

"Owe *her*?" he questioned.

"Aye. Her 'honest wage.' Your brother won't need it for her keeping, now that she won't be going back to him."

Alicia blinked her eyes closed, hard, fighting tears. Earlier, as she had bundled her few belongings together, she had felt such optimism and hope, but then Culver Perry had been a long way from her memory. It wasn't until Armand taunted her with her folly that she felt fear and apprehension rise within her at the thought of leaving the village with Rodney. It was possible that this man was no more trustworthy than Perry. But it was too late to take the easy way. She would go. And if being left by the roadside was to be her lot, she'd drag herself up and manage from there.

Armand opened his mouth to protest Rodney's request for payment and Alicia held up her hand to stop him. "No debt, Armand," she said. "Put what I've earned toward what you lost from the nobleman who didn't pay you."

Rodney looked at her with a slight frown. He detected the sadness her features had taken on. He shrugged and climbed onto his horse. "Then let's be away. Enough on the matter."

Rodney took the reins from Alicia's mount in his free hand and, clicking his teeth and spurring his horse, they started away.

"Ye'll not find the promises answered, miss," Armand shouted at her back.

Alicia blinked back tears. There had seldom been promises made to her. Only once, and Armand was right. She'd been a fool. She'd been used and cast away. The first illusion that this would be a dream come true was struck from her mind, and she willed herself to strength. She would take her chance in any case, and hope there was something more down the road for her than a straw-filled attic and regular beatings. Something more than being abused and unwanted.

"Ease your mind, maid Alicia," Rodney said. "You're deserving of a great deal more than the innkeeper would have you believe."

She smiled her thanks for his soothing words, but inwardly she feared that this journey would be only the beginning of her challenges. With a sigh, she took her own reins from him and edged her mount along beside him.

three

*A*licia stood by the window of the inn and looked down into the dark street. The only lights came from the windows of the tavern below her and what little brightness broke through from behind covered windows along the street.

A loud crash and subsequent shouting from below caused her to jump in surprise. She rubbed her upper arms with her hands and shivered, both cold and a little frightened.

The journey to London had been uneventful, Rodney carefully looking after her food and lodging along the way, and she traveling easily and silently beside him. They had rested the night before in a lodging house (it could not be called an inn by any measure, though rooms were rented to travelers) and left early in the morning before having anything to eat. They arrived in London early in the day. Rodney had explained that they were near enough to the city to have traveled the entire distance without stopping for the night, but he preferred to have her come into the city with him in the light of day.

She could plainly see his wisdom in this now. The inn near the wharf where he had placed her was grim enough in the morning. Had she been brought through the wild common room below her in the evening, she would have been too frightened to stay in this room alone. The Ivy Vine had its share of drinking and trouble, but from the sounds in the common room tonight, it was nothing compared to a London ordinary.

In this meager setting, there was the nearest thing to a raised bed, one leg missing and replaced with a rough chunk of wood. It wobbled piteously as she tested it, but it still outshone any sleeping arrangements she had ever had. There was one stool, and a table used for eating as well as holding a washbasin and pitcher and one stubby candle. A dirty and ragged towel had been tossed into the empty basin. Not even water and linens had been delivered to her since Rodney left her hours earlier.

Alicia moved to the table and plucked at the filthy rag that was meant to dry her whenever she was lucky enough to wash. "Your great wealth comforts me, milord," she whispered to the empty room.

A cracked mirror without a frame hung from a nail on the wall. She looked into it but found the image lacking. It was a poor reflection and she couldn't plainly see the dirt on her face, the snarls in her hair, or the disappointment in her eyes. Squinting, she looked closer, touching the long and tangled hair that dropped around her shoulders. Combs, she thought despairingly. A brush and combs would greatly improve her looks, but in the inn, she had shared the one brush with three other maids, and, though she might have made away with it without being caught, it had not occurred to her to take it. She wished now that she possessed a more devious and self-serving mind.

"He won't find much to delight himself in," she told the mirror quietly. "When he spies this wench he'll likely keep running for days."

Anticipation had churned within Alicia's stomach several hours earlier when Rodney delivered her to the inn. He had a meal served to her and explained that his young lord's ship was nearby, and he would hasten to him with the news. "I expect to be bringing Lord Seavers here to meet you very soon." Anxiety drove hunger away and she was unable to eat her meal. Regret grated like rough wood inside her stomach now, for she was very hungry and dinner time was long past. Rodney had been gone for hours.

The crashing of glass below her caused her to start again, and this time she rushed to the bed to grab hold of the leather pouch that held her coins. There was no place within the practically naked room to hide her fortune, and she greatly feared being robbed and molested while alone in this place. She tucked the pouch into her modest bundle of clothing and gave it a pat, finding the hiding place unreasonably insecure.

"Fine bargain, this," she hissed. "A hundred pounds'll fit me fine when I'm dead and thrown in the street."

The sound of a key in the lock seemed to show her fear was justified, and she turned toward that portal with immediate terror. The clicking, turning, picking, and grinding seemed to go on forever, while Alicia grabbed her small bundle and backed away from the door to the farthest corner of the room. When the door finally opened, she saw the reason for the lengthy fumbling. The man opening the door could barely stand and leaned against the frame for badly needed support. Her first thought flashed: If he can't walk he can't kill me.

"Aha," the man said when he saw her.

She retreated even more, her back flush with the wall.

"Ah, yes," he said, his voice slushy. "Aye, you're the one. And you'll make a mighty fine bedmate once we get you washed."

He entered and turned to the door to close it and began fumbling with the lock from the inside. Alicia's heart was pounding mercilessly as she watched him attempt to lock them both into the room. The process of locking the door took nearly as long as unlocking it had, and when he turned to face her again he had a smile of victory on his face. He looked not vicious but boyish with his grin. She could not help noticing that he was dressed richly and was quite handsome. Mother of God, she silently prayed, do I give thanks that it is not a wretch who attacks and robs me?

He dropped the key into his jacket pocket and looked her up and down, his grin vanishing and a look of consternation replacing it. "God's bones, where're you from and who, heaven help me, is your seamstress?"

Alicia's brows drew together in a frown. Then that vanished into a look of astonishment as she wondered how she could be insulted in all her terror.

"Even your shoes..." he started, halting abruptly to belch loudly. He swallowed and regained his attempt at dignity. "Even your shoes are worthless. Did you slop hogs 'til coming here?"

"Leave me alone," she said quietly. "Go away."

"But I can't, maid," he said, spreading his arms in mock helplessness. "Destiny brings us together and we are meant ...umm...destined to be together...you and I." He shook his head, and his sandy-colored hair flopped about like a thatched roof in a rainstorm. "We need each other."

"Don't touch me," she begged, her bundle clutched tightly to her chest as she attempted to melt into the wall.

"Don't worry." he grimaced. "God's blood, would I be here if touching you before you're bathed were part of the bargain? It's hard enough to look at you."

"Then go," she insisted loudly.

But he paid her no attention. He looked her over again, and again he grimaced. Why, she wondered, had he troubled to break into her room if he found her so unappetizing? Could he possibly be aware of her large sum? She wondered if she had worn her concern with keeping the money safe while eating in the common room, thereby alerting some thief that within the carefully guarded bundle of clothing there was wealth.

And this, she quickly reasoned, was a successful thief, for he was well dressed and articulate. He certainly robbed and assaulted only rich people.

"You'll never do," he said, slurring his words and shaking his head again. "Can't see how you'll manage. No breeding whatever, dressed to slop hogs and empty chamber pots, and without washing for a score of years."

Alicia stood a bit taller. She was not in dire need of bathing, though it had been a couple of days. She did not think she smelled. But then she remembered the odor that greeted her when she entered the room and reasoned that he mistook the stench for her. God above, she thought, do I worry over insults made against me by a thief?

He took a few steps toward her, wobbling dangerously, and she edged along the wall to a safer distance. Catching her was going to be his problem, she could see that. His vision was not clear and his movements were disadvantaged by too much liquor. "Come here, wench," he barked.

Alicia made a quick jump to the other side of the room, not having much difficulty dodging him. Again he advanced, the boyish grin adorning his face, and his eyes barely slits in his effort to clear his vision. Alicia stood still, waiting for him to get closer before quickly jumping away again. But this time the sodden assailant surprised her, making one deft and speedy lunge. He caught her in arms that were strong but clumsy with drink, and caused her to drop her bundle as she struggled to get away.

"Be still, wench," he ordered. "Hold still so I can look at you. I can't see you clearly."

"Let go of me," she said through clenched teeth.

"Now, how can we get to know each other if you fight me?" He let out a laugh that was not much more than a drunken giggle. "If you hold still I'll let go," he offered.

She stopped struggling suddenly and stood very still, nodding her head slightly. His arms dropped to his sides and she skittered out of his grasp immediately, dashing around the table, keeping that as the barrier between them.

"Damn wench," he muttered, turning to locate his disappearing catch. "Don't make me mad," he cautioned, his smile gone.

"Don't touch me or I'll scream," she warned.

"Scream," he told her. "And I'm sure the castle guard will come running. Now, behave or I'll have to beat you."

As he delivered this last threat he stumbled slightly, and she saw that he was so sodden that with luck she could outwit him; and though she feared his strength, she was more angry than afraid.

"Lay one hand to me and I'll kill you."

"Kill me, eh? I see my work's cut out. I'll have to throw up your skirts and give your wretched arse a swat or two. Now come here."

"Never. Get out."

"Bitch," he mumbled, rubbing his neck and looking as though he'd forgotten what he entered her room for. "All right, have it your way . . . with a fight." He stumbled toward her and grasped the opposite side of the table, his eyes fully open now and fixing her with a glittering stare filled with determination. Alicia's mouth opened slightly and once again she feared him. As he made to pull the table from between them, she grabbed the pitcher by the handle, and with no aforethought, she reached over the short distance between them and laid her mightiest blow to his head. The crockery gave way immediately, crashing to the floor all about him.

His eyes grew round and shocked just before they gently closed and he melted to the floor in a heap. She stared at him for a moment, the porcelain handle of the pitcher still in her hand. He did not look dead, but her first thought was that she had killed him. Yet he seemed peacefully asleep. A look of contentment seemed to rest over his eyes and mouth like a warm blanket.

Ah, he was handsome.

A handsome fool, her anger answered loudly. He deserved at least a bump on the head for what he might have done.

There was a knock at the door and Alicia's eyes jumped from the sleeping form on the floor to the sound. Her heart began to pound again, for now she was caught. Though she did not think herself outside the law in defending herself, she did not expect to be let out of blame easily once it was discovered that she had wounded this man. His clothes were rich. It was possible he was someone of importance, robbing and assaulting women for sport rather than for sustenance.

Again the knocking. Her eyes began to sting with tears. There was no one to help her. "Blast that oaf," she muttered under her breath. "He promised to be near."

And at the moment Rodney crossed her mind, she heard his voice outside her door. "Alicia?" he questioned from the other side.

She went to the door quickly and attempted to open it, grateful enough for tears to spill just because of his presence outside. She wiggled the latch once before she remembered that her attacker had the key safely tucked in his pocket. She went back to the unconscious man and frantically searched through his coat until she retrieved the key. It took her, in all her sobriety, nearly as long to unlock the door as it had taken her intruder. She actually frowned over her shoulder at the man, for it had not occurred to her that it was a difficult lock. She assumed his clumsy drunkenness made the task time-consuming.

Rodney carried a tray of food which he nearly dropped when he saw the body on the floor. Alicia watched him as she saw, for the first time, a look of absolute fear on his face.

"What has happened?" he whispered as he studied the broken crockery and the injured man.

"He's likely as dead of drink as of the blow," Alicia said quite easily. "He meant to do his worst."

Rodney shook his head and kicked the door closed before setting the tray on the table. He knelt by the injured man and opened his eyes and checked his head.

"I thought I'd die of hunger, and now you've brought something, I doubt I can eat it. Where have you been?"

"In the common room for the most part, explaining you to Lord Seavers. He had a mite to drink, but when I left him, his condition was not this poor."

"I was afraid this man would take my money," Alicia explained, still uncertain what they should be doing about this situation.

"He wouldn't have taken your money, lass. This is the man who gave it to you. Geoffrey Seavers."

"God above," she sighed, dropping heavily to the stool by the table. That explained the insults perfectly. He was appraising her to see how she would fit that part they planned for her to play. And judging by his earlier reaction, she didn't fit the bill. She sighed softly and looked away from the sleeping noble. "I suppose I'll be on the next coach."

"If luck is with us he won't remember clearly," Rodney said, rising. "You say he was fairly drunk?"

"Not fairly, sir. He could barely stand without the wall."

Rodney fought to keep from chuckling aloud. "I don't suppose you could have dropped him so easily were he able to walk."

"Don't be too certain," she said wryly. She nodded toward him. "Is he drunk often?"

"Seldom. I should have expected this. He was ... ah ... upset with the circumstance."

"Then he will have none of me?"

"I think he'll come around to it, lass. He is honest to a

fault, and therein lies his problem. Robbing the crown of an inheritance does not sit well with the man. He's the most loyal man Charles has at the moment."

"You're wrong, sir," she said very quietly. "He did not find me good enough in any way. He said so."

Rodney stood and looked down at her. Her eyes were lowered and looking at Seavers. She studied his face carefully and it tugged just a bit at her heart. She had not liked his behavior, but he was actually more amusing than frightening. Beneath his thick hair the color of sand and wheat, his closed eyes looked peaceful. They sported thick, dark lashes, but she clearly remembered the green color. They had sparkled with excitement, delight, and fury, all within the short span of time she had dodged his arms. And the arms — though clumsy, as they clutched at her they were not cruel or careless but strong and gentle. Aside from the drunkards who had lunged at her when she served at the Ivy Vine, there had been only one other pair of arms to hold her . . . and those had been strong and demanding. Culver Perry was at least as handsome, possibly more so, but there was nothing as boyish and comfortable about his face and body.

This man, she thought, is appealing in many ways. He is handsome and strong. And though he had not been kind or compassionate, neither could she be sure that he was vulgar and mean. Perhaps when he was not swelled with drink he could be tractable . . . even loving.

Her lips curved in a half smile and she felt moisture come to her eyes. What would it be like to have a man like this actually love her?

"Did he hurt you, maid Alicia?" Rodney asked softly.

"No," she whispered. "But 'tis truth that he said he did not want me for his bargain." She looked up into Rodney's kindly eyes as her own were quickly welling with emotion. "He said I wouldn't do at all."

"That was more the ale talking than the man, lass. He's a bit plagued by the circumstances, but he's not one to purposely hurt a woman. Even one he does not like." By the way she lowered her eyes, Rodney could see that she could not easily quell her disappointment. She believed the bargain was no longer being offered. "You had your heart set on a fine home and decent clothes."

Alicia looked up at him again, and for a moment she made no response. As she considered his statement, she remembered that her hundred pounds would certainly buy more in the way of lodging and clothing than she might ever have had as a farmer's wife. That would not be taken from her. But her spirit was drained by yet another rejection. There had been so very many in her short lifetime.

She almost had to laugh at herself. He had stumbled into her room drunk and presumptuous, looking like a criminal, and yet the fact that he found her an unsuitable maid had hurt her. And further recollection made her see that she had not been at all terrified of him but just cautious of his intent. She thought perhaps she had been immediately taken with him. Sometimes she didn't understand herself at all. He was drunk, outrageous, and insensitive. Had she simply liked his face?

A low moan came from the injured man. "Yes," she said to Rodney. "I had great hopes for the riches you promised me."

The manservant frowned slightly. Her answer lacked a convincing tone. He puzzled at her manner. This did not fit the proud image he had of her. In his mind he suspected that Geoffrey had already pinched at the maid's heart, even in his clumsy first impression.

He moved to the groaning man and lowered himself to look at him closely. Over his shoulder he addressed Alicia. "Eat something, lass, and have patience with my cloddish master. The game is not played out yet."

With a sigh, she picked up her utensil and stared into the plate of stew.

"Once you have some decent clothes and the benefit of

grooming, I wager he'll thank us both for this opportunity."

She chewed thoughtfully on a mouthful. Then she swallowed and returned her knife to the table top and looked earnestly to Rodney. Her eyes seemed cleansed of misery and held only rueful acceptance. "I'm a foolish wench, sir. I've long held to a hope that one day I'd meet someone who would look beyond my poor style of dress and lack of legitimate family name — and still find me suitable." She shrugged and picked up her cup of wine. "I suppose I have proved my ignorance in that."

"The game is not played out," he repeated.

In a section of the city not far from where Alicia waited out her bargain, another young woman paced a small rented room atop a clothier's shop. Her agitation was more intense than Alicia's had been, and her furnishings were finer. Although she was a maid alone, she did not flinch at every sound from below. She was preoccupied with her lack of food and drink and her anger was mounting.

The sound of footsteps on the stair colored her face with hopeful anticipation. The unlocked door opened and a sigh of relief escaped her. The tall and handsome man thrust a basket toward her.

A somewhat chubby hand grabbed the basket with eager lust, and without a word, the woman was digging through it, withdrawing bread, meat, cheese, and wine from the inside. She did not labor with the tablecloth and utensils but chewed off a generous bite of cheese and poured herself a full cup of wine from the half-empty bottle. Her gluttonous movements brought a grimace to the man's face.

"It's not an easy task to keep you in food and drink," he sneered.

Though her mouth was full and a bit of wine dribbled to her chin, she did not wait to answer him. "You don't keep me all that well, milord. Hold your complaints or I won't hold my tongue."

"You know what to say to silence me, Charlotte. I wouldn't have guessed you knew such designs."

She laughed and her dark curls bounced with the action. "I'm intent on doing as well as I can for myself. That's all. Lord above, no one else is going to give me anything."

"You stand to gain a great deal this way. Considerably more than you would have in marrying Seavers. It's plain truth to everyone in London that he wants to get his hand into your pot for his ships. You'd be a pauper with a title in six months."

She swallowed more food than would be allowed a normal throat, and a look of disgust came over her face. She did not pause in her feast to answer him, but her expression clearly showed that she would not have been content with such an arrangement.

"I think with a little time on our side we can find a way to reject the king's proposal of marriage for you without offending him badly. For the moment, I fear, he won't be too happy with you. When Seavers's man can't find you, they'll all assume you've fled the betrothal. We'll come up with a better story, and you can escape his wrath and perhaps turn his mind toward another suitor." He paused in his oratory and looked at her. He smirked and shook his head. "Madam? Did you hear me?"

"I hear, Culver. Haven't I already told you that I'd marry you if the king allows?"

"Yes, madam, you did indeed. And I'm counting on you to keep yourself from being swayed by the courtiers. They play a lot of pretty words on attractive young virgins such as you are."

Her eyes narrowed slightly as she studied him. "And you play a pretty word or two, Lord Perry. When you're sure of me I have no doubt your love may suffer just a mite. Just a mite. So I'll take my chance on you till you show me I'm foolish." She smiled, and in her teeth there happened to be slivers of meat that detracted from the smile. "I think it may work out, Lord Perry. Unless you've lied to me."

"Why would I lie? By the time you're at court a day you'll hear from every wagging tongue that Seavers has been hard at work to finance ships. And I? I told you honestly that I need money to back my influence at court, but I've no intention of spending it all — only holding it for the influence it gets. And remember, Charlotte, you can cause me a great deal of trouble by spilling the truth about our alliance, but no less than you'd cause yourself. Charles doesn't *have* to give you your estate."

"I'm not going to spoil the lot, love," she said, her smile quick and still speckled.

"Good. We're of like mind."

"Are you staying here the night?" she asked.

"Much as I'd like to, love, I still have a great deal of business before I rest. And I wouldn't want anyone seeing me with you until you've been able to reject Seavers successfully."

"What business? Another woman?"

He smiled devilishly. "I'm counting on your fortune to help, Charlotte, but there's still quite a lot I can do to improve my lot before we exchange vows." He paused and looked her over, forcing himself to smile. He was not attracted to her, but lying beside her for a brace of years in exchange for a decent amount of money would not pain him much. "I'll either be here once you're asleep or in the morning to bring you something to eat. Remember, don't go out."

"Like yourself, milord, I'll go where I please. I hadn't thought you desperate enough to sell favors. Who're you sleeping with and what's her title?"

Lord Perry frowned. "I didn't say I was sleeping with anyone, Lady Charlotte."

"No, you didn't. And I don't care who you're with, but don't expect to hold me to a different plan. I'll have your promise in writing that my money is my own, and once we're wed and I have the Perry name, we'll each do as we please. And I'll be careful enough to see that my inheritance doesn't disappear into the ocean, but should it please me to go out and stroll about a bit, I'll do so." She bit off another large piece of meat and chewed it greedily. "You don't own me, Culver, nor will you ever. And when you start to act as though you do, I'll tell His Majesty that you've kidnapped and beaten me, and in fear of my life I've followed your orders."

Culver Perry watched her as she settled herself on the only chair in the room to finish her feast. She did not trouble over his comings and goings so long as he kept her in food and visited her bed regularly. His plan for hustling Seavers out of the Bellamy inheritance had been much more appetizing before he had realized that Charlotte was as devious as he.

But there was a bright light in any storm. "At least we understand each other, madam. Let's just be cautious that no other understands us as well."

"Fair enough, milord," she said with a mouthful of food. He smiled at her, turned, and gratefully took his leave of the room.

Alicia came awake at the sound of a moan. She sat up on the bed and took notice of Geoffrey stirring from his sleeping place on the floor. He shook off the cover that had been thrown over him and sat up, rubbing his head. Taking a cautious look around the room, he spied Alicia, still in her clothes, sitting up on the small bed. Rodney had also taken possession of the floor for his sleeping. Seavers had no way of knowing that Alicia would not allow the servant to leave her alone with him. All were clothed and apparently passing Geoffrey's unconscious state as best as could be allowed.

With a pathetic-sounding grunt that spoke loudly of stiffness and ill health, Seavers rose to stand on shaky legs. Gathering strength, with a hand on his belly he headed for the door without looking back. His pace quickened, judging by the sound of his footfalls, as he rushed down the hall and stairs.

"You see," Alicia said, "he's not dead. But I wager he regrets last night."

Rodney struggled to his feet, his problem being age and the hardness of the floor. "I for one am grateful for his malady. He'll blame the drink and not you for the condition of his head."

Rodney walked to the door and on the way dropped the key on the table. "Lock yourself in and I will see to his lordship. I'll see that you're delivered some meager comforts before you have to deal with my young friend another time."

The meal was the first such comfort to arrive at her door. The tired-looking and unkempt maid who served it further depressed Alicia's spirit. She wondered if she could ever endure that way of life again. It was the first time since she was a child that she had been served, rather than having to work from early morning until late at night.

When her meal was finished, she paced the room and expected to be seeing Rodney again, but instead the next knock at the door brought a heavy brass tub and buckets full of hot water. A package arrived soon after: scented soap, large linen towels, a generous sponge, and a brush.

A bath of clean hot water, one of the first she had enjoyed since leaving Osmond's home, eased her mind and body, and later, wrapped in towel, she sat on her stool and brushed her wet hair.

Another knock interrupted her grooming, and she went over to the door. "Who's there?"

"Geoffrey Seavers, madam. May I come in?"

"You'll have to wait, milord. I've only just come out of the bath."

"Stand behind the door then and let me come in. I've

brought you a dress and shoes." He paused and cleared his throat. "I won't look."

Alicia thought for a moment and then put the brush on the table and took up the key. She struggled with the difficult lock, and as the door creaked open, she very quietly asked him to honor his word. "If you'll put the dress on the bed and leave, I'll be most grateful."

She held her linen towel around herself and watched his back as he moved to the bed. His hair was pulled back and tied with a ribbon and he had changed to a fresh coat. His steps were slow and cautious ones and he seemed to hesitate. He finally rested a bundle on the bed and painstakingly undid the large package, withdrawing a rich-looking gown. He draped this on the bed and withdrew shoes — expensive-looking ones — which he set beside the gown.

He cleared his throat but did not turn. "I'm told I made a miserable fool of myself last eventide and you were frightened." He cleared his throat again. "My apologies."

"And I am sorry that I proved such a disappointment to you," she replied in a quiet voice.

Geoffrey turned abruptly and startled a gasp out of her. The towel covered her nearly to the floor and did not leave her badly embarrassed, yet she had expected him not to turn. When he realized his error, he cast his eyes resolutely to the floor.

"Again, madam, I'm sorry. I did not think. It's only that I couldn't remember your face, and your voice surprises me."

"What surprise is in my voice?" she asked somewhat harshly.

"It's gentle," he said, still looking at the floor. "And pleasant. Not what I expected."

"Well, at least I'm not totally unfit in your estimation," she countered.

Geoffrey's hands went into his coat pockets and he raised

his eyes very slowly. Alicia did not gasp and clutch at her cover this time, for his action was so deliberate. She had plenty of time to call out to him not to look at her, but she wanted to see his eyes again. Though she had not suffered ill with drink the night before, she found in the morning that she could not clearly remember his face.

Seavers's memory was badly impaired and he could not separate in his mind one foul and ill-kept barmaid from below from the parcel that Rodney had delivered, both being women he had encountered the night before. Though he'd arranged the bath, soaps, and clothes, he couldn't carry the idea a bit further without seeing her face. And the face he was seeing now was lovely. Her hair hung in dark, wet ringlets over her shoulders and down her back, and her face glowed with a freshly scrubbed flush. Slender fingers held the cover in place over her breasts, and drops of moisture from her hair caused the linen to fit her more as skin than cover. What he saw pleased him a great deal. "On the contrary, Alicia," he said hoarsely.

He cleared his throat and began to pace about the small room.

"What we shall do first, Alicia, is teach you all we can of the Bellamys. It shouldn't take very long. A letter has been sent by courier to the king explaining that the delay in your arrival at court is for the purpose of burying your aunt, the old woman having just been laid to rest. Then, with a few gowns to see you through, you will be given apartments in Whitehall, and our betrothal will be announced. I think it should fall into place nicely."

She nodded at his words, only half of which she heard, and kept her eyes glued to his. The recollection was clear now that she saw him again. His green eyes glittered and danced as though within him there was joy, but the heavy brows countered the joy with a look of sternness. He was most handsome, and when sober, his voice had a pleasant and comfortable sound.

"Do you need anything more of me?" he asked.

"No, milord," she said.

"Then I'll leave you to your grooming and take the noon meal with you, if that is satisfactory."

"Aye, milord," she responded.

He moved to the door and stepped out, closing it behind him. Alicia moved slightly and looked at the closed door, remembering the face and voice. The door suddenly popped open and he startled her again. "Lock the door, madam. I wouldn't want anything to happen to you now."

"Yes, milord," she said again. The door closed and she did as he ordered. Then she looked at the door again. A slow smile crept over her face. "Yes, milord," she repeated, her eyes beginning to glow with pleasure. "Oh, yes, milord."

four

𝒯he life of Charlotte Bellamy had been completely dull, from the point of view of Alicia. Geoffrey Seavers sat across the small table in her room at the inn and told her all he knew of the young woman. She had lived in the small farming village, remained mostly uneducated but for what her aunt was willing to teach her, and had few friends. She was virtually unknown until it was discovered that she was due an inheritance.

Seavers had made it his business to talk to those few men who had known Fergus Bellamy closely during his service to the crown. He asked after the knight's reputation and had expected to learn something of this woman he was seeking to wed. But the questions gained him few answers. Fergus seldom spoke of his daughter and did not visit her or bring her to London that she might be introduced to his friends. It appeared likely that Fergus used the presence of offspring to facilitate the restoration of the lands he felt he deserved. It was poor timing on the knight's part, in that case, to die so abruptly and never have the chance to enjoy his estate.

"Little enough for me to remember," Alicia reported with a shrug when Geoffrey had completed his story.

"Aye, there's little, but it would do nicely if you could make attempts to remember your father regularly and with sadness."

"And the aunt?" she questioned.

"From what Rodney was able to learn, she was not fond of Charlotte and they did not share much love. Much mention of her seems unnecessary." He looked at her across the short distance and nodded once. "You shall have to accustom yourself to the name, however. And with all due respect, I shall be addressing you as Charlotte from now on. Even in our private moments."

"Our private moments, milord? I didn't think there would be many of those." Geoffrey's look was somewhat puzzled, not confused by her statement, but certainly at a loss as to how to deal with it. "I understood I was to play the part of Charlotte, not become her entirely."

"We shall have to share rooms," he said. "Surely you understand that."

Alicia simply met his eyes. She was not prepared to face his anger, but neither would she let him think that any desire he harbored would be met by this eager slave. She recognized his plan — and had one of her own.

"I hope you have prepared yourself to play the part of a wife, Alicia. For what all eyes see, you should be devoted to my needs and dependent on my strong arm. That certainly requires that we at least share rooms. For the sake of talkative servants, if nothing else."

"You will not be disappointed in my performance, Lord Seavers, but do you expect too much? Am I to live the part I play, or simply play the part well?"

Geoffrey smiled lazily. He leaned back from the table slightly as he studied her face. "Business shall prevent me from spending a great deal of time with you. Indeed, Alicia, our private moments together should prove to be few. I doubt you'll be worn out by my presence."

"And is that in keeping with what should appear to be a 'loving marriage'?" she asked innocently.

His eyes darkened somewhat. "It is well known that this is not a marriage built on a foundation of love, but one of inheritance. Still, I think it behooves us both to show those who will look closely that there is a certain fondness between us, once we take up the roles of man and wife." He leaned closer again. "I am not a man bent on commitments or attachments, Alicia. Not at this time in my life. My purpose is to remain free of bonds and ties. Do not fall in love with me or you will be hurt."

"You worry without cause," she returned with bravado.

"You are very young, my dear," he said in a condescending tone. "I suppose you dream of love and castles and many children, and perhaps you'll find all that at some future time, but —"

"I dream of a fair amount of work in return for freedom and my hundred pounds, Lord Seavers. That is all."

"Then you should be prepared to give me as much as a year of your time, madam, and I will give you aid in seeking some new location and identity."

"That will be fine, Geoffrey," she said. His eyes sparked slightly at the sound of his given name, the reaction she had hoped for. "The name, Geoffrey. You should become accustomed to hearing me use it. Even in our most private moments."

His brows raised slightly and a half smile was his answer. Yes, she was quick. Quick enough to carry off this masquerade without difficulty. He admired her for protecting herself, but a small part of him would not trust her. A better bargain might buy her betrayal. He made a mental note to watch her carefully.

The time that Geoffrey spent with her was minimal, but he was careful, at least, to see that she was not left unprotected at the inn. When he was not there to escort her in and out of the building, Rodney was with her. Only short and carefully guarded walks for exercise and fresh air were allowed and meals were delivered to her room. When the sun was lowering and the men in the tavern became loud and energetic, Rodney was with her through the night.

Little was needed in the way of educating Alicia in better speech patterns, for it was well known that Charlotte would be at a temporary disadvantage in the court. In fact, Charlotte may not have done as well, for Alicia was not only well-spoken, but had a special knack for adapting herself to a new situation. And though no one was quite certain how much personal wealth Charlotte had enjoyed, it could be assumed that her aunt would at least have made sure that she would have some decent clothes and shoes for her journey to London. Only four days were needed to accumulate those things and the other small accoutrements of a lady and make ready for another journey — this time out of the city.

Early in the morning, before the sun was risen, Rodney and Alicia mounted two horses and rode south of London to yet another inn. With a scant amount of baggage tied to the animals, they made a hurried trip. After a brief night in a country inn, they stabled the horses and waited for a London coach. A convenient tale to the driver got them quick service. Rodney explained that he was delivering Lady Charlotte to Whitehall, where she would be given over as ward to Charles himself, but their coach had broken down and would take days to repair. The sympathetic driver offered his services directly to the palace.

Alicia had thought herself well enough prepared, especially after days of discussion and anticipation. But that was before she had even seen Whitehall, the monstrous palace that seemed, from her small window in the coach, to stretch for miles. Her stomach lurched and she felt as though she would be swallowed alive by the building, the people, the plan.

Rodney jumped from the coach and helped the driver get the luggage to the ground. "My lady," he urged from outside. The door stood open and Alicia made no move. "Lady?" he questioned. He looked into the coach and saw that she sat back in the seat, her hands folded in her lap and her eyes focused on the opposite seat. She had expressed no fear or apprehension until now. He understood immediately what he must do. His hand rested lightly on hers and he leaned into her gaze. "Lady Charlotte," he urged gently. "We've arrived." And in a very soft voice he added, "I won't leave you right away and I promise you'll be all right."

With a deep breath she prepared to disembark, holding on to Rodney's steady hand the entire time. Her trembling was hidden in the large hand that helped her. Her knees threatened to buckle as she stood on the ground before the palace, but true to his word, Rodney did not allow her to test her strength. He tucked her arm in his and gave her a moment to judge the huge structure and gain her composure.

Alicia had no way of knowing what portion of the palace they entered. Her wild imagination insisted that just inside the double doors she faced, there would be a huge gallery and a great king on the dais at the end. What she could plainly see were several handsomely garbed gentlemen lounging and laughing with two elegantly gowned young women. The finest dress she had ever worn in her life seemed a rag in comparison. She had risen early in the morning to labor over her hair, for the use of ribbons and pins was new to her, but she could see from the modern and artistic coiffures of the ladies that she was nothing more than a peasant. Her trembling hand uneasily touched what had earlier seemed a daring curl.

Her eyes met Rodney's. She was feeling physical pain in her back and legs just from the fear of passing them to enter Whitehall. His eyes were warm and reassuring, his mouth firmly set in a confident smile. He patted the hand that touched his arm and took a step, refusing to delay any longer lest she faint from fear of the unknown.

Alicia had expected the nobles at the door to present their backs as she passed, so weak was her self-esteem at the moment. But to her surprise, plumed hats were swept off and bows greeted her.

Rodney bowed in return. "I've brought Lady Charlotte Bellamy by His Majesty's request," he announced loudly. "Can anyone direct me to her apartments?"

One handsome young man spoke out quickly. "I can't say where she's lodging, sir, but her arrival is all the talk. The guard will know and will take you himself." The man then bowed again, and addressed Alicia. "Welcome, my lady. Your servant."

Alicia smiled nervously, feeling her normal breathing return for a moment. She detected a kindness, and some of the fear dissipated, but quickly returned when she noticed one of the young maids speaking behind her fan to the other, and the laughter was loud in their eyes. Here, as at the inn and other places, she would be cut apart from the other young women and ostracized. Her heart began to flutter anew. But to the young man who had been pleasant, she smiled again and nodded once.

Within the palace, the galleries were large and spacious, but there was no great hall just inside. Rather, there were bustling servants, lazy guards, and dogs flopped on the floors. The driver of the coach gawked and moaned so as he entered with the baggage that Alicia's staring did not look so obvious. After questioning several people just inside the door, a uniformed footman went off to ask where the lady was to be taken. Rodney and Alicia were left to wait and watch people pass without a nod or word of greeting.

Rodney was beginning to chafe at the wait when a servant, not the man sent, but one wearing different livery, approached them in the gallery. He looked the three of them up and down, smirked slightly at the worn baggage, and faced Rodney to ask, "Lady Charlotte Bellamy?"

Rodney's eyes glared at the man's careless manner, and he took a breath, his frame looming larger. There was only one woman present and she had not been acknowledged at all. Rodney did not know if his anger came in defense of Alicia, of etiquette, or of respect due the young heiress. "I am Lady Charlotte's escort, man. *This* is Lady Charlotte." He lifted Alicia's hand as if to present her and made it clear with his eyes that he would not allow her to be treated with such nonchalance again.

"If you'll follow me, madam."

They traveled through what seemed miles of corridors and galleries, Alicia's shoes clicking on the floors and the driver gasping and exclaiming behind them at every turn. She tried to memorize their journey, fearing she would never find her way out of the maze, but after the first few moments she gave up and simply followed. At the entrance to what was to be her living quarters, Rodney turned to the servant and asked if the king would be notified of Lady Charlotte's arrival. And after a brief nod they were abandoned.

The space that had been allowed Alicia was minimal in comparison to what prestigious guests and tenants in Whitehall received, but for a simple country maid it was a castle in itself. Seven beautifully furnished rooms lay before her eyes. Among the furnishings were a four-poster in her bedchamber, a huge dressing mirror, and thick draperies. Two of the rooms had rugs, a luxury she had never before known. The high sheen on the dining table shocked her, and the padded chair before the hearth left her breathless. She had never in her life seen such wealth.

Rodney followed her from room to room after he had dismissed the gawking driver. She was too overwhelmed even to smile but meandered from wall to door, chest to table, touching and testing. It was safe to assume that Alicia did not even ken what all these rooms were for. Entertaining was something she had never done, but for the entertainment she provided the men in the tavern when she walked from table to keg to table.

Rodney saw that those who had prepared her rooms had neglected what was possibly the most important article Alicia would be needing.

"When you're somewhat settled, lady, I shall have to find you a woman."

"A woman?" she questioned.

"Before long you shall have several, I am sure. For now, you will need one. And quickly."

"She will clean?"

Rodney chuckled slightly. "She will help you dress, fix your hair, serve your meals, and accompany you whenever you go abroad. A companion of sorts, madam. If I am lucky, I will find a woman who has served noble ladies before."

It took just a moment for this to register, and then with a smile she said, "That is a position I would have liked to have."

There was such delight glowing on her face that Rodney could not hold back his grin. He looked at the slender form before him, and at the excitement in her eyes and natural poise with which she held herself, and he knew he had been right to choose her. "I think, my lady, that your future bodes much better than that."

"Kind Rodney," she said softly. "You have so many hopes for me, so much kindness and patience . . . but must you be reminded that this is not really different from what I have always known? I travel from one life to another, fitting myself into a place as best I can for a short time and then moving along to the next. The people I have known I give up, for they do not follow me to the next place. The rooms where I've slept I never see again, and the clothes I've worn are given to me and then taken away." She gestured with an arm to the beautiful surroundings. "It is grand, sir, but it is not mine and it is not for long." She reached out and touched his hand. "Sadly enough, you will not be my friend for very long. It will be hard for me to say good-bye."

"Madam, I think it a bit soon to talk of good-bye."

The glitter of excitement vanished from her eyes and with a look of sadness she answered him. "But I must not let myself forget, dear friend, that this will not last long. I cannot let myself learn to love — "

Before she could finish her statement, there was a loud knock at the door and Rodney looked in that direction. He did not rush to see who called, for he wanted her to complete what she was saying. Love riches? he wondered. Love the fine lodgings? Servants? Lord Seavers?

"The door, Rodney," she said. "Shall I?"

"Allow me, madam," he said, turning toward the door. Alicia was close behind him, curious about the visitor. They found the same servant that had directed them. "His Majesty has many appointments and bids you be comfortable until he can come to welcome you himself."

"My lady would be pleased to go to the king," Rodney offered. Alicia listened raptly, these courtly manners intriguing her. Certainly she would be pleased to go to the king, but it had not occurred to her to offer.

"He has no time to see her now and the wait could be a long one," the servant replied. "Take your leisure and he will come when there is time."

Rodney faced Alicia again when the man had gone and the door was closed. "You were saying, madam?" he questioned.

She laughed lightly. "I just heard that the king is coming to call and you expect me to remember what I've been saying?"

"Understandable, madam. You'll be needing some things that I can send for if you'll be all right alone here for a time."

"Will Lord Seavers be coming here soon?"

"I think not, lady. You see, he does not know you yet."

A strange and almost victorious look crossed her eyes. She glanced around the room and a smile played on her lips. "That's right. He does not know me yet."

Rodney studied the expression and recounted the words of just moments before; her declaration that she would not allow herself to be attached to any of this — any of these people. Floating around in her mind somewhere, Rodney guessed, there was more hope and fight than she would admit to or allow to be seen. And he reckoned it was not the fine furnishings or the prestigious position she was aiming to secure for herself. He thought perhaps this young woman before him, now an unblossomed rose, sought the love of a man and the commitment that could accompany it.

"I imagine there will be a formal introduction," Rodney said, unable to suppress a sly grin. Alicia merely lifted her eyes in his direction, showing little, saying naught. "Do your worst," he advised in a knowing way.

"Kind sir," she returned indignantly, covering her inner longings as best she could but concealing them from Rodney very poorly, "I assure you I shall try my hardest to do my *best*."

"I am Lord Seavers's man, madam, and he depends on my loyalty, but there is a thing I would have you know: I would not betray him or lie to him, but whenever you need my aid, I am your servant."

Alicia's heart grew soft and pliant as she luxuriated in a fatherly concern, the likes of which she had not known before now. "I promise you, sir, I intend only to serve Lord Seavers as faithfully as you do."

Rodney nodded and departed, and Alicia took a moment to wander around her splendid new abode, touching the rich coverings on the furniture and turning full circle to take in the four walls and ceilings of every room. When she finally paused in her tour, she did so before the dressing table and mirror in her large bedchamber. She pulled pins from her hair and let the shining tresses fall to her shoulders. She reminded herself that there was work to be done on her stylishness, but what she saw in her reflection now, for once in a decent mirror that did not mar her complexion, was pleasing to the eye. And she would pay close attention to the ladies, learning from them how to make the most of her appearance.

She smiled at the new face — rosy cheeks, light lip paint — and the clean, shining hair falling in thick curls about her shoulders. Charlotte Bellamy would certainly be recognized as fair of face, and with the proper clothing her figure would be greatly enhanced.

"Everyone knows this is a marriage of convenience." She smiled into the mirror. She sighed deeply and focused on her blue-gray eyes. "Do not fall in love with me, Lord Seavers. You might never survive it as the same man."

The apartment at Whitehall grew into a lonely place as Alicia stayed mostly alone, with Rodney popping in and out to bring her food and news. Two full days passed with no other word from the king, and Alicia was afraid to leave her rooms for fear he would come in her absence. Rodney seemed reluctant to leave her totally unattended there, but there were many things needed for her comfort. He spent hours of each day ordering food to be delivered and looking for at least one servant to aid her.

It was while she was alone in her rooms that a man came to her door. Though it was early evening, it had not occurred to her that anyone who meant her harm might come to her rooms, and for that reason she opened the door quickly and was scolded by her visitor. "Odd's fish, haven't you a care for your safety, madam? I might've been anyone."

She looked in surprise at the tall, bulky man in a dark, thick periwig. He had a harsh-sounding voice, yet a mirth lay hidden in it. Though his eyes were dark and commanding and his full lips set sternly, fear was not her reaction. She felt at ease with his presence.

"Who calls then?" she asked, still holding the door.

"I am Charles; for the moment, your guardian."

With a gasp, she let go of the open door and retreated slightly, her hand first going to her mouth, then both hands going to her sides to hold back her skirts as she began a curtsy, then without completing that she looked at him again, judging his rather casual attire and lack of robes or scepter. "Good Lord, are you *that* Charles?"

He smirked slightly and entered without ceremony. "I am known as the king here, my dear," he said lightly, turning to close the door. "I hope I'm not coming at your inconvenience, I —" As he turned toward her again, he found her finally accomplishing her curtsy and she was indeed bowing low before him. "Here, madam, rise before you hurt something."

Rising from this new acrobatic was nearly as difficult for Alicia as getting down had been. She was not accustomed to the heavy clothing or the undergarments these genteel ladies wore, and her movements before becoming "noble" had been mostly trotting, stooping to clean, and carrying things back and forth. A hand quickly gave aid. "Thank you, sir," she said.

"Sire," he corrected. "Or 'Your Majesty,' or some other appropriate title, whichever you like."

"Yes, Sire," she mumbled.

"Not so much for me, dear, but I imagine everyone about will be watching you carefully, eager to throw stones at you for every error in etiquette that escapes you."

"Oh my," she breathed. "Sire," she added belatedly.

Charles chuckled at her. "I know I'm bound to make you jitter a bit. Call me Charles and let's sit down someplace. I've been running about all day long."

She stood gawking, trying to think of what she should

say, how she should lead him, where she should take him, and above all, trying to remember everything that she had been told about the Bellamys.

Charles raised an arm in the direction of her sitting room and his look was impatient. "Madam?" he questioned.

"Sire, I'm sorry," she gasped. "Please . . ." She moved toward the sitting room, where a settee and a chair sat opposite each other in front of the hearth. He paused inside the room looking at each.

"Where do you like to sit?" he asked her.

For a moment she considered, and the answer was the chair, for it was more comfortable. "Please take the chair, Sire," she said quickly.

Charles sat down so that she might also sit, and once seated, he confronted her. "I see my judgment was right this once, my dear. I decided to meet you privately rather than have you presented at court, knowing that this is all a bit new to you." She fidgeted on the edge of her seat, hanging on his every word. "I hope you'll relax in a moment. I'm too tired to watch you tremble and I swear I haven't killed a maiden in at least a fortnight."

She took a deep breath to still the excited fluttering of her heart. Inside she wasn't sure his attempt at joviality was pure jest. She didn't know him, she barely knew of him, but if anyone could slay a maid for jitters, a king could.

"I thought your hair might be red," Charles commented. "And I heard that you were . . . ah, well fed."

"Heard?" she repeated.

"Well, your father, you know. He spoke of you from time to time, when he was petitioning for his lands, and while I know he did not see you often, he described you as beautiful though generous of body."

Alicia looked nervously at her hands. "What father doesn't think his daughter beautiful, Sire," she said quietly.

"It's plain to me that he was being very modest. So, are you ready to make the acquaintance of your groom?"

"Yes, Sire."

"He's quite handsome, and the women consider him something of a rogue, as he seems to need them a good deal less than the rest of us do. What strange creatures we are, chasing all the time and loving resistance best. Ah, well, he's escaped the ladies quite successfully, as I'm sure you've been told."

"I've talked to no one, Sire," she said a bit quickly.

"I would have hoped his man, that huge old war-horse, what's his name, would have sold his lord mightily to you."

"Oh, yes, Sire," she replied. "Rodney, Sire. He did tell me Lord Seavers is handsome."

"Unfortunately, Seavers expects you to be rather unpretty. There's one or two here that claim to have made your acquaintance not long after my return and had not the best report. But that was a while back and you were much younger. Women, I realize, do a great deal of changing as they approach womanhood. Your changes have either been tremendously good ones or I heard only jealous tongues wagging."

"Jealous of me, Sire?" she asked innocently.

"Madam, your wealth is not great, but it has received some attention, since a number of men at court have less. And having a king take care of your inheritance makes it seem even more important."

"My thanks, Sire. It's kind of you to bother."

"Don't thank me too soon, madam. If Seavers is able to do half of what he intends, I'll be getting a goodly share back."

Her attention was snagged immediately. "Sire, please, what does he intend?"

"His shipping venture, my lady. He plans to establish himself on the sea, beginning with one ship. And not much of a ship at that, since I only recently toured it. Sadly for you, it's my right to arrange your marriage, and I've arranged it to Seavers because I wager the man can do well

69

whatever he takes on." He leaned back in his chair and looked her over. His dark, lazy eyes studied her face and she felt herself glow under their intensity. "I've gambled your inheritance for you, Lady Charlotte. And before you let the fact insult you, let me assure you, I've been a fairly good gambler in the past. I think I can place a bet at least as well as you can. Probably better."

"I'm satisfied, Sire," she said softly, getting at least one clue as to why the real Charlotte had fled. She might well have been hysterical at the thought of what she might face in the king's gentle care. Seavers could have been a wretched, lying, aging horror.

But he was not. And Alicia guessed the king had gambled wisely.

"I shall see that you meet him immediately. I will present you to him myself on the night after next in my chambers. There will be many guests, though only my usual ones, and my lady Castlemaine will hostess the affair. Is there anything you need while you wait?"

"I don't know," Alicia said honestly. And again as an afterthought, she added, "Sire."

"Well, clothing. Do you have suitable clothing?"

She lowered her eyes. "I'm not sure."

"I'll send someone to help you with that. Did you bring servants and a coach?"

"Only myself, Sire."

"Odd's fish, you *were* poor." He scratched his chin. "I imagined Fergus did as little for you as possible. I'll send someone to help you with your staff as well."

"That's very generous of you, Sire."

"You're to be my ward, which makes this my obligation, but the money will be drawn from your estate before Seavers begins his spending, which I'm certain will quickly follow the marriage. When should you like that to take place, madam?"

"At your convenience, Sire," she replied.

"In a week? Month?"

"I . . . I . . ." She stopped the stammering and simply shook her head in wonder.

"Of course. You'll want to meet him before you give an answer. Very well." Charles rose and Alicia jumped to her feet. "We'll talk of this when you've met your betrothed, but I pray you get this marriage done quickly. The gossips can't stand the wait."

"Yes, Sire."

He strode quickly to the door without turning. When he arrived and his hand found the latch, he turned to look at her again. A puzzled frown creased his brow. She looked nothing like Fergus, for that much he was most grateful. He wondered for a moment if she would find any old friends at court and as quickly he realized she would not, for no one knew her, including himself. Then his expression suddenly changed and his smile was devilish. "Oh, you're going to greatly disappoint them, madam."

Panic filled her eyes. "Oh, how, Sire?" she asked impetuously.

"You're really quite pretty," he replied with a shrug. "They'll hate you for it. The women at least." He chuckled again and opened the door. "The men will hate Seavers." He started to duck out of the door. "I won't be far if there's any real trouble," he said. "Good evening, madam." And the door closed.

Alicia turned away from the closed door. "The king," she said aloud to her walls. "Dear heaven. The king thinks I'm pretty." Her mouth curved slightly. A weak and nervous laugh escaped her. She considered that he would be clothing her and hiring her servants out of the inheritance that Geoffrey had worked so hard to get. She laughed again. "Perhaps in a month, Sire," she said with feigned innocence. With the laughter coming more easily and the lilting feeling filling her stomach, she picked up her skirts and began to dance around the room.

five

*I*n the captain's cabin of the *Patrina*, there existed a bunk, large desk, and chair, shelves lining the walls, stacked coffers, and a general mess. Amidst rolls of plans littering the desk top sat a barely touched tray of food. Behind the desk was a small stand that held a basin of water and a mirror leaned against the wall. Geoffrey Seavers attempted to fit a periwig to his head in front of that mirror.

The door to the cabin opened and Rodney entered carrying a dark blue satin jacket. Glittering buttons graced the breast and Geoffrey looked over his shoulder and glanced ruefully at the garment. Shirtless, unadorned, and riding the back of his ship, hard at work, was how he liked himself best. The pomp of court life grated on him.

"The tailor managed nicely on the short notice," Rodney offered.

"This is Charles's idea of fun," Geoffrey grumbled. "He likes to watch his puppets dance about and prove their adoration of one another." He scowled into the mirror and adjusted the wig another time. "He'd have a jolly good time if he knew I was making the acquaintance of a tavern wench."

"His Majesty would enjoy that mightily," Rodney laughed. "And I think all the better for Charles if he knew. But no more of that," Rodney said, approaching with the coat. "I think it'll be clear when you see her that she's no longer a common serving maid."

"Clothes and manners help, but there's no changing the person who wears them. I only pray she can convince the gossips, or I'll be out to sea, but not with a fleet." He turned and shrugged into the jacket. Now there was a smile. "The building of the next ship is well under way — on my personal note."

"I've seen that for myself," Rodney returned. "I hope the building can be continued."

"And why wouldn't it? The introduction is tonight, the betrothal will be announced and posted, and the marriage soon. Charles cannot sit on the land and taxes for long. The goods and workers will be paid for."

"Are you aware that Preston will be with you tonight?" Rodney asked.

Geoffrey chuckled at Rodney's question. "His timing is so perfect I almost think he planned it this way. Blast the blackguard, he's here purely to laugh at my foibles."

"He's here on his father's business," Rodney corrected.

"A ruse," Geoffrey insisted.

Preston Tilden, longtime friend to Geoffrey, had left England with the rest of his family during the Commonwealth to begin building a new life in the Americas. Letters he'd written to Seavers told of rough wilderness that had to be cleared, slaves that had to be bought for endless work, shortages of food and supplies, and various adventures the family had had. But the Tildens had prospered. Five sons and considerable money had procured a fine home on a large portion of Virginia soil. The family's interests lay in mills and farming, shipping and badly needed trade to other countries. Geoffrey, too, had been offered a plot of this new and uncivilized land across the ocean, but had chosen to make his way in England. He envied Preston his early success, but knew that without the financial backing and numbers of family members that Preston had, he would still be chopping down trees.

Preston was the youngest of five sons. He and Geoffrey were nearly the same age, Preston being just two years younger than Geoffrey. Their fathers had been neighbors and longtime friends as well, and the families had been close for years.

Though Tilden ships arriving in port were not uncommon, Preston's arrival was a complete surprise to Geoffrey. Rodney had carried the news earlier in the day that Preston himself commanded this Tilden vessel, and Geoffrey had to curb the urge to swim out to the approaching ship for the reunion. The sight of his friend waving from the bow brought back memories of adventures shared, loves fought over, and laughter that went late into ale-ridden nights. Having Preston near was the balm for Geoffrey's anxiety over his dream of a fleet and his precarious betrothal.

When Preston arrived on the *Patrina*, he had wine and a block of cheese with him, bursting into the cabin with a loud laugh. "Behold, the groom," he goaded.

Geoffrey scowled and eyed Preston's goods. "We can drink later, when this ordeal has ended."

Preston turned to Rodney. "He does not sound like a man in love, eh?"

"And you would know what a man in love sounds like?" Geoffrey asked before Rodney could answer.

Preston set the cheese and wine on the desk and spied the tray of untouched food sitting there. "Ah, this is more the rote." He grinned. "No appetite, surly mood . . . aye, perhaps there is hope for the man."

"I have not met the wench yet."

"Wench, is it. God's bones, you'll land in the gutter for that slur, should anyone hear."

74

"The lady," Geoffrey corrected. "I have not heard the best things about her. 'Tis her dowry that is attractive to me."

"That's a start," Preston conceded. "And whatever other troubles you find with her, work them out quietly and with care, lest some better-mannered knight takes her away from you."

"I've seen you practice your lessons well," Geoffrey laughed. "Remember the friend that rode and sailed with you — and watched you play the ladies and toss them away."

"Ah, but now I have a wife."

Geoffrey looked up in surprise. "A wife? What madness possessed you to take a wife so soon? Your family has money."

Preston laughed good-naturedly. "A pretty vixen crossed my path and schooled me in when to dally and when to make a contract. She would have none of these courtly games."

"And so you're caught." Geoffrey smiled. "A family man at last."

"Indeed, a family man. Just as I prepared to leave, Brianna told me that she intends to present me with a child next summer. Our first."

Geoffrey extended his hand. "Then we'll make time to raise a glass. To your dynasty."

Rodney looked around the cluttered cabin for cups, and wine was poured all around.

"I'm the last of my brothers to marry," Preston said. "And while the Tilden men are often bending their backs or out to sea, it has not kept the family small. We seem to have a knack for finding fertile women who grace my parents with new grandchildren yearly." He raised his cup and drank, sighing in appreciation. Geoffrey looked at his friend's face. Fulfillment seemed to show there and envy presented itself again. "Another addition to the house will be needed, but then I laid brick and wood for my brother's additions."

"You've acquired your fortune, Preston," Geoffrey said. "I wish I thought my future would bring as much."

Preston sighed deeply. "I hesitate to damage my reputation, but in all truth, wealth does not mean as much to me as it once did. Brianna has taught me something of the value of women that I did not know." He raised his glass as if in silent toast to her. "I wish you luck, friend. I hope your contract bodes as much."

"I doubt that is possible. While you look well enough for your bonds, being so tethered does not have any appeal for me." Geoffrey took a long pull on the wine, and his eyes glittered when he looked at his friend. "If she is not shrewish, I shall survive it, but I tell you, I see no great love brewing here. 'Tis a profitable arrangement. That is all."

"Then enjoy your misery." Preston shrugged. "You seem most intent on it."

"My appraisal as well, sir," Rodney put in. "Though I think the boy spoiled and sullen. Lady Charlotte is lovely and kind."

Geoffrey only smirked. There was little about the maid that he disliked, but the idea that this could be a fulfilling arrangement had not occurred to him. He mentally counted his money and time. What Preston had acquired, his land, income, and family, was desirable to Geoffrey. This marriage scam would aid him in getting a start on a decent shipping enterprise, but it was another year out of his life, another temporary situation that he would have to see finished before he could settle himself to a decent family life with a wife and children. He felt a long way from having what Preston had.

"And to think," Preston mused, "had my younger sister survived the wars, she'd be a good match for you."

"The child who died when you were small?" Geoffrey asked.

"Aye, and I hope to uncover some of the mystery of her death. It was while my parents were having her spirited away to my aunt that she disappeared, and all efforts to find her failed. It was a dangerous time. All of England was at war with itself. She could not have survived. . . ."

Geoffrey became solemn. When his father and brother died, his mother and sister became his responsibility. A strong sense of failure overcame him whenever he thought of them, for they had died within a year of each other. His sister, Andrea, betrothed to the flamboyant courtier, Culver Perry, had died quite suddenly while riding. His mother became ill soon after Andrea's death and, he reasoned, found little reason to go on — she had lost all of her family but Geoffrey.

"You've had a few years to recover from that loss," Geoffrey said with some bitterness.

"Aye, friend," Preston answered compassionately. "And on the eve that you'll meet your bride it's rude of me to bring up our sisters. Forgive me."

"Can you imagine who might have argued most heartily for the hand of Lady Charlotte?" Geoffrey asked his friend.

Preston noted the fury in Geoffrey's eyes and knew from whence it came. "I had heard that Perry made his request for a rich bride well known. I am surprised he survived your wrath."

"I am certain he believed our family would have large sums and plentiful lands restored when he asked for Andrea's hand in marriage. He courted her too well — but loved her too little." He downed the last of his wine and slammed the cup onto the desk. "I never saw his grief."

"Culver Perry cannot take anything from you now, Seavers," Preston said slyly. "Unless, of course, you foolishly leave unattended what is yours."

Geoffrey's green eyes were sparked with hatred as he looked at his friend. "Should he give me the slightest excuse, I will kill him. I hate the man more than I allowed I could."

Geoffrey tugged on his jacket and took a breath, trying to still the emotion that seemed quickly to fill the room. Even Rodney moved away from the conversation a bit and Preston did not encourage any more expression. Geoffrey had lost too many that were dear to him. Had Perry at least suffered upon the death of his betrothed, Geoffrey might have been able to abide him, but he immediately began his courtship of any available dame at court, including old dowager baronesses whose ears were turned toward the flattery and whose purses were not yet empty.

"The oaf would marry the king's mare, were she well saddled," Geoffrey said.

"The name Perry brings much attention in England, since his brother still has land and influence. But I understand there is no family love there and Perry can get nothing out of his brother's fortune," Preston said. "And though I have no respect for the man, it would do you well to remember that he is handsome and suave. Take care that he does not easily usurp what you already consider yours."

"He will not," Geoffrey promised. "This once I believe I've outwitted him. Lady Charlotte will marry me."

The galleries in Whitehall were chilled and dark, the drafts causing draperies and tapestries to shiver. Lord Seavers and Preston Tilden set a good pace along the corridors and through halls to the apartments of Lady Castlemaine, Barbara Palmer. They walked in silence, with only the sound of their heavy and hurried footfalls echoing in the passageways.

Lady Castlemaine would immediately recognize Seavers, for she had, a time or two, flirted with him. There was no reason to assume that she was interested beyond an innocent affair, for it was acknowledged that she was the king's, and one did not toy with the king's mistress. Yet Seavers had willingly accepted her attentions as a compliment and recognized that it did not hurt his case with King Charles to be in Castlemaine's good favor. And no one, least of all Geoffrey, was surprised to see that Barbara Palmer hostessed the affair that would present Lady Charlotte to Lord Seavers.

Lady Castlemaine utilized her liaison with Charles to secure for herself fine furnishings for the large living quarters she inhabited. Gifts to her from those seeking favor with the king decorated her walls and tables, and jewels from her admirers sparkled on her throat and wrists. Preston and Geoffrey were admitted and announced by a servant, but it was only moments before Barbara glided toward them with a greeting on her lips. Her hand briefly touched a pendant that she wore about her neck: a cluster of small diamonds gleaming around a sapphire. Geoffrey smiled, but a small flush threatened to mar his rugged appearance. He had given the pendant as a gift and assumed it would be lost among the many richer tokens she had acquired. Obviously she wore it and drew his eyes to it with her hand to establish their alliance.

Seavers was not as well practiced with the ladies as many seemed to believe, and in fact, aggressive women, like Barbara, caused his stomach to churn. As luck would have it, his habit of drawing back within himself and giving little or no recognition to the many flirtations only made him that much more desirable to the women. No one seemed to be aware of his shyness. His aloof manner drew them like flies to honey.

He steadied himself internally, not at all sure he could handle the situation to his satisfaction. If there was a woman alive who could paint him into a corner, it was Castlemaine.

"My lords," she purred, lowering herself into a bow that threatened to spill her round breasts out of her gown. The fact that she was with child did not detract from her sensuality. Both men took mental note that Charles did indeed have exquisite taste in women.

Geoffrey extended his hand to take hers. "Lady Castlemaine," he said, his voice smooth and controlled. For all appearances they were old friends delighting in the reacquaintance. He kissed the back of her hand and, upon raising his head, found her eyes glued to Preston. "Allow me to introduce Preston Tilden, lately arriving in London. Preston's father, Lord Tilden, has made his home in Virginia of the Americas and Preston is in the business of trade."

"A pleasure," Barbara said coolly. "Then merchanting is your family business," she said, seeking clarification. That a merchant would presume to come to her affair without a special invitation was an affront.

"In essence, lady," Preston returned quietly.

Geoffrey presented his arm to Barbara and they preceded Preston to join the other guests waiting in the sitting room and dining room. When they had gone but a step, Geoffrey leaned close to the hostess and whispered, "His family is very rich. Very rich indeed."

Barbara's eyes lit ever so slightly and she glanced over her shoulder to appraise the young guest again, this time with a half smile and raised brow. Dining with a merchant was not prestigious, but a very rich merchant with a nobly bred family was not exactly an embarrassment. "Tilden, you say. Seems I remember a Lord Tilden. . . ."

"Perhaps, lady," Preston returned. "Though when my parents left England permanently, I'd say you were but a child."

And to that Barbara smiled brightly. Youth was the most precious commodity in all London. Still in her early twenties, Barbara feared age more than anything. And she was not unlike the other court ladies in that.

Charles stood off in a corner with Buckingham, courtiers lounged about half at attention and not yet totally inebriated, ladies fluttered fans and fawned over each other's jewels and gowns, and Geoffrey tried, inconspicuously, to scan the room for some sight of Alicia.

Charles glanced over his shoulder and spied Geoffrey. Their eyes met briefly. Charles smiled knowingly, turned away to whisper something to George Villiers, and then turned abruptly toward Seavers.

Geoffrey's acknowledgment of the king was slow. He felt that creeping sensation when he first spied Charles, for the fact was that the king completely controlled his future at this point and could at any moment change his mind about letting the young noblewoman advance her inheritance through marriage to him. But he caught himself, remembering courtly manners and being very much a man comforted by rules. Much of the comfort came through the reckless feeling of breaking them and never letting on that he'd escaped. Inwardly, however, he never stopped feeling unsettled by lying and cheating.

He checked himself and bowed deeply. "Sire."

"In a hurry, no doubt, to make the acquaintance of your future bride," Charles drawled.

"Is she here, Sire?" Geoffrey asked.

Charles scratched his beard, his fingers gliding up his jawline to give his mustache a tug. A smile played at the corners of his mouth, and his eyes glittered mischievously. "I've enjoyed myself a bit with this chore," he confessed quietly.

"I thought you might," Geoffrey slipped out without thinking.

Charles was not offended but intrigued. "It occurs to me that everyone knows me better than I like. Ah, well, so what? The truth is I can't remember when a secret's been more fun."

Geoffrey's face darkened somewhat and his eyes narrowed. He hated to ask. "Secret, Sire?"

"Well, everyone — that is, everyone but you — has asked

how I found Lady Charlotte. Though I haven't made her a prisoner at all, she's kept to her rooms entirely, getting herself ready for tonight."

"That isn't good news to me, Your Majesty," Geoffrey sulked.

Charles laughed uproariously, drawing eyes sharply toward them. "Not to rectify a disaster, Seavers, good God. The lass arrived without servants, clothing, or any knowledge. You were warned that while she's due some money, her youth was not spent in riches and education. She was needing the preparation."

"Am I to thank you then, Sire, for helping her to acclimate herself to Whitehall?"

"I think not, Seavers. I asked Lady Castlemaine to send one of her own servants to assess the lady's needs, and Barbara took it upon herself to look in on Lady Charlotte." Charles cleared his throat. "Your young woman is now ready with a staff, wardrobe, coach, and other essentials."

"I appreciate that very much indeed, Sire. I did not know how poor her state was."

"It was no problem at all, Seavers. Lady Charlotte could well afford it."

Charles watched dubiously as Seavers's smile vanished. As Seavers mentally figured the approximate cost of Alicia's refurbishing, the damage to his purse sent pain shooting like a knife to his stomach. His pupils shrank as he wondered if it would match the cost of outfitting an entire ship. Would there be much left for his business ventures?

"I didn't want to leave you with so much to do for the lady that you couldn't see about your own affairs," Charles said, finding it hard to conceal his amusement with Geofrey's agony. Charles did not play at dressing and teaching ladies, but in this instance, he imagined that without his intervention Charlotte would be left no better dressed than she was when he first met her, and would be as sleeping prey to the court. They, he knew well, would bludgeon her with careless criticism. He gave Castlemaine the chore of outfitting her as a lady, and Barbara did as he expected she would; Charlotte was now Barbara's pet and project.

"Don't pout so," Charles told Geoffrey. Geoffrey straightened himself abruptly, piqued at being treated like a child. "Thank me for seeing that it was Barbara taking care of things," he whispered. "I could have asked the queen."

Geoffrey nodded in agreement. He found a great many qualities in Catherine to admire and he pitied her in a great many ways, but it was true that when it came to stylishness she was a failure. Yet what else could be expected of a woman whose husband's mistresses were flaunted before her continuously?

Geoffrey glanced over his shoulder and found Barbara still fluttering her fan over her voluptuous bosom and chatting amiably with Preston. Catherine had the political interests and title Charles needed to marry; Barbara Palmer had the passion and sexuality that kept that smile playing about the king's lips. Seavers pitied Catherine, but he didn't deny that Charles's need for Barbara was real.

And yet he had heard that Barbara was losing her appeal for Charles. Frances Stewart, a rather new beauty to arrive at court, had the king in chase while she flirted outrageously and hung desperately to her virginity.

Such was the way of the court: to fill the night or the month or perhaps a few years with one person, but to answer nature's call without overburdening oneself with commitments. Charles had set the standard himself. Who would argue with a king?

"Thank you, Sire," he mumbled, though gratefulness was not something he was feeling. "When will the lady arrive?"

"I've sent for her, now you're here," he replied, moving away from Seavers and toward Barbara to make the acquaintance of Preston, whom he would realize he knew, once they were face to face.

Seavers stood alone, wanting conversation less than anything. Charles was playing the game to the hilt, holding back the woman to the last moment, setting the stage so that everyone within a mile could watch his face as she entered and quietly but clearly gave the information that a good deal of her money had been spent on dressing her for her new position.

I'll be damned, Seavers thought, if he isn't playing me like a puppet. Have fun, Sire, while you can. Before very long I'll be running this —

His thoughts stopped abruptly as he heard the doorman's announcement, and all heads turned. "Lady Charlotte Bellamy."

From where he stood, it did not seem to be the same woman. Perhaps Charles had found an impostor of his own. But a closer look told him that Alicia had been groomed, exquisitely, to compete with the most beautiful women at court.

Her gown was close-fitting velvet, lavender and deep, rich purple, snug through the bodice and waist and flowing in graceful pleats to the floor. Her slim figure and long slender arms gave her the look of a dancer. Her wrists glittered with bracelets and her neck shone with precious stones. Over one arm, she carried a black fox fur that a servant quickly took from her. Her gown was cut in a deep V, and her breasts, round and plentiful, rose and fell gracefully with every breath.

It was her face; that much he could recognize, though he feared he had gone partially mad. It was the difference of seeing her hair so perfectly coiffed, with small glittering stones tucked here and there among the curls. And her manner was so different in this setting. She stood taller, almost commandingly, her every movement poised and confident. As the king approached her, she gave him a quick and natural smile, her even white teeth gleaming and her eyes coming alive with a special excited light.

Geoffrey felt an urge grow within him the moment he had taken in her entire appearance. She was more than lovely: she was magnificent. He tried to recall the tavern wench he'd met: a slender and unkempt brown-haired girl. He had thought her fair, but the potential had never occurred to him.

But it was not the clothing alone, he assured himself. There was something in her demeanor that made her very different from the wench in the inn. He had seen her clamber into the coach with Rodney, and now he was seeing her glide across the room on the king's arm, her smile soft and sweet as she acknowledged the sighs from the courtiers as she passed them, and seemed to take as much pleasure in the lack of comment from the ladies. Indeed, the only woman in the room to be the least bit appreciative was Barbara Palmer, and that was because of her contribution to this maid's attractiveness.

Charles stood before him, his ward on his arm. "From your expression, Seavers, I'd say you're pleased."

Geoffrey shook himself and reached to take her hand, placing a courtly kiss on it. "Your servant, madam," he cooed.

"There are a great many eager for your acquaintance, lady," Charles told her. "I think your escort can manage that, if you'll excuse me."

"With pleasure, Your Majesty," she said, her voice lilting.

"I'll be announcing the betrothal after dinner and I hope you'll be telling me the wedding date before long."

"I'm certain we can settle on a date soon," Seavers attempted.

"I think it shan't take long for me to get to know the groom, Your Majesty," Alicia said.

"Didn't I promise you all the time you need?" Charles asked her. She nodded as though they had indeed had a long conversation on the matter.

As Seavers attempted to hide his frown, Charles left them. Though they were hardly alone, they were isolated enough to exchange a few words, if quiet.

"Quite an improvement, lady," he whispered.

"I might say the same, milord," she returned.

The shock nearly set him on his ear and he quickly tried to remember what he was garbed in when last they spoke together. He had not considered that his appearance was ever less than debonair.

"We shouldn't need to keep the king in suspense, should we, madam? I think the wedding can be soon."

"Let's not worry with that tonight, milord, please. I'm interested only in getting to know you better."

"Madam," he pressed, prepared to argue. But as he would have begun, he noticed that the gallants would not allow him privacy. And he understood their motivation, for he had to acknowledge he had indeed been lucky.

He made several introductions and found himself pressed out of a tight circle as Alicia was put upon by every curious spectator within the room. Behind him he heard his friend's familiar voice. "I should like to hear your miserable complaints *now*," Preston whispered.

Geoffrey was silent. He stared jealously at the backs of nobles and ladies that surrounded his betrothed.

"Pity you've had to sacrifice so much. Poor wretch; only money and beauty and, from what I can see, a sweet disposition."

Geoffrey turned to glare at his friend.

Alicia found no use for her rehearsed smile and nod of acquaintance at each introduction. She was carried away by the fuss and compliments, and her own natural happiness rose to the surface. Could she have seen the difference between the rehearsed acceptance she had practiced before her mirror and the beauty of her simple joy, she would not have recognized herself.

It was not until a familiar voice touched her ears that her confidence was shaken. "Your beauty far surpasses any tales brought to court about you."

Her eyes grew wide and she fought to suppress a gasp of surprise as she recognized Perry's voice and looked into his glittering blue eyes. The anger she saw there threatened to shatter her. She tried to smile. "Thank you, milord," she murmured.

His voice was low and menacing. "How you've managed this is a complete mystery."

Alicia cast a quick glance around her to see who might have overheard. There were several gallants and maids close at hand, but their laughing and tittering with one another had left Perry's words unnoticed.

"Beg pardon?" she breathed, panicked. The last thing she wanted was to hear him repeat himself, but she was at a complete loss. Her worst fear had been realized. She knew in her heart she would be exposed as the tavern wench Perry had lain with last summer — and here, before the king's court.

"If you have any wits, madam, flee quickly. Be in another county before a day passes."

Alicia was frozen to the ground. She could do nothing but stare at him in frightful wonder.

"I *know* Charlotte Bellamy, madam. You are in dire straits. It is only a matter of time before Seavers finds out you have tricked him."

Alicia took a deep breath and looked past Perry to where Geoffrey stood with another man. She decided quickly: she would rather go out in a surge of flames than be inconspicuously drowned and unnoticed. "What *do* you mean?" she asked with as much courage as she could muster.

Perry forced a smile for onlookers and took her hand in his as if to kiss the back of it in courtly grace. "Would that I knew who you are and how you've managed this — I would expose you tonight!" The low rumble of his laughter terrified her. "But, alas, I have no desire to *help* Seavers. Flee madam, before the added sin of marrying Lord Seavers belongs to your list of crimes."

Alicia heard herself laugh, the sound nothing more than a distant noise to her own ears. He did not remember her! He *knew* Charlotte Bellamy, though no one else did . . . but he did not remember a woman he'd seduced, lied to, and left.

Geoffrey was suddenly at her side, a perturbed frown on his face. "You've met my betrothed, Lord Perry?"

"At long last," Perry simpered, his angry eyes turning to Seavers. "You're very fortunate, she is beautiful," he said, the displeasure obvious in the voices of both men.

Alicia feared she would fall to the floor. The only thing that kept her on her feet was the protective arm about her waist. The tension was not hers alone. She could feel the tightness in Geoffrey's arm and she could see the anger in Perry's features. She felt, quite suddenly, that this entire situation had very little to do with her.

"I agree, of course," Geoffrey proclaimed.

Alicia leaned against Geoffrey without realizing she was doing so. Perry nodded again, excused himself, and melted into the crowd beyond them.

"Are you all right, madam?" Geoffrey asked. She looked up at him and saw that he looked not at her, but in the direction Perry had gone.

"That man," she began, her voice quavering. "He frightened me."

"Beware of Culver Perry, madam. He is a liar, and worse."

"Is there any possibility he *knows*?" she whispered.

His eyes snapped to hers. "He knows about your fortune. He bid mightly for your hand."

She felt herself sway slightly.

"Madam, have you need of a chair?" Geoffrey asked her.

"Is he very important here?" she asked tremulously.

"Perry? He has very little influence here. Fortunately, much less than I. If he's made you any promises, be warned, he will not keep them."

"I know that," she said, her voice sounding very far away. He did not *remember* her! He had lain with her, sworn his love, and quickly forgotten! Her fear nearly dissolved in the presence of her hatred of the man. She quickly decided she would see this through a bit farther. If not to help Lord Seavers, possibly to hurt Lord Perry.

She looked up at Geoffrey. "I could tell instantly that he is a vulgar, hateful man," she said.

"You are very perceptive, Charlotte," Geoffrey said. His eyes still held that suspicious and threatening gleam. Though Alicia did not know why, she knew Geoffrey hated Perry as much as she did. "Very perceptive indeed."

six

s it came like a breath through the open window, the evening breeze billowed the shabby curtain. The light from a single candle fluttered slightly. A man's low mumblings brought a rattle of giggling from a woman and then a gleeful laugh.

"Lawd, gov'na, you do play a word with a maid," a woman's voice said as she flopped the heavy comforter about a bit.

"God, I mean it all," he argued.

The slamming of a door below and heavy footfalls on the stairs caused them both to sit upright. Charlotte ran one hand through her tousled curls and clasped the cover to her breasts with the other.

"Is that the man's got you in keeping?" her panicked partner asked.

"Gor, he said he'd be gone hours," she breathed.

"I'm hoping he rounds yer pretty arse and not mine," the man said, easing quickly from the bed and searching for his pants.

"'At's a love," Charlotte seethed vindictively. "One moment, you'll give me the world, and next, sell me for a beating." She threw her legs over the side of the bed and reached for a simple dress that had been hastily thrown to the floor and lay amidst apple cores and orange peelings. She gave it a shake. "Jackanape," she muttered. "I hope he breaks your head."

The door was thrown open with a bang and the intruder walked to the lone candle, using it to light another, brightening the room. He seemed not to notice the man struggling into his breeches or the toss-and-tumble bedding and naked woman until the room was more brightly lighted.

"Been amusing yourself very well, I see," Perry said, eyeing the disheveled lovers.

"Don't make no trouble, love," Charlotte said easily, stepping into her dress. "He's leaving."

As she straightened herself and looked at Culver Perry, she actually took a step back from the furious gleam in his eyes. His fists were clenched at his sides and his face was reddening. "I told you to have no one in here."

"He's leaving, milord," Charlotte said a bit tremulously. "I won't do it again."

Perry's stare was fixed on Charlotte, and the man took the opportunity to gather what was left of his clothing — shoes, shirt, stockings, and jacket — and start to ease himself cautiously toward the door.

"Find a stallion in any gutter, eh, love?" Perry asked with a sinister sneer. He abruptly grabbed for the young man, catching him about the neck and hurling him out the open door. "Was it worth your time?" he asked the rattled fellow.

"No, milord — I mean, I didn't know . . ."

"Don't come here again, you hear? If I see you within a mile of her, I'll kill you."

"Aye, milord," he said, trembling.

Perry gave him a shove and, with a firm kick in the pants, sent him rolling down the stairs, his clothing scattering along the way. Without looking to see if the man survived the fall, Perry came back into the room and slammed the door.

"Didn't think you'd get yourself in a snit about it, love," Charlotte said cautiously.

Perry walked briskly to the decanter of brandy he kept for himself and poured a stout portion into a dirty glass, downing the spirits more quickly than usual. He turned on Charlotte with a curse.

"I don't give a damn that you're a whore, but I can't have you spending time in the taverns and bringing strange men here with you. Does he know who you are?"

"Of course not. I told him I was in keeping." She laughed suddenly. "But then I'm keeping you, eh, love?"

The glass came flying through the air like a shot, smashing on the wall behind her. Charlotte ducked the vessel and rose again with wide eyes.

"You bloody whores are all alike," he blustered. "You'd be naked walking the streets if I hadn't dragged you from the worthless farm you were raised on, and brought you here."

"Wrong, gov'na," she said angrily. "I'd have Lord Seavers."

"You're wrong, bitch," he shouted. "Seavers met his bride tonight at Whitehall. Lady Charlotte Bellamy. A beautiful and elegant woman, obviously Seavers's own design. He'd not have spent a farthing to make you right for the title."

"What?" she asked, aghast.

"There was a woman there tonight, the mysterious bride: Fergus Bellamy's daughter." He strode toward her, grabbed her by the upper arms, and stared into her eyes. "Tell me truthfully: was the knight your father or are you some farm wench who played a tale on me?"

"I *am* Charlotte Bellamy," she insisted. "You *know* that."

He released her abruptly. "Aye, you couldn't have fooled me on that score. I was there to see where you lived and how you lived." He walked away from her and spoke without looking in her direction. "Then it's as I thought. Seavers couldn't find his bride and so has an impostor playing the role."

"Damn me, he won't for long," she huffed behind him. "And whether it suits you or not, I'll not let another wench claim my father's money. I tell the — "

"You'll tell no one!" he barked. He looked her over, from tousled head to filthy bare feet. "What d'ye think, darling? You'll stroll into the king's bedroom and tell him you're the heiress — having come here with me to trick Seavers out of his fortune? Charles would have a good laugh on that, a filthy whore claiming the prize." He picked up the decanter of brandy and took a long pull from it. "You don't seem to understand, my dear. Lady Charlotte's made a smash at Whitehall. She's beautiful and appears to be gently bred."

"Gently bred, by God," Charlotte laughed. "In that barn I was raised in?"

"Fact is fact," he said. "They've accepted her. And I can't present you without giving myself a great deal of trouble from Charles." He took a long breath, letting his anger and frustration cool. "We'll have to find another way to get to Seavers. Perhaps a bit a planning can cause him to trip over his own lies."

Alicia sat before the dressing table in her bedroom. Behind her Margaret Stratton, the woman Rodney had hired to be Alicia's personal maid, fluttered about the room putting everything in order, chattering all the while.

Margaret, or Maggie, or Meg, whichever Alicia preferred at the moment, was a heavyset woman in her early forties. She had been widowed several years back and spoke frequently and with fondness of her late husband. She spoke also of the son who served in His Majesty's Horse Guard.

And there were countless sisters, brothers, cousins, and others that she chattered about endlessly.

Alicia found her to be an absolute delight, a knowledgeable caretaker with an eye for fashion, though she wore nothing particularly fashionable herself. She showered Alicia with motherly concern that gave her a sense of being home that she had never before known. Alicia felt the woman's immediate loyalty.

But this morning she half heard all of Mrs. Margaret's chatter, and quite often, when she realized she'd missed a direct question, she would turn with a rather preoccupied "Mmm?"

"Not a thing, sweetheart," Margaret would say. "You're all caught up with that handsome lord you're t'marry and can't give me a spot of time. . . . I know that. Old women cluck like old hens. Never mind me."

"But you're not old," Alicia returned.

" 'Tweren't much more than your age when I married Mr. Stratton and had myself a baby, to boot. I remember, love. I remember clear as if it was yesterday." She shrugged and fluffed the pillows. "Couldn't give the time of day to those bantering old hens myself." And she would laugh with genuine amusement.

A knock at the door sent the woman rushing to answer for her lady and she accepted the quick message.

"His lordship is here to see you, love," she relayed.

"Now?" Alicia asked in astonishment. "Oh, blast him, I'm not even dressed."

Margaret laughed. "Barely out of bed, at that. Well, then, let's get you in something comfortable and comb your hair. See him in here, if you like."

Talking all the while, she picked through the wardrobe and finally pulled out a heavy scarlet dressing robe that was lined with white lace. "This will do nicely, eh?" And then, stooping, she retrieved a set of slippers from the floor of the wardrobe — a velvet pair that had tiny pearls sewn around the edges. "Aye," her woman said. "This will warm his heart on a cold day."

Alicia eyed the garment and smiled devilishly. In helping to choose Alicia's clothing, Lady Castlemaine had selected gowns of daring and sensual design.

While Barbara was as friendly as any sister might be, and had been helpful during a confusing time, Alicia was wary and a little frightened of her. It was Margaret who explained the reason for Barbara's almost dotish help. "Frances Stewart's all but taken the king away from her. She's been declared the most beautiful woman in England, you know. And if Castlemaine can pry his eyes away from Frances for even a minute, it's worth her time. She'll make you the competition. She's not afraid to deal with you."

Alicia could see the probable truth in that at the dinner where she was formally introduced to Geoffrey. Lady Castlemaine remained the center of attention only as long as she was able to take credit for Alicia — Lady Bellamy — and Frances did suffer a lack of recognition that evening.

The fact that Alicia received so many adoring remarks, her beauty being commented on loudly and frequently, did not cause her head to swell. She wanted to be considered beautiful and desirable. But when this play was done and the glitter of court life gone, so would the favor disappear.

She slipped into the dressing robe and slippers, sitting again at the table and handing a brush over her shoulder to Margaret. She pulled at the bodice and low neckline, satisfying herself that her bosom looked plentiful, yet demure enough to attract his curiosity and not a lustful attack. "This will do," she told her woman. "But I'll see Lord Seavers in the sitting room, not in here."

"I should have known that, mum. It's not fitting where you come from."

Alicia struggled not to laugh. Where she came from, she had a difficult time keeping men from dragging her into their rooms at night — and not for a social call. She knew

95

Margaret would not fawn over her had she known she was not the genteel lady she pretended to be.

She willed herself to be poised, and walked down the hall toward the sitting room without disturbing a curl. She moistened her lips repeatedly with her tongue, and she had pinched her cheeks to give them a flush — something she only had to do when apprehension caused her to go pale.

She could see Seavers's back as he leaned on the mantel and stared into the fire, and for a moment she didn't want to disturb the picture. His tawny hair was pulled back and tied with a ribbon at the base of his neck. She took a moment to study his broad shoulders and thick-muscled legs, for when he turned, she knew she would be absorbed by his eyes and would search her memory later for his other features. Before she spoke his name she reminded herself again to be coy — he was not wont to be captured.

"Geoffrey?"

He turned and she watched his features. A slow smile touched her lips as she noted that his eyes warmed, his pupils dilating slightly, as he looked at her. With studied care, she turned and closed the sitting room door, turning back to him again.

"My apologies," she said, her manners rehearsed and delightful to her. "I'm afraid I stayed abed longer than I should have."

"Quite all right, my lady," he said, looking around to be certain they were alone. "I should have asked permission to call on you."

"There's no need," she laughed lightly. "This is as much your home as mine, since we are to be married soon."

"That's why I've come, Ali — Charlotte. I don't want to be put off. I want the wedding to take place immediately."

"Very well," she said easily.

"I think it can't be — " He stopped his argument abruptly and looked at her in wonder. "You are agreeable?"

"This is more your wedding than mine, milord. I am simply a bystander as you marry a fortune. I imagine you wish to begin building your ships."

"I've already begun, madam. On a note. And that is why I cannot allow a delay." He waved a hand about him, indicating her fine surroundings. "But you, it seems, hold all the cards."

"Nonsense. I am only doing all I possibly can to bring credit to your name. I didn't think it polite to look too eager to the king."

Geoffrey relaxed somewhat, though not entirely at ease with the situation. He feared to trust her.

"Then let us discuss marriage plans. With your permission, I should like to rent a house on Tiller Street, a fashionable part of town. Likely you think this fine lodgings, but I prefer living someplace else."

"Whatever you wish," she acquiesced.

"The furnishings are at least as fine, most of the furniture having been brought in from other countries. It's larger and you wouldn't be under the constant surveillance of courtiers and ladies, a situation that no doubt makes you somewhat uncomfortable."

"On the contrary," she returned. "I find it easy enough to bear. But if it makes you uncomfortable, Geoffrey, do let's move."

He inhaled sharply, looking her over carefully. What plot is this? he asked himself. She seemed to be playing the part of every man's ideal mate. "What is your game?" he asked her.

"Milord," she breathed, her brows drawing into a frown, "I beg your pardon?"

"All this cooperation? What is it you want?"

"I only hope to please you," she said quietly, the wind suddenly going out of her sails. This man was certainly the hardest to please, never happy with anything. If she was not groomed in dress and manners, he was upset; if she did her very best, he was suspicious. She felt the insult and it stung. "Would you have me confine my good manners to public dinners only and behave as a tavern wench in private?"

Geoffrey's scowl remained. "No, of course not. I'm sorry — but you've changed so greatly, so quickly, I'm not prepared at all."

"But I haven't," she argued softly. "I've only learned to speak more appropriately, and I've learned what might be expected of me at court. I thought you'd be happy and here you're — "

"Don't go to tears over it, Charlotte," he commanded none too gently. "Let's just sit down and get on to the business about the wedding. I'll hear your ideas on it, since you'll have to do the planning."

"Very well," she sighed, walking the short distance to the settee and dropping gently onto the cushions. "It's getting late in the year and I think it best not to have a fuss. Truth is, I've talked to some of the women about weddings and it seems there's too much detail to remember, so I'd rather have it small with only a few present. Mrs. Stratton, the woman Rodney employed for me, can handle the arrangements." She shrugged and looked down. "I'll only botch it if I try."

"Somehow I don't think you would," Geoffrey commented dryly from his standing position. She looked up at him hopefully. "I should commend you," he continued. "You're coming off looking like the genuine article. Just don't become too confident."

Inside, Alicia knew there was little hope of that, but she hid it well and demurely replied, "I shall take the greatest care."

"Is a fortnight too soon?" he asked her.

"It needn't be that long if you're in a rush," she told him.

"I think you ought to ask for that much time," he said. "You're the one who's supposed to be controlling this, since you'll have to tell the king when you'd like to be married. Can I trust you to do it at once?"

"If you'll tell me the time and place, I'll speak to His Majesty. He's promised to see me this week for that very purpose. I think he's eager to be done with it."

"Good, then, we'll keep it small and trim in money, entertain only a few, though they'll be a rich few and will cost something magnificent to entertain. We'll take a short holiday — that will be expected, though I can't see how I can spare the time — and settle on Tiller Street at once. I think you'll appreciate the lodgings. I chose the house carefully."

As he spoke, Alicia watched him with something akin to disappointment in her eyes. His marriage was such a business affair, and something told her it would not be terribly different if she *were* Charlotte. In fact, she wondered, would he be very different if he loved his bride?

There was a brief tapping at the door and Margaret poked her head in. "Beg pardon, madam," Margaret imposed. "You have a visitor. What excuse would you have me give?"

"Who is it?" Alicia asked, considering the possibility that it was the king, though later she realized Margaret would surely have said so.

"Lord Perry, mum."

Geoffrey immediately stiffened, an action that drew Alicia's eyes to him at once. She had no idea what brought the ill feelings Geoffrey had for Perry — she had her own, and with good reason. She instantly feared the worst; that Perry had recognized her and would expose their plan.

She looked back to Margaret and steadied herself. There was no need to face the prospect alone; no need to hide from Geoffrey the fact that she was a maid pulled out of a country ordinary.

"Did you tell Lord Perry that I am with my betrothed?" she asked Margaret.

"No, mum, but I'll be happy — "

"No," Geoffrey said sharply. "No, indeed. Show his lord-ship in. You needn't even tell him I'm here. I'm curious with his coming."

Alicia looked up at Geoffrey. It was clearly hate and nothing less that Geoffrey felt. It occurred to her that if she confessed that Perry not only knew her, but had stolen her virtue, it might lead to Geoffrey's hatred of her, too. She was not sure how well she could lie. And for how long.

"I wonder what Lord Perry has done to you," she said softly.

"He was betrothed to my sister."

He did not look at her, and for a moment she saw something of pain cross his features.

"I know nothing of your family," she prompted.

"There is none — now." His gaze dropped to her, and for a moment there was a gentleness mixed with remorse in the soft gruffness of his voice and in the way he looked at her. "He was betrothed to my sister — a contract made without the consent of either me or our mother. I'm certain he thought the Seavers family enjoyed wealth, as in the days before the Commonwealth. I think even Andrea thought we would have our lands restored and with them a sizable amount of money."

"And there was nothing?" she asked.

"Nothing restored, and worse; a near guarantee from Charles that it could not be gotten back."

He turned from her and seemed to speak into the mantel of the fireplace. "We were cast to make our fortunes back, as were many others. No money for Perry to wed, and my sister dead, quite suddenly, of a fall while she was riding with her betrothed."

He turned back to her. "He did not grieve."

His eyes grew hard and impassive. "And further, he argued heartily for the hand of the orphaned daughter of our knight, Fergus."

As he finished his statement, the door to the sitting room opened and Culver Perry took a step in, halting suddenly as he spotted Geoffrey. The two studied each other brazenly, rather heatedly, as if the hostility from being in the same room was mutual.

Alicia quickly took note of them; they were equal in many ways. Perry's handsomeness was dark and somewhat sinister, but pleasing to her female eye nonetheless. Geoffrey was fair of hair and his eyes glittering green, but his skin more bronzed than Perry's. Perry was taller; Seavers more solid and muscular. They both commanded with their eyes, but Perry's command seemed plotting, while Seavers dealt from strength.

She understood Geoffrey's reason for hate, for she knew Perry to be a user. He had, after all, used her.

But then, she could not say Geoffrey was innocent of that very flaw.

Perry bowed elaborately, first toward Alicia, speaking with a lilting grace. "Your servant, madam." And then, oozing melodious charm, he turned to Geoffrey and said with familiarity, "Greetings, Geoff." Alicia nearly jumped at the shortened version of his name; it was a first to her ears.

Geoffrey bowed, though stiffly, and made no verbal greeting.

"I was not aware you were here," Perry said to Geoffrey, his eyes gleaming somewhat, his smile almost believable.

"I thought not."

"I called to ask your bride to select her wedding gift, since I'd like to make it something special." He turned his attention to Alicia immediately. "It's not that he's spoiled a surprise, only that I'd have given the choice to you. It seems fitting that the bride make the selection."

"No gift is necessary, Lord Perry, but I thank you for your thoughtfulness."

"Unnecessary? I protest, madam, I — "

"The fact is that we've only just decided the wedding will be a private affair, since neither of us comes from a large family. Aside from His Majesty and whoever he wishes to attend with him, there will be no guests. I apologize." Alicia forced a smile. "I do hope you're not offended."

Her smile became more natural as she realized he certainly was. Mortified, in fact, as she judged from his shocked scowl. "I see," he said rather blandly. He took up another pose, his acting ability nearly matching Alicia's. He *would not* be offended, but gracious to a fault. "Certainly, madam, I understand. Of course you would choose such a wedding. But then, my gift cannot be discounted because of the circumstances. I wish to give you something in any case."

"How very nice. Well then, what is it I am to choose from?" Hands folded in her lap, she watched his gaze settle on her bosom and heard him nearly stutter.

"There are a few things I would offer: a silver service, a chest of great value made in India and lined with the finest silk from the East, or a collection of rare gems taken off a Dutch vessel and brought from Africa."

Alicia looked up at Geoffrey and found he glared at Culver Perry still, but looked to be more in control.

"Geoffrey?" she questioned.

" 'Tis your choice, Charlotte," he replied easily.

"Very well, the chest then," she said quickly. "I think I would be envied to have such a treasure in my home."

"The chest it is, madam," he promised. "It shall be delivered to you posthaste. Am I to assume the wedding will be soon?"

"Very soon," she fairly crooned, making the most adoring eyes toward her intended. "And with all due respect, sir, hereafter you must give me some warning of your visits. It just isn't right for a new bride to entertain a man without a chaperone."

His eyes narrowed slightly, but he smiled. "Of course,

madam," he said in a strained voice. "Then, I'll be going." He turned and quit the room.

A stillness prevailed as neither moved, each contemplating what had just taken place. Alicia gave a barely audible sigh, a silent vow that never again would a man to whom she gave herself forget her so easily. She felt a strange emptiness; an ache that grew within her. She could not bear to think of herself as a passing fancy to be used and tossed carelessly from a man's mind. And yet the culprit had done just that. And he would never know how deeply she hurt.

Seavers simmered inside. He had seen Perry's attention to Alicia's full figure, the light in his eyes as he studied her delicate features. There was no question that his disappointment at not having won the maid was now intense, for she had become a greater prize than any at court imagined she could be.

All the ladies and courtiers had expected Charlotte Bellamy to be most unpretty and crude of manner. Alicia acted the part as a beauty with delicate etiquette and gracious bearing.

Geoffrey looked down at her. Aye, she was perfect. Pity she was an impostor. But then, no one would know. . . .

"It's clear, madam, that he was here to woo you. His offer of a choice of gift was a ruse."

Her soft blue-gray eyes rose to look at him. "Perhaps not, milord," she said.

His hand came out to point at her attire. "Have you nothing more modest to wear?"

She self-consciously gave a tug at the lace bodice. "I'm afraid not. Lady Castlemaine chose most of the gowns. Mrs. Stratton tells me it is her plan to keep the men from staring at Frances Stewart."

"Aye, and I'm certain you are greatly pained to have their eyes on you."

"I don't mind that they find me pretty," she replied.

"Pretty?" he laughed. " 'Tis not the way of the courtiers to look and not touch, *chérie*. Even Perry," he said, raising a hand toward the closed sitting room door. "Had I not been here, your virtue would not have been protected."

"There are servants in the house, milord. He would not have been allowed to hurt me."

Geoffrey turned away and grumbled. "I doubt what he had in mind resembled pain in any way."

"Is there something I have done to offend you?"

He turned back to her, and, as he looked her over, he wore a mixture of lust and anger. "I would see you more suitably gowned, Charlotte, once the wedding has taken place and you live with me."

She laughed suddenly and stood up, walking casually around the settee, thus putting it between them. "I thought the marriage purely a means to an end for you, Geoffrey. How I dress and what I do should not matter to you as long as I *appear* as the wifely sort."

"And you think exposing most of your flesh wifely?" he countered. "Charlotte, it is dangerous to appear too inviting."

Her head dropped and she looked down.

"You see what I say is true?" he asked.

She raised her eyes to meet his. "I don't mind what I do for you — this marriage thing." She took a slow breath. "I don't like the name."

"Name?"

"Charlotte."

"It's only a name."

"But not mine. I feel as though you're talking to someone else."

"I thought it was understood it would *become* yours, even — "

"Never mind," she interrupted, bolstering herself for a more serious subject. "The clothing," she said, returning to the cause for his ire. "I'll wear whatever you like if you'll

104

have it made for me. But pray don't be too dotish in your style. I should not have to suffer too greatly in this position."

His jaw set. "You enjoy the attention."

"Aye," she returned enthusiastically.

"And how can you play wife to me while the men ogle you?"

"As planned. Let them look; it should not matter. You will have your ships. And the envy of the court."

He moved closer to her, looking at her over the settee. "And with that I would have respect. I won't be laughed at, nor will I wear a cuckold's horns."

"You are a jealous fool!"

"And you act a harlot."

"No. A woman — and you cannot appreciate it."

"A wife is modest and loyal."

"A husband is loving."

"Love? This has nothing to do with love."

"Then there is no cause for your rage," she said, turning her back abruptly.

Geoffrey's heart began to pound. He felt certain he'd lost control of her, for she showed the greatest contrasts: warm and cooperative one moment, sassy and presumptuous the next. He walked around the settee and, grabbing her shoulders, turned her around to face him.

Surprise was etched on her features and he relished it. Her mouth was half opened in astonishment and she watched him in stunned silence as he spoke.

"We have a bargain and you will play my wife for the court, for the world. And you will play it by my rules or not at all. Do you understand me?"

He noted her expression of fear and not just surprise. "Please don't hurt me, milord."

A puzzled expression came over his face. Nothing akin to fear possessed her moments ago; why now? He wondered if she expected a beating. Her past was much a mystery to him. Perhaps beatings were a regular part of her life before now.

He loosened his grip on her arms but his gaze was intense. He saw her features relax somewhat.

"Is that how you are controlled? By beatings?"

She shook her head. "I do not wish to be beaten, milord."

"There is a better way to teach you what I expect," he said hoarsely, and, with no hint of his intention, he slipped an arm about her waist and covered her mouth with his.

Alicia's eyes flew open wide and her hand instinctively pushed against his chest, trying to resist him. But he seemed to enjoy her resistance and held her closer, pressing against her, molding her velvet-clad body to his. Her pushing ceased, but she dared not embrace him lest he become aware of her immediate defeat.

She could not be captured.

Her lids gently dropped and she tried to resume the fight, but he must have thought her weak or foolish, for happily, she did not succeed in moving him a breath away.

His lips released hers and he dropped a kiss to the rounded knoll of her heaving breasts. Then his mouth was poised close to hers again.

"While you live with me as my wife, whether in truth or by bargain, you will do my will."

"In truth, your will," she whispered. "By bargain, *our* will."

"I will return you to your tavern lovers," he warned.

The jibe dug deep. He truly believed her a whore.

"You cannot," she breathed. "You love your ships too well."

"I will not fight you long, Alicia. I will win."

He released her and strode quickly away from her. At the sitting room door, he paused and looked at her.

"Set the wedding date with His Majesty. And have a care with your behavior."

She pursed her lips and would not reply. He left without another word and she stood still, but for the transformation her lips made from a stern pucker to a lazy half smile. Trembling still possessed her and her fingers brushed the place on her bosom where his lips had branded her. She was profoundly aware that as he had touched her so intimately, so passionately, he had called her by her given name.

"Perhaps the fight will be longer than you expect, milord," she whispered to the empty room. "But I think you unclear as to the winner."

seven

On an afternoon that was wet and cold, when even a short walk about the palace was inadvisable, Charles, his son James, duke of Monmouth, and George Villiers, duke of Buckingham, stepped from the royal coach and began to walk toward the chapel. The queen, though compassionate by nature, would not attend a Protestant service of any kind.

Charles looked up at the sky and examined the moisture collecting on his hat, coat, and arms. "Beastly day for it," he remarked. "Can they blame me for the weather, George?" Charles asked with some humor.

"They shouldn't, Sire," Villiers replied, speaking of the subjects Charles ruled. "But I think they will, just the same."

"I doubt not," the king muttered, taking long strides to the chapel door. The constant downpour of rain, the frustration of not putting a quick end to the Dutch conflict, one mistress pregnant, a heatedly pursued woman still a virgin, and countless other miseries did not plague him overmuch. But the damn rain spoiled his walks in St. James Park, and that had made him a trifle cross.

The chapel was dim. Inside, the others waited: Castle-maine, Frances Stewart, a minor few courtiers and ladies; and near the front of the chapel stood Lord Seavers and his friend Preston Tilden. All rose and curtsied or bowed as the king entered.

As if to still any apprehension, Charles put forth his hands to pat down nervousness. "She is on her way. She'll arrive any moment."

The round-faced chaplain smiled and bobbed and others either relaxed in their stance or sat down again. Charles took note that there were no special provisions made for the day; no special bouquets or streamers, no musician or reader. He scowled slightly, shook his head, and considered the waste of space he viewed. This wedding of Seavers's could have been done by contract and no ceremony. Charles thought Geoffrey would one day regret being so damned tight-fisted and uncaring.

Charles left Lady Charlotte's apartments just ahead of her, allowing her to finish her primping and preening with just her women, and thought he had beheld perhaps the loveliest bride he had ever seen. But as her women fussed all around her, he had not seen her smile. Indeed, she looked deeply saddened, though he couldn't imagine why. Seavers, he guessed, had been oafish in his courtship and the bride had second thoughts. Charles's next emotion was an intense desire to get the thing done before any more time was required of him. He wanted this ward married, the ships built, and as little trouble as possible.

There was the sound of the heavy oaken doors opening, and the look of relief on the face of the priest told Charles that Charlotte Bellamy had at last arrived and his part in all this would soon be over. He turned to behold her, a striking creature done from head to toe in white, with lace trimmed in silver thread adorning her gown. Ahh, Charles thought appreciatively, Barbara ought to dress all the women at Whitehall.

The bulk of Alicia's hair was pulled sharply away from her face and fell to her shoulders. Tiny curls framed her face. Transparent lace covered her from her breasts to her neck, allowing for a deep plunging V. Her slim waist was caught by a silver chain and her tiny slippers glittered as she took a step. A black cloak lined with silver fox was pulled off her shoulders by her woman, and then a long lace veil that fell from her crown was lightly fluffed. Charles caught the sound of a sigh and turned quickly to look in the direction of Lord Seavers, hopeful, as hopeful romantics often are, that the sigh had come from him.

But Seavers's expression was serious, if not stern. He stood as he would while commanding a ship, hands behind his back and legs braced slightly apart. The man had gained a reputation in warfare that was nothing less than fantastic, and he held claim to several victorious moments in battle; but Charles feared he was slightly daft if the sight of this bride did not even warm his cool eyes.

Preston Tilden, on the other hand, smiled openly, and his pale blue eyes shone as he beheld the beauty before him.

Well, thought Charles, something exciting may come of this yet.

It was not as if Geoffrey Seavers were seeing something other than what the other men beheld; it was the feeling in his gut that caused his slight scowl and cool eyes. Aye, she was beautiful, and the plan he had been talked into by Rodney had seemed a simple and temporary project, until this transformation in Alicia.

The first inkling that it would not be so simple and impersonal an arrangement came when he viewed her in the inn, garbed in only her linen wrap. Later, at their introduction, he recognized open desire in himself. And when he tasted her lips, his agony heightened. He had not lost sight of his goals. But he did not know how to keep himself from an irrevocable involvement with her. Even now, as she approached him, her shining eyes somewhat sad and uncertain, he fought the urge to cradle her in his arms and comfort her. He had been plagued, since early in his youth, with the dramatic longing to take care of the women whose lives he touched.

And this one was no exception.

They knelt together, exchanged their promises, hers all done in the name of Charlotte Bellamy, and rose to seal their marriage with an embrace and kiss.

Alicia faced her husband, a husband only in a play to entertain those present and to secure an inheritance. Tears clung to her dark lashes and her lips trembled. She had done well to conceal what her heart cried throughout her life, but this once it was more than she could hide.

True, all of her life she could do what had to be done, behave the way she was expected to behave, feel nothing — or at least let nothing she felt show; whatever role was required of her, she could perform. It kept clothes on her back and food in her stomach. Even this wedding was a means to a specific end: life would be comfortable on her hundred pounds.

But this thought did little to console her. This wedding was like a dream she had nurtured; a dream that one day she would be loved, wanted. That it was just another role for her to play hurt her deeply. And though the final plans had not yet been made, their arrangement would end and she would leave. How, she wondered, am I to leave? Feeling what I've come to feel?

His lips released hers and she looked for a moment into his concealing eyes. He seemed to reconfirm for her that all her longings would be unmet; that for this union, tickets should be sold as in the Duke's Theatre. A tear dropped from her lashes and coursed its way down her cheek. For an instant, through clouded vision, she thought she saw a change in his eyes, something close to compassion.

His hand came up to brush the tear from her cheek and then he kissed the same place. His voice came lightly into her ear.

"It's all right, Charlotte. Brides are oft sentimental on their wedding day."

"Oaf," she muttered back to him.

His earlier sternness returned, and within she felt a certain victory. She had, after all, forgotten her place. Her eyes quickly dried as she took pleasure in teaching him just how well she would play the willing chattel.

A brief though formal supper in Lord and Lady Seavers's apartments followed, lovingly prepared and displayed by Mrs. Stratton and a staff of giddy and excited servants. To serve an intimate crowd of under thirty people, with the king and his competing mistresses among them, was a feather in any servant's cap. And while courtiers' curiosity had peaked when Lady Charlotte was summoned and just arriving at Whitehall, most were satisfied now to have seen her. Since the wedding was done and the newest beauty at least temporarily locked apart from the admiring courtiers and jealous ladies, this group had bored of the folly and did not stay long. The night was young when Charles said his farewells and was followed by his train of faithful pups to a rowdier dinner elsewhere.

"Let me ready you for bed, love," Margaret murmured in Alicia's ear the moment the door had closed behind the guests. But Alicia did not look at her serving woman. Her eyes were fixed on Geoffrey, who swirled brandy in his glass and looked into it pensively as he stood in front of a blazing fire. She could not pull her eyes from his broad shoulders, his lean thighs.

This was, in all its absurdity, her wedding night.

"Come, love," Margaret said again, this time pulling at Alicia's sleeve.

This time, at the sound of the voice, Geoffrey turned. For a moment, as their eyes locked, Alicia thought they might be of like mind: that perhaps they should carry on with the play. A timid smile crossed her lips and her voice came softly.

"Mrs. Stratton is eager to help me out of my gown, milord."

The hand holding the drink came out abruptly in her direction and his voice was also quiet, though impatient. "Go ahead, then. I'll be along."

Alicia donned a daringly transparent sleeping gown and covered that with a dressing gown of the same pink hue, though less revealing. While her heart thumped out a rhythm that spoke of anything but fear, she was not certain that consummating this bargain was wise, though she desperately wanted him to make love to her.

Am I his bride? she asked herself. Am I his love or his servant or his desire? Will he make me his whore?

And then her thoughts quickly raced to a possible consummation and she wondered how she was to explain that she was not a virgin. He did not expect her to be, his words had proven that. But she wished him to know that she'd lost her virtue to a misguided moment of love and passion and not to paying tavern patrons. She had not been used for sport by drunkards and thieves, though she had been betrayed once before.

There had been moments, though brief and fleeting, when she had seen compassion and caring in his eyes, when she felt like a person and not a possession in his presence. She prayed she would find another such moment as he approached her. Otherwise, she was not sure she could let him touch her, however intense her own desires.

Her hair was brushed out and lay across her shoulders. She arranged herself on the daybed, the large four-poster seeming too real for her, and excused her one servant. Wine, she thought, would serve her now, though she'd already had more than she was accustomed to. Geoffrey did not enter her bedchamber for a very long time, and the time clawed at her nerves. She was on such a ledge of apprehension when he did enter that the sound of the latch and the opening of the door caused her to jump.

His periwig had been discarded and his coat was slung over one shoulder. He looked ready for a comfortable evening; he looked ready for bed. He still carried the glass of amber fluid in one hand but he was not drunk — Alicia had come to know.

His coat was tossed onto a nearby chair and he came to sit on the edge of her settee.

"You've done a masterful job of the day, love," he said with pride. "I'm pleased."

"Mrs. Stratton deserves your thanks," she said.

"For the dinner I've thanked her and given her a little something extra. You, on the other hand, were magnificent."

This form of seduction was very new to Alicia. She lowered her eyes and mumbled her thanks.

"I have all the papers the king was holding. There's land in the country that I doubt Charlotte ever saw and I think it will be quickly sold. But before that we should visit the manor — when the weather clears. Are you agreeable to a trip?"

Her eyes came up and her apprehension about their possible consummation fled. He was again bent on business. "If you wish."

"I think it would be wise at least to look at the property, though I need the money as quickly as possible."

Muted by his cool reserve, she simply looked at him.

"We will move from this house in a few days, and may I suggest as little entertaining and gadding about as possible until then."

Not the slightest discomfort from longing showed on his face. "Whatever you wish, my lord," she said, though her voice was becoming less timid and more perturbed.

"Very well, we'll keep it simple and stay away from the curious, since there's no honeymoon."

"And is that in keeping with the custom, sir?" she asked coldly.

"What exactly were you expecting, madam?" he asked.

"Not very much more," she snapped.

"Well, my dear, you've done a fine job and I hope you know how pleased —"

With a huff, Alicia drew herself from the daybed and stood glaring at him. "I'm certainly glad you're pleased."

He took on an expression of complete confusion. "What's got your wind up now?" he asked. "God's bones, I can't seem to pay you a decent compliment without getting your nose out of joint, nor can I —"

"Decent compliment? You mindless oaf, what compliment is this? Where does your great plan end and your own mind begin?"

"I haven't any idea what you want," he returned, nearly as angrily.

"Is there any part of me that doesn't fit your *plan?*"

He stood and once again they glared at each other over a piece of furniture.

"Your constant complaints don't fit my plan," he blustered.

"Is there a man under that armor, or are *you* a ship and a contract? What flows through your veins, my fine lord? Blood or oil?"

He placed his hands on his hips and met her, blow for blow. "Well, my fancy harlot, is it love you plead for now?"

"Never have I had to play the harlot until now," she shot back. "Even through the years I served the ale to men, never did I sell myself. Does any woman know my lord Seavers's love — or do they all show their pretty smiles and best manners, only to be met by your cold eyes?"

"I think perhaps I've been better appreciated before now.

You might thank *me* for your gowns and jewels and fine lodgings."

"I could as easily thank Charlotte Bellamy, poor wench. She'd have found something lacking in *this* marriage."

"I see the newer gowns have done little for your morals. Are you so starved for a man that you taunt me now? I thought you wanted nothing more of me than my hundred pounds and a few months of courtly life. But I see from your antics that I was wrong to trust a tavern wench to act the lady. I —"

"You slimy son of a guttersnipe! How dare you treat me as you would your whores! Who would do for you what I do? Who would play your game as well, fool so many with nary a flaw? 'Sdeath, you're a wretched blackguard hiding in a sea captain's coat."

"Lower your voice, bitch, before you bring out the guard —"

"I wager you throw the whores in the streets orange skins and blow them kisses."

"Enough of your slurs, wench, or I'll see you driven out of your fine lace and jewels, and slinging ale for your drunkards again."

"And you'll rot in Newgate, fool, for laying a finger to my lace." She turned angrily away, presenting her back, her arms crossed over her chest. Ignorant, iron-blooded imbecile, she silently raged. Could he not see what she would trade for a kiss? For one show of affection in lieu of his constant patronizing of her acting ability? "*I* am the fool. I thought there was more flesh in you than silver." She turned back to him. "You are a clout-headed, self-centered —"

"Alicia," he warned, his green eyes blazing.

"— lying, scheming jackass." She took a breath. Her anger, as much with herself for wanting him as with him for rejecting her, did not allow her to see how close he was to losing control. "And never," she sneered, "have I known such a tight-fisted bastard as you."

The glass he held broke in his hand, and quickly, both hands were on the daybed as he easily slid it away. With a squeak of fear, she picked up the lacy folds of her dressing gown and made to get away, but before she took two steps, he had grabbed her arm, spun her around, and thrown her on the bed. He pounced atop her and held her pinioned. No amount of struggling could free even her arms, and when she ceased her fight, she was forced to look into his angry eyes.

"I allowed you more words than good sense said I should," he told her, his voice deep but controlled. "Now listen to me and hear me this time, for I won't say this again. You've a certain right to be angry, for truth, I use your beauty, charm, and wit to gain my fortune. But I gave you the terms and you agreed, so I'll not take another tongue-lashing from you."

Tears came to her eyes as a thousand emotions built within her. She was ashamed of the slurs she'd cast on him, and, from her point of view, he had been entitled to the oaths he had hurled at her; she had goaded him so. Further shame filled her that she had been angry at not being wanted to fill any physical role for him. And more than that, it still stung her so deeply to want him, while he continually assured her that she filled only a temporary and detached role in his life. She blinked her eyes hard and the tears flowed across her temples and into her hair.

"I don't want you harmed or scarred, but I'll see you taken quickly and quietly away from here if there's any chance you'll scare off my money for ships, Alicia."

"I am a person; not a dog to be whipped for growling," she sputtered.

"And so you've had a hurt or two, wench. Do you think that you alone have suffered disappointments? Been used and tossed aside?"

"Nay, I think not I alone," she stammered. "But never did I choose to give that back to another." She sniffed and choked. "You are cold, Lord Seavers."

"Aye," he said, brushing her hair from her brow. "Perhaps I am that, but I've more on my mind than a toss in bed with a tavern wench."

"And if I were Charlotte Bellamy? What would you give me then?" she asked with a sniff.

"Not a great deal more," he assured her. "Except perhaps a good lashing for your foul behavior."

He pulled himself from atop her and stood looking down at her. "But you are not Charlotte," he said in a voice that was low and soft. "You are Alicia, a lass spirited away from a country ordinary. And unless I make some arrangements for your existence here to be short, we'll all rot in Newgate. Or worse."

She covered her eyes with the back of her hand as she considered her outburst and the strength of her words. They might've been *heard*. And she could not think of a way to undo that.

"Now, Alicia," he fairly whispered. "Can I trust you or must I send Rodney to fetch you away on the very night of our wedding?"

She shook her head. Though it was difficult, she struggled to sit up, and faced him. "I — I'm sorry, my lord. I promise you — I won't question our agreement again."

Through her blurred vision she could see some softness in his gaze. "And I am sorry, Alicia. I had hoped you would not be hurt. I believe I warned you from the beginning: I belong to no one. I will have no ties now. You should not have let yourself love me."

Her mouth dropped open slightly and she stared at him aghast.

"You cover it very poorly." He shrugged. "Indeed, you cover it not at all."

Surprisingly, she did not feel another surge of tears. In a manner, the confrontation was mostly comfortable to her. "And you, Lord Seavers," she said with amazing calm, "can you love no woman?"

"I think perhaps I can't," he replied. "But be assured," he went on with a smile that was rueful, "if I do learn that I can love a woman, I hope she is as lovely as you — with a bit less belligerence."

She turned her head away. "I hope for your sake, Geoffrey, that you live long enough."

The rain mingled with snow and sleet through the Christmas season. It was a time when most of London preferred to hover around blazing fires and exchange their gifts. With the coming of the new year the weather cleared somewhat, though it remained frightfully cold. Roads were passable and lodging available for the most part. It was just after the new year that Preston Tilden began sending couriers out of the city on a route that took them all the way to Portsmouth and spread them generously across the southeastern portion of England.

The couriers Preston had hired were told to ask after a small child who had been separated from her family in 1650. Lord and Lady Tilden, Royalists, could no longer stay in England safely and had to plan their flight out of the country. But then the revolution was young and the noble couple clung to their optimism, hoping the war would be short-lived and they would be able to return to England soon. They had no way of knowing it would be years before Royalists could reclaim their England.

Lord and Lady Tilden packed up what they could carry, and at Lord Tilden's insistence, their five sons fled with them. "The Commonwealth may claim my land and home and arms, but by damn, they will not cost me my sons. If death lies upon the road, they'll go with me." It was only through Lady Tilden's pleading that the baron allowed their baby girl, Letty, to be spirited away to an aunt in the south of England for her safekeeping until they could either return for her or pay her passage to some faraway place.

But the child, just a toddler, never arrived at the aunt's manor and no trace of her passing was uncovered. It was to find the whereabouts of at least a grave to end this mystery that Preston planned an extended stay in England. And the wharf remained his concern, on behalf of his father and brothers, whose ships were regularly in and out of port, until the couriers he paid had some evidence of her passing for him to investigate himself.

During the weeks that his misfit band of detectives questioned the south of the country, Preston worked and entertained himself with the regular court parties and activities, such as dinners, trips to the theater, dances, and gambling. He tried mightily hard to stay out of the way of his friend Geoffrey and his new bride, for he remembered well how grateful he was at the end of a day when he could nestle his own Brianna in his arms and close out the rest of the world. But he soon suspected that his etiquette in this was not appreciated.

When the sun was setting and he would have left the wharf for some evening entertainment in the palace, he went instead to the vessel on which he knew he would find Geoffrey. The *Patrina* was now the favorite but not the only ship that Lord Seavers possessed, and Preston had heard it was also his home. Apparently Seavers lived on his ship while buying, refurbishing, and repairing more vessels, stocking them with arms, and eager to be setting them out to sea.

Seavers's crew was busy clearing the deck of ropes and building materials as they ended their day. Rodney stood looking out over the men, his hands plunged into the pockets of his heavy woolen coat, his cheeks bright red from the cold, and steam coming from his nose. Preston came on board and lifted a hand to Rodney, to which the manservant-mate nodded once. In question, Preston pointed toward the captain's quarters, to which Rodney nodded again. They passed each other in the cold twilight without another word.

Preston gave two sharp raps to the door and heard Geoffrey's terse welcome. "Aye."

Preston scowled slightly at the sight within the small room. Geoffrey sat behind his desk virtually hidden among rolling plans and litter. His clothes were draped recklessly about the cabin, a bed made out of a windowseat still lay in rumpled disarray, and nothing about the man or his habitat resembled the Geoffrey he had known for so long.

"You?" Geoffrey said. "What have you about this part of town? I heard you entertained yourself mostly at Whitehall."

"Someone let it get about that I have the means to gamble well, and true, I've been welcomed into their circle. But I find their games tiresome at times." Preston looked around the disheveled quarters. "Are you so eager for your fortune that you need sleep here?"

"It's proven efficient enough," Geoffrey said, rising and reaching for a skin of wine that hung from a nail near his desk. He poured some into two cups and held one out to Preston. "Now there's the money, the time is what I grow short of. I've waited a mighty long time to get this fleet together."

Geoffrey raised his cup in something of a toast and Preston complied. "To your industry," Preston offered. They both drank. "But what'll you spend your fortune on?"

Geoffrey shrugged and turned away. "More ships, I imagine."

"What of pleasurable things? Have you given them up altogether?"

"I've no taste for dancing and the Duke's Theatre."

"I was there just today," Preston said. "With the lovely Lady Seavers."

Geoffrey glanced up with something of a start, then quickly accepted his friend's news and walked back toward his papers. "I thank you for escorting her. She's been left alone a great deal."

"She did not tell me how much, but from the looks of this place, it seems you see your wife but little."

"A busy time..."

"A beautiful woman, to be abandoned in London, at the whim of the court and all their vultures?"

Again Geoffrey shrugged and did not meet Preston's eyes.

"Would you like to tell an old friend about your troubles?"

"What troubles? I'm a busy man and can't find the time to play honeymoon at the moment. But once the work is done I can settle myself into more pleasurable games." He smiled and pointed his cup toward Preston. "You've grown more solid since your marriage."

Preston did not smile. "I've been here since November and with luck I'll leave in early spring. Since that time I've seen you betrothed, wedded, and acting the part of a hermit in your ship's cabin. What ails you? Do you hate the lass?"

"No, I have work," Geoffrey insisted very loudly.

"No man has work so urgent that he can't spend a few minutes in a coach to sleep in a decent bed with a beautiful woman, rather than taking up sleeping in a sty such as this. Not even the king."

"I've been with my wife," Geoffrey lied.

"She's not a very happy woman," Preston informed him. "Though she pretends to be."

"She has money, beautiful clothes, plenty of invitations to dinners she can handle quite well, and I'm near enough to be called. If she's not happy, I'd say it's her concern, not mine."

"Why do you scorn her?"

"By God, what is your interest in my private life? In where I sleep and when? In my wife's *happiness*?"

"There's a bad smell in the air, Lord Seavers. If you have a problem, let me share it."

"No problem," Geoffrey insisted, turning away from his

friend again, his face reddening and his muscles tensing more as each moment passed.

"Is it a whore who needs to be dealt with? This urgency with money — is there a problem I can help you solve so you can live a normal existence? Money I have and whores I've dealt with before."

"Money I married and whores I have no time for," Seavers barked. "Leave off."

"I'm not here to pry, but to help. If there's something —"

"Christ, leave off I say. There's nothing." Geoffrey set his mug down with a clunk and ran a hand through his tousled hair. "Look, friend, I appreciate your concern, but it's for naught. There are plans that need work, workers that need pay, a war that needs ships, and foul-smelling Dutchmen lurking on the seas. I have no time for parties and court games. Mayhaps when I have twenty ships ready to sail and a pregnant wife, I can wander about and worry about other men's personal problems."

Preston put up his hands as if to stop Geoffrey or at least soften his tenseness. "I only wished to offer aid — if there is a problem. I did not intend that you should be angry with me."

Geoffrey shook his head. There was no hiding his troubles; it was clear and probably all about London that he saw his wife almost not at all, barely maintained the house on Tiller Street, and since his wedding had not been seen at any functions. He did not know how much gadding about Alicia was doing; he had assigned the chore of watching her movements to Rodney and did not want to hear about her unless there was urgent trouble. From what he had gathered, Alicia did little more than wish away her days in their house.

His growing desire for her pressed down on him every time he was in her presence. He found himself wanting her, and the feeling shook him to the core. If it was not enough that she was a common tavern wench, an unlikely match for a noble bred through a long line of aristocratic ancestors, she was also his pawn in an illegal scheme to trick himself into some quick money. Becoming at all attached to her now would be a disastrous mistake; it could only lengthen the time he had to fear discovery. He could not even consider his own emotions. He forced himself to disregard her. She was the means to his fleet and work became his life.

He popped in and out of the house, checked on the servants and the condition of the property he rented, and then went back to work. He worked continually, often through the night, and thought about the woman who was known as Lady Seavers as little as possible. True, there were a great many times she arrived without notice into dreams that left him weak and breathless, but he vowed that in time he would control even those.

"You're right," Geoffrey said reluctantly. "I'm working too hard . . . and there's no great reward in never having a day off. What say I clean up and we'll take Lady Seavers to dinner?"

Preston smiled and shook his head. "I'll beg off this time. I've made plans to meet a group for more dice and there's a pretty wench to bring me some luck." He laughed. "Luck only, Seavers, I promise you — I don't play the ladies since I can't find one in all the world looks better to me than Brianna. I'll leave you to have dinner with your lady alone." He nodded once and his smile was sincere. "You look as though you could use it."

He turned to leave, but at the sound of his name he turned to look at his friend once more.

"Preston, I regret that I shouted. I appreciate your offer of help, but the truth is there's nothing I need but to get my work finished and my ships on the sea. Then I imagine I can enjoy myself more."

Preston nodded and left the cabin and the ship, and went on to his evening of throwing dice. His nights were spent mostly on his favored vessel, the *Letty*, though there were offers aplenty of more comfortable lodgings, and occasionally he took rooms elsewhere.

It was past midnight when he'd had enough gambling and drinking and hired a coach to take him back to the wharves. He bade the driver pause at a certain place and asked him to wait a moment.

Preston walked slowly toward the *Patrina* and a young sailor jumped up from the deck at the sound of Preston's close footfalls. The man shouted down, "Who calls?"

"Captain Tilden. Is your captain aboard?"

"Aye, come up, sir."

Preston paused, gave a long sigh, and called back. "I'll see him tomorrow, lad. Good watch. Good night."

"Thank you, sir," the lad called back.

Preston took his coach the rest of the way, damned if he could figure it. Poor bastard, he thought in perplexity. Suppose he wants to use her — and *can't*.

eight

The one advantage of the house in Tiller Street was that there were gardens; lovely, quiet gardens. When one inhabited apartments in Whitehall there were also gardens, but they were filled with maids playing games, suitors playing suit, the royal family abiding there, and, on several occasions, political conferences meant to be secret: the plotting of plots and the scheming of schemes.

Spring was not exactly on the horizon and the weather had a strong tendency to be nasty, but Alicia was a country girl, and so was accustomed to being outdoors in any kind of weather. She'd played, eaten, and even bathed outdoors. She was more familiar with the elements than she was with the functions of a noble's house in the city. For that reason, she considered herself fortunate that, between Rodney Prentiss and Mrs. Stratton, she was not needed to oversee any household projects. They did ask her, on a regular basis, what her preference for cleaning, decorating, or cooking would be, but if she only shrugged, the chore would be completed just the same.

There were spaniels that belonged to the driver of their carriage and the dogs sometimes played in the garden.

Alicia could easily have had them driven away, for this was her home now, but she enjoyed the dogs and would sit for hours throwing sticks for them, patting their heads and stroking their backs.

She was sitting on the marble bench in the garden with her friends when Preston called out to her. At the sound of his voice, she turned with a bright smile to greet him.

"Those dogs will dirty your skirts," he said, smiling. "But I don't think that matters much to you, does it?"

"Not a bit," she laughed, jumping to her feet and brushing off the deep green velvet that covered her. "Mrs. Stratton enjoys fussing about it and then cleaning the clothes." She giggled a little. "Sometimes I think she's the mother I never knew."

"That's right," Preston said, scratching his chin. "Your mother died when you were born."

And it quickly became Alicia's moment for surprise, for she was so comfortable with Preston that she had forgotten he knew nothing of her actual past. He only knew the past of Charlotte. A very strange feeling crept over her at the realization of that, since she felt more of a kinship with Preston than she did with Geoffrey. "Yes," she murmured. "That's right."

"I've come to say good-bye. I'm going to be out of the city for a while — not long. I'll be back as quickly as possible. I think I told you that my wife will deliver our first child this summer."

"Then you don't want to be away too long," she responded quietly.

"I'll hurry business if I can, but it isn't a thing that can be hurried."

"Trade? Are you buying —"

"No, Charlotte, it's the business of my sister that takes me out of the city. The couriers I sent in search of information have returned to tell me of a few things I would like to investigate."

She tilted her head slightly and peered at him. She had no idea what business this was.

"Geoffrey did not tell you?" he asked.

"He said nothing of your sister . . . only your shipping and your brothers and . . . the fact is, he's been so busy that . . . well, we hardly find the time . . ." She let her voice trail off, for she had not yet complained of a lack of attention from Geoffrey. She felt she had no right to. Things were progressing just as had been planned; she played the wife and he played lord, merchant, and sailor. There was nothing in their agreement that said he would also play the husband.

"I think you need say no more. I know that Lord Seavers spends very little time with you." Preston lifted her chin with a finger and looked into her eyes. "He seems greatly troubled, Charlotte. Do you know why?"

She shrugged and shook her head. "He speaks often of pressing schedules; work to be done."

"I suppose that is the extent of it. I always had my family and we shared the work; sometimes without pause for enjoyable things. Geoffrey has only himself."

He needn't be alone, Alicia thought. If he would but make me his helper rather than —

Alicia had come to the conclusion just after the wedding that they need not make this a temporary arrangement just for the dowry. She had already fooled the court and been accepted as well as Charlotte Bellamy ever would have been. There was no need for her disappearance or simulated death. If Geoffrey felt anything for her at all, and there were times she believed he did feel something, they could go on with their play forever. All she needed was to be told that it was *she* and not the ghost of Charlotte and a fortune that he wanted.

"Tell me about your sister, Preston," she said. "What happened to her?"

He took her elbow and, kicking away the spaniels, led her to the marble bench where they could sit and talk.

"My family fled England just after the king was murdered. My mother, father, and five brothers. Mother pleaded for the baby, Letty. She feared taking her abroad to parts unknown. The rumors were wild then; stories of fleeing nobles being murdered on the road and worse. Mother's sister could take Letty until the worst was over, and we could send for her or return for her.

"But Letty never arrived." He shrugged. "A letter followed us for almost a year before we knew that the youngest and safest of us all had not made the journey."

"And since? No word?"

"The driver of the coach that took her away and the maid who tended her were married and had no children. It was always our hope that they'd claimed her and settled someplace in the country. In that case they could eventually be found. But never did my father or any of his men find any couple with a child that could be my sister. There has been no trace until now."

Alicia sat on the edge of the bench with her elbows on her knees, listening intently to every word. Her own background being so hazy, the strong sense of family that Preston exhibited was wonderful to her. That he would be moved to pursue the fate of his sister filled her with envy; she had searched for a sense of belonging, a sense of family for a long time. "And now, Preston? What trace now?"

"There a village of not more than a hundred people in the south that has an old coach they've used for fifteen years. It was a rich coach when it was first found, and the smith repaired it a hundred times over the years so it could be used. It has a family crest on the door that's marred, but possibly recognizable. If it's a Tilden coach I'll know it. And if it is the coach, Letty must have been found nearby. I'll at least know where she is buried."

"I imagine if you can find that much, there should be an entire story to go along with it. Oh Preston, I do hope it's good news."

"I think that's a little too much to hope for. I'll be content simply to know what happened to her."

Alicia felt a lift in her heart, a kinship of souls with Preston. He portrayed for her the type of family she would choose for herself, if that were possible. She felt her eyes grow moist with the emotion. "That you would even search for her past, Preston, is so noble, so . . ."

Preston laughed at her and touched her nose, a gesture that made her smile in spite of her deep feeling. "Of course, you would understand: your mother was lost to you early and your father left you soon after. Not many understand as you and I do, since our families have both been separated and spread apart.

"And that is the thing I consider now; that we have no evidence concerning what became of my sister. I think the matter cannot be put to rest in any of our minds until every effort is made to uncover her story."

"Even though she had a very short life, I find I envy her, Preston," Alicia said with a sigh.

Preston delighted in her. "You're the perfect audience, Charlotte. But let's remember, *chérie*, it's very likely the best that can be done is to be pointed to an unmarked grave. I don't know how an infant would survive . . ."

Her eyes began to water slightly. "You *shall* find her, Preston. I just know it! And please, hurry to tell me. Please."

Preston rose from the bench and looked at Alicia with open adoration, he was so moved by her sensitivity. "Thank you for your encouragement, *chérie*. I will send word. And I won't be away long."

Preston started toward the house with Alicia close behind him, chattering all the way. "And if she isn't married, Preston, what do you suppose? What if she's turned awful and mean? What'll you do if she's fat and ugly?"

Laughter rippled through the house as they walked toward the front door where Preston would take his leave. "If she's horrible, fat, and wretched, she'll be a damned good sight if she's alive. If she's a murderess, I'm prepared to buy her freedom, and if she's indentured, I'll break her bonds."

"You'll be her knight," Alicia laughed excitedly. "You'll find her and take her from all her miseries of the years and deliver her to her rich parents and . . ." Again she laughed, her heart glad and her imagination wild.

Preston paused before the front door and leaned down to kiss her forehead. "Sweet lady, you are the only person I've known, including my own family, to see any hope in the situation."

"Of course, I am, Preston, but look: nothing wonderful should've happened to me, but I am here, wearing gowns — the king's own ward for a time." She shrugged. "Why wouldn't I imagine the very best? Hurry and go so you can tell me what you find."

He started to leave and then turned to her again. "Lucky you caught your lord, darling. If my sister had not been lost, you can be sure I'd have seen her married to Geoffrey. Thank the stars it's too late for him to speak for Alicia."

First a puzzled look and then an overall sensation of pure shock settled over her. She leaned unsteadily against the doorjamb, but Preston did not notice, for he had tipped his feathered hat and turned to go.

"Preston? Lord Tilden?" she called weakly. He turned to look at her. "Alicia?" she questioned.

"Aye, though she was Letty to the family." He shrugged and smiled, still exuberant because of Alicia's excitement. "Do you think she'll want to throw off that pet name?"

Alicia shook her head dumbly. "I think Alicia is a beautiful name," she whispered. "Go with God."

He raised a hand to her and walked briskly down the street. As his broad shoulders disappeared from her sight, a tear glistened on her lashes and her trembling lips whispered another farewell. "Go safely — my brother. . . ."

For endless days and longer nights Alicia's mind was totally consumed with the probability that she and Preston were related by blood, that she was the sister he sought. The only tokens of her childhood, her links to him, were the similarity in the way his sister had disappeared and the small toddler's gown that she was found wearing when the Thatchers took her in. She still possessed the gown, though it was nothing more than a tattered rag now. And it bore no evidence of being something of the Tilden family; there was no crest or initial anywhere on the garment.

The dream that had once comforted her now plagued her. She strained to make every detail more clear and was convinced that Preston was the older brother who had tended her, scolded her, and loved her. And the fair-haired woman who cried: she must certainly have been her mother. The red cloak — why had she not worn the red cloak? And what time of year was it? She remembered cold and rain, but she wasn't sure whether the memory was of traveling or of another time and place. But the name was hers. And it was not a common name. Her looks were not unique; many English girls had brown hair and blue eyes. She had no marks on her body that would have been there since birth.

"But I am his Letty," she told herself. "There is no doubt."

Where the doubt loomed large was in what to do about it. She troubled for only a short time on whether to tell Geoffrey. There was no point, since he rarely took the time to talk to her about anything at all and clearly was not interested in Preston's business in England. His biggest concern seemed to be in quickly spending Charlotte Bellamy's dowry.

She thought of confronting Preston with the possibility, but the thought of being shown to be an impostor was terrifying. Preston might well be prepared to pay Alicia's bondage, free her of debts, and help clear her name, but was he ready to face the king with her treason?

Her fear became more real when she went with Margaret to the Exchange. It was an outing she had not allowed herself often, for she was still a bit at odds as to how she was supposed to act in public. On this trip abroad she had it in her mind to buy linen and thread to try her hand at needlework: something Margaret wanted to teach her. "All the high-bred noblewomen do it," Margaret had said. And it was perfect for lying deep in thought without drawing too much attention to yourself, Alicia thought.

And so the things were purchased, and Alicia was lingering over a display of lace and ribbons when she heard her name called. "My lady Seavers, dear heaven. How marvelous you're looking; how grand."

As she turned she was amazed to see Lady Castlemaine, complete with her own entourage of courtiers and servants, and with her vizard held up over her eyes. Barbara was done in the face patches that were so popular, and her belly swelled with child, for she was preparing to deliver her fifth. Alicia stood shocked for a moment, for the attention took her by surprise.

"You *must* come to supper, my lady. Why, you're all the talk of Whitehall since you're seen about so little these days."

Alicia smiled then and curtsied before her ladyship. She had heard that Barbara's popularity was slipping and that the suppers Frances Stewart gave were packed with all the important people. With some pride, Alicia thought Barbara wanted to draw people with Alicia's presence.

"I'd be honored, madam," she replied demurely, wondering how she would dare find an excuse for not going. She was not sure whether she liked or hated Barbara Palmer, but she surely feared her. Being her protégé in a manner was fun, but being her enemy must be terrifying.

"Then I'll call on you soon, madam, and we'll arrange it. I've been so aflutter with invitations myself that it takes some doing to plan a party. But I will manage something very soon."

Barbara's departure was carried out with as much aplomb as her arrival, her servants and admirers trailing along behind, giggling maids and mincing fops all in a line at her back.

Alicia turned back to the lace and ribbons, not quite seeing them, a light glow creeping to her cheeks. She was somewhat embarrassed by the fuss and took just a moment to focus on what had interested her earlier. She shook off the slight daze and was about to turn to Margaret with a request to go on home, when she met with angry eyes. She found herself face to face with a lass of about her own age, though she was a good deal larger. The eyes bore down on her and the copper curls seemed to tremble.

Alicia's mouth stood slightly open in wonder.

"So ye'r the one," the girl growled. "Ye'r the one what calls herself 'Lady Seavers.' "

"Margaret?" Alicia said, looking around.

"I don't know who you are," the girl spat, "but I know who you *ain't!* You ain't Charlotte Bellamy, that's sure." With that the young woman snatched at the purse hanging on Alicia's wrist, and the cord bound and tore at her gloved hand as the purse was pulled off. Alicia gave a cry and a shriek, and Margaret dropped what she was holding to join the fight, but the girl grabbed the article and ran through the crowd of people, quickly disappearing from sight.

"Stop the thief!" Margaret screamed, half chasing the woman. "Stop her, she's taken milady's purse! Catch her, the fat one!"

It was then that Alicia realized who that had been. From the king's own words, "*I thought your hair might be red. And that you were well fed.*" Alicia prayed they would not catch her.

"Margaret, please, let's just go . . ."

By that time a crowd had gathered, and Rodney, their driver and escort, having heard the screaming and seen the commotion, had pressed his way through the people and taken Alicia by the arm.

"Please, Rodney, take me home," she pleaded weakly. No further request was necessary. He pulled her out of the crowd, while Margaret gathered their packages and followed.

Alicia said not a word. The complexity of her mixed identities grew beyond any sense in her mind, and silence was her only friend.

Geoffrey Seavers walked briskly into the house on Tiller Street, taking off his hat when he entered. He looked about and noticed that it was well kept and orderly. There seemed no one about, so he stood admiring the sitting room for a time. The house was comfortable and clean and had a nice smell. Even though he had his own chamber here, he chose not to use it. Being in this house reminded him all too often that he had lied and cheated the crown, and had a great many knots to untangle.

"Afternoon, milord," came a voice. "Nice t'see you about."

He smiled at Margaret as she passed him and went in the direction of the stairs.

"Is her ladyship in?" he asked.

"Aye, sir. In her rooms."

"Ask her if I may come up."

"Aye, milord," Margaret said, continuing away from him.

Within moments she returned to send him to Alicia. As he entered the chamber, he found her sitting behind a frame, her forehead furrowed into a few troubled lines and her fingers playing havoc on a piece of linen.

"Come in, my lord," she beckoned him. "I'll be glad to put this damned thing aside."

He frowned slightly at her language but appreciated very much the sight of her pushing the frame away from her chair and standing. She must surely like to primp, he thought. He never found her less than perfectly gowned and coiffed. He forced himself to remember that there was nothing about their relationship that was anything but business. He tried to consider her one of his staff; someone he was paying to do a chore.

"How have you been?" she asked.

"Quite well. I understand you've had some trouble."

"Trouble?" she asked, looking puzzled.

"At the 'Change. Something stolen?"

She looked away. "There was nothing of value taken. The thieves are running the streets. I won't go out as often."

"You go out hardly at all as it is."

"By your request, my lord," she reminded him.

"Yes, of course. Well, I have only a little time but I think since the weather is warmer now we should travel to the country to look over the land Fergus Bellamy left. I'd like to see it sold before very long."

"I've been told there are revenues to be had from the land since there's farming there. Are you sure you wouldn't do better to keep it?"

"I'd rather get rid of what was the Bellamys and begin building for the Seaverses."

Alicia looked at him closely. "And who will that be, my lord?"

His confused look answered her, and then, as he caught her meaning, he turned away from her.

"There should be no reason why we can't talk, my lord. Tell me who you think will be 'The Seavers Family.'"

He responded with a mumble and she took two paces to touch his shoulder and turn him around. "I imagine I'll marry someday." And then at the pained look in her eyes, he pleaded, "Alicia, please, don't do this. . . ."

136

"Will you look for yet another rich woman?" she asked.

He shook his head. "I shouldn't have a great need for money, but there needs to be blood in her name." A heavy sigh escaped him. "Enough blood to satisfy all my dead ancestors."

Alicia turned and walked toward the window, pulling back the heavy velvet drape and looking out. "I wonder . . ." she started, not looking at him. "I wonder: if I had a noble family, how would you treat me then?"

Geoffrey came up behind her and put his arms on her shoulders. Her curls tickled his nose and her sensuous fragrance tempted his desire. "I think, *chérie*, considering your life before we met, you should be a little grateful for this much. And it would be helpful to me if you would punish me with your sadness a little less."

She turned abruptly, practically into his embrace. "But you are not happy, my lord."

"No, Alicia, my love, I am not. But do you see what I face? I've bought this bargain for myself, and the sooner it is done and there is no risk of losing all I've struggled to gain, the sooner I can stop fearing discovery." He sighed deeply and his green eyes were sincere. "I will look upon that day with gladness."

"Had you never thought that our bargain need not end? If I were in truth Charlotte Bellamy it would not end — and who could prove otherwise?"

He softly touched her lips with his. "You tempt the saints," he whispered. "But this lie sits ill with me, and a lifetime of it I cannot abide."

"Then there is something of love between us, Geoffrey," she murmured.

"I want you. I do not know love."

"You will chance nothing on it," she told him. "Not a farthing."

His eyes grew dark and his lips fixed in a stern line. "Nothing."

She turned away from him and looked out the window again. His mind was made up and she would not ask him again. But when and if he changed his mind, she would listen.

"How soon can you be prepared to travel?"

"At your convenience, sir."

"Two days?"

"How shall we go and what should I bring?"

"We'll go by coach. Bring only traveling clothes and essential servants."

"Two days will be fine," she said, turning back to him. The hat he held in his hand was turning in his grasp. "I will be ready."

"Thank you. And good day."

"Geoffrey," she called. He turned to hear her. "Will it be very long before I am — before this is done?"

He looked down, fiddled with his hat a bit more, and then looked up at her. "I think not terribly long. Perhaps by the fall. Are you eager?"

"No," she breathed.

"We may need longer, to assure those — to be certain there is no suspicion."

She nodded and bit her lip, a gesture that caused him to feel some pain. He hated for her to hurt. He could do nothing to help her but perhaps free her soon.

"There have been deaths in the city," she remarked. "They say it's plague."

"Every death is called plague. It's nothing."

"It frightens me."

"There are more important things to fear. The Dutch. The truth."

"I don't fear the truth, my lord. It has never harmed me before."

He put his hat on his head and tapped it once. "This once, Alicia, it could."

nine

The property that had been restored to Fergus Bellamy lay west of London. The roads as far as Newbury were decent, but as the need to leave the well-traveled path and ride slightly northwest arose, the roads became wretched. Geoffrey rode alongside the coach while Rodney sat with the driver. Two horsemen, a meager number for a lord, accompanied the travelers, and Alicia rode within the coach with Margaret, her only servant. All in all, this prestigious family did not travel with as much pomp as usually accompanied nobles, and therefore did not get much recognition along the road. Innkeepers did not bow and scrape at their approach; while Geoffrey would have preferred more attention for himself and those with him, he didn't get it, since it was not apparent that he was wealthy. He made his journey more in the manner of a tightfisted merchant.

The manor and surrounding land had been called Belle-rose when it belonged to the Bellamy family, but the name had fallen away when the last Bellamy to own it, namely Fergus, left it to be looted and taken by someone else.

The road to the manor house was miserable, for it had been a long time since it had been tended. As the coach jounced toward the house, Alicia clung to the seat fighting regular attacks of nausea. "This 'rose,'" she groaned, "should be a sight to see!"

When they finally halted and she threw open the coach door to look, she sighed with joy. The manor rose in red brick from the ground to four or five stories. The grounds were certainly neglected and tangled, but she could see that among the overgrowth were rosebushes and trees. Having been deprived of a life filled with wealth and castles, and having little other than Whitehall to compare this property to, she thought it beautiful. Her opinion of Whitehall was that it was a slice of city mess she could do without. The country talked to her; spoke her language.

"Bellerose..." she murmured, a smile coming to her lips.

"More thorn than rose," Geoffrey grumbled. "It won't get a good price at all. Who would want it? I would fain see the villages around it."

"But it's wonderful!" she insisted, jumping down from the coach without assist. Her slippered feet immediately found mud and she picked up her skirts with a curse. "Drat! I've never learned prudence."

Geoffrey indicated the remainder of the road with his hand and smiled at her. "How do you propose to get the rest of the way to the house, madam?"

Alicia formed a pout and looked up at him. "Since there are no gentlemen on this trip, I am in a quandary, sir."

Geoffrey chuckled and dismounted, leaving his hat on the saddlehorn. He sloshed through the mud to where she stood and scooped her up in his arms, carrying her to the house. The mud rose up his black leather boots and the filth from her gown and shoes scraped against his breeches. "We'll have a mess to clean up once we get inside."

"I've got to preserve my gowns," Alicia told him. "Once you've thrown me over for a new baroness, I'll have no one to buy me clothes."

"You taunt me in my darkest hours," he scolded.

"Finally, my lord," she told him as he mounted the stairs to the landing, "after all these months I feel like a bride."

He set her down quite firmly on the slab, a jolt that caused her to look at him with some disapproval. "I spoke too soon," she grumbled.

Geoffrey couldn't help laughing at her, for she had held up very well through the whole of the trip. Less than satisfactory lodgings did not upset her — she was used to worse — and never had she complained about their meals or hard traveling. Even the house, which was, in his opinion, a complete disaster, pleased her. Aye, there were advantages to having partnered himself with a resilient tavern wench. She had an honest and delightful excitement and took pleasure over the simplest things, and when he least expected it, she would laugh at their troubles.

"Just keeping you in line, madam," he said with a bow. He looked over his shoulder and saw that Rodney was in a spot because of Geoffrey's gallant action, for Margaret hovered in the open door of the coach with something of expectation on her face, and Rodney was flushed scarlet at the thought of having to carry her to the house. "Do you imagine he'll follow suit?"

Alicia looked toward the coach and covered her mouth as she giggled. Geoffrey began pounding on the manor door, while Alicia's attention was held entirely by Margaret and Rodney as they looked at each other in confusion. At her further laughter, Geoffrey turned. Margaret was not a small woman, and while Rodney was a large man, he had met his match. Though he was prepared to try, it was possible they'd be sprawled in the mud in no time. Even the horsemen were struggling to keep their faces composed.

"Rodney, you fool, make her a chair; use the other men!" Geoffrey shouted.

The ensuing scene brought more mirth, but only from those not participating, namely, Alicia and Geoffrey. The horsemen could not laugh, for they were required to clasp hands between them while Rodney directed Margaret as she left the coach backside first and dropped her large, round bottom on their arms, an action that nearly toppled all four into the muck.

By the time the six of them were safely landed, Alicia was holding her sides and Geoffrey was coughing loudly into his handkerchief. He wished, for a moment, that he'd been raised in the simple life so that he, like Alicia, could laugh openly without the worry of displaying poor breeding.

After a fair amount of pounding and attempting to jar the heavy oaken doors of the manor, it was clear that the place was barred from within, but no one would answer.

"There was to be a caretaker here," Geoffrey grumbled.

"I wager he absconded, milord," Rodney offered. "Dropped the bar in place and went out another door or window."

The women stayed near the front door while the men, properly booted and brave, looked about the rest of the outside of the building. It was quite a long time before the sounds of the board slipping and the hinges squeaking could be heard. Geoffrey stood in the opened door with a sour look on his face, practically glaring at Alicia. "My lady," he crooned sarcastically, "Bellerose."

Alicia gingerly stepped inside. There was dirt nearly as thick inside as out, broken and useless furniture, evidence that animals had roamed through, rags that might have covered windows at one time hanging from the walls, and a smell that would insult the laziest nose. "A rose indeed," Alicia hummed.

She stood with Geoffrey just inside the door while the

others wandered through, the men looking upstairs, and Margaret, muttering her disgust, examining the downstairs rooms. Lord and Lady Seavers stood quiet and contemplating for a while, listening to the echoes of footfalls upstairs and Margaret's moving around downstairs. "How did you get in?" Alicia asked.

"The door to the gardens was not bolted. The caretaker, the good man who was to clean and protect the place, scooted with the money I gave him."

"Was it much?"

"Five pounds, ten more of which he'd get on my arrival when the place was presentable."

Alicia began to laugh.

"Five pounds amuses you, madam?"

She shook her head, but could not stop her laughter. "I imagine it was the easiest five he's ever earned, and he was quick to see that there was no way to earn the ten you promised."

He put both hands on his hips and stared at her. "And you find that a good jest, eh?"

Giggles overtook her and she blinked away tears as she tried to explain. "This fortune, my lord. You've paid so much, so many times over, to have it. A hundred to a wench, more for her gowns and so billed to you by the king, a caretaker that steals, and God knows how many more debts before you can count your gold."

He screwed his face into a pout and looked around. "I admit it's funny as hell."

Alicia laughed the harder at that. "No only did you have to marry," she stammered. "You had to capture, educate, dress, and fight your bride."

He looked at her in complete confusion, but she was not intimidated by his stare. While he stared, she controlled her laughter. "Fight?" he asked.

"Aye, my fine lord," she said with a nod.

"How do I fight my bride?"

"You're afraid to be my friend. And more afraid to be my lover."

"Be damned," he argued. "I do as I please."

"Liar," she said, arms crossed and small foot tapping.

"You are an ungrateful wench," he scolded, but it was hard to look at her without a smile. She was so full of herself this afternoon. "Never have you thanked me for all you've gained through this alliance. And admit, my fair lass, I've thanked you aplenty and you've been angry with me for that."

"I don't feel appreciated." She shrugged.

He threw his arms wide and looked at her in dismay. "Tell me, maid, what you want?"

She chuckled again, covering her mouth. Her eyes were alive with mischief as she looked at him. "It is great fun watching the pain on your face as you unleash every farthing for what you want. Yet I can't say why you continually *thank* me. You're unhappy most of the time."

"I have a great deal on my mind," he said in defense. "I will be happy when this is done."

"I'm not sure, my lord. When it's done it may simply be — " she shrugged and went on, " — done."

"What do you prattle about, wench?" he demanded.

She looked at him with a wisdom that made him uneasy. "Did it ever occur to you that what would make you happiest is something you cannot buy?"

His expression closed, for it was a thing he had not considered. At least not for now. Right now all that he wanted had a price.

She laughed and danced away from him, going in the direction of her woman. A sharp thwack on her backside put a jump in her step. She turned with a frown.

Geoffrey raised one eyebrow and leered, his eyes roaming from the top of her head to her toes. "One day you may regret taunting me so."

"Be cautious, my lord," she warned, shaking a finger at him. "Don't run up any more debts."

The house was a big disappointment to Geoffrey. And its run-down condition caused him to walk about and mumble to himself for the better part of an hour, until he sent Rodney to fetch a flask of whiskey from the baggage. No one was quite sure what was going on inside the captain's head while he drank and contemplated, but the rest of the group let him be and set about making the best of a bad situation.

Rodney found a decent supply of dry wood in a building that was a poor excuse for a barn, and Margaret was able to fashion a light meal out of food that had been brought along for the trip. Alicia decided the only decent room on the lower floor was probably a sitting room, and it was not long before a fire was blazing to warm it.

Alicia tucked up the hem of her fine velvet gown, pinning it up and letting her petticoats hang below to catch the dirt. She found a broom and began to clear some of the filth off the floor. She caught sight of Geoffrey as he passed the room, his drink in his hand. He was deep in thought.

In a bedchamber, Rodney found a mattress that did not seem to be inhabited by creatures, and he dragged it down the stairs and set it in front of the fire. While the horsemen took care of their animals, Rodney, Margaret, and Alicia sat before the fire to partake of bread, fruit, and cheese. Geoffrey entered with his drink and looked at them from the doorway.

"Some garden party," he commented dryly.

"Are you hungry?" Alicia asked, holding a slice of bread and cheese toward him.

"The sight of this place has taken all thoughts of eating from my mind."

"Will we be finding an inn for the night?" she asked.

"We'll stay here the night and leave early in the morning."

Margaret gulped hard and began to cough, but neither Alicia nor Rodney was surprised. They did not really expect Geoffrey to part with more money for lodging when there was a roof and fire here, however mean the accommodations.

"Where will we sleep?" Alicia asked. It seemed she was the only one who would question him.

"The women, here. The men, wherever each one finds his comfort."

Rodney rose with a snort, his mouth full of bread and cheese, and pulled his coat tighter about him. "I'll find my comfort in the barn. There is at least a pile of hay there." He chewed and smiled down at Alicia. "I've made the best of a pile of hay before."

"Can some be spared from that pile?" Alicia asked. "Mrs. Stratton deserves better than the floor, and this feather tick won't do for us both."

"Aye, lass," he said appreciatively. "I'll fix something up for her." And with a nod toward the serving woman, he quit the room.

Alicia looked at Margaret with a smile. "I think he's grown quite fond of you," she teased.

"Bah!" she coughed, her cheeks brightening somewhat. Alicia could only giggle, a thing that made the woman flush the more, and shortly she rose to leave the room to conceal her embarrassment.

Alicia remained on the tick, nibbling at her bread and cheese, while Geoffrey looked in from the doorway. With a sigh, he moved toward her and picked a crust from the basket that had been carried in.

"If I didn't think it quite insane," he said with a mouthful of dry, hard bread, "I would think you find this enjoyable."

"It doesn't distress me, Geoffrey. Why should it?"

"It is a filthy sty. It is not an inheritance but a joke. A very bad joke."

"But since it is not mine, why should I be troubled? And

though you have to worry with what to do with this, you've been given a good deal of money to start your shipping, so what does it matter?"

"I shall have to have the place refurbished before it can be sold."

She shrugged. "You'll make it up in the price you get."

"It is not a serious thing to you, is it?"

"I think I am lucky I was poor," she confided. "You rich nobles have more problems than I could bear."

He relaxed back on his haunches and looked at her, shaking his head. "Alicia," he murmured, "I think perhaps you are right."

Her eyes warmed and her smile was soft and sweet. "I like it when you use my name," she whispered.

He turned away uncomfortably and looked into the fire. "I forgot myself," he grumbled.

"Yes," she said, her smile still directed at him. "I know."

It would have been convenient for all six travelers to stay in one room for the night, the room that had been partially cleaned and warmed. But Rodney and the horsemen chose the stable, for the hay was soft and the coach and horses could be watched. Margaret fashioned a comfortable mattress of hay on the floor in a far corner of the sitting room and lay down exhausted the moment the sun was low in the sky. It was not long before her snores could be heard throughout the room.

Geoffrey had gallantly offered to stay inside the house for the night to see to any needs the women had, and though he was tired, he sat on the feather tick beside Alicia and looked into the fire.

"I'm sorry you're disappointed, Geoffrey," she told him. "You've gone through a great deal for very little."

"I complain too much," he conceded. "What has come of this marriage gives me a decent start. But it's a hard pill to swallow," he said with a laugh.

"How so?"

"I find myself almost wishing that Perry had managed to take it away from me."

"That again. Well, what do you suppose he'd have done with it?"

"Hard telling, but I assure you he wouldn't be grateful for it. And in some devious way he'd have turned it into money and got himself a large estate to sit and rot on." He shrugged. "Perry hasn't had enough power to suit him for a very long time."

"I don't seem to understand why he is poor. His father was an earl, was he not?"

"Aye, and his brother holds that earldom still, but Perry has wasted and lost what little was given to him. His family has left him to find his own means — and clearly he intends to come by it as easily as possible, through marriage."

Alicia turned her head sharply to look at him. "And aren't you proud that *you* didn't choose such an easy escape!"

"I give you that, lass. I couldn't see a better way for myself either." He pointed a finger at her. "But I began my shipping and fought hard for the king." He paused. "I needed more."

"Aren't you afraid, Geoffrey?" she asked him, her face wrinkled into a frown. He almost answered her, thinking she was talking about the danger in war and privateering. "Aren't you afraid there will never be enough?"

He studied her for a moment before answering. "There are so many times I can't bear to be near you," he said softly. "I envy so much about you."

"Envy me?" she laughed. "You are not only ruthless but foolish!"

But Geoffrey was serious, and for the first time since they'd met, he was actually finding himself wanting to share some of himself with her. He was comfortable talking; the brandy had soothed, the fire was warm, and but for the regular snorts from the sleeping servant, the room was quiet.

"It does not take much to make you happy. Indeed, the simplest things amuse you."

"That's not completely true, my lord," she said with a hint of guilt. "I left the inn with your man because I could not be happy in the country with a simple farmer."

He reached out and touched her cheek. "And was there a farmer, Alicia?"

"No," she said with a sigh. "No, there was no one. And I had no dowry, no family, no schooling but for some simple reading and ciphering when I was very small." She looked up at him and raised her eyebrows. "I would have nothing if it had not been for Rodney ... and you. You're right, I should thank you more often and ask you for less."

"I can't believe the country lads did not chase you from brook to woods."

"Believe!" she laughed. "There were no combs for my hair, my clothes did not fit, and most of the time I did not have shoes to put on my feet. Aye, there was not much to chase.

"Yeomen are like nobles, my lord. They, too, look for a wife with money or land or at least one cow to bring to the marriage."

"Most country girls and especially tavern maids can find ways to better their lot."

"I know you think I'm a whore," she said quite easily. "But the truth is that I was not. Armand held quite a stick over the head of every maid who served for him. A pregnant lass was not as quick on her feet."

"He beat you?"

"Regularly."

"But he did not sell you to his customers."

"No, he did not do that, but then most of us sold ourselves, but not for gold." She laughed ruefully. "I don't think I know of a lass who did not fall in love with at least

one courtier passing through. They lied so well; promised a
life of ease in London with such perfection." She sighed
and played with the hem of her gown. "What poor shoeless
wench wouldn't want to believe?"

Geoffrey was quiet for a moment. "And is that what happened to you?"

"Yes. And it shan't happen to me again. Your hundred
pounds put me above that trickery."

"I think I see the bruise of your last beating," Geoffrey
said with affection. "Your broken heart."

"But it is mended," she said defensively. "I name myself
as much the fool as my vanishing courtier, the blackguard.
I had seen the same happen to maids before me, yet held
myself as something special."

The fire gave off sparks as a log fell, and Geoffrey moved
to the hearth to throw on another log. Alicia shivered and
pulled her cloak tighter around herself, tucking it in around
her knees. As he moved back to the feather tick, Alicia
appeared to be a small bundle of misfortune needing his
care, and he put an arm about her, pulling her close.

"Perhaps things will go better for you from now on," he
said.

"And for you," she said.

"True," he returned. "We have helped each other. Let
us take great care not to hurt each other."

"And how could I hurt you, my lord? You have had my
word that I won't confess the truth of our arrangement. I
can't leave you and I can't stay with you. There is nothing
I can do to hurt you."

"I don't believe that you have accepted the conditions
of this marriage, Alicia," he whispered, his lips against her
ear.

"What matter in that," she said, somewhat breathless
from his nearness.

His arm went around her waist and his lips touched her
neck. "You must remember everything we share is for *now*.

You must take what you can from me and let go when the time has come. Or you will be hurt."

She pulled away from him a very little bit so that her lips were close to his and her voice was soft, her breath in his half-open mouth. "And you, Geoffrey. You must let go when the time has come. Do you think you can?"

His mouth came down on hers and they tumbled onto the feather tick, caught in a passion that surprised neither and delighted both. Alicia circled his neck with her arms and held him fast, for this was no test or game; she would not release him. She meant to know how far he would take this bargain.

Geoffrey felt her response and a wanting grew in him. He cautioned himself to move slowly, to conceal his desperation if he could, to love her gently. But he was a man starved, and control was difficult, for he had suppressed his hunger for her so completely that he had not taken any woman since Alicia came to London. He had not acknowledged how passionately he wanted her. His fingers moved along the buttons on the bodice of her gown, and a groan escaped him as he touched the soft skin of her breast.

"Please, do not expect to find me a virgin," she reminded him.

His hands worked a magic on her and he ignored her quiet plea. The only sound from him was the soft murmuring of her name. "Alicia. Alicia . . ."

"I am not your bride," she whispered. "This is not a part of the bargain."

"Don't deny me, Alicia. Don't deny yourself. Love me."

Her body needed only what he offered, but her heart needed something more, and though she made no effort to stop him, she let her lips break from his to voice her questions. And while she felt the hem of her gown sliding up to expose first her knee and then her thigh, she whispered to him.

"Am I to *take*? Or am I to give?"

"Love me, Alicia. I've wanted you for so long."

"I do love you, Geoffrey. But do you know who I *am*?"

He rose above her slightly, looking down into smoky gray eyes, her hair loosed and tousled on the feather tick. He felt as though his breeches were a vise, needing to be loosened, but she stayed him with her words.

"Alicia, you are noble, strong, sweet . . ."

"A tavern wench — already used and cast aside."

"That was another time, another Alicia. It matters little. You're the woman I've come to love."

And with that, the last stronghold she claimed as her own tumbled down, for she had heard the words that made her heart give way. And then she felt his hardness slide up between her thighs and she pulled him closer. She would bind him to her, and then what he chose to do with her love would be left to his honor. She was, to all the world, his wife.

"And can you let go, Geoffrey?" she whispered.

"Nay," he moaned. "Nay, how can I? You've cast your spell."

ten

*A*licia stirred as she felt the warm presence leave her side. She opened her eyes to see that Geoffrey was putting another log on the fire, and she sighed contentedly. With a little shifting, she was able to take the cloak she lay upon and draw it over herself. As he turned back toward her, she lifted the cloak invitingly and he slid down on the mattress, taking her into his arms.

"We are foolish," he said. "How long can the woman sleep so soundly?"

"A little longer, I pray," she sighed, drawing him closer.

"I would not have thought this haunted old trap could provide so much comfort on a cold night."

"Ha! You give credit to the house!"

"Come, wench, until we see the sunlight, do not taunt me. Give me ease of your complaints."

She ran a finger around his ear and smiled at him. "I do not complain so much, Geoffrey."

He had not conditioned himself to so much affection in one night, and for a brief moment he feared that it would be too much for a man who had lived, eaten, and slept mostly on the ship. But at the touch of her lips, and with the feel of her arms around his neck, he found he had more stamina than he had given himself credit for.

Women were not strange to him, but the truth was that he had always worried so with his performance as a lover that he was somewhat intimidated by them. Something in the way Alicia responded to his touch fed his masculine pride and he could barely contain himself. She was someplace between his last enthusiastic whore and a vestal virgin. She was neither aggressive nor acquiescent. When his touch thrilled her, he heard her sigh. When he moved against her, she moaned softly. With his hands on her hips she moved with him. She made him master and slave.

The urgency of lovemaking was gone, and he leisurely worked the buttons that went the length of her gown, laying it open to his gaze. His mouth tasted the sweetness of her skin and his senses were tuned to the texture and scent of her. While he believed he controlled her every quiver, something in him wondered if she perhaps controlled him.

"What a witch you are, Alicia. You've taken possession of my soul. I cannot ever be without you."

"And you need not, Geoffrey."

"How could I think it?"

"From too great a distance, I think."

With his fingers woven into her hair and his body hovering over hers, he claimed her leisurely, moving carefully, slowly, until he had to cover her lips with his to cease her soft moans. He felt the power of the captain of a fleet, for he could moor her now, halt her, send her home, or take her to the sea.

"Please . . ." she begged softly, and a low chuckle rose from his throat, for he was not the captain at all. The velvety softness of her and the sweetness of her breath had poisoned his will, and he could do nothing but end the agony of waiting. She made him *feel* powerful, a feeling he knew himself to need heavy doses of, but he was not in power at all. She held the power. He had, in their first coupling, tasted her ecstasy, and he knew he would not be satisfied unless he could feel that again. He held himself until he felt her trembling nearly out of control and then let himself match her.

She lay quiet and pliant in his arms, her breathing even and shallow. Geoffrey had thought himself to be lucky in his encounters with women and he had indeed lain with experienced whores earlier in his manhood. But what had happened with Alicia had surpassed anything he had ever known. It did not occur to him that this was his first encounter with the emotion — love. He laughed to himself, for he thought he had had lovers, but no lover gave him the joy this woman did.

The thought struck hard. Lover?

He had not intended to make her his lover, though for a long time he had longed to touch her, hold her. And he'd held himself away from her because of the complications making love to her might involve. During those times he could not control his fantasies, he had been able at least to promise himself that he wouldn't commit himself any further until he could see a way out of the tangled mess of lies he had begun.

He moaned softly at his own discomfort, and Alicia moved trustingly nearer. The softness of her cheek was pressed against his lips and he wondered which would be worse: asking her to leave with her hundred pounds, or rotting in Newgate without her.

But for the moment he could think of nothing but her presence and the comfort he felt in holding her near. With a sigh, he tightened his arms around her and joined her in sleep.

At the first faint glow of dawn, Geoffrey jostled Alicia. "Madam," he beckoned. "Come, Charlotte..." Her eyes opened and she looked at him in some confusion. She had nearly forgotten that name existed. Geoffrey tilted his head in the direction of the sleeping servant, and Alicia smiled. "Clothe yourself, *chérie*," he whispered. "Before the others are upon us."

Disappointment slowed her movements and her face formed a pretty pout. Nothing would please her more than to doze longer in the arms of her lover, but they'd spent their moment too publicly already, and she reluctantly pulled her clothes around her, her fingers lazily doing the buttons.

"Madam, please," Geoffrey begged, giving assist with the buttons. Alicia's soft laughter was his answer and he did more of the work of garbing her than she.

He held up her cloak for her and helped her to her feet. She sighed as she pulled it around her and frowned as she looked around the room. There were no luxuries for nobles here; no dressing table, basin of hot water, or chamber pot. Alicia shrugged and resigned herself to the very chill outdoors.

She lollygagged along the path, took her leisure in the convenience, and when she would have returned to the house, she found Geoffrey leaning against a tree, waiting for her. She smiled her appreciation and moved sleepily toward him. She did not recognize his tenseness.

"Alicia," he fairly whispered, looking over his shoulder suspiciously. "I must apologize for last night. I am sorry."

Her perplexed look caused his heart to plummet.

"I had no right — and you tried to caution me when I would not hear you. It was not a part of our bargain."

"No, it was not," she said evenly.

"I should not have used you without . . . I should have given greater thought to . . . That is, I was taken with your softness and the brandy and —"

"Pish," she said, stopping him. "That is not what you said."

"I know I spoke words of love and made promises that

I'm not sure I can keep. I beg your forgiveness. I would have you forget — "

"What are you telling me?" she questioned, her ire raised. "That you lied to me?"

He scuffed a foot in the dirt and cursed himself for having woven yet another web for himself. "They did not feel like lies."

"But in the morning, is that what your words have become? Lies?"

He could not look at her. "Aye, I said words I was not sure I felt and made promises I am not sure I can keep. I promise you this in sound mind; it will not happen again."

He looked at her and saw her eyes darken. Anger was etched into her delicate features. "What did you expect would happen?" he asked her. "Did you expect this could go on?"

"Aye," she answered. "And why not? If that is what we both want, to be wed and to carry on, why not?"

"Of course, you would expect such, what have you to lose? You do not risk your fortune or your title. You have everything to gain if we never end this — this *arrangement*."

"Lord Seavers," she whispered in barely controlled rage, "what will I gain by allowing this *arrangement* to go on? A life as an impostor, with the world about to come down on my head at any moment? The constant worry that fear will force us to separate and plan a 'death' to relieve the threat of being imprisoned? Aye, I could play this charade forevermore, and when there are children, I could be forced away from them for fear of exposure."

"Then you agree — it is foolish to — "

"I agree that it is foolish! Coming to London was the most foolish thing I've ever done. For now, when there is risk, you think that you alone — " She stopped and let out a heavy sigh and looked at him in the most complete frustration. She thought he had come to a decision; a time of knowing what he wanted. "You are the most complete fool."

When he looked into her eyes, he felt for a moment like a small boy looking into his mother's eyes. A few hours earlier he had felt like the most powerful man in the world and he hated to let go of that feeling. Rebellion rose within him. "I hope you are not hurt," he said rather tersely.

"You are finished with me, then?" she asked caustically.

"I will keep my word, but I will not be bound to a woman now."

"And I will hold you to your word. You will not touch me again."

She lifted her skirts and took long, quick steps into the manor house, tears stinging her eyes.

Oaf! Beggar! Thief! Bastard! Her mind railed on and on. Passion in the nighttime and cold calculating indifference in the morning. But she stopped short as she arrived in the room where their coupling had occurred. She moved slowly to the feather tick and dropped to her knees to touch the place where they had slept.

"I pressed him for promises and words of love he was not ready to make," she reminded herself. "And now he would have me believe it was lust and brandy that brought him to me. And harden yourself, heart, for his ships are his love and he may *never* be ready. He warned me that this was only for now, and now — the moment has passed."

She heard his footsteps and turned to see him standing behind her. Tears coursed down her cheeks. She turned away.

The sight of her tear-stained face ripped through Geoffrey's heart. He wanted to run to her, take her in his arms, and beg her to be patient, he would find a way to ensure their future so that they might never again live with fear. But he found himself afraid to comfort her with those words. He was afraid he might fail to find a way to safely keep her.

He moved toward her slowly and lowered himself to kneel on the floor behind her. He rubbed her upper arms with his hands. "You will not feel this hurt for long, *chérie*. I promise."

She sniffed back her tears and straightened her back.

"Tell me you do not love me, Geoffrey."

He sighed and struggled for the words. "What matter love, Alicia? That I love you enough to buy you the moon and the stars would matter little if the king locks us both away. That I love you beyond the value of every ship England owns would buy neither of us freedom from the charge of treason against the crown." He used a finger to turn her face that she might see his eyes. "If I tell you I love you, Alicia, it will not change the fact that our bargain could turn on us at any time and devour whatever love we thought ours."

She stared at him with angry eyes, her pupils sharp as pinpoints. "I pray you take care with what you so carelessly claim and throw away. One day you will regret that you are not a man who knows his mind."

The coach was loaded with baggage and the group made ready to depart, their visit to Bellerose cut short by days because of the condition of the manor. Alicia sat within the coach with her cloak pulled tight, a veil from her hat covering her face. She pulled back the drape from the window of the coach, and tears gathered in her eyes as she looked at the disheveled building and overgrown lawns.

As she looked at the manor through a veil, she thought how she had looked at her life through a similar veil. She had allowed all of her needs and desires to seem real and attainable without considering they would not mesh with what Geoffrey needed for his life.

"A woman with blood in her name; a family that is *known*, whether they be dead or alive." She sighed heavily as she considered that the Tilden name would do nicely now, but for the fact that it pointed her out to be no relation whatever to Fergus Bellamy. That would not sit well with the king. Being a Tilden now would not help her secure a true marriage to Geoffrey.

She saw him mount his horse and raise an arm to the driver, and the coach gave a lurch. Pity it is ships he loves to ride, when he looks so dashing astride.... Her mind wandered. Ah, dear Geoff, poor man. You love so well and such fruits of passion spill from your lips when you are caught in love's spell, but you cannot see it through. And what are the chances, dear man, that you'll stumble upon a woman with beauty, passion, family name, money, and a devotion to you? She chuckled at her thoughts. Alicia Tilden, perhaps, should you ever be fortunate enough to make her acquaintance.

And then the tear fell from her eye because she knew more of Geoffrey than he gave her credit for. She knew he had not lied to her as he loved her, but simply couldn't bear the responsibility of his words and actions.

She had considered the many ways she could pursue him, make it easy for him to claim her. But all that she really wanted from Geoffrey was to be claimed for the person she was; love not hinged on jealousy, blooded ancestors, dower lands, or a successful seduction.

Again she pulled back the drape and her eyes found her lord, his cloak blowing in the wind and his hat pulled down over his brow. I will not fix it for you, dear Geoff, she silently pledged. You are almost everything I need in a man. But you are not wise. She sighed. Even with your courtly upbringing and fine manners and reputation as a grand warrior, a simple tavern wench could teach you lessons in life that you've gone this far without learning.

She let the curtain drop and leaned back into the velvet seat. She knew that Geoffrey had a very short time to come to terms with what he felt for her. If the decision to claim her was not his and his alone, she could never trust him. If he would not risk one farthing now, what would he wager to keep his fortune in the future? He needed to learn that the joys in life would be more plentiful when riches were a little less important.

Nothing about her life had ever had any sense of permanence. Over and over again she'd been cast aside, pushed out, sent on her way. And over and over again she had survived.

She would give Geoffrey a little time, but not a lifetime. And when the time for her to go was upon her, she would know it. With her hundred pounds, she would move along yet another time, and she knew she would not lose hope. And someday, she told herself, when the time is right and there is no need to fear the king's wrath, I will present myself to the Tildens. Even though she couldn't count on permanence there, it was not too late to know them.

The coach slowed to a stop and the door was opened. Geoffrey looked in at her, though he could not make out her features behind her veil. "Are you comfortable, madam?"

"Aye, milord."

"We'll be stopping in the village where it will take some time to try to find workers I can hire for Bellerose."

She gave her head a slight nod.

"I think we'll travel a bit farther for a room for the night. There is little protection along this road and I'd prefer to see you housed in a safe place."

"Worry not, milord," she said, lifting her veil and looking deeply into his eyes. "I assure you, I'm quite accustomed to taking risks."

His eyes narrowed as he felt the jibe, but said nothing. He closed the door and saw the coach jerk into motion again. He held his horse back and watched for a moment as the coach preceded him. He continued to frown. "Patience, Alicia," he said to the departing coach. "If you will just be patient, perhaps there is a way I can minimize your risks."

Work at both the wharves and at Bellerose kept Geoffrey away from his house on Tiller Street most of the time. He made token visits to assess that all was going smoothly, but he did not stay.

On one such visit, he brought a package for Alicia. She opened it to find a beautiful necklace of sapphires, set in gold filigree among tiny diamonds. She gasped at the sight of it. "It was found in a hidden safe at Bellerose and must surely have belonged to a Bellamy woman some years back. The jeweler was able to clean and repair it."

"And would you like me to wear it?" she asked.

"Certainly. Don't you like it?"

"It's lovely," she said softly.

He lingered for a while, questioned her about her activities, and inquired if there was anything she needed. And though she answered him politely and asked him about his ships and the manor, his tenseness was increasing and she couldn't say why. Finally it erupted. "Do you hate the necklace I brought you? Is there some flaw or scar on the piece?"

"It's perfectly beautiful," she answered in confusion.

"Why, in heaven's name, don't you *thank* me?" he stormed.

"You mean, it's mine?" she asked.

"I gave it to you!" he blustered.

"I didn't know that." She smiled. "Thank you."

"Didn't know? How could you not know?"

"I thought you'd made the gift to Charlotte," she informed him. "And, of course, Charlotte would wear it and then, one day, leave it behind. But if it is mine . . ."

He scowled blackly. He looked around to be certain they were alone and then let his gaze bear down on her. "This business of speaking of two women, Charlotte and Alicia, is enough to make any man wild. I have given the necklace to *you*, whichever name you might be wearing. No matter who you are when you wear it, it is yours!"

She smiled softly into his eyes. "Thank you, milord. It is precious to me."

"By damn, you insist on punishing me. You will respond to me with warmth only when I address you as Alicia, and when I use the name you are to *wear*, you treat me coldly. I don't know how I am to face you."

"I think you do the very best you can, milord," she said with a smile, turning away from him and going to the dressing table to fit the necklace around her neck. He moved behind her to help with the clasp. "I do love the necklace, Geoffrey," she said, meeting his eyes in the mirror. "And when we are far apart and no longer know each other, I will treasure this as part of the memory."

She saw him wince slightly.

His eyes moved down from hers to the necklace that dropped into the deep V of her gown, and his eyes were dark emeralds of wanting. He took his hands off her shoulders and moved away. "You wear the piece beautifully," he said, his voice more of a mumble than anything.

She watched him in the mirror, and when he turned to look at her again, she smiled at his sultry expression. "Do not fall in love with *me*, Lord Seavers. I don't think you could survive it."

He quickly picked up his hat and left her room without a word.

His visits were regularly of that order; his rather sheepish entrance, his struggle for a comfortable way to converse with her, and then, shortly, his discomfort in her presence and his abrupt departure. He would not stay to sup, slept in the house very seldom and only if he entered long after she was asleep, and seemed to deal with their relationship more poorly every time they chanced to meet.

Alicia was not in any way fooled by what was happening within Geoffrey's mind. His entire plan had gone awry when he fell in love with the woman he was paying to play his wife. His determination to maintain emotional detachment in this business arrangement had failed, and he could not see how to deal with his failure.

The problem was with her daily, and daily she schooled herself in how *she* would deal with him. Harden yourself, heart, she would think constantly. He may choose to punish himself and deny himself forevermore . . . and in that there is no room for a lover or a wife.

She had not thought that things could become any more complex than dealing with the truth of her identity and feeling she must stay silent, having seen a woman she believed to be the real Charlotte Bellamy; and being in love with a man who would undoubtedly cast her aside soon. But as she sat in the drawing room fumbling with the needlework she forced herself to do, bigger problems presented themselves in the form of Culver Perry. He was announced by Margaret, but there was no welcome in her voice.

"Shall I send him away?" Margaret asked hopefully.

"No, I'll have to see him."

"But why, mum? His lordship will not like it, not a bit."

Alicia sighed and pushed the loom away from her. "Bring us something to drink, missus, and let him come in. It's better knowing what's on his mind than wondering."

Mrs. Stratton shook her head in complete disagreement, but Lord Perry entered just the same. He put on his courtly show of kissing her hand and posturing about the room a bit, asking how she was liking London, why had she not been about to the theater, whether Bellerose was found to be fitting or falling apart, all questions he seemed to ask with the answers already in his mind.

"The mansion is not fit?"

"Indeed not. It is a shambles."

"A great disappointment to you, no doubt. Tell me, did you remember any of it from your younger days there?"

Her eyes narrowed. "I found I did not, my lord."

"Your father could have made it mighty easy for you had he at least brought you to London before his death, but he did not. The last time you saw your father, how did you find him?"

"I thought he would have a great many more years than he did. His death was quite a shock, for he did not look unwell. When you last saw him, Lord Perry, how did you find him?"

"The same," Perry said, picking up a cup and sipping tea. He peered at her over the cup with the same strange sneer he wore throughout this visit. Alicia knew beyond doubt that he was up to no good, but gave not a clue that she was highly suspicious of his presence. And thanks to Geoffrey's story about Perry and his sister, there was no need to be overly gracious. She would not be expected to coddle her husband's enemy.

He set his cup on the small table beside his chair. "I think we may end the game here, lady. You are not Charlotte Bellamy, as we both know."

She raised one brow and smiled. "Who am I, then, milord?"

"I'd give a ransom to remember the name, but without returning to the country and finding the inn, a place I barely remember, I cannot retrieve the name." His smile was cold and calculating. "But I remember well the body."

Her cheeks felt hot, but it was anger and not embarrassment that caused her slight flush. "You will have to leave this house if you are determined to take such a disrespectful course with me."

He laughed outright. "Bright for a tavern wench, love, but you'll not frighten me away. I've come to bargain."

"There are no bargains here," she said, and nearly chuckled to herself as she heard her own words.

"Ask your husband for a ship in my name. That will do for now. I'll take the half of the booty on one ship that was to be his."

"How is it you claim this as your right?" she asked with calmness she did not feel.

"I know you're not who you pretend to be."

She picked up her cup and sipped, willing it to be still in her hand. "And how is it you came to this conclusion, my lord?"

He leaned back in his chair. The contest was a good one. Neither would display the slightest trembling to the other. "I stopped at an inn more than a year ago. I was in fact in search of Charlotte Bellamy and, as luck would have it, found her there. True, she's nothing to you; she's fat and filthy and has all the grace of a drunk jackass . . . but to double my luck, I courted a serving wench at the inn for a night or two.

"You looked mighty familiar to me the moment I saw you, but damned if I could place where I'd seen you before. It was you I courted at the inn on my way home to London."

She smiled as if amused by the story. "If you have truly seen a woman claiming to be Charlotte Bellamy and feel certain I am not she, why have you not made your claim to the king? He would be very interested in your story."

"You know why," he said, his frown appearing and his superior smile vanishing. Alicia willingly took the upper hand for the moment.

"Pray explain, milord. I fear I am most confused by your facts."

He leaned forward, elbows on his knees and a serious, if not angry, look on his face. "Because, my lady, I was betrothed to Andrea Seavers, the wedding to take place soon, when I learned of the Bellamy inheritance. I could not speak for Charlotte because of my contract, but the Seaverses played me false. They had nothing to offer me in a dowry. Andrea was poor, as you were at the inn, but her brother simply laughed at my poor judgment and threatened me regularly with trouble should I fail to support her and treat her well. My position when I found Charlotte at her aunt's manor was not a good one."

Alicia's smile was bland and tolerant. "It appears your position is no better now."

"Somewhat, dear. I doubt my crime would be as serious as yours, should I produce Charlotte Bellamy for his majesty."

She shrugged. "I think there is no crime anywhere, except perhaps the uncertainty surrounding Andrea's death. . . ."

His jaw muscles tensed and his face became red. There was fury in his eyes that caused the pupils to shrink, and his dark brows dropped low over them, making his expression fearful. Alicia steeled herself for whatever would come next. "Did you not say you were betrothed while searching for Charlotte, while lying with some mysterious serving wench? How soon after that affair did Andrea Seavers die in her riding accident with you?"

He popped to his feet. "I will find out who you are, madam, and make you regret that you threaten and taunt me."

"What will you do, Lord Perry? Travel to some inn to learn some wench's name? Bring a farmer or innkeeper to London to swear I am she?" She leaned back and looked up at him. "Will you tell your king that you sought the hand of Charlotte Bellamy while you were already betrothed to another, and how quickly and mysteriously your betrothed was killed? Who *will* you say I am? And who will believe you?"

"You forget, bitch. I have Charlotte Bellamy."

Alicia laughed softly. "I believe you told me about this

woman you claim is Charlotte." She laughed again, her eyes alive with amusement. "Will you present this fat, dirty, graceless creature at court to discredit me? I know you are fond of thievery, Culver, but I must urge you to find a better way to steal yourself a dowry, for your plan would surely point you out to be a fool."

"This game you play with me will not last long, madam," he sneered. He stomped toward the sitting room door and turned on her angrily. "For the moment you have stalled me, but I am not stopped. Tell his lordship that I know his secret and will have payment for my silence."

"Tell him yourself," she snapped back.

He nodded with a silent chuckle and a smirk. "You will be more cooperative in time, my dear."

"I do not fear you, Culver. I shan't make the unfortunate mistake to go riding with you. I already know what you are capable of doing."

He pulled the door open with a jerk and went out, slamming the door behind him. The moment he was gone, Alicia began to tremble and tears threatened to spill. Margaret immediately entered the room to see about her mistress's condition and was rattled at the upset Lord Perry seemed to have created.

"What's he done to you, sweetheart? What's he said?"

"Never mind, Margaret."

"I'll get his lordship from the — "

"No, missus, you will not!"

"He's a lazy man, his lordship is, not seein' to his lady nor to his house. Time's come for him to protect his wife."

"Missus, I will not *beg* you to obey me," Alicia said, mouth set and eyes angry. "I will discuss Lord Perry's visit with his lordship when it is right to do so and you will *not* call him home!"

Margaret shifted uncomfortably in front of Alicia. It was the very first time the young woman had ever barked orders at her servant. She could not argue further, but her loyalty to Lady Seavers ran so deep and was so protective that she would not answer her with an assent.

"The brandy that is kept in the study for his lordship," Alicia said. "Do you know of it? Bring me a small glass."

"The brandy, mum? You're sure?"

"I'm sure. If it works for his lordship in his darkest hour, it will surely serve me now."

eleven

*A*n early morning fog still hung in the air, but by midday the sun shone down on London and the air warmed. The crowds mingled about the docked vessels, while workers hauled their tools and merchants sold their wares.

The *Rose* dropped her garnish of ropes, sails billowed, and oars moved. She was out of port and on her way, the wind taking her quickly. Within a brace of moments, the *Thora* was moving away, her solid sides bulging with expectation, her guns sitting like erect antennae in anticipation.

Geoffrey Seavers felt as though his chest would burst as he watched them depart — his first two trading ships setting sail, their destination: New York. He was hopeful they would encounter and attack Dutch vessels en route, sink the blackguards, and bring back their booty. He longed to be aboard, to be present for the first adventure. But there were more ships to ready and his battles had already been many — he could wait for the *Patrina* to sail.

Seavers stood in good company to watch the departure of the first two vessels of his potential fleet. Charles, his brother James, duke of York, and Buckingham watched the first of a fleet leave the wharves. All the men enjoyed the sight of a new ship going, for her return would bring riches and victories to the English, and to the king and Seavers personally.

"They all bear women's names," Charles pointed out with a smile. "Fitting. Never is there anything so skilled in fighting, so pleasurable to ride, nor so eager for wealth as a woman."

The men chuckled in agreement, while silently each thought no man knew women so well as Charles. He took them very seriously and then not seriously at all. Charles loved them, pursued them, pampered and ignored them, gave them expensive gifts, listened to their complaints, and bought them off. He could not live without beautiful women, but he never allowed them to become so important that they might interfere with the business of running a country.

"How many more ships are being rebuilt?" Charles asked Seavers.

"Six more, Sire, and the *Patrina*. She's ready enough to sail, but I claim that as my ship and she won't go without me."

"And which of these are to be a part of the royal navy?" James asked.

"All, in event of war."

"The event of war, my lord, is upon us daily," James retorted.

Charles clamped a hand on James's shoulder and laughed. "I own fifty percent of the booty on these vessels, James. Let's not tie them up permanently. Seavers sails in occupied waters. He'll take a few Dutchmen — and bring us valuables as well."

"There will be ships anchored off the coast and ready to sail at the first call, my lord," Seavers told James, prepared to answer to his own commitments. "You need never fear that I am first a merchant and privateer; I pledged my fleet to His Majesty a long while ago, and so it is first for England."

Charles cleared his throat. "Just the same, my lord, let them never be idle creatures. I wish to see them busy, riding the sea and doing their work."

And Seavers nodded then to his king, straddling the fence perfectly, serving James, the naval commander, and the king, whose need was definitely for money and victory.

Charles had been in England now five years and his financial situation was not good. He called himself the poorest king in all Christendom and was no doubt accurate. His flamboyant way of life and the many encounters with the Dutch and Spanish that he had to endure had been costly. He needed several constant sources of revenue and he was pleased with the sum Seavers would supply when he was actively sailing.

"I have not seen Lady Seavers, my lord," Charles began, walking away from the dock and expecting the others to follow, as they did. "Is she well?"

"Quite well, Your Majesty."

"You don't bring her around, which I suppose is wise, considering the attention she would get."

"On the contrary, Sire, I don't keep her away from the court. My obligation is first to these ships, and my lady is content to be at home. She was not bred for the court and I fear she worries with her appearance."

"She needn't. She's beautiful and well-mannered. I think you are a lucky man."

"Aye, Sire."

"And I am a lucky man, I realize that."

Geoffrey stopped and looked at the king in confusion. "Lady Charlotte is an investment, Seavers. Certainly you realize that."

"Certainly," he said, though he hadn't.

"Well, good work, my lord," the king said, reaching his coach. "And good luck."

"Thank you, Sire."

Charles looked around before entering his coach. He loved the business of sailing and shipping, but at the moment, with talk of plague and no one quite certain how rampant the disease was, he did not tarry about the wharves. Sailors were known to carry the disease from port to port. "Guard your health," he said, ducking in and allowing York and Buckingham to get in behind him.

Seavers stood, looking out over the water and catching a final glimpse of his lovely ladies, their sails full as his heart. New York, he thought, Africa, the West Indies, Virginia. . . . He loved the thought of what his men and his vessels would procure for him.

He had fought in New Amsterdam, now New York. He had fought off the coast of Africa. He had not lost his taste for fighting, and he'd captained ships before, but they had not been *his*. And now he employed captains who sailed for him, rode his ships. His legs ached to be on the deck of the *Patrina*, his flagship, with several others keeping pace, but for what he wanted for his future, this place was better for now; watching them go off to trade and fight.

And later, when there was sufficient money, he would take advantage of the land offered him by the king and build in the Americas. He could import indentured servants from England and Africa and begin a farming and trading industry. He would perhaps be a neighbor to Preston and they would rekindle their friendship and sail and trade together.

The *Letty* was not in port, but anchored not far from sight. Preston's brothers did not return to London often, but ships belonging to the Tildens put into port regularly. England was not home now, but it was their port and first allegiance. Yet their family did not have to live, eat, and breathe courtly politics and schemes. He would be glad to remove himself from the English court and seek out adventure in a new land. Indeed, a new life, once he could bring luxuries so hard-earned to a new place.

Before he could stop the fantasies of his future, his own coach entered the shipping area and Rodney climbed down from his seat next to the driver to hand Geoffrey a sealed message. It was Perry's seal and Seavers frowned as he ripped the parchment to see the scrawl.

> A meeting, Lord Seavers, might serve to establish the credibility of your marriage to Charlotte Bellamy.

A flourishing *P* ended the note. Geoffrey's eyes blazed. "How did you come by this?" he asked Rodney.

"Delivered by a page, my lord, from Lord Perry. I thought you should see it at once."

"Do you know what this is about?"

"Aye, sir. Lord Perry visited Lady Seavers not long ago and threatened to expose her as an impostor. He instructed her to ask you to put a ship in his name — for now."

"A *ship?*" he blustered. "For now?"

"Aye, sir."

"And Lady Seavers thought it unimportant enough to keep silent on the matter?"

"Indeed, sir. And I agreed. She informed me of his visit immediately and I have hired a man to watch his moves."

"I should have been told at once. What evidence does he have to hold against me?"

"None, as I can see. I think it fair to say that Lady Charlotte handled him beautifully. She encouraged him to take his tale to the king and showed not an ounce of fear of exposure. He left your house in a very angry mood."

"She encouraged him? Where is her brain?"

"In quite the right place. Perry said that he found Charlotte Bellamy on her aunt's farm before your betrothal to her was granted. At that time Perry was himself betrothed, to our fair Andrea. I think you'll agree, sir, Perry cannot speak out against you — it would implicate him in a conspiracy a good deal more serious than yours."

"I should see him . . ."

"Beg pardon, sir, but I disagree. There seems no point, not so long as he's being watched. I feel certain he will try to blackmail you, but he will not show his cards. Ignore him. For now."

Seavers's face was red with rage. Perry was the kind of man who would use any means to intimidate and blackmail him. He would take the profits of one ship! "Does he think I will not fight him for this fleet? Does he think I'll answer to his blackmail?"

"Undoubtedly, sir," Rodney replied.

"Is it time for Charlotte Bellamy to die?" Seavers asked.

"It indeed is time for her to live, sir. And thank fate that a woman capable of not wilting in the face of trouble is at your side. I think Perry would attempt these manipulations even if you were wed to the genuine article, and no doubt the real Charlotte could not maintain her composure as well as our Alicia does."

"I'll be mighty glad when this is done."

"Aye, sir. Go to work and consider it done now. I perceive no danger in Lord Perry."

"I only wish I were as confident as you, Rodney. I am never surprised by Perry's mischief. He may yet find a way to get his hands on a fortune."

"I've stepped up protection for Lady Seavers, sir. I've employed another steward and am keeping myself mostly at the house."

Geoffrey nodded, trying to hide his embarrassment. He had been concerned with the profits of his ships and had not thought that Alicia might be in a compromising position. "Keep her safe, Rodney," he said as an afterthought.

"Of a certain. And at the risk of being too bold, sir, may I suggest you look in on her from time to time?"

"Ah, yes, of course. . . ."

The king's coach rattled on its way to Whitehall, and within, the men laughed over the escapades of the king's previous evening, when he'd taken an outrageous actress from the Duke's Theatre to supper with him. The actress entertained a group with her obscenities and flirtations, and then rumor had it that she'd visited the king's bedchamber for yet another entertaining job. Charles would not admit or deny the fact, much to his friends' frustration.

"I think it a dangerous game to upset Barbara so close to her lying in, and Madame Stewart so close to her deflowering," Buckingham taunted.

"Madame Stewart is no closer to losing her maidenhead than ever she was," Charles assured them.

"It was kind of you to ask after Lady Seavers, Sire, but it would please me more if you'd insist on her presence. Some of us could use something new to look at."

"Odd's fish, haven't we enough trouble over women? Let Seavers keep her to himself for a while."

"If she is your investment, why not profit more by her presence?" George asked him.

"She's nervous with the court. Barbara fawns over her and it seems to make her quiver beyond anything I'm able to bear," Charles answered. "Let her be. She won't be around long."

"Where the devil do you think she'll go?" James asked.

"Can't be sure, but likely Seavers will move his industry out of London and take her along. He's selling Bellerose when it's refurbished, which is what I expected him to do."

"How sits your shipping if he leaves?"

"Quite well, I imagine. He cannot do without England, but he need not play parties and gamble when he could be working." Charles peered at his friends with that dark-eyed wisdom that no one quite understood and dared not question. "I'd been looking for a way to stuff Seavers's pockets with money for a long while, since there's no one at court more eager to lose himself in work than that one. Lucky for us all that Charlotte Bellamy and her inheritance happened along. Now Seavers builds a fortune for us both."

"There's talk about Lady Seavers, Sire. No one can quite believe the good fortune and untimely death of Sir Fergus. Truth to tell," George said, "I don't either."

"Fergus was a good man, though not worth all that much. As for his daughter, sweet and lovely as she is, I would not have taken up her cause had it not put money directly into the pocket of a privateer seeking the greatness Seavers expects."

"Aha," James laughed. "Had there not been a good sailor with far-reaching dreams available, poor Charlotte would be selling oranges for her bread."

"No doubt."

"And the fortune?" George asked.

"With as many bastards to support as have I?" The king chuckled. "I imagine I could have easily found a place to drop the inheritance Fergus left. But sad to say, none of my children would work half so hard to make money for me as Seavers will."

"Why didn't you finance him long ago if you were so sure of him?"

"There had to be money first, George. And I had at least to grant myself the amusement of watching him go after it." Charles laughed. "I love his lust for gold. It's marvelous!"

"I wonder if his lust for his wife equals it," George said.

"If it doesn't, he is an idiot. I have seen her," Charles said.

Alicia spent an unusually great amount of time out of doors, but she did not go abroad at all. Since the day her purse was torn from her wrist, followed not too long after by the visit from Culver Perry, she had begun to fear being out in the teeming London streets, regardless of the protection Rodney offered.

Alicia had been informed that Geoffrey had been confronted, via message, by Culver Perry, but thankfully he had chosen not to respond. "He must be wild with fury," she told Rodney, speaking of Culver. "No one will give attention to his tale."

"We will not, madam, but tales are plentiful here and no one seems to grow tired of them."

"I have not left the house and already this week I've heard the king is a confirmed Catholic, that he was married to Monmouth's mother, and that Barbara Palmer is paying an acrobat to sleep with her. Rumors, it seems, are the best-loved things in London."

"You are not concerned?" Rodney asked her, marveling at her composure.

"I'm deeply concerned, but I am not foolish. At this moment, I think Perry would have as much success in saying the king is not who he pretends to be. There is only one thing I fear: that Perry has some evidence that we know nothing of, some property or paper that could only belong to Charlotte Bellamy that I do not have."

"There's no way to prepare for that, madam, other than what we are already doing."

"I'm quite sure that Lord Perry is holding the woman whose right it is to be in this home, wed to Lord Seavers. If he has her, we should know it. It is easier to deal with the trouble if we know where the trouble lives."

"And if we find her, madam, I assure you Lord Seavers will throw himself in the sea in pure panic."

"If Charlotte has trusted Lord Perry, Rodney, she needs our sympathy. Let's carry on the watch and pray that Culver grows tired of this method of making money."

It was less than a week later that Rodney informed her

that Perry had been seen on New Street, visiting an apartment there, where a heavyset, copper-haired wench was living. There was the distinct possibility in Rodney's mind that it was indeed Charlotte.

Without giving the matter much thought, Alicia asked him to find a hell cart to replace the family coach and take her for a tour of the place. "I suppose you'll be angry that I had not mentioned this to you, but the woman who tore away my purse accused me of being an impostor. I'm quite certain she is Charlotte. If we should happen to see her, I could tell you for sure."

"Why did you say nothing?" Rodney asked her.

"And borrow trouble for your troubled lord? He is so frightened now that he can barely stand to look at me."

Rodney helped her on with her cloak and lifted her chin to look into her soft eyes. "And you, lass. Are you not a little frightened of Newgate for yourself?"

"Kind sir, you brought me away from a prison yourself. How can you think Newgate would frighten me more than anything else has?" She shrugged and pulled on her gloves and picked up her vizard. "I have an advantage that Lord Seavers does not have; I have never known where I would live next and even now do not know. Whether prison or palace, I will manage somehow."

"His lordship fails to thank you properly," Rodney told her.

"Not so, sir. He does not thank me at all."

The hell cart bounced along the London streets past the 'Change and through the Jewish quarter. As they pulled closer to New Street, Alicia pulled back the dark drape and, with the vizard over her face, she peered out. She hoped to catch a glimpse of a woman who could be Charlotte, but another sight caught her eye. Crosses on three doors on the street caused her blood to run cold and made it difficult for her to breathe.

The church bells had tolled three more deaths this morning, and the crosses were moving across town with frightening speed. The first registered plague death had been taken lightly; the second, third, and fourth were generally ignored. But now there could be no doubt that plague was in the city and it was creeping closer and closer to the rich. Many nobles were already leaving London for their country estates to escape the illness.

"We won't stay here and wait," she said abruptly. "Show me which apartment it was and let's be away."

Rodney pointed to the building, a shop below and four stories of living quarters above, its sides flush with the building beside it, many shops and houses stacked together like logs. "If that is where she lives, she may not be here long." Alicia gulped. "I don't like feeling responsible for her nearness to disease."

"You are in no way responsible, madam," Rodney argued. "Had she not fled her betrothal to Lord Seavers she would not be residing in a plague neighborhood. It is her doing."

"No, good sir, I think not. I think if I am not to be blamed, then Lord Perry should be. I am sure if she is here it is because he brought her."

"Still, madam, she had a choice."

Alicia thought for a moment, and at a lift of her hand, Rodney called out to the driver to take them out of the streets and home.

There was no stopping the flood of memories Alicia had of Culver Perry, his smooth tongue and his incredible sincerity. There were things that Culver was expert at: lies and the ability to seduce a woman. Wicked and hateful as he was, he was handsome, articulate, and a consummate actor. He could charm the hide off a wild boar.

Alicia did not blame Charlotte, even though she thoroughly blamed herself for having once fallen prey to his charms.

"Who is the man you've hired to watch Lord Perry?" she asked Rodney.

"Mr. Scanland, a retired sea captain I've known for some years. He is not young, but he is capable."

"Ask him to take special care of his health; but if it is possible, he should speak to the woman on New Street. She may be inclined to tell a friendly old gentleman her story."

"Aye, madam." Rodney smiled and patted her hand. He had guessed she would be a fitting woman to help young Geoffrey, but daily she amazed him with her wit and intelligence.

"And we will not frequent this part of town," she added.

"Worry not, madam. I've an idea you could survive anything."

Rodney's confidence in her was a thing she did not always understand, for she often saw herself as very vulnerable. And the emotions involved in working herself into her role as Charlotte, Lady Seavers, were very taxing, and it was a piece of work that many times left her exhausted.

When they returned to the house on Tiller Street, there was yet another challenge awaiting Alicia.

Margaret hurried to the door as they entered, and, with a great deal of excitement, she presented Alicia with an invitation bearing the king's seal. Alicia opened it with anxiety pounding in her chest; she'd much prefer, especially right now, to be nearly invisible in London.

"It's an invitation to sup with His Majesty," she told Rodney quietly. "It says nothing about Lord Seavers. . . ."

twelve

argaret, please," Alicia begged as she was jolted about by another sharp pull on the strings of her corset.

"Don't fuss so, madam. You've got to be at your best for the king, madam."

My best? she wondered. What on earth for? She did not think he was calling her to Whitehall to incarcerate her for fraud — he wouldn't have to waste any food on her for that. But it was clear something was up. Perhaps she had not been wise to stay so far away from the court activities. Perhaps that in itself made her appear a suspicious person.

For the very first time since playing the part of Charlotte Bellamy, Alicia was not gaining much joy from her primping and dressing. With the pressure applied from Culver, the certain presence of the true Charlotte in London, and now this special invitation from the king, her position felt more precarious than ever.

But she did not dare beg to be excused from the dinner and she did not dare arrive late. She mustered all her acting ability, dressed as well as she could for the occasion, and allowed Rodney to take her to the palace.

That Frances Stewart was the hostess was her first surprise, for she had assumed she would be Barbara's pawn once again — a slim figure to keep the gallants from fussing so over Frances. But there were few gallants. The dinner was a small, intimate affair.

And she was greeted, almost personally escorted, by the most powerful man in England.

"My lady," Charles drawled. "Such a pleasure to see you again."

"My thanks, Sire," she murmured, sinking into a curtsy before him.

"Odd's fish, you've nearly got it right," he chuckled. "Come now, we'll have no bowing and posturing tonight. We'll concentrate on pleasure, if possible."

"I don't know how it's possible," Frances said, quickly sidling closer to the monarch. "I don't know when London's been more dreary than this."

Charles nearly ignored her remark, but for the scowl. He took Alicia's hand, tucking it in the crook of his arm, and led her farther into the room. "I'd rather not talk of plague and war tonight," he confided. "Just for a moment, I'd like to forget it's out there. And you, madam, have been away too long. Your presence is sorely missed."

"I apologize, Sire," she said meekly, her confidence suffering a bit. "It's only that Lord Seavers is so . . ."

Charles waited a moment. "So . . . ?" he urged.

"He's very busy with his ships, Sire," she said.

"That's no reason for you not to be enjoying yourself. You aren't still frightened in a pack of fools, are you, my dear?"

"Fools, Sire?"

"I've left you mostly alone and insisted the others do, as well, knowing how nervous this whole scene seems to make you; but I can't hold them off forever. They *demand* pretty things to look at."

Alicia heard herself laughing at that. Was that why she

had been invited? To add another female to the bouquet of flowers the courtiers plucked from?

"Come and amuse yourself with Buckingham for a while. He's the one who's been asking after you most often — though it pains me not at all to admit I've been eager to have you about."

And with that, she was led to a settee where George Villiers was seated, and he promptly rose, kissed her hand, and asked someone to fetch the lady a glass of wine. Within a short period of time, she was introduced to the earl of Rochester; James, the duke of Monmouth and the bastard son of King Charles; and a few other notable, powerful members of the ton.

Though this was a dinner, Alicia noticed how squeamishly the people around her picked at their food. The roast of duckling was not as good as her own cook could have produced. The usual for a dinner at Whitehall was a lavish and expensive spread of foods, fine wines, and brandies. But the dinner Frances provided was adequate, and that was all. It was, no doubt, a sign of the times; delicacies were harder to come by these days. She was seated between George Villiers and Monmouth, who likewise pushed their food around.

"How do you find the duckling, milord?" she asked Buckingham quietly.

"Half good, lady, that is all." He sounded somewhat terse, and Alicia prompted him no more, but turned quietly back to her own dinner. The duke leaned closer to murmur again. "Perhaps if *she* wouldn't trifle with her meal so, the rest would feel safe to eat," he said, indicating the fair Frances with his eyes.

Alicia looked at their hostess and found, as Buckingham had indicated, that she played with the food on her plate and looked less than gay. But then Frances was given to fright easily and worried herself nearly ill over the reports of sickness in the city.

"I think you should feel safe, milord," she said with a smile. "His Majesty would not partake so courageously if there were anything wrong."

They looked together toward the king, who chatted with the woman beside him while heaping generous portions of food into his mouth, undaunted by Frances's delicate and suspicious attention to her own plate.

"There's a thing you should know about him, my dear," George reported. "It takes a good deal worse than bad food to cause him to lose his appetite."

Frances rose from her seat long before the others when one of her servants whispered in her ear. She returned to the long table to urge her guests to finish.

"Our entertainment is ready," she smiled, throwing an arm out in the direction of two midgets garbed in entertainers' chausses and vests and colorful shirts, with bells on their stockings.

"Do let them perform," Charles said, his fork still in his hand.

Frances frowned slightly. Apparently it was not her plan to have the miniature acrobats tumble about her dining room, but she took her seat, turned her chair slightly, and, with a bow, the little fellows began to hop around, climb atop each other, and toss one another into small aerial flips, their bells tinkling as they popped up and down. After each trick, they paused, took a little waist bow toward their audience, and, without the benefit of applause, went on to the next trick. Frances seemed to be slightly amused with the performance, though Alicia watched them with rapt interest.

By the time the performance was over, the dinner was also finished. Frances excused her midgets and stood at the head of the table, while her guests rose from their seats.

"Now shall we play blind man's bluff?" she asked them.

Alicia thought she noticed at least two women clap their hands together as happily and childishly as Frances, but she couldn't be sure, for it was Buckingham's voice that over-rode. "Good God! Again?"

Charles laughed in good humor. "Why is it you want to deprive Frances of her fun, George? You know how she loves the game."

"May we, Sire?" she asked him, her eyes shining.

Even Alicia could see Charles soften and begin to glow at the sweetness of her plea. "Of course, my dear. This is your dinner."

Frances happily fluttered in the direction of a larger room, the guests following her along. By the time Alicia arrived, Frances already had a blindfold over her eyes and Rochester was busily tying it. George Villiers hung to the back of the circle, an unhappy expression on his face. Rochester began to turn her about to make her quite dizzy, and the people in the room pulled back from her so as not to be caught by her flailing hands. As Alicia herself backed away, she noticed Buckingham making a dodge for the door. She heard the king chuckle behind her.

"That's the way he never gets caught," Charles said, pointing to Buckingham. "And poor Frances will never realize he's gone, but wonder only why he's never blind-folded. Come," he said, taking her elbow, "let me show you something of interest."

"What is it, Sire?" she asked excitedly.

He pulled her along with a devilish smile on his lips, and led her to a sitting room in Frances's apartments. A small marble table stood in the center of the room, and on the table was a perfectly constructed miniature of a ship with *The Royal Escape* painted on its side. "This was made for me," he told her proudly. "It is an absolutely perfect rep-lica of the ship I left England on after the battle of Wor-cester. I imagine you've heard the story a hundred times at least."

Alicia smiled. "I never grow tired of hearing it, Your Majesty."

"This is priceless to me," he confided. "A work of art."

"Why do you keep it here?" she asked, and as she met his eyes and saw his smile, she immediately blushed scarlet. She had practically asked how intimate his relationship with Frances was. And the talk was that Frances was still a virgin, after being pursued by the king for nearly two years.

"I don't *keep* it here, madam. I had it brought here tonight to show it off. I daresay everyone's seen it but you."

"Forgive me, Sire, I didn't mean to —"

"Lord Seavers, madam — does he leave you completely unattended?"

"Sire?"

"The talk is that he does not live with you at all, but on his ship. True?"

"Sire, I . . . I have no complaint . . ."

"Complaints I have no time for. And you are no longer my responsibility, but Seavers's. I think perhaps you don't follow the reason for my questions. There is talk, madam, that you are an impostor. Is Lord Seavers aware of this?"

Suddenly Alicia knew why she had been called to sup with the king, why she had been coerced into the sitting room alone with him, and, vaguely, what was coming. She did not know how to meet the questions, but bolstered herself to realize the game would end here. "I'm certain he is not, Sire," she said with evident shock.

"Has there been any threat made to you?" he asked.

"No, Sire. Please, I don't understand . . ."

He patted her hand affectionately. "There's very little to understand, my dear. This was bound to happen, and with any luck it will end here, die a natural death. Since no one knew you, grew up with you, or could identify you, someone was bound to suggest that you are not who you are. I thought only to ask after your safety. In the event that your husband is not closely protecting you."

"I assure you, Sire, there is no truth to the rumor that Lord Seavers does not live in his home. I would know."

The king cocked a brow. "He is not with you tonight."

"I didn't know the invitation included him."

"An invitation was sent to him — at the *Patrina.*"

Alicia felt her cheeks grow hot. "I can't imagine why he didn't mention that, unless..."

"Unless he was 'busy'?" the king attempted.

Alicia opened her mouth as if to reply, but the king went on. "I find myself mighty attracted to you, madam, and see no reason why you need sit and rot in that wretched house if you'd prefer to be — that is, if it would suit you to be — in better company."

"Your Majesty?"

"Is your time your own, lady?" he asked.

"Of course, Sire."

"So that you could spend it otherwise without doing injury to Lord Seavers?"

Alicia straightened abruptly and a knowing look came into her eyes. "Your Majesty!"

Charles shrugged and a half smile played on his lips. "Some women are actually flattered..."

Alicia found herself suppressing a giggle and she couldn't keep the smile off her lips. "And I am," she confessed. "But for a moment I thought you'd called me here to reprimand me for something."

"Only for being beautiful and lonely at the same time, which there is no reason for any woman to be."

She looked down into her lap, for she didn't know what to say next. This was not charity work on the king's part; there were enough women in all of England prepared to jump into his bed. He not only desired her, but would probably continue to pursue her. He had, after all, chased Frances around the palace for two years now.

"Ah," Charles breathed, knowingly. "So you love the rogue, eh?"

She slowly raised her eyes to his and felt herself strangely near tears. She gave her head a slight nod, terrified that she had deeply offended him.

"But, does he love you, madam?" Charles asked.

"I believe he does, Sire," she said softly.

Charles rose abruptly, as if to say he'd spent all the time on the matter he intended to. "Well, I don't know that you're right on that account, madam. Seavers isn't showing it in the way I would. But I think we can continue this discussion on our next encounter, which will be soon, won't it?"

Forcing a confident smile, Alicia rose to stand beside him. She hoped she looked as if she was tempted in the direction of the king, if only to buy time. "I hope so, Sire," she said softly. "I do hope so."

"Next week, perhaps?" he asked.

"I can't say you nay, Your Majesty." He held out his arm to walk her back to the party. "This business of my reputation, Sire, what do you suggest —"

"Don't worry yourself over it, madam. It was bound to happen." He turned to look down at her and she could clearly see warmth in his dark eyes. "Didn't I tell you you'd drive them to distraction with your fresh looks? And see, you have us all. . . ."

For two days Alicia thought about her encounter with Charles, picking it over in her mind until she could think of it no longer. She sent a message on each day to the wharves asking Geoffrey to come to the house and see her, and each day Rodney returned to tell her that he simply couldn't break away from his work.

Fear of discovery might have been foremost on her mind, but waking each morning to the sound of bells ringing out death in the city made her fears rise higher, until she thought she might go mad with fright. And this closer kinship with the king was a thing she simply couldn't handle without a husband. She knew the time was here. And she dressed carefully for an outing.

She was lifted into her coach by a very reluctant Rodney. She had pleaded with him until he could do nothing but consent to take her to the wharf, a place that in the midst of plague would be considered the most dangerous part of town. But dangerous or not, that was where Geoffrey insisted he was needed, and he would not abandon his men or his ships for safer ground.

She saw from her coach that three of Geoffrey's ships were being loaded with great fervor; this would not seem unusual, except that one of them was the *Patrina*. She had been told that Geoffrey would keep her in port as his base until all the work was done and the other ships he had purchased or leased were ready to sail.

With all the hurrying and running around, the coach could not get very close to the wharf. Rodney stopped and jumped down, immediately snapping open the door. Alicia made a move to disembark. "Nay, madam, I forbid it."

"But I know where to find him," she offered.

"I'll not let you wander the planks with all the sickness about."

"I'll be quick," she promised, trying to leave the coach.

"With all due respect, my lady, his lordship will defend me if I have to tie you to keep you off the dock. I'll fetch him to you or take you home."

Alicia opened her mouth to protest and Rodney began to close the door. "Home it is," he said.

"No, Rodney, please . . ." she begged. "Please ask him to come to the coach. It *is* important."

A childlike and wistful look came over her face as she sat in her lonely vehicle, wondering what would pass between them this time. Would there be kindness, impatience, or anger? She could not predict his mood, but she feared this would be the last time she would see him.

Moments later the door bolted open and she looked into

Geoffrey's green eyes, which had tired lines surrounding them. Perspiration stained his linen shirt. She couldn't remember ever having seen him look so frantic.

"For God's sake, madam, what are you doing *here?*"

"It couldn't wait, Geoffrey, and I didn't know if you would ever come home. Please, a few moments."

"I honestly cannot allow the time, Charlotte," he said rather loudly. She flinched slightly at the sound of the name.

"I must insist. It is urgent."

"Quickly, then," he barked, still standing in the open door.

"Privately," she muttered, more than a little piqued at his attitude.

Geoffrey took a deep breath, irritated to be faced with her now. He climbed in and sighed loudly, restlessly, as he simultaneously noticed the color of her gown, the plunging neckline, the sparkle of her eyes, and her general tempting appearance. He wanted to grab her and pull her to him, giving himself a moment of passion to take with him, but the icy fingers of control held him in check. Later, he told himself. Just a little while longer. . . .

"Madam, please, hurry. I'm leaving immediately."

"Leaving?"

"Aye. We are meeting the Dutch. War."

"War? she breathed. "My God, Geoffrey, I —"

"I have very little time!"

"This cannot wait for the war to be over, Geoffrey. Our situation becomes worse. I had dinner with the king just two nights past — he told me you received an invitation as well. Why did you not attend?"

"I don't have time for this, madam."

"He asked me if you were aware that the talk is that I am an impostor."

She dropped her head and looked into her lap. If only he would reach out to her quickly, now, before his battle. She could not await a better time in hopes that something of love could be brewed between them.

There is always war. Or shipping. Or politics. There is always delay; something that would allow Lord Seavers to postpone dealing with his personal problems. Many things can wait; but she could not wait any longer.

"And what did you say, madam?"

"I told him I was certain you were unaware. I asked his advice and he seems, for the moment, completely unconcerned. But, Geoffrey, he made advances. He thinks I am lonely."

"It is not your loneliness that attracts him," Geoffrey said, his voice grating out the words as his eyes roved over her partially exposed bosom.

"The plague in the city is worse. There is talk that the gates will be closed and no one will be allowed to leave."

"It is only talk," he said heatedly.

"I am ready to leave," she said resolutely. "I have stayed here long enough."

"I *cannot* leave," he said between clenched teeth.

"You need not," she said simply. "But I must leave the city before plague strikes me down. There is too much danger here. And I prefer to be as far as possible from Lord Perry."

"I perceive he is no threat; he has no proof of what he prattles about."

"His word is more dangerous than you know. He has Charlotte Bellamy in his custody and he knows who I am."

"How is it I am never told —"

She shrugged. "There is no reason anyone would believe Perry over you," she started. "But I will not play these games any longer, my lord. Culver Perry knows who I am because he is the courtier who seduced me and robbed me of my virtue over a year ago."

Geoffrey's eyes opened wide, shock etched into his features. He stared at her in wonder. He could not respond.

"I see no immediate danger, but I think it most unwise to court trouble. It is time that I leave London, and the plague is good reason to leave. Then there are choices..."

"Choices?" he questioned.

"It would not be unusual to begin your merchanting trade in another port, with this one still seeing much of you, and your king continuing to profit from your trade. Your family can reside elsewhere."

"What do you babble about, wench?" he snarled.

"Speak for me now, Geoffrey, or give me up. I can't go on with this game any longer."

The shouting outside the coach gnawed at him that the battle with the Dutch would not wait for him. Within their private cubicle he was learning that a man he hated more than the devil himself had come before him with the woman he loved. And their life together, the interwoven mass of lies and confusion, he must speak for *now*.

"Perry," he growled. "I would have preferred you *had* slept with the king."

"What matter the name, Geoffrey. What he had he took. You have had more of me than any other. Do you cherish it? Will you claim me as your wife?"

He was speechless and his brow began to sweat.

"Geoffrey," she breathed. "Do not hate me for that, I pray. Your own sister loved him."

"Be glad he used you and left you. Had he been tied, he may have killed you to free himself."

Alicia looked away from his face, for the pain etched there caused her blood to run cold. "It is that possibility," she said quietly, speaking of Andrea's untimely death, "that holds Lord Perry at bay. It is clear that Andrea had her fatal fall from a horse at the very moment Lord Perry was seeking a way to wed the Bellamy inheritance." She looked back at him. "He cannot speak as long as I play the part of Charlotte. His plan is thwarted by the foul implications of his game. There is no doubt, Geoffrey," she said, touching his

193

hand and looking earnestly into his eyes. "There is no doubt: he killed Andrea."

"And Charlotte Bellamy? If he has her, what can he do with her now?"

Alicia shrugged. "I pity the girl, but she forfeited her father's money and land for a chance with Lord Perry. She may in time betray him and confess who she is, but, poor thing, I doubt she would be believed."

Geoffrey looked at her, anger burning brightly in his eyes. He did not know if he loved or hated her; it wounded his pride to have shared her with Culver Perry. And to have had his hide saved by her finesse as an actress, appearing devoted and loyal. She was right. No lesser woman would be believed now. He was indebted to her, and not the other way around. She made the entire play work for him. But the pressure of loving her was killing him, for she was desired by many and he had not yet found the way to secure their future together. His words were angry when he found them. "I have *you* to thank for that, madam. You are very skilled at illusions."

She sat back slightly, hurt in her eyes. "At least there is no danger to you."

"No danger but that I am to be bound to thieves and liars all my life and caught tightly in their bonds. A fancy party, this: you, Perry . . ."

"I am not a thief and I lie at your command!"

"And very expertly."

"Will you leave London with me? Will you leave this place and make a place for your family?" she insisted.

"This is my home! This is where I will make my fortune!"

"And so you are determined? This play will end and so will we?"

"I see no alternative to that," he said, looking away from her. He did not want to be caught in this tight enclosure with her, and now, while his pride bled and jealousy threat-

ened to erupt into rage, he did not want to face her, speak
to her, or make any plans with her.

"No matter what you say, Geoffrey, I know that you have
loved me. Will you throw that away now?"

"I did not know *who* I loved!"

"You loved Alicia," she whispered in taut aggravation.

"Whose Alicia?" he asked savagely. "Culver Perry's or
mine?"

Alicia straightened herself and looked at him through
cool blue-gray eyes; eyes he recognized, but glistening with
a new, firmer determination. He held silent as he faced a
woman completely controlled and determined.

"Until someone speaks the binding words of love and
devotion, Lord Seavers, I belong to no man. While I serve
you with my acting and my lies, I am used by you as I was
used by Lord Perry." She looked at him closely. "And when
I gave you my love and you gave me yours, there was no
bargain nor bond. Will there be now?"

The shouting on the wharf grew louder and the sound of
running feet confused the already jumbled emotions Geoffrey struggled to untangle in his mind. Her distant eyes
and her heaving breasts excited and terrified him.

"I will not be cornered. I will not be pressed. I have a
war to attend."

"Speak your mind, if you know it."

He grabbed her by her arms, and his flashing green eyes
glittered into hers. "Cease your demands! I will settle this
score with you when I am ready. Now my country goes to
war."

"There will always be war," she said gently. "What of
our war?"

"I am not a child to be scolded and pressed. I will deal
with you later."

He made a move to leave the coach, but she stopped him
with her soft voice. "I will not stay here."

He jumped down and turned abruptly. "Go where you will," he said with a dismissing wave of his hand. "You have the time to worry with plagues and assignations and bonds of love; I do not! Those problems will have to come another time!"

And the door of the coach slammed in her face. She pulled back the curtain and watched him stomp away from her, his strides long and angry, his hand flying this way and that as he barked orders at people he passed. While he had dallied in the coach, the loading had been nearly completed, and a page held his surcoat for him to pull on.

A tear glistened on Alicia's cheek as she watched him, his face red with anger and his mouth moving rapidly with shouting she could not hear. "Be safe, my lord," she sighed to the faraway, agitated figure of her love.

A trunk lay open at the foot of Alicia's bed and two young maids worked at filling it with gowns and grooming articles. A smaller case sat on the bed and Alicia filled that herself with personal things, including the carefully guarded hundred pounds that she had coddled and protected since leaving the Ivy Vine. A knock at her door announced Rodney. She looked across the room at him, silent for a moment. She thought perhaps he read her sad expression and knew her mind.

"Leave us alone, please," she said to the maids. The two girls scurried out of the room and Rodney stepped in. He stood looking at her as she stood with one hand resting on her small case and the other holding her brush. She shrugged and her teary voice came lightly. "I see no reason that I need leave this behind," she said, lifting the brush a bit.

"You need leave nothing, madam. Everything that has been yours is yours now."

She moved away from him and he watched her back as she spoke. "I would like you to send a coach and cart to Bellerose with the servants and most of the things that are packed. When they are gone I will need you to help me find passage out of England under a name that will draw no attention. I think I can supply more than enough money if it proves difficult."

"You could go to Bellerose and allow Lord Seavers to join you there when this skirmish is over. It shouldn't last long."

"When I am gone you can join the rest of the staff in the country or wait here for Lord Seavers, whichever you prefer," she continued as if he had not spoken at all.

"You need not leave the country yet," Rodney informed her again. "You need not flee Lord Perry. I doubt he can hurt you."

She turned abruptly and Rodney saw the tears in her eyes. "Geoffrey would offer no solution save ending our bargain as it was meant to be. I will not let him tarry with his confusion while my risks grow." She swallowed and tried to control her tears. The gunfire from the battle at Lowestoft could be heard in the city and people rushed by land and water to get closer to it.

"I will go away. Lord Seavers can bury his wife and get on with his life. Perry can go straight to hell."

"Lord Perry may search for you," Rodney offered. "He may not accept your 'death.'"

"In this time of plague? Let him search. I wish him luck."

"Reconsider, madam. The boy needs time and patience to —"

The brush she still held came down with a smack on the table beside her bed. "The *man* has had time enough!" she stormed, though her words came in a hushed whisper. "I think it time I set my sights on men and not boys!"

"He's dealt with so much chaos and —"

"He's *dealt* with nothing! That is why he is still a boy — because he cannot deal with his chaos and his problems." Her eyes watered and her expression grew softer, though troubled. "Good sir, I know you love him, but do you not see? He cannot act on his own mind, his own heart. I cannot wait upon our young lord's whim. I cannot look into his cold eyes again and wonder if he will let himself love me or hate the very sight of me. . . ." She shook her head. "It is time for me to leave. Find me passage or I shall have to do it myself."

Rodney dropped his head in disappointment. "I would prefer to change your mind, but if I cannot, then I am forced to make this as easy for you as possible. Your passage is arranged."

"Thank you, Rodney, I know it is difficult —"

"You have a visitor."

"No visitors now. Tell whoever calls that I'm preparing to leave the city because of —"

But even as she spoke, Rodney was pulling the door to her bedchamber open. There stood Preston, his hat in his hand and his rumpled light brown hair soaked with sweat. He must have only moments ago climbed down from a horse that brought him back to the city after his search for his sister.

As she looked at him, tears came again to her eyes. The expression on his face showed a wealth of knowledge. Rodney stood just paces aside as they looked across the room at each other.

"Alicia," Preston said, his voice soft and filled with emotion.

The brush fell from her hand and, with a cry, she flew across the room and into his arms. Through her mind flashed the memory of the boy who scolded, buttoned her red cloak, and helped her into a waiting coach. As he held her she imagined herself as a child; her tears were both fearful and elated.

"Alicia," he said softly. "My Letty. . . ."

thirteen

ot another day, lovey, not another minute. I've had my fill of your schemes and deals and should've known before I left the country that you toted a pack of lies from the first."

"There's no place for you to go, save the streets, Charlotte," Perry said coolly. But for all his calm exterior, there was a rage burning inside of him that he found more difficult to control with every passing second.

"Ah, you're wrong about that, love. I'm taking myself to the court and I'll find someone there who'll listen —"

Perry's loud and cruel laughter rang through the small, filthy room. "You honestly think anyone will listen to *you?*"

Charlotte's chin began to quiver, a thing that rarely happened to her. She was usually tough and clever enough to make the best of her hard luck . . . but now she was frightened. Every morning and every evening, the death cart moved through the street she lived on, and Perry was doing nothing to see to her protection. "I've a strange feeling you hope I die of plague," she told him, her voice softer than it had ever been.

Again he laughed, a low, sinister sound. There was a gleam in his eye. He looked around the room and reached finally for an orange that sat in a bowl filled half with fruit and half with garbage and rinds. He plucked a cloth article from the bowl and looked at it. "What is this?"

"Her ladyship's purse, that's what," Charlotte said.

"How did you come by it?"

"I saw her at the 'Change and plucked it straight off her hand, that's how. And told her I knew she wasn't who she said she was." Charlotte gave a nod. "Scared her plenty, too."

Perry's brow wrinkled as if in thought. The bitch had become a little too brazen for his purposes. "Did anyone see you?"

"No one knew me, Culver, thanks to you."

"It's not my fault it didn't work out better, but there's still time enough to —"

"There ain't no time, Culver," she said shortly, spreading out the sheet that covered the bed and throwing a dress onto it. It took Perry a moment of watching to realize this was Charlotte's way of packing. "It's true I'll have me some trouble getting anyone to pay me any mind, but there's things of my father and his father that I'm the only one to know; and once someone will listen, I'll at least get my money."

Culver heard the bells tolling outside for the dead and shook his head sharply to remove the sound. He felt unusually hot, and he knew it had little to do with the weather.

"An' if I can't get anyone at the court to hear me, I think I'll take myself to the chaplain. Or Lord Seavers. I don't want to cause no one trouble — she can rightly have his lordship — I just want a piece of what my father —" She broke off.

"Damn me, Perry," she cursed, turning on him. "Do you have any idea how I hate you for the lies you told me? That Seavers was a wasting old man, that he'd spend all his money on ships — that one, that 'Lady Seavers,' she don't look like she's done without."

Perry watched her with a calmness that belied his inner turmoil. "I imagine you'll be wanting your vengeance."

"I'd be the happiest woman alive if they'd hang you," she spat, turning to pick up an article of clothing from the floor and toss it onto her pile on the bed.

Perry began to open and close his hands, stretching his fingers and then making a tight fist. "You're not the only one with regrets, pet," he said viciously. "I regret ever laying eyes on you."

"I don't wonder at it, milord," she huffed, beginning to pull the corners of the sheet around her clothing.

Perry felt the knife from the fruit bowl in his hand before he realized his own intention. He moved toward her back.

"I've got to blame myself for listening to you, but everything else bad has been your —"

Her words stopped with a grunt and a foul gurgle as her hand went to her throat and she felt the knife piercing her and the blood running over both their hands. Her head turned slightly as she looked at him, her eyes glazed and wide, a trickle of blood coming out of the corner of her mouth. And then she fell motionless to the floor beside the bed.

Perry stood for a moment looking down at her lifeless body and the bloody knife in his hand. He had no regret for killing her. He also had no plan. His movement had been spontaneous, unplanned. She caused more risk to him than she was worth. And the sight of the purse — she was not afraid to get too near the Seaverses. She would not be afraid to confront Geoffrey. Or the king.

He could not be ruined by a filthy, stupid whore.

"Bring out your dead. Bring out your dead," called the driver of the dead cart from the street below.

Perry wiped the knife on Charlotte's dress and rushed to

the window. "You," he called. "You there! Come up!"

"I don't go in no plague house," the man cried back.

"There's no plague here. I need help. I'll pay."

The man driving the cart looked around briefly. The streets were nearly deserted.

"Don't worry, man," Perry called. "No one's going to *steal* it."

He reluctantly got down and walked toward the building, and Perry heard him coming up the stairs. The door was opened for him as he reached the apartment.

"Where do you take the dead?" Perry asked anxiously.

"For burial," the man answered, astonished at the question.

"Will you take this one and call it plague?" Perry asked him.

The man looked at the body on the floor and saw the blood soiling her. He looked back at Perry with wide, horrified eyes.

"Aye, she's been stabbed. But I'll pay you better money than you've seen picking up plague deaths if you'll take her and forget my face."

"Be glad to help, gov'na, but if I takes a bloody body, somebody's likely to ask me questions."

"We'll tie something around her neck and you can say it was a lanced plague boil."

"Like to, Gov'na, but —"

"Twenty pounds," Perry said, knowing it would nearly wipe him out of funds.

The little man shivered a bit as he stood there. He was faced with a murderer, he knew that. Maybe the man would kill again. And twenty pounds was more than he'd earn this year.

"All right. Let's hurry with it, chap."

Perry stooped over the body, pulling the sheet off the bed and tearing a long strip of it off. He wrapped the linen around and around the neck.

"They don't usually get boils on the neck, you know," the man said.

"You can sneak her past," Perry said without looking up.

"Truth is, no one much likes t'look at 'em."

"There. Take her out."

"You'll have to carry her down. She's a mite much fer me."

Perry grumbled and started to lift the heavy body.

"Ah, first me money . . ."

Perry halted his action and stood to dig through the inside pocket of his surcoat, pulling out a pouch and shaking its contents out on the bed. He separated two coins for himself and gave the rest to the little man.

The man smiled and counted while Perry struggled with his burden. Down the stairs and out onto the street he walked, looking about suspiciously, but seeing no one about. The man jumped back on his wagon and resumed his shouting without giving Perry a thanks, good-bye, or any further recognition. "Bring out your dead! Bring out your dead!"

He moved his cart along down the street for another few minutes, grateful that no one had answered his call. From behind him, a man's voice called to halt him and he reined in his horse, turning to look.

"That body you brought out," the man said. "I'd like to see it."

The little man on the cart paled slightly. "I don't have to show the dead," he argued.

"I'll pay to look."

The man sighed and jumped down, going around to the back of the wagon.

"She's not plague, is she?" the man asked.

"She looks like plague to me," the driver insisted.

"What did he pay you to put the body on the dead cart?"

The man shrugged. "I couldn't take no pay."

"I'll pay you double to hold the body back from burial just long enough for my employer to get a look at her. It won't take me more than an hour to find Mr. Prentiss."

The dead-cart driver scratched his chin in confusion.

"My name's Scanland. I've been watching the lass. I know she hasn't been sick."

"I can't tell plague. I just take the dead."

"How much?"

"Just to keep them from burying her? For an hour? I won't even be done in an hour."

"How much?"

The little man broke into a broad grin showing his missing front teeth. "Forty pounds."

"I'll give you twenty. And if you keep that body warm, there will be another twenty from Mr. Prentiss."

The man smiled and opened his palm. He took the money and climbed back on his wagon. He clicked his tongue and resumed shouting. "Bring out your dead!" And then he chuckled and talked to the horse. "Plagues been mighty good payin' today. . . ."

The duke of York had commanded the English fleet, chasing the Dutch for over a month, sighting them at Lowestoft. Word was delivered to the palace by Pepys, the king's diarist, that the two fleets faced each other. Seavers did not hear of the impending battle until after midnight, and then he questioned the rumor until sunrise.

Workers had been huriedly put to the task of loading his remaining vessels, ships he had deemed nearly ready to sail, and his crews were pulled from inns, bawdy houses, taverns, and street corners. Some of the crew who appeared drunk could have been sick with plague, for they wobbled on board and perspired piteously, but Seavers concerned himself only briefly and let them either sleep, vomit, work off their drink or illness, or flee. Illness was everywhere; it would not stop for war. He would join the battle, however disabled his forces.

By morning he was nearly ready. The brief and anxious

visit with his "wife" had slowed his pace briefly, but the moment she left he donned his coat and strapped on his sword. The *Patrina* pulled out and down the Thames ahead of three other vessels; the channel was crowded and confusing. He could already hear the gunfire, as could most of London.

As the *Patrina* drew nearer the battle, the explosions became deafening and Geoffrey's pulse raced. By late afternoon he could see the fighting. A huge warship lay tilted on its side, fired, sails and masts dipping down into the sea. Specks scattered about the water proved to be human life struggling toward upright ships. He was still too distant to see blood, but he felt the blood of the wounded and his chest swelled with excitement, his cheeks flushed with the thrill of war and adventure. The sinking ship belched and jolted: her flag was Dutch.

His first time at sea he had puked for seven straight days. On his second voyage he had climbed the mast, and the sea winds burned his face and warmed his soul and he found his sustenance. Not very many years later, he was sailing on his own captaincy on a ship that rode proudly behind Prince Rupert. Just over a year ago he had sailed for England to New Amsterdam to fight the stinking Dutch, finding when he arrived that Tilden ships, outfitted primarily for trading, had joined the fight. They took the Dutch then and left that port with the name New York.

Geoffrey stood at the helm getting directions from the lookout and surveying the sea, counting the ships, identifying the English. He looked for the *Letty* all through that day and the next, but did not really expect to see her in the battle. Prince Rupert joined the battle late, and he, the greatest of Charles's sailors, contributed mightily to the sinking of Dutch vessels.

Seavers fought both by fire and hand for four filthy days and nights and saw one opponent kiss the sea good morning: the great Dutch warship tilted in flames and sank out of sight within a short time. Blood stained his right side from a Dutch seaman he had stabbed as the vessels came abreast of each other, and a painful red flow stained his left side from the blade of an aggressor. His face was blackened from powder and soot, his clothes torn, his belly empty, but his spirits flying high. His guns breathed fire, and his men screamed battle cries and fought like Vikings.

Although the Dutch surpassed the English in ships and wealth, at the end, the English sent the Dutch fleeing in their broken ships to report thousands of Dutch sailors dead. Nine Dutch ships were taken and more were sunk.

The English vessels returned home in victory, but they were wounded ladies of the sea as well. Filled with joyous and sunburned sailors, their bulging sides charred and split from the battle, the ships were welcomed by an ecstatic town of London. Bonfires lit the horizon and church bells tolled. It did not resemble the plague-torn city they had left behind.

Seavers could not let the excitement of battle fade from his soul, for it was that that sustained him. But there were times during the fighting when a vision crossed his mind and he had difficulty turning his thoughts elsewhere. He shrugged off this image of a dark-haired maid, with soft blue-gray eyes — his high-spirited lover — and raised his sword and barked his orders.

But on the return voyage he could do nothing to erase the pictures in his mind. He saw her clearly, her bright smile and her turbulent tears. He felt his emotions rise and fall as he thought in turn of her standing up to him and calling him a fool, and of her lying beneath him with her arms encircling him and her body moving with his.

She will not let me be, he cursed silently. She will never let me be!

During the hours his men needed his attention, his command, he could barely give them answers to their questions. He watched the sea, the scattered clouds, the crippled fleet returning with victory, and in everything he saw Alicia. He shook his head, but she would not fade.

"They'll send me straight to Bedlam," he growled.

"Sir?" a passing sailor asked.

"Nothing. Nothing at all," Geoffrey insisted.

And the vision of Alicia in his mind laughed in good humor. *"Do not fall in love with me, Lord Seavers. You may never be the same."*

"I do not love you!" he insisted to the face locked in his mind. But he saw her eyes grow cool and controlled, her face stern. She looked him square in the eye, a thing that many of his men could not do. *"You are the most complete fool,"* her voice said. And he felt as he had that day as she walked away from him.

As if his suffering with all that had passed between them had not been enough, he saw a vision of her holding a child — his child. And a stricken look came suddenly over his face. What if he'd left her with child?

"Cap'n, sir," a man beckoned. "Let me see t'your wound now, sir."

"Of course," he said thoughtfully, a rueful smile crossing his lips. "Then I would be trapped . . ."

"Sir?" the sailor asked. It was only then that Geoffrey realized the man was tugging at his shirt to bandage his wound. He sighed and raised his arm that the man might bandage him, but his mind was elsewhere.

Not trapped, Lord Seavers, his conscience said. And his conscience looked like Alicia. *You're not trapped at all. You've lain with maids before and for all the world knows, you've fathered sons in several ports. Throw her off and make your way alone.*

His heart heaved and his stomach burned. He could not be alone again. She was the woman he needed. She'd made him feel alive and elemental. There was warmth in her presence and a fire that lit their arguments and their passion. She was naught but a simple tavern wench, but he knew there would never be another like her. And what he felt when he was near her would never come again.

Something settled over him that warmed his soul for the first time in many years. I'll build a house for her in the Colonies, and not long after there will be children, he thought. It will be ready if I begin at once. If she understands the risk and my love, she will not chafe so at the name Charlotte. I will find a way to make her glad she chose to take it.

The London streets were filled with sailors who could not be induced to help mend the wounded ships without first celebrating their victory. There was no Seavers coach waiting at the wharves to take Geoffrey to his house, but why should there be? He had not used his house since he'd moved Alicia into it. He had had no use for transportation before, and now none was provided.

A hell cart was hard to procure because of the chaos clogging the streets, but finally he found a coach to take him home. As he passed the houses on Drury Lane, the red crosses on the doors lunged at him and he found himself feeling guilty and worried. He had not protected Alicia in any way, but had ordered his man Rodney to see to her needs. Even now she could be lying sick with the plague.

"*I will not stay here,*" the memory of her voice said to his troubled mind.

Geoffrey's pulse picked up and began to race. He didn't know whether he preferred to find that she'd left the city or that she was still there, with her things familiarly scattered atop her dressing table and the soft, sweet scent of her filling her chambers.

The door was bolted when he arrived, and he pounded on it and shouted to be let in, but to no avail. Passersby looked at him strangely, recognizing that he was a returned sea captain, and afraid to speak to him. Everyone knew that sailors carried plague. It was the better part of an hour before he could persuade two passing hearties to help him break into the house, and even they were most reluctant and had to be promised a substantial reward.

The heavy oaken door took a great deal of battering and hammering before the hinges yielded and the house was vulnerable. Leaving his helpers in the doorway, Geoffrey took the stairs two at a time and found Alicia's chamber stripped of her personal possessions. The only thing that remained was the necklace he had given her, lying atop her dressing table. He picked it up and held it for a moment. She had purposely left it behind. It was valuable beyond anything he had ever given a woman — she could have sold it for its worth — but she left it. She must hate me more than I allowed, he thought.

The furniture had not been covered or taken, but the food and clothing for her and the servants were gone. It looked as though the household had moved from the city hurriedly.

"Do you know this house?" he asked the men who had helped him.

They shook their heads dumbly and put out their palms. Geoffrey dropped a few coins in each hand. "The woman I left in this house was my wife," he told them. "I've been at Lowestoft with the fleet."

He noticed their eyes coveting the furnishings of the house and knew if they had not supported themselves as thieves before, this would be a good time for them to start. They faced a vacant house rich with furnishings. Half of London would be looted before long, with nobles leaving the plague seas for higher ground.

"I imagine I'll wait here for word of her." Seavers shrugged, hoping he had convinced the men the house would be protected from now on. "My thanks," he said to them, and without a word of reply, they left him standing in the broken doorway.

All through the night the bells rang and bonfires lit the sky, but in Whitehall there were quiet corners for those who grieved friends lost in battle. While some mourned, others there were wont to celebrate, and still others skittered about wondering when the court would give up the plague-torn city and leave for safety. Word was that Charles was determined to stay and show his people that there was no need to fear. Nevertheless, there were too many who could not watch the dead cart move through the streets and remain calm.

Geoffrey walked through the halls of the palace in search of a familiar face; a person who would have word of his household. He had not bathed or changed his clothing and was still charred, thick with dried blood and sweat, and red as a tomato from the sun. Charles was with his ministers and friends and could not be bothered. Castlemaine could not be found, and her steward would not allow Seavers to enter her apartments. A group of ladies walked down the gallery and, when seeing him at a distance, recognized a seaman and widened their path to pass.

"Madame Stewart," he called out, halting the young woman.

She looked at him queerly, tilting her pretty head and peering at the dirty, injured man.

"Lord Seavers, madam," he said, bowing clumsily.

"Of course," she replied, making a slight dip in response.

"My house has been vacated and there is no word of my family."

A pained expression crossed her face as she looked at him.

"There was no one there to keep the house?" she asked uncomfortably.

"No one, madam. Have you heard where Lady Seavers might have gone? Bellerose?"

She frowned. "There have been horrible rumors, my lord," she quavered. "Have you asked about her elsewhere?"

"I've been able to see no one, madam."

Frances sighed and closed her eyes briefly. She was held

as the most beautiful woman in England, and, truth to tell, she must have been, but she was not made of the hardened stuff of most courtly ladies. Frances was very sensitive. When her eyes opened to look at him again, he noted that they were tearing.

"This dreadful illness," she exclaimed. "I'm so frightened of it, I wish we would leave. I swear if His Majesty wants to stay another day, I'll go mad."

"Lady, have you heard —"

"I heard a rumor. I've heard so many rumors," she sighed, shaking her head. One of her ladies patted her arm while Geoffrey stood in stiff anticipation for the reported rumor. "I heard that the household left and Lady Seavers was stricken just as she would have entered her own coach. They've buried her."

"*Buried* her? Five days ago I spoke to her, before I —"

"Less than a day. I think she did not suffer."

"But word is that the plague lasts for weeks!"

"Weeks or hours."

Geoffrey swayed slightly on his feet. He'd been days without any comforts, and the pain in his side had begun to worsen, since the wound had not been tended for some time.

"Milord?" Frances questioned.

He pressed his side with the palm of his hand and brought it away covered with fresh blood. He smiled somewhat sheepishly, embarrassed before these ladies. "Lowestoft," he mumbled. His vision began to blur and he noticed through a haze that Mistress Stewart and her ladies retreated slightly. His thoughts flashed rapidly back and forth, from the fire of battle and the spit of the sea, to the vision of Alicia that had floated before his eyes for days; from the blood of battle, to the softness of his woman; from the charred and desolate remains of sinking ships, to her bright eyes and smile . . .

Blackness swallowed him in one large gulp. The cursed visions stopped.

The sky and the sea blended together and one could not discern the beginning or ending of either. The rocking motion of the ship quieted the nerves and the cool sea breeze stung the cheeks.

Alicia leaned on the rail, her hands clasped in front of her and her eyes searching the horizon for some sign of life. The new land was a million miles away. She mumbled a prayer. Two firm hands grasped her arms and the comforting voice invaded her moment of devotion.

"Perhaps you should not have left him," Preston said.

"Will you get word that he fared the battle with his life?" she asked.

"He is alive, *chérie.* I vow he sank a thousand Dutchmen himself."

"Will you get word?" she asked again, turning.

"Word will be a long time in reaching America, but I've been with him in battle before. He is well, I promise you."

Alicia nodded and her eyes were downcast.

"I'm not sure this is the best way," Preston said. "I'm not sure you should have left him with no word."

"Geoffrey did not ask for word. I told him I would not stay."

"I will not defend him." Preston shrugged. "But your love for him worries me. Perhaps he should know —"

"He does not deserve to know who I am, where I am. Once again, Preston, my life is my own. I belong to no one.

Preston frowned slightly. "You have family now, Alicia."

"Aye." She smiled. "Will they want me?"

"Of course."

"But you are the only one who searched —"

"Wrong! Father sent searchers out more than once, but no trace was found. I am the only one who would not give up." He touched her nose and smiled. "And you would not tell me and save me the trouble."

"I could not tell you. I worried that I would be imprisoned or worse for my lies."

"You could have depended on my silence and protection, *chérie*."

"It was better for you to learn in your own way, Preston. I shudder to think how closely we came to being separated again, but then I couldn't abide being called an impostor in yet another role."

He sighed and shook his head. "It was not very long before I found that Letty was a name that didn't stay with you long. But that you clung to Alicia through your youth helped me considerably. You left a mighty angry innkeeper at the Ivy Vine. I had to buy him off before I could learn a thing."

"He had no right to money from you. I worked hard for him and he still claims me as a debt. I took not a farthing of his money when I left."

"He has no claim on you now, love. And you'll be well taken care of. Your mother will be greatly relieved when she sees you."

"I don't want them to know about Geoffrey," she stated firmly.

"And where will you say you've spent the last few years?"

"At the inn, I suppose," she said with a shrug.

"Ah, yes, the inn. And when your new family suggests marriage, what will you say? You are not a virgin."

Alicia's eyes widened briefly. She had not considered that it would matter, but of course it did. It always had. And she would shame her new family if she was discovered to be a sullied bride.

"I don't want them to know of this business with the king — with the Bellamy money. I want only to forget that."

"Very well, but I would think more lies would be unattractive to you now."

"I'll have to hope they don't ask. If you're right that they will pass no judgment on what my life has been apart from them, let us leave it behind."

"Have *you* truly left it behind? There's always a good chance that you'll see Geoffrey again one day."

"He cast me aside. Perhaps the law would say we were not legally wed, for my name was not used, but in my mind we were not illicit lovers but husband and wife. He chose to be finished with me. And so he is."

"And you'll give him no rights?"

"Charlotte Bellamy is dead, Preston. A dead woman can give nothing of herself. Alicia Tilden is alive and beginning a new life. Geoffrey Seavers does not know her. Where is his claim?"

Preston looked into her eyes and smiled. "He claimed your heart a long time ago, *chérie*."

"You promised me, Preston. You promised I could start anew with my family. Will you betray me to Geoffrey?"

"No, sweetheart. I'll let you do this your way."

"You act as though you pity Geoffrey! He does not deserve your pity, Preston. He would not claim me when he could. I assure you he does not care what happens to me now. He will be greatly relieved that his lies are buried so that he can find himself a woman worthy of his title and wealth."

"He loves you," Preston said.

"Aye, I believe he does. But he will not speak of it. Nor will I."

She turned away from him and looked again out at the sea. Preston's voice came softly to her ears.

"Time, Alicia, will prove the worth of those words."

fourteen

*J*t was first the feeling of a cooling rag on his fore-head that Geoffrey Seavers noticed, and then slowly and with great care, he opened his eyes. He lay on a soft bed in a darkened room. He did not recognize the canopy above him nor did the draperies or tapestries look familiar, but it was clearly a rich place.

He sat up very cautiously and looked around. His shirt had been stripped from him and his wound was dressed. He touched the spot tentatively. It had been little more than a cut, but the lack of attention and the dirt and sweat had chafed it and caused it to become infected. He'd learned that lesson quite a few times and always swore the next time he sustained an injury he would take the time to have it tended. He laughed to himself, for it was likely he never would change his ways. He was impatient and too involved with whatever problem or battle was at hand to see to his own needs.

With that thought, the memory drifted back to him; he had plunged into blackness from the weakness caused by battle combined with the news that his wife had been buried. He lifted the coverlet to ease himself out of the bed, noticing that not only his shirt had been removed but his breeches and stockings as well. He did not see his clothing anywhere about the room.

He was sitting on the edge of the bed as the door opened. A young maid spied him and, with a gasp of surprise, flew across the room. "Into bed with you, milord, and I'll tell her ladyship you're awake."

"Her ladyship?" he questioned, obediently lying back into the rich pillows and allowing the maid to cover him.

"Aye, she asked to be informed. She'll be here soon as I fetch her."

With a flurry of cotton skirts and the hard click of her shoes, she was gone, and Geoffrey lay there in confusion. Her ladyship? he wondered. Frances Stewart? Had she seen to his care?

But it was not that fair lass who entered the chamber moments later, but Barbara Palmer. Smiling and carrying a tray with an herbed wine for him, she drew near his bed.

"Haven't been taking very good care of yourself, have you, my lord," she purred. "Here's something to pick you up a bit."

"My lady, how —" He found he didn't even know what question to ask.

"You'd have likely been taken out on a dead cart if left in Madame Stewart's care. That witless twit's scared green of plague, and every headache she gets she thinks is going to be her death. And does she get headaches! She gets them every time His Majesty steals a kiss."

Geoffrey's eyes grew wider as she talked. There was definitely some serious competition between the two women, but Castlemaine usually held her tongue and spoke cautiously, as if Frances were her dearest friend. Rumor had it that was by order of the man in the middle: Charles.

"The moment you fell, Madame Stewart started to shriek,

certain you were another plague victim. Had I not heard the commotion, you'd have been in the street." She paused a moment and smiled at him. "I've sent someone in search of your man, what's his name. 'Haps he can tell you something of your household."

"Madame Stewart said —"

"I know what she said: she said Lady Seavers is dead. Truth is that no one saw her dead and the rest of your household left the city, including your man, as far as we've heard. And the other rumors are flying about, but you've nothing to worry over till you see your man. He'll know."

"Other rumors?" Geoffrey asked.

"Surely you've heard them. Lady Seavers is an impostor, her death a hoax —"

Geoffrey began to cough and choke on his drink, spitting and dripping as his face reddened. It was some time before he was able to control his fit, but the red in his face would not dissipate. He faced her with question in his watering eyes, but Castlemaine laughed at him.

"You're wise to the gossip, my lord. I won't ask you the truth of it, ease your mind. I'll get my duchy another way, so I have no need for your fortune. His Majesty gets impatient with me from time to time, but he's had no success in throwing me over for another in these many years, so I doubt he ever will. This tiff won't last any longer than the last."

Geoffrey blinked. He tried another sip of wine to take the tickle out of his throat. "You've had a falling out?" he ventured.

"I've heard the court's getting ready to leave for Windsor. I'm going elsewhere. Let him have his witless virgin for a while and see how he likes it."

Geoffrey smiled at Barbara. There was anger in her green eyes, but he could sense her control of the situation. He disagreed; he did not think she could hold the king forever by having child after child, but Barbara would never give up. And she'd play him carefully, besides.

"He'll be coming here to see you when he has the time, so you're to stay and begin to recover."

"I'll report to His Majesty but I've got to —"

Barbara was shaking her head. "You misunderstand me, my lord. You're not allowed to leave. The king has business with you. Your rumors, you know."

A creeping sludge filled Geoffrey's gut and his face lost its flush.

"And I imagine he wants every detail of your part in the battle. I doubt you have much to worry about, but just the same, leaving now would not be wise. Let's not make him any angrier than he already is."

Lord Seavers gulped hard and set the wine on the tray.

"Well, I admit," she went on casually, "he's more angry with me than just about anyone, but when he's angry with me it's already got a good start, you see. You'll want to handle him gently for now. He's lost friends in the battle, you know. And he doesn't have a farthing to pay his navy."

"The rumors, lady. What rumors have found Whitehall?"

"Perry, the jackass, is in a fit over Lady Seavers's departure, shall we say. Seems he has the worst possible timing as ever I saw. While Charles refused to eat, sleep, or speak to anyone, Perry insisted on seeing him and telling his story, the most ridiculous story about Lady Seavers being a country wench trumped up to get the inheritance. Charles was closer to sending a man to Bedlam than ever before."

"Then he does not believe . . . ?"

Barbara rose from his bedside, brushing down her skirts and looking bored as she could be. "I think he doesn't *care*, my lord. And I think if anyone is going to get stuck with the problem, it's bound to be you."

She chewed her finger as if deep in thought. "Well, I've a hundred things to do if I'm moving this household before they're all rotting of the plague. There's none in the palace yet, from what I hear, and I've set my own spies to that bit of news. If there's plague here," she said, shaking her finger at him, "I'll be the first to know it."

"You weren't afraid I was sick with plague?" he asked.

"Only a bit." She shrugged.

"But you took a grave chance."

"A small chance, my lord. His Majesty would not likely come to my apartments for a while since I told Mistress Stewart I'd like to have her nose slit. I told you, he's angry with me. But your name's gotten some attention around here the last few days and I knew if I had you here he'd want to see you."

Geoffrey reclined with a smirk on his lips. "You've got something going all the time, haven't you Barbara."

"There's a thousand people in this town who'd see me burned in a trice. I'll warrant you I can take care of myself well enough, but I've got to keep my wits sharp."

And, Geoffrey thought, you've got to keep your lover in check. He smiled slightly with the thought and, as if she'd heard it, Barbara responded with her own smile.

"How do you suggest I handle these rumors, lady?" he asked slyly.

Barbara laughed and turned toward the door. "If there's any truth to them, my lord, I suggest you do a damn good job of lying."

Lord Seavers sent word to his mate that he'd taken up residence at Whitehall in the hospitality of Lady Castlemaine and all messages for him should be forwarded to the palace. It was only one full night's sleep and a day later that saw him feeling fit and restless, but still he was cautioned by Castlemaine that leaving would be a huge mistake.

In another part of the palace there was much more excitement than that caused by Geoffrey Seavers's problems, for the king had gone through about as much as a king could without cracking. The plague was on a vicious rampage through London: crosses marked more doors every day, while graves were being left unmarked and often were filled with more than one body. Sailors rioted in the streets in fear and anger, for none had been paid and all had earned bonuses; and, while the war had been a victory for England, her ships were suffering the wounds of battle and would need heavy repairs.

It was not strange that in all this fervor Charles paid little attention to the problem of Lord Seavers's wife and the legitimacy of her inheritance. He might have been particularly interested had he been grotesquely bored.

He received several requests from the young lord for an audience and ignored every one. The end of June was drawing near and he was concerned with moving the court, placating the sailors, and perhaps getting out of London with his health. He was fiddling in his closet with medicines that a visiting Jew had given him the formula for, when George Villiers, the duke of Buckingham, entered and caused a slight frown to cross the king's face.

"It had better be urgent," Charles said without looking at him.

"I confess it's not the least bit urgent. It's my cousin again. Lady Castlemaine."

"How is it she can creep up on me when I least expect it? And not even in the flesh."

"In the flesh would please her best," George said.

Charles sighed and mixed his potion. "Only because she thinks it's likely to make a difference in how I'm feeling." He turned toward the duke with his noxious mixture in front of him. "I promise you it won't."

"I know that and you know that, but Barbara's probably going to drive us both crazy if we don't do something about her condition."

"Another condition, is it? Well it's not mine."

"Not pregnancy, Your Majesty."

"Try this, George. Guaranteed to relieve anything, and with any luck at all, it'll take care of your pox as well as my fear of plague." Villiers wrinkled his nose in stark refusal, and Charles shrugged and downed the brew. It could've tasted like a cesspool and he still would have smiled. The man liked nothing so well as his own medicines, except perhaps chasing women.

"I think, George, that perhaps we ought to move to Hampton Court tomorrow. What do you think?"

"Sire, I beg your indulgence this once but —"

Charles scowled and moved out of his closet and away from his toys. Whenever George begged his indulgence it was sure to be something distasteful.

"Give it to me quickly, it's got to be worse than that concoction I just swallowed. The plague might be better, for that matter." He sighed. "What does she want this time?"

"She'd like you to give her guest permission to leave so she can have back her apartments with some privacy."

"Aha," Charles brooded.

"I think he is afraid to touch her and she can't get about as she likes with him there. Sire, you instructed her to keep him until you could see him."

"I know," Charles said, moving toward his fruit bowl and picking up an apple that had spoiled. The sickness in the city not only carried the constant fear of contamination, but servants in the castle were afraid to go out to purchase food, and many of the merchants had closed down their stands and shops to flee. And when food could be found and bought without fear, it was of a quality far inferior to that of healthier days. "Damn me, it'll be a long time before we can enjoy decent nourishment again, I vow," Charles pouted, dropping the rotten apple back into the bowl and shaking his head in frustration. "To be a common man and helpless is one thing," he told George. "But you can't imagine the pain of being a helpless king."

George got a bit bored with following his king and finally took himself across the room to look out the window. There he stood quietly, knowing better than to push Charles for a response. They had been good friends for many years, alternately fighting and playing together. This happened to be a good period for their friendship; but Charles was always the king and George the faithful servant.

"Well?" Charles finally said.

"Well, I'm curious as hell and could care less about Barbara's predicament."

Charles laughed in good humor, for he liked George best when there were no protocol barriers between them and they were simply friends. Charles was cautious, however, because no one was to be trusted. Especially George. Charles never did blame a man for trying to get the best he could. He tried not to tempt George into betrayal by giving him too much inside information.

"Tell me what's got you by the tail, George."

"This business Perry carries on about; that Charlotte Bellamy is not Charlotte Bellamy and that she's not dead but run off and that the real Charlotte —"

"I've never heard such a lot of garbage in my life," Charles said, pouring himself and George some wine from a decanter that sat on a nearby table.

"Then you think there's no truth to it at all?" George asked.

"I imagine it's all entirely true."

George rose and accepted the proferred glass, a look of complete perplexity crossing his face.

"True?" Buckingham asked.

"What I can't believe is that Lord Perry expects me to spend any time thinking on it."

George raised the glass to his lips and downed much of the contents. He absolutely never got on the upper side of Charles. Once again he couldn't come close to understanding Charles's position on the matter. It looked to George as if the king had been cheated and taken advantage of and should be mad as a hornet.

The king let himself drop into his chair and muttered. "Hampton Court. Or perhaps Salisbury . . . but I don't want to get too far away, and damn me, I hate this running about. I traveled enough in my day. I like the idea of staying put, don't you, George?"

"Sire, you think it's *true?*"

"That again? Yes, I suppose it's true. I quite imagine that Seavers took one look at Charlotte Bellamy and thought that even for a fortune he couldn't bear the wedding night. That's not how Perry tells it, but it could be the fact. And I imagine he brought his own Charlotte from some decent household; she's a lovely creature, don't you think? And I imagine if she didn't in fact die of the plague, she's off somewhere where we won't see or hear of her again."

George swallowed the rest of his wine in confusion and held his empty glass toward Charles. "Sire, may I?"

Charles chuckled. "Be my guest."

Villiers poured again.

"I think this has you in more of a knot than I, George. Would you like to handle the problem for me?"

"Sire," he said, turning back from the decanter, "I can't for the life of me imagine how that could be done to please Your Majesty."

Charles loved to play this game, and with George it was especially amusing. Poor Buckingham needed to be on the better side of his king and never knew from one moment to the next if Charles would be laughing at a plot, or having a man's head for it.

But Charles wasn't likely to spend a great deal of time

with this amusement, since there were so many serious things to deal with. He controlled his laughter and composed his face.

"Simply, Buckingham, I was looking for a way to drop an inheritance in Seavers's lap. I considered one or two estates that could be given as rewards, but there are always so many of higher rank asking and I'm not the fool to anger the few good men I've got in this country. When Fergus died and left a tidy sum for his daughter, I thought it might get Seavers started on his ships."

"You never had any intention of letting anyone but Seavers marry Lady Bellamy?"

Charles let his brooding eyes drop and he shook his head.

"But you put her on the block and let the gallants all have their bid for her."

He nodded.

George began to laugh. "And Seavers bargained himself into the money with a promise to make his venture joint with you. God's bones, but you're a crafty fellow." He raised his glass in a toast to his king, impressed and a little jealous. "And what about Perry?"

"Perhaps he has something, perhaps not. I told him I particularly admired the lady in question, and if he brought his gossip through my chambers another time, he'd be buying his way out of Newgate."

George laughed uproariously.

"As for Seavers, if you like your head you would do well to hold silent. I don't think I'd like him to know I don't give a damn who he's married, I want him on the seas earning a decent wage, half of which belongs to me. Let him stew awhile and then I'll let him out of his hole." Charles laughed. "Spending a few days with Barbara should be sufficient punishment, especially if he's frightened to death to crawl into her bed."

Buckingham's loyalty to Barbara didn't go very far, and

certainly no farther than his king. He laughed in good humor when the king, presently angry with his mistress for her bawdy behavior, criticized her.

"She rather expects that keeping Seavers warm for you will cause you to visit her apartments, Sire."

"I know that, too. Why is it I'm the smartest one here and always taken for a fool?"

"Beyond me," Buckingham laughed. "Completely beyond me, Your Majesty." He laughed for a moment longer, Charles enjoying his own humor all the while as well. "Sire, you'll pardon me if I wonder what will happen next."

Charles shrugged. "I don't see how it matters much, as long as Seavers is alive enough to sail. Odd's fish, I don't think a better sailor has come along since Rupert." He took a long pull on his wine and grimaced slightly. "You may tell Barbara I wouldn't discuss Lord Seavers, and be sure and let me know how bad her tantrum was. I enjoy hearing about them a great deal more than witnessing them."

Charles rose from his chair and moved to the window. The sun was setting and his city was in for another fitful night, with the church bells tolling for the dead and the stink of disease floating through the air. It pained him a great deal to think of death and suffering. It hit him in the stomach and head, and he ached with a longing to have powers beyond that of a mortal, but his gifts were few and his money less. Once again his hands were tied and he punished himself and his inadequacies as little as possible. He turned back to George.

"I do hope Lady Seavers is not dead, George. She seemed a decent woman."

George nodded his agreement, though he didn't really have an opinion. She wasn't dreadful, but he hadn't seen the challenge as Charles had.

"I suppose I won't know the truth unless I'm of a mind to punish someone for lying — and I'm not. Pity is, I could easily have endured a bit more of Lady Seavers," he said, raising one knowing brow at George. "But my poor circumstance insists I give a mind to money, and Seavers can't earn any for me if he's dead or in jail. As long as I'm left out of it entirely, I'm just as happy." He looked out the window again, then turned quickly back to his friend. "Let's leave tomorrow. Or the next day. I've had enough of those damn bells."

The plague did not confine itself to London. Many of the small villages began to report cases soon after droves of Londoners fled the city for the safety of the country, taking the infection along with them and spreading it from town to town.

Charles came to a decision and the court left Whitehall on the first day of July and moved just twenty miles away to Hampton Court. Lady Castlemaine went with them, though it looked as though that might not happen. Seavers was told by Barbara that the king was not interested in his story or lack of it, but simply sent his regrets if Lady Seavers had in fact died, his congratulations for Seavers's part in a victory over the Dutch, and his best wishes for his sailing.

"And what of Lord Perry's tales?" Seavers asked impatiently.

"His Majesty quite expected Perry's jealousy to appear a good deal sooner; he did bid for the hand of Lady Seavers before the king gave you permission to marry her."

"If he's chalked it up to jealous lies, why has he kept me here for so long?" Geoffrey stormed.

"Very likely to keep me occupied, the rogue...." Barbara pouted.

"But you've at least seen him. I —"

"I haven't seen him at all," Barbara retorted. "Buckingham came to tell me we are moving and you can go where you please. He said the king's message to you is that he'd like to see Perry handled, and out of his chambers, with as little attention drawn to him as possible. I fear for you both if Charles hears any more about digging up graves to prove identities."

"What?" Geoffrey blustered. "What is this? I am not even certain my wife was ever ill."

Barbara gave an impatient wave of her hand. "How would I know what the fool prattles about? I am leaving, Lord Seavers, and you can find your lodging elsewhere. I have a bone to pick with Madame Stewart. If you've any sense you'll leave London too. This bloody city is crawling with death."

It cost a decent sum to get a courier even to visit the wharves to see if any messages of any kind had been left for Lord Seavers, that being about the most dangerous place in the city.

The house on Tiller Street was looted, as could be expected. Most of the furniture was still there, the heavier pieces, but everything else was gone. Geoffrey's spirits sank as he thought of the silver and other small valuable items, and he hoped that Rodney had had those things moved, and they were missing from the house for that reason and not because they had been stolen by scavengers. It was with a heaviness in his heart that Geoffrey closed the door and headed for Bellerose.

With the threat of disease all about, inns were dangerous places to stop for the night. Traveling on horseback, with a small packet of food and some water, and sleeping on the ground, were the best safeguards against the risks of eating infected food and sleeping among other people, who might no longer be alive by morning.

As he rode, he passed people moving from the city to the country, some of them taking plague with them. Some weary travelers held pomanders over their mouths and noses as he rode near, in case he was carrying the infection. He saw carts and wagons stopped because one of the members of the family was sick, and he witnessed a burial more than once. His heart ached anew as he wondered if there was any truth to the rumor that Alicia was just about to enter the coach that would have carried her to safer territory, when she became ill. And with that thought he quickened his pace.

The sun was hot and high when he neared Bellerose. The grounds and house were quiet; work on it had ceased, probably because of the heat and illness. He pounded at the front door of the mansion and heard his man's voice answer his knock. "Who calls?"

"Lord Seavers — if you remember me . . ."

The door creaked open and Rodney stood in the doorway, a huge smile on his ruddy face. "Good to see you, sir."

Geoffrey walked through the door, glancing around and noting that the place was a good deal cleaner and some progress had been made in its restoration. He saw no other people. "Where is everyone?"

"I've given Mrs. Margaret leave to go to her son and am keeping the steward and a few maids here. There are no workers now and I imagine new ones will have to be found."

"Lady Seavers?"

Rodney sighed and rubbed his sweating neck with one hand. "I can tell you about that over a bite and drink, if you like."

"I'd like to hear about it at once; food can wait. Is she dead?"

"Charlotte Bellamy is dead, sir. Alicia booked passage to America."

"How did you allow her to do that without waiting for word from me?" he stormed.

"I was told you gave her permission to go wherever she pleased."

"I was due out of port when she began babbling about —"

"About her marriage, my lord," Rodney said, his face growing stern and implacable. "She said the bargain was over and you were not interested in the marriage — or her love."

Geoffrey turned away and sulked, then turned back to his servant and blustered, "Love, so she says . . . but how am I to know . . . any of a hundred men could have. . . ."

With a movement too fast to predict, he found himself seized by the front of his linen shirt and backed up to the wall. He was not as tall or as strong as Rodney, but had the circumstances been any different, Geoffrey might have given him a good fight. His shock at being so handled by his own servant and friend was so great that he simply stared into Rodney's angry eyes.

"My lady served you truer than any and I pledged her my aid when you failed to care for her. 'Twas I who brought her from the country for you to use, and it was meet that I should help her to leave and find people who would give her a home and a chance to start over."

"Aye, Mr. Prentiss," Geoffrey said, trying to soothe him.

"Do no decry her again. Speak as if she is dead, for there lies a grave on this property and Lady Charlotte Bellamy is gone."

"Aye. Let go of me."

"The loyalty she carried was to you and no other."

"Aye," Geoffrey said calmly. "I know that."

Rodney loosed his grip and let Geoffrey stand free of the wall. Geoffrey looked at him first with a frown and then let himself smile. "She certainly got under your skin, didn't she?"

"She deserved better than she got here."

"Aye," Seavers admitted. "But how do I rectify that? You've let her go."

"Perhaps this time it is too late," Rodney said, turning away from his young lord.

"I don't like the sound of that, Mr. Prentiss. Now come, help me find something to eat and show me this grave that holds Lady Seavers."

A courtyard for burials had been cleared years before by one of the Bellamys, and within it there was a grave, still not covered by a decent marker.

"It is, in fact, Charlotte Bellamy," Rodney told him. "I'd hired a man to watch Perry and the woman he had in keeping on New Street. It wasn't until the crosses appeared on that street that Perry panicked, for he'd gotten nothing out of you or Alicia. He went straightaway to the king to report that you'd likely hired an impostor, and that he had kept Charlotte Bellamy in lodgings in the city. They fairly laughed him out of Whitehall."

"And the death?"

"For your purposes, sir, we'd planned to bribe a body off the dead cart to be buried here when Alicia sailed. But our work became easier then, for just as Alicia was due to leave, Mr. Scanland reported to me that Perry had just the opposite plan. He bribed the man pulling the dead cart to call the death in his house plague. The girl he had them haul away was dead of stabbing. I feel certain it was Charlotte, though Perry is the only one to know."

"And Perry?"

"I have no idea. I had the body shrouded and carried to Bellerose, with a statement from the man I bribed to get the body, saying it was yielded to me to bury and the death had been reported by Lord Perry. That done, there's more than one witness to the fact that Perry killed the lass, and we buried her on her own rightful property. No one can accuse you of murder. It cost a good bit."

"I'll see you settled with, not to worry. Where do I find Alicia?"

"Left to her, you don't."

"So, she plans to punish me with a great deal of style. And whom do you serve now, Prentiss?"

"I gave my word to her."

"Will it help her to keep it?"

"You cannot get your fleet out of port, my lord. You likely cannot get back into the city, for that matter."

"I can make France and book passage from there, if I know where I'm bound. Did she have arrangements at the other end?"

Rodney turned and started to walk back to the manor, not giving Geoffrey any answer. "Rodney," he called, causing the man to turn and look at him again. "So I've bought this trouble with dishonest fare, but tell me, she *is* alive?" The man nodded. "And it *is* to America I'm bound if I mean to find her?" Again the man nodded and then walked back toward the house.

Geoffrey stared at the simple grave for a while. The relief of knowing that Alicia was still well and on her way out of the country felt a damn sight better than wondering if she could actually be dead of plague. And Rodney would see her taken care of; his loyalty would not have allowed her to be placed on a dangerous ship with a less than honorable captain, which ruled out most of the ships leaving London.

And then it hit him: he had not seen the *Letty* in port. A slow smile spread across his face and he chuckled to himself. He couldn't arrange to leave England without seeing to a good many details, which gave him some time to think on it and time to work his way back into Rodney's loyalty. Finding her seemed less of a problem than he'd first thought. But still, he was not wise enough to realize that, although finding her could be easy, winning her back might be difficult. After all, the lass loved him, but he'd hurt her deeply.

Whistling, he walked back into the manor to find Rodney and began to mend the damage their friendship had suffered.

Culver Perry sat at a lonely table and had drunk the best part of an ale when the serving maid approached him. "'E'll see ye when 'e can gov'na. 'E's in the stable."

"Tell him my business is urgent," Perry said. "I can't wait while he plays with his animals."

"I said I told 'im," she whined. "Wait or go, I doubt Armand cares at all."

"Tell him it's urgent," he insisted.

The wench smirked and moved away from his table and out of sight, muttering as she went. "Bloody 'igh and mighty nobles ain't got nothin' better to do but order simple folk . . ."

Perry nursed the rest of his ale and waited, his anger having subsided not at all since he left the city. He had worked and worried with the best piece of evidence against Geoffrey Seavers that ever he could have found, and what good had it done? Seavers would not respond to him, the wench he married would not give him so much as her worry, and the Bellamy bitch had done nothing but hound him and screech at him for months on end.

He remembered the night he returned from Whitehall, the sounds of the guns of the fleet of Lowestoft still sounding in the city. The king had told him in a near rage that he found Lady Seavers to be everything he had hoped for and would hear no more slander against her. Perry was ordered out of the palace and preferably out of the city.

"While my navy is fighting and dying at the hands of the Dutch bastards, and my city is being eaten alive by disease, you are here complaining about some fortune you missed, when I never would have allowed you within a mile of that money. Haven't you had a bit of ill luck with brides as it stands?"

Charles's words had been clear enough. He was not about to investigate the legitimacy of the inheritance, and he had no patience with Perry's claims. When Culver argued that the king had been cheated, Charles shouted loudly enough for every courtier and lady within the kingdom to hear. "I don't care if it's an orange girl he's wed, the contract is made and I am done!"

Regardless of the shape of it, Perry was not done. He would find a way to remedy his loss. He'd gone back to the apartments on New Street and told Charlotte of the situation, but the maid got out of hand and talked too much. From where he sat, he was the only one to know that he had killed twice in his life; both victims were young women who were counting on him to bring them the happiness they deserved.

The innkeeper approached Perry's table, using his towel to wipe off his balding head. "I'm Armand, innkeeper here."

"There was a wench here nearly two years ago, her name escapes me."

"They come and go," the man said.

"This one was tall and slender, brown hair and light eyes. I remember her clearly as being quiet and bright for a tavern wench. She would have left here almost a year ago with a nobleman bound for London."

Armand sat down at the table and eyed Perry suspiciously. "I can't say I understand why so many men ask after her." And then he was silent.

Perry pulled the leather purse from his belt and took out a couple of coins to toss onto the table. "Is she back?" he asked the keeper.

"She won't come back here, I warned her of that. I won't have her."

"Who else asks after her?"

"Don't recall the name, says he was from the Colonies, he says." Armand snorted. "The ones that come, they got money, that's sure. They plop down their gold to ask about her."

"Colonies? What does he look like, the other one?"

"Your age, nearabouts. Lighter hair maybe. Taller, maybe. Can't recall much. Ordinary sort, but for his clothes."

"Nobleman? Merchant? What, man?"

"Can't say..." Armand stalled, scratching his chin. Perry pulled another coin from his purse. "He has ships, he says. From the Colonies. Says he'd take her to the Colonies if he could find her. Puts into port here regular and makes it his business to find this wench."

"Merchant, then. Did he give any name at all?"

"No name for himself. Calls his ship the *Letty*."

"Tilden," Perry said. "Tilden came looking for her."

"Maybe her, maybe not. He was looking for a woman he thought was his sister, lost in the wars. Said he knew where to find her."

"When she left here, the nobleman who took her: was he light-haired and young? My age or younger, with what some maids think a handsome face?"

Armand began to laugh. "The man who took her was hardly handsome and he was my age or older. Huge monster of a man with red hair gone thin and gray and arms big around as your legs."

"His man Prentiss, the mongrel."

Armand shrugged. "I never heard the man's name, but I let him take the wench. She was no good to me and caused naught but trouble in my tavern. What's she done?"

"Done?" Perry asked, rising to leave.

"Aye. You're not the first come asking after her. There was that noble from America wanting her."

"Bit of dumb luck is all," Perry replied. "But at least I know where she is."

"And you aim to find her, too?" Armand asked, gathering up his coins and counting his money.

Perry didn't answer, for in truth he wasn't sure what he meant to do about the girl. He walked toward the door of the inn.

"I hope she's got a few more on the way to ask after her," the keeper said. "I've made a bit more money since she's gone than I did when she worked. Lazy whores."

Perry looked over his shoulder at Armand and raised one noble brow to peer at him.

"You're the one," Armand said in realization. "You're the one what courted her and made off without paying your keep."

Culver first smiled and then laughed loudly, leaving the inn, and he was still laughing as he mounted his horse and rode away.

fifteen

*D*o you have any idea how long you've been standing there?" Preston asked.

Alicia turned to face him. She had been watching the beach as the *Letty* rocked along the home stretch. The trees that lined the shore seemed to wave in the balmy breezes. Her stomach jumped in anticipation, fear, and hopelessness.

"Are we very close?" she asked.

"Our home is farther inland, upriver. It will take us another full day of traveling by barge to get there."

She turned back to watch the shoreline with a deep sigh. She had quickly changed her clothes to come and stand at the rail at the first sight of land because she assumed that this shipping family must live right on the ocean. But she saw only unattractive shacks that looked nothing like the houses in England.

"I want to see the savages and the blackamoors," she said, a lilt of excitement in her voice. "And the woods and beasts."

Preston chuckled. "It's not the wilderness you've been

led to believe. We have Negroes and bondservants who do most of the difficult farming and loading for us — and who take care of the house. The Indians trouble us very little and indeed have moved themselves as far from our populated areas as possible. They like the fighting as little as we, I imagine. As for hunting, it differs little from England, except that game is more plentiful here."

"Negroes and bondservants," she thought aloud. "How many?"

"Only a couple of hundred," he replied casually.

Her head came up with a jolt. Geoffrey employed a total of seven servants for their London household.

"The plantation is so large and the fields so endless that it would be impossible to manage without slaves or indentured convicts." He shrugged with an air of acceptance. "Without at least two hundred, ours would be considered a modest farm."

"You *live* with the blackamoors and convicts?"

He laughed a little at what he imagined must be going through her mind. "It takes on a strangely different meaning than in England, love. My father only buys indenture papers on those convicted criminals whose crimes are not atrocious. Murderers, for instance, don't work on our land, and thieves that steal again simply add more time to serve without pay. The Negroes stay mostly in the fields except for the ones who are bright and quick enough to speak the language well and can work in the house, docks, and warehouses. And they have their own homes, their own villages, away from the big house."

Her brow was furrowed in confusion. Servants' quarters were familiar to her, but special communities for the servants and laborers was something she couldn't comprehend. "When I worked for Armand, we slept in the attic so that our presence did not cost one space that could be rented to guests."

"I suppose it's something like that. You'll understand the workings of it in no time. And I imagine your new home will be a busier household than even the Ivy Vine. Nearly as many abide there."

She recounted in her mind the names and pecking order of the brothers. Wesley, the oldest, who bore his father's name, had moved up the James River with his wife, Sarah, and their three children. There they built a mill. Next came Robert, married to another Sarah, and their son, who lived south of the family. Milling was their occupation also. Next came Stephen and Melanie and a daughter, living in the city. John and Sylvia lived in the family home, as did Preston and his wife. Both women were expecting babies soon.

Preston watched her counting off on her fingers, her lips silently moving with the names. He had explained that even though the three eldest lived away, when they visited they stayed for days at a time. And the house could accommodate them all and would stretch for more. She finally shook her head in dismay at the size of this family.

"Father has always been accused of being overzealous in his undertakings. The size of his family bears that out."

"I'll never remember the names when it comes time to meet them."

"Anxious?" he asked.

She nodded with a nervous smile. "I'm a little afraid."

"You needn't be."

"Preston, what if — " She stopped and thought hard for a minute. And then very weakly she let her question out. "What if they don't like me at all?"

"They are good people, Alicia. If you give them a chance to be your family, I think you will be glad you did." But still he saw her worried face looking past him, her thoughts serious and troubled. "You can tell them honestly about your past if you choose to."

"You gave me your word . . ."

238

"Aye, and I won't break my promise. But if you change your mind, it will be all right."

"I won't," she said with finality.

Preston leaned toward her and kissed her cheek. "Tell me what you want, Alicia, and I will provide it. Shall I bring the rogue to his knees? Shall I command the pirate from England to right the wrongs against you and make honorable his misuses — "

"Cease to speak of him, if you can," she interrupted quietly.

The cool seriousness in her eyes held him from any jesting. What abided behind those steeled, concealing eyes was a pain that she would not share and could not cast aside. "All right, darling," he said. "But I'll warrant this bargain you've struck is far from over."

She turned back to the rail, looking over the new land. "You are wrong," she insisted. And Preston noticed that she gripped the rail so tightly that her knuckles became bone white and the veins in her delicate hands stood out.

He stood there behind her for a long time, looking with her at the shoreline. He realized she had just cause for her grief, and he thought she dealt with her misfortune with courage and daring.

But he knew something of Geoffrey as well. He knew that it was not the man's way to deal dishonorably with women and that lies were impossible for him to bear gracefully. He surmised, once he knew the game, that Geoffrey had found himself in love with a tavern wench and had imagined himself face to face with a monster he'd never before challenged: true passion. Preston recognized it because he had struggled with that demon himself; and finally, after much confusion, had put the demon to rest by settling himself in marriage with the woman he loved.

Geoffrey, apparently, had not been able to wrestle his demon to submission in time. And his game had fled.

"If you ever find you've changed your mind and wish me to get in touch with Geoffrey, you have but to ask — "

"Never," she insisted, and again her pale, porcelainlike hands gripped the rail.

The *Letty* dropped anchor outside of Hampton, not venturing upriver in the dark. The shallowness of the water and the many sandbars made an adventure a bit too risky for Preston, especially with his precious cargo. Even though they were all ready to feel solid ground under their feet again, Preston insisted on another night on board.

Early in the morning the mate was sent to procure a barge while the ship was docked and unloaded. The personal belongings of the captain and his passengers were then loaded onto the smaller vessel, and after a quick breakfast at a dockside inn in the wee hours of daybreak, they were moving along again. This time Alicia's attention was more rapt than before, taking in the very breath of the land. The river gradually narrowed and was flanked by trees that formed a canopy over the shore. Every few miles a huge brick mansion rose out of the earth, and the land had been cleared to the shore.

The barge crept into a spacious dock and she could see another mansion, some distance from the river, settled back into the trees. Her breath caught at the sight; this was their home.

A Negro ran from the wooded beach to the shore and began to ring a huge bell. More people appeared as the barge moved sluggishly into its port and all hands threw ropes to tie up the little boat.

Preston presented his arm to help Alicia move across a narrow but sturdy plank and finally onto solid ground. An exquisite barouche pulled down the road through the trees, the driver jumping down without a word to help Alicia into it.

"Send a cart down for our things. We'll go straight to the house," Preston directed.

Alicia was silent and speculative, her eyes taking in the land, the road, and the looming house before her. Her heart pounded mercilessly within her breast as she tried to steady herself to face them: her family.

It was only moments before the barouche came to stop before the huge brick house, which had a vast porch stretching the length of the house on the front. Large polished oaken doors marked its entry and a tremendous circular drive wound up to the front of the house. It appeared as rich a structure as any English country manor she had seen. Little black faces peeked around the sides of the building to see who had arrived. Alicia looked at them queerly. She had seen a blackamoor before, but never so many at once.

She turned to look at Preston and found that he was not moving to get out and he was frowning. "It surprises me that no one has come out to meet us," he said. "At least Etta should be here."

"Etta?" That was a name she hadn't heard.

"The housekeeper," he explained as he climbed past her out of the coach. "She rarely leaves the house and is the first one to know who's come to call."

Alicia stepped onto the porch on shaky legs, holding her trembling hands together in front of her. She worried over her appearance. She had tried to select a conservative, high-necked gown, something she imagined a *daughter* would wear. She'd let her hair fall loosely over her shoulders, hoping she looked innocent.

Preston held open the door and she meekly walked through, finding herself in an entry hall from which there stretched a long, high staircase to a second floor. Preston looked around the entry. Something was different from the picture she had painted for herself. This was not a busy, bustling household filled with many people, but was morbidly quiet.

She jumped in surprise as a woman of about fifty came flying around the corner with an armful of linens. "Preston!" she gasped.

"Madam," he smiled with a half bow.

"You barely made it in time," she said, resuming her quick pace to the stairs. "It's Brianna . . ."

"Her time?" he asked, astonished.

"In moments," she said, heading up the stairs so swiftly that Preston took them two at a time behind her. Alicia was certain she had not even been seen, though she stood directly beside her brother. She heard a door open and close above her and found herself to be completely alone in the large entryway.

There were two straight-backed chairs and a table in the generous hall. She walked slowly over to one of the chairs and took a seat. She was curious about the house, but didn't dare look around without at least an introduction. The woman, she thought, might be Etta . . . but then Preston would not call Etta madam. She must be Marguerite: her mother.

It seemed a very long time before the door opened and closed again and she heard the sound of footsteps coming back down the stairs. Alicia felt herself stiffen and her heart pounded anew.

As Marguerite descended, she pulled down her rolled-up sleeves and buttoned them at the wrists. Her hair, a mousy, brownish gray, was pulled back in a tight bun, but wisps of it fell down her cheeks and back. She looked as if she had worked hard. And she was smiling.

"There," she said in a breath. "A fine boy. A fine welcome-home present."

Alicia nodded and watched her face.

"I hadn't forgotten about you, dear. Preston brought you?"

Again she nodded. Words failed her completely.

"Did he bring any others?" she asked.

Alicia was confused and her brow wrinkled. She responded, though she didn't understand the purpose of the question. "No, madam. I don't think so."

"Well," Marguerite continued, her voice businesslike but warm, "I don't know how you got here and we don't have to talk about that immediately, but I can briefly tell you the rules of the household."

"Yes, madam," Alicia said as politely as possible. My goodness, she thought, there certainly will be no wondering about my place.

"You're very polite. I like that. And young. Perhaps we can find some things in the house for you; you look a bit too frail for fieldwork."

"I wouldn't mind, madam," Alicia said, eager to please. "I like being out of doors."

"That's very nice of you, dear, but we do need help in the house. Lord, the family grows out of all reality." She laughed lightly. "It's a blessing I like a large family. I certainly have one!"

"I'm glad you do, madam. And I'll do anything in the house you ask of me."

Marguerite looked at her queerly. She was not accustomed to new servants speaking to her. They were usually a little more frightened, and it had become Marguerite's job to allay their fears and show them they would be treated kindly and fairly in return for good service.

"I think you should know one thing," Marguerite said. "I'll give you a chance to settle yourself into our household and make some new friends without pressure from Mr. Tilden and me, but in due time you'll be expected to give us the personal details of your past. I have to know where my girls have been and what they've been through if I'm to help them start — "

She stopped abruptly at the sound of a slamming door in

the back of the house and turned to smile at the large, bearded man who entered. His linen shirt was wet with perspiration and his riding boots were caked with mud. His hair was graying, his cheeks were pink from the sun, and there was an anxious look in his eyes.

"A boy, Wesley," she said to him, smiling. "And Brianna is fine. She's a strong woman."

Without a word, the man turned and looked at Alicia. Marguerite followed his gaze.

"And Preston is back! He arrived just in time for his son's birth and is upstairs with Brianna now."

Wesley's eyes appeared slightly glazed as he looked at Alicia. She felt the penetrating warmth and understanding coming from him. He could not remove his eyes from her face, nor could he seem to close his mouth.

"Preston's brought this girl and I was explaining the rules of our household just as you — Wesley, I think it impolite to stare so — "

He looked back at Marguerite and then again at Alicia.

"Preston's brought her?"

"Aye, and I told her we'd keep her in the house. She seems a bit slight to be working outside, though she's content with any — "

"Marguerite," he said, his voice slow and tender, "have you looked at her?"

Marguerite sensed nothing amiss. She smiled with sincerity at Alicia. "Yes. You *are* lovely, my dear."

"Marguerite, Preston brought her. Have you asked her name?"

"My heavens," she said, aghast at her own bad manners. "I'm sorry! The birth and all the excitement and Preston's return — "

"Your name?" Wesley interrupted, slipping a strong arm about his wife's waist and waiting expectantly.

Alicia looked past them and saw Preston slowly making

his way down the stairs, obviously having heard the very last of this conversation.

"Alicia," she replied very quietly.

"Oh, my," Marguerite said. "Why that was our daughter's — " And then she stopped short and covered her mouth. She looked at Wesley, who had finally managed a smile of recognition, and back to Alicia. Preston came quickly to his mother's other side. "Alicia?" she questioned in a weak, disbelieving voice.

"You could not see her resemblance to you?" Preston asked.

"Fortunately I saw it," Wesley said, "before Marguerite had her waxing floors and chopping vegetables."

Marguerite still could not smile, nor could she move closer. She stood shaking her head and staring. Alicia sensed that her mother's discomfort was even greater than her own and she rose from her seat. "I'm pleased to meet you," she said, her voice quiet and tense.

"Pleased to . . ." Marguerite mimicked, shaking her head in wonder. Finally the smile and the tears came and she carefully embraced her daughter with trembling arms. "Fifteen years of thinking you dead," she cried. "And you are pleased to meet me . . ."

"And I'll be glad to do any work you — "

"Hush," Marguerite said, embracing her more fiercely. "I've waited for years just to hold you again." But she let go suddenly and looked at her son. "Preston, are you *sure?*" she asked cautiously.

"Positively. You have only to look at her."

And it was true, Alicia greatly resembled her mother. It was what had stopped Wesley short in his tracks. Alicia could have been brought out of the past and been the twin of his bride.

"I cannot believe you're alive," Marguerite breathed.

Alicia could not speak; she felt awkward and was fighting her own tears.

245

"Alive, well, and returned," Wesley said. "Well, mother, let's feed her, show her the house, and give her her list of chores."

Preston explained that the house was always under construction because as the family expanded additional rooms were needed. No such addition was necessary for Alicia, however. There was a single bedroom, generous in size, that was immediately allotted to her. And for the remainder of that first day she was with her parents, Marguerite was especially reluctant to leave her side. In fact, she insisted on tucking her into bed that night, as if she had her little girl again.

"Fifteen years," Marguerite sighed. "And you realize, when Wesley's couriers could find no trace of you, I was forced to accept your death."

"And I had to accept yours," Alicia reminded her.

"Of course, you did. I just don't know how you've survived it all — family after family, working you to death in a tavern. . . . Why, I hardly know you at all. Alicia, before you left England, were there gentlemen calling?"

"Madam?" she asked.

"Had you been thinking of your marriage? Is there a young man in England whom you love?"

Alicia sighed heavily. "Oh, madam, I've talked so much of my life already, I can scarce think of another thing to tell you. No, there were no gentlemen."

"Surely someone courted you."

"I had no dowry, madam." Alicia suspected that would end the subject.

"Well, you have one now. And you will see, darling. There will be gentlemen."

And she kissed her daughter's forehead and blew out the candle in her bedroom. The only thing Alicia thought about before drifting to sleep was that it would be most unfair for her to accept a dowry. She still possessed, carefully tucked away in her belongings, a hundred pounds. She felt she had well earned every farthing.

The Sunday after her arrival was the first day that the entire family was pulled together, for a lavish dinner party. She met all her brothers and their wives and children. They approached her carefully at first, but gradually they — the women especially — found her stories about the many families she had lived with and her work in a country tavern to sound wildly adventurous. "I promise you, it was not adventurous," Alicia proclaimed. "If Preston had not found me, I would be married to a poor old farmer now; my only usefulness would be in my ability to clean and cook for him and produce many children."

As that statement left her lips, she caught sight of Preston out of the corner of her eye. He raised one brow, smiled knowingly, and rose to leave the room lest he laugh out loud.

"I am surprised it didn't happen already," Marguerite said. "You are much older than most country girls are when they marry."

Alicia made no comment, but she was aware that it was the second time Marguerite had referred to her marriageability and the absence of suitors.

Alicia's mind was in a whirl over the activity in the house when just the family was together; when Wesley announced that invitations had been sent to neighbors and friends for a party at which Alicia could be introduced to the entire community, her head began to spin. And so the wives and children of her older brothers stayed on in the big house and helped with all the preparations, while the men rode off to oversee their mills and crops, intending to return for the festivities.

Under the heat of a summer sun, carriages and barges full of guests converged on the Tilden home. Pits were set to roasting pigs and beef, and chickens were boiled, stuffed, and baked. Long tables of food were set up on the lawns, and

Wesley Tilden put out some of his best and closely protected home brew. Neighbor after neighbor paused before Alicia for introductions, and it did not even occur to her until the sun was nearly setting that she'd met many more single men than single women. And she might never have realized the reason if Preston hadn't told her.

"Are there not many women of my age in Virginia?" she asked.

"Of course, there are many: the daughters of plantation owners and visiting cousins and friends and — there," he said pointing. "Gloria; have you met her?"

Alicia followed his finger. "No," she replied, looking toward the pretty young woman standing with a young man under a tree, a parasol over her head.

"Well, I don't doubt it. I imagine the women are a trifle jealous. They'll come around."

And bearing that in mind when she looked, she spotted several other pretty young women who were keeping their distance. Some of them she *had* met, but on recollection she remembered them to be somewhat cool toward her. But the men had not.

"Alicia, at last you're unprotected," Bryson Warner said. "And I can have a minute of your time."

"Of course, Bryson," she said sweetly. Alicia did not even pretend to dislike the attention. She looked over her shoulder toward her mother. Marguerite sat with a group of women who were straining toward their needlework in the setting sun. She watched her daughter. And gave a slight nod.

"I think since we're neighbors, we should see more of each other," Bryson said solicitously. "There's a dance next Saturday, and I'd like to take you."

Bryson had taken her arm and began walking with her. She went along because it seemed the natural thing to do. "I should discuss that with my parents," she said. "And I think I should tell you, I've never been to a dance — "

Bryson laughed and assured her she'd be the most beautiful there. He was a tall, good-looking man in his early twenties, and of the several she'd met that day, he was the most aggressive. "I have my own home, my own farm, and over a hundred Negroes," he was saying, listing his assets.

"That's very nice, Bryson," she commented.

"And I've invested heavily in some Tilden ships — but of course, they would be Tilden ships . . ."

"You must be very wealthy," she sighed, somewhat bored with his monologue.

"Not rich, mind you, but I'm capable of getting mighty rich someday. And with the right woman at my side . . ." And he went on and on and on. Alicia knew that what she was hearing was a downright good bid for the Tilden dowry that would be laid on her head. She knew how she would have felt had she been present when King Charles put the Bellamy inheritance on the block. But she could not encourage Bryson. It would be a very long time before she would have the courage to pass herself off as a bride to any of these young settlers.

"The truth is, Alicia," he said, stopping her under a tree well away from the close scrutiny of the other guests, "I think you're the most beautiful woman in Virginia — and mind you, I've seen them all. I'd be honored if you'd allow me to call and — "

"Bryson, you're sweet to be so kind to me, but I don't think you should make any plans. I'm new and — "

"Alicia, I won't let you put me off. I won't wait in line behind all the bungling fops that will come begging for your favors. I'm the richest bachelor for hundreds of miles, and if anyone is going to court you, it's going to be me"

"I've only been here a short time!" she snapped. She was not at all ready for a rush of suitors.

He maneuvered her so that her back was against the tree, and he placed his hands on her waist. When she looked into his dark, earnest eyes, she could clearly see that he was serious about wanting her. And he was kind and handsome, but she was not the least bit moved.

"I know that, darling, and I'll give you time, honestly I will. But I won't back away and let the other men trample you in their ardent courtship."

"Courtship?" she questioned. "Are women to court so *scarce* here?"

"Oh, sweetheart," he laughed. "You are precious..."

She frowned as he stole a kiss on her cheek. She was anything but innocent, she knew that. And she resented his solicitous behavior. It would be different if she felt any attraction to him.

But apparently the feeling of her flesh on his lips had inflamed him, for he pulled away from her cheek looking slightly flushed and glassy eyed. "Alicia, I must see you again. Soon."

"I'm not sure that —"

She was stopped in her response by his lips on hers, seeking some passionate kiss that she did not have the energy or desire to give him. She tested the lips, opening cautiously for a deeper kiss, but she felt nothing. She was a little repulsed and pushed at him, but he refused to release her.

"There is a better way to control you" came the memory of Geoffrey's voice beating in her mind. And the feelings within her when she was scooped into his unyielding embrace and had tasted of his passion threatened to come back to her. She gave Bryson a hefty shove, unlocking their kiss.

"I want you *never* to do that again!" she insisted loudly.

"I'm sorry, Alicia. You made me forget myself."

"I will not fight you for long, Alicia. And I will win!"

She looked at the young man, his head down and his apology sincere; and he was completely unattractive in his submission. "You take a great deal for granted, sir, and I'll thank you to mind your manners better!" And with that she picked up her skirts and huffed into the house.

The inside was as busy as the outside, and she passed

through the hall as swiftly and silently as she could, making for the stairs to find the solace she needed in her room. She locked the door and sat heavily on the bed.

"*Go where you will!*" The words would not stop. She could hear his voice and feel his presence. It had worsened tenfold with Bryson's kiss. She feared she would never again feel what Geoffrey made her feel. Her stubbornness, his strength, the way he played her body against her will ... she thought she would surely die if those feelings never came to her again.

I am shameless, she thought. He cast me aside and I long for him still. How *can* I be such a fool?

She felt a tear wetting her cheek and brushed it away impatiently. She could not fathom the reason for her surly mood. In all the excitement of her reunion she should be wild with joy, but instead she felt a sullen tugging at her heart.

There was a tapping at her door and she asked who was there.

"It's Etta, honey," she replied. "You all right, honey?"

Alicia felt herself nearly smile. Etta had come to Virginia as a bondslave and had worked out her indenture long ago. She had managed the Tilden home — indeed, she had managed the Tildens — for the past many years. And now she was doing what the entire family had predicted she would: she was making Alicia's settling in, her own personal affair.

Alicia opened the door for her. The huge woman's appearance had at first been almost frightening, she was so imposing and her face so stern. But it had taken only a couple of days to become aware of Etta's gentleness. "Did that Bryson hurt you, girl?"

"No, Etta, he was really very polite."

"I saw him lookin' you over, lass. He'll mind his good breedin' here or ...."

"He wasn't out of line, honestly. I don't know why I'm so moody. I'm sorry."

Etta patted her head. "Does something ail you, lass?"

Alicia nodded and felt another tear in her eye. "I should be happy, but I seem to feel like crying."

"Ah, missy, you just let it come," Etta said, holding her and patting her back. "There's ever so much goin' on in this house and maybe it's yer time . . ."

"Yes, maybe," she sniveled.

"You lay down, missy. Lay down and rest yerself a mite."

Alicia nodded and moved slowly to her bed. She flopped down on it and heard Etta softly close the door behind her. And then she wondered; her breasts were tender and her moods were up and down: maybe it was time for her menses.

But she couldn't remember the last time — it was long ago — before she left England. She sat up with a start and her hand went instinctively to her flat, firm tummy. It was before Geoffrey.

It was certainly before they spent the night at Bellerose. And that was more than two months ago, nearly three. "It couldn't be," she told herself. "It's only the traveling, the excitement . . ."

She had an hour or so to lie in the peacefulness of her room before her mother came to see about her. She entered quietly and sat gently on the edge of the bed.

"Is all this too much for you, Alicia?" Marguerite asked.

"No, madam. I just needed a — a moment. That's all."

"Is there any need for your father to take a young man to task?"

"No, madam," she replied listlessly. "Bryson was very well mannered. He's just more — more *interested* than I am, that's all."

"Alicia, you've told me about the families, about the inn: is there anything else you want to confide to me?"

Alicia thought for a moment. She knew her mother loved her and would do nearly anything to protect and keep her now, after all these years. But she wasn't sure she would still be accepted here if they knew everything about her.

"There's nothing, madam. Truly. I'm just a little tired."

"Well, if you need me, Alicia, I am here."

Marguerite left her daughter and returned to the guests. At the bottom of the stairs, she nearly collided with Preston because her thoughts preoccupied her and she had not been watching.

"There, madam, you're in some dreamland."

"Excuse me, dear," she said in a distant voice, and then changed her mind about passing him in the hall. "Preston, does something we don't know of trouble your sister?"

"Beg pardon, madam?"

"Won't you tell me what you learned of her before you found her? Something that can help me understand her now?"

"Don't worry about her, madam. She'll make the adjustment in time. This is all very new."

"Preston, dear, did your sister leave a man she loved to come here?"

"Mother," he said with seriousness, "Alicia will confide in you what she wants you to know."

"You will not help me?"

"I cannot, madam. Alicia's life has been her own for many years. She must be the one to tell you about it."

"I find myself badly confused about my own daughter's life."

"I think you are no more confused than she," Preston laughed. "But fear not, madam, Alicia is beautiful and bright, and a handsome man of good breeding will come for her and she will be powerless to refuse him." He shrugged and smiled. "Now what else could happen?"

"You speak more as a prophet than her brother." She frowned.

"Do I, now?" he asked playfully. His mother sighed and went back toward the lawns and her guests. Preston laughed to himself again. "Do I, indeed."

sixteen

*W*hile Alicia may have fantasized a quiet new start
to a quiet new life on a country manor in Virginia, she couldn't have been more inaccurate.
It was anything but. There was more of a demand on her
time than ever before in her life. The Tildens were an ac-
tive, involved clan whose doors were always open to guests
and whose family members were constantly on the run.

Wesley handled farming and shipping and financial man-
agement with his sons. The men were either riding out to
the fields; or taking trips to Hampton, sometimes staying
for days to complete loading, warehousing, and other duties, and always bringing some business acquaintance to the
house for dinner. There would be a merchant from the
north, a sea captain from another port, or a banker from
out of town. At least once a week there was a party, social,
or dance at one of the plantations. Locals sought out Wesley Tilden to ask for loans, jobs, or advice. Wealthier
friends were constantly interested in joint investment ventures. The dinner table was almost always the scene of
some hefty discussion and plenty of gossip.

On one such evening, Bryson had wangled an invitation

to join them. Marguerite passed him in her carriage on the way to visit one of her neighbors, and he bemoaned his lack of good company and expressed his desire to call on her daughter again. She was quick to decipher his ploy. "Then you'll join us for dinner tonight, Bryson, and I won't be refused."

Alicia was not very surprised to see him there, and even less surprised to find he was seated next to her. There were more gentlemen asking to call and requesting a dance and offering their services, but Bryson was the only one to make clear to her parents his desire to be in her company.

Among other guests were Captain Horatio Pelt, a merchant from England; Reverend Jody from the church, and his wife, Beatrice; and Carlisle Brandon, a merchant banker.

Several conversations seemed to be going at once, and Alicia listened with half an ear to all of them.

"A baptism will be your next order of business with me, I imagine," Reverend Jody said to Marguerite.

"We should have a yearly date selected for such an event," Marguerite suggested.

"I would guess an investment of a thousand pounds would cover the cost of rebuilding the ships . . ." came from the other side of the table.

"And the cost of transporting them to Virginia?" was Wesley's question.

"That would be additional, I'm sure. . . ."

"Would the bank be willing to invest in a partnership in a mill?" Bryson was asking.

"Better that you find an investor the likes of Tilden," the banker replied. "He wouldn't scoff at another mill in the family."

"Just such a proposal was on my mind. . . ."

"A letter of marque from the king is what this family is needing most," Preston said. And Alicia's head came up as she listened to her brother.

"Aye, it wouldn't hurt," Wesley replied. "Our ships are

often attacked for their goods, and taking their remains is illegal without royal permission. But I doubt heartily that the Tildens have enough influence at court to get privy attention."

"Pirating goes against the Good Book," the Reverend added.

"Getting attacked without preparation goes against good sense," Wesley argued. "Aye, a letter of marque would at least turn the fight into profit."

The visiting captain laughed loudly. "I swear I can't believe the Tildens suffered unduly from attacks by Spanish and Dutch vessels. Tell me, Tilden, that you *don't* counterattack and strip the ships and keep the booty."

"I won't tell you a damn thing, Pelt, except that pirating without the consent of the king and a letter of marque is against the law. We defend ourselves against pirates — and some of them have been English."

"I have friends at court," said Preston. "A couple of close friends with just such papers from Charles. I care not to return to London, with plague and war in her town and waters, but I could send letters."

Alicia gulped at the thought of letters being sent to Geoffrey. Preston would not hesitate to summon his help in getting royal permission for better shipping conditions.

"Shouldn't amount to much trouble once we get around to it. The Tilden ships have been lent to war before and will be again. The booty would have to be shared with the crown."

"London's our port as it is."

"If you could persuade your daughter to marry a decent pirate it would make things easier," Captain Pelt laughed.

"And after the baptism . . ." Reverend Jody was saying, ". . . perhaps there will be a wedding to perform."

"We haven't discussed weddings of late, Reverend."

Alicia felt her head begin to swim and took a small sip of her wine. Her stomach was jumping and queasy. She didn't know if it was the discussion of privateering; the notion that perhaps Geoffrey would come to be involved in this family, just when she thought she was through with him; or this idea that, now that there was an unmarried Tilden woman available, a wedding was the next topic of concern.

She rubbed her abdomen under her napkin and hoped she wouldn't be sick.

"You can joke about weddings to pirates all evening," Bryson said in good humor. "But I insist on being consulted before any such plans are made. I've a right to my bid."

Several people chuckled. Alicia took another sip of her wine and tried to laugh with the rest, but her smile was strained and nervous.

"You'll have to bring more to the bargaining table than a farm and half a mill," Carlisle suggested. "These Tildens are damned hard to please when it comes to business."

"Will you be at the church on Sunday afternoon?" Reverend Jody was asking Marguerite, in a separate conversation.

"Of course, I'll be there. Harlan Townsend has been a friend of the family for years. His son's wedding is of personal interest to us."

"Pitiful affair. Lacks decorum, if you understand what I mean."

"I don't think I do," Marguerite responded coolly.

Beatrice Jody snorted. "There's a lot going around about the bride. No one knows her family and she's got that brat hanging on her skirts. Claims she's been married, but who's to know? And young Townsend says he'll adopt the child. But a sailor from up north says the girl supported that child serving in a common tavern."

"I think the fact that Jim Townsend loves the young woman is as far as our concern should go," Marguerite exclaimed.

"Decent marriages don't seem important to our young people anymore," Beatrice went on. "The lad's embarrassed his father and his friends by bringing home a common tramp with a bastard child and trying to pass her off as — "

"I met the young woman at church," Marguerite interrupted emphatically, "and the only thing she can be passed off as is a very kind and lovely young woman."

Beatrice huffed, and picked at the food on her plate. Reverend Jody recognized the disapproval of his largest tithing member. "I'm pleased you'll be there on Sunday."

Those at the other end of the table still talked ships and mills, oblivious to the gossip about the upcoming wedding. "We'll break out some of my private blend and come to a better price on those ships," Wesley was saying.

"If it's your stock, I think the terms will be more pleasing," the captain replied.

Alicia thought the room would close in on her. She was grateful to notice the men standing and excusing themselves. The women would follow shortly.

"Bryson?" Wesley invited.

"Thank you, sir. Yes." And he, too, moved in the direction of the study. Reverend Jody stayed abstemiously with the women, but from the look on his face even Alicia could see the liquor beckoned, and if he could find a good excuse, he would join the men.

"Madam, may I be excused?" Alicia asked.

Marguerite nodded and frowned slightly at her daughter's pallor.

Alicia sat on the veranda and let the cool night air relieve the heat on her cheeks. Her stomach settled and the sound of the men laughing in the study relaxed her somewhat. She had damned those lonely dinners in London when Geoffrey was too busy for her, but she had to admit that the loud and confusing conversations at the Tilden dinner table were almost more difficult to bear.

She was quickly learning the order of things here and it did not differ greatly from in England. Marriage was the topic of concern for any maid over fifteen years of age, virginity was still the second most sought after commodity, closely following the size of the dowry and the best financial arrangement. And women who had not been closely guarded by their parents were assumed to be of a low and suspect class of people. She wondered how Beatrice Jody would feel if she knew that as she criticized the young bride of Jim Townsend for serving in a tavern, she might as well have applied all those unkind words to Alicia.

And if there had ever been any temptation to bare all the truth to her family, it had been removed. Whether or not her parents could sustain the burden, it was certain the community could not. The Tildens would have to accept shame if they accepted her true accounts.

She stood to say proper farewells to Reverend and Mrs. Jody, feeling a little sorry for the preacher. The tightness of his jaw indicated he had not found a way to get to the study to sample the liquors.

As she stood with her mother on the porch, Bryson was the next to appear.

"I have to say my farewells, ladies. My work won't let me lie abed in the morning."

"I'm glad you could join us, Bryson," Marguerite said.

"And thank you, madam, for your superb hospitality." He turned to Alicia and reached for her hand. "I have a great deal to accomplish before Sunday, Alicia, but I think I can leave my work for at least that afternoon. With your permission, I'd like to call on you then."

Alicia quickly took a sidelong glance toward her mother for some answer, but found that she had tactfully moved to the door to leave Alicia and Bryson alone.

"I heard my mother say we are committed to the wedding on Sunday, Bryson," she said, trying to stall.

"It's a small affair. I doubt you would be missed."

"I think I should join my family."

"I could meet you at the church, then. And drive you home. I only like to talk to you."

She pitied him somewhat. He was clearly afraid to make his moves too dramatically because of the vast Tilden protection surrounding her. But she knew her parents approved of Bryson. And the thought had crossed her mind that he would not be too quick to judge her, given the family ties he would acquire if she were to find him to be a favorable groom sometime in the future.

"Very well. I think you may."

His face broke into a grateful grin; a boyish and toothy smile that told her he was ecstatic with her permission. He squeezed her hands tightly.

"Most country girls and especially tavern maids can find ways to better their lot," Geoffrey's voice intruded.

"I'll live for Sunday," Bryson told her.

She laughed lightly. "Bryson, you're a dear, but just a Sunday drive can't possibly mean so much to you."

"I think, Alicia, that it is only the beginning of something more permanent between us. I haven't asked you about your past, you know, but in your eyes I see your need for a man to love and take care of you."

"I think I see the bruise of your last beating," Geoffrey had said with affection. *"Your broken heart."*

Alicia felt herself stiffen at Bryson's words. "Be careful that you don't mistake what you want for what you think you see in my eyes, Bryson. I feel no such need."

"I'm not worried, Alicia. I think in time we'll become closer."

"Perhaps. Until Sunday, Bryson."

"Alicia," he began haltingly. "Alicia — may I — I wouldn't want to offend you again, darling — may I kiss you?"

"Bryson, I — "

"Alicia, if you let yourself, you may come to feel as strongly for me as I feel for you."

260

"Don't deny me, Alicia. Don't deny yourself. Love me."

She sighed and tried to relax her tense shoulders. She let her head drop back slightly to look up at him, and her eyes gently closed. Bryson's arms went around her waist and, taking great care, he pulled her nearer and gently kissed her lips, moving over her mouth with delicacy and caution. And then, ever so gently, he withdrew his lips and kept his face close to hers.

"Alicia," he breathed. "Oh, Alicia . . ."

"Alicia. Alicia . . ."

Without warning, Bryson covered her mouth again and kissed her more fiercely, his lips opening over hers and his tongue attempting to thrust within her mouth. His body pressed hers tightly and she could feel the tensed muscles in his thighs and a growing thickness in his pelvis. She groaned and struggled against him, pushing him away. He released her reluctantly and she could see him struggling to control his emotions.

"I had better reconsider the drive . . ." she began, brushing at her hair.

"Again I must apologize, Alicia. It is most difficult to remember my honorable intent when faced with your beauty. Forgive me."

"I'm not certain I can trust you to remember the next time," she said a little impatiently.

"You have my word," he said with a slight bow. "And should I fail you, you have every right to refuse to see me. But I shall count on Sunday, darling. It means everything to me."

"And I'll count on your honorable intent, Bryson. It means everything to my father." She felt her stomach lurch at her own words. Inwardly she knew she had no right to use Wesley Tilden's leverage on this young man — she was not exactly a virtuous maid. But the Tilden name controlled Bryson better than she could.

He clicked his heels together and lifted her hand to his

lips, placing a respectable kiss on the back of it. And she returned to the chair on the veranda to watch him as he rode away from the house.

For a long while the sounds of the men's voices from the study, and the pots and pans in the kitchen — the distant laughter and clanging — consoled her. She mulled over Bryson's kiss and the way Geoffrey's words flew into her mind at the most inopportune moments, causing her chest to tighten.

A decent and honest young man sought her love, and Geoffrey had spoiled even that. Here was her chance to fulfill her plan and marry well, and nothing inside of her would support that ideal. She had felt a gnawing emptiness when Bryson touched her, and the thought of a lifetime with him did not seem hopeful.

The night was clear and the stars sparkled as her thoughts wandered and she struggled to drive Lord Seavers, pirate, liar, thief, from her mind. But the harder she tried, the more clearly she could see him.

She could see him upon the rocking ship, and as she sank farther into a dream state, the scene changed and she was walking through a cloud toward a garden. The mist cleared and her beloved stood waiting for her, his tall frame exquisitely garbed in tight-fitting breeches and blue satin surcoat. The ruffles at his throat and wrists accentuated the dark tan of his face — the tan he'd earned by strutting half naked on shipboard while he worked.

His arms were outstretched to her, and with a glad cry she was in them, falling with him to the soft earth, feeling the strength of him holding her, loving her, his whispers coming softly into her mind. *"I cannot ever be without you. . . ."*

She sighed, rolling her head from side to side as her lover possessed her in fantasy. She softly moaned as he touched her, tempted her, teased her. And then she was alone. She sat up on the bed of grass and looked around this mystical garden but saw no one. She could hear the sound of guns in the distance, but she could see nothing beyond her cloud-filled garden.

"Geoffrey," she called, her heart wrenched and aching for a sight of him. "Geoffrey."

There was no sea, but he stood on shipboard, his sword strapped to his belt and his hair blowing in the wind. She called to him again and again, but he turned his back on her. "Don't go. Please, there is a child, Geoffrey . . . your child . . . please . . ." But he turned only to wave her off with his hand. And as she watched, she saw his body jolt and blood stain his coat as he slowly began to fall toward her.

Screams threatened to escape her but she only trembled and brought herself quickly back to the reality of the sparkling stars and the cool night air. She was alone on the veranda in Virginia, and he was miles away — possibly dead.

"I hate him," she whispered. "I hate him for what he makes me feel. I cannot drive him out of my mind, no matter how I try. Even in my sleep I —"

"Hate who, darling?" Preston's voice interrupted her.

She turned to notice Preston drawing nearer to her. A look of sympathy and understanding was etched into his features.

"You shouldn't creep up on me, Preston." She impatiently wiped a tear from her cheek.

He knelt beside her chair and touched her hand.

"It sounds as if you must have loved him very much," he soothed. "Very, very much."

She rose and looked down at him. She thought about talking this over with her brother and then simply sighed and went into the house.

Preston took her place in the chair, swirling the liquor

around in his glass. He looked out at the velvet sky and began to whistle a melancholy tune.

Alicia found that her drive with Bryson was exactly the battle she had expected it to be. He stopped his carriage in the countryside, prompted her to walk with him for a while, and proceeded to beg kisses. She feared to consent; she feared not to. Of the gentlemen she had met, Bryson was the most desirable, and, in fact, most of the young ladies turned their heads his way as he passed. His deceased parents had left him a considerable estate and he was well-mannered and handsome.

But his kisses were either bland or overzealous. She knew by the time they finally returned to the Tilden home that she would either have to refuse to see him apart from chaperones, or else consent to marry him. Of course, he had not proposed, but every syllable of his dialogue led her to believe that was all he wanted in the world: to marry her — and the Tildens.

Her parents had returned from the church hours before, and Marguerite was seated on the veranda snapping beans into a pot when Bryson drove her up. He said a few passing words to Lady Tilden, tipped his hat, and was on his way.

"Did you enjoy yourself?" Marguerite asked.

Alicia sighed, unsure. "Yes, madam," she replied, going past her mother into the house.

She was moving listlessly up the stairs when her father called to her. "Alicia. Do you have a moment?"

"Of course," she answered, turning around and walking toward him.

"Come into my study. There's something I'd like to discuss with you."

She followed him and was a little surprised, at a loss, when he closed the study door behind her. He didn't mince words.

"The subject of your marriage has arisen, Alicia."

264

"Why?" she asked quickly.

Wesley laughed a little. "Because of the amount of time you're spending with young Bryson. Is he your choice?"

"I plan to lessen that time. No, he is not."

"Whom do you prefer?" he asked bluntly.

"I prefer things as they are," she insisted, her mouth becoming dry and twitchy.

"I don't want you to feel that just a short time after we've finally got you home we're pushing you out, but you're eighteen and marriage is inevitable."

"Inevitable, perhaps ... but, sir, I haven't had time to consider it at all."

"Bryson is a fine man and would take good care of you."

"I've taken care of myself all these years!" she heard herself nearly shout.

"I regret that you have," he said softly.

"I can manage a few more," she insisted tersely.

"You must bear in mind that people here expect a woman to marry when she's matured, and people will begin to wonder why you delay."

"I don't delay." She felt the sting of tears reach her eyes. "I simply don't love anyone. . . ."

"There's a considerable dowry provided for you. The men in this community have their eyes turned to it."

"Aye," she said, a tear touching her cheek. "I'm waiting for the man who doesn't desire the dowry, but wants *me*."

"Alicia, you are my child and my responsibility, and seeing to your proper marriage is part —"

She blinked her eyes tightly shut and a tear collected on her lashes. She could not drive away her past. And now she would have to disgrace her new family, a thing that caused her incredible pain. And that pain turned to anger toward her father.

"Your responsibility! I have been my own master for eight and ten years! I've made my own decisions and planned my own life! Damn your dowry! How can I even know the man loves me, with your dowry hanging over my head!"

"Alicia!" her father cautioned.

"I *can't* talk of marriage," she sniveled, hot tears coursing down her cheeks. "I *can't*."

"It's a matter of propriety —" he began.

"I'm certain, after hearing Mrs. Jody, that I am *anything* but proper bridal stock!" She rose and walked toward the study door. She turned and faced her father. "Don't you see? It's too late for you to take care of that for me."

She opened the door and began to exit, her father's sharp, commanding words at her back.

"By God, my daughter will be properly wed when I deem the time right and the man honorable."

"I will not!" she shouted.

"Will!" he rejoined.

"You can't," she cried, her tears and her anger equally strong. "You have me home, but I am not your little girl. I've been my only counsel for most of my life. You can't tell me what to do with my life now."

She was moving to the stairs, and her father, angry and red-faced, was close on her heels.

"You will abide by your father's wishes as the other children have or —"

Alicia turned and faced him brazenly. Her cheeks were moist and her eyes blazing. "I respect your wishes in your home where I can, sir, but you cannot make me marry a man I do not love."

"You can learn to love your father's choice for you."

"I will leave this house first," she promised, and turned from him, dashing up the stairs toward her room.

"Letty!" he cried after her.

Alicia felt a pang when she heard him use the shortened version of her name, but she did not pause. She fled from him, from the Tilden dowry and the respectable reputation all the Tildens had. She couldn't face him. And she couldn't dodge her own hurt.

Wesley Tilden's face was pink from the heated exchange. He had managed, he thought, to maintain some control over his children, until this sprite came along. She was headstrong, stubborn, and would not be properly parented. He was at a loss as to what to do with her.

He would have gone back to sulk in his study, but he found his wife staring at him from the open door to the veranda. Her face was grim and set.

"What have you done, Wesley?" she asked.

"I spoke to her about her marriage," he said defensively. "She thinks my opinion hardly worth her time —"

"If you drive my child from her rightful home," Marguerite said very slowly, "I think I shall never forgive you."

Wesley opted for fewer words on the subject. His wife seldom turned a completely rigid expression to him, but this once she was adamant. And with her jaw set so, she looked remarkably like her daughter just had. He grunted. "Damned stubborn women..." And he turned to walk back to his study.

The bell at the river rang several times every day, and usually it was some merchant wishing to discuss the goods that Wesley Tilden and his sons had warehoused for sale or trade. The small Negro children dashed to the dock to see who was arriving, but the women had become accustomed to frequent guests. Only the children were the ones always excited about new arrivals.

Alicia stood in the kitchen with Brianna and some of the staff, snapping beans to be boiled, her hair covered with a kerchief and an apron covering her rounding belly. A small black child tugged at her skirt and she looked down into his bulging white eyes.

"A *sea* captain, mum," he said. She nodded and smiled at him. "And they say he's the *lord*."

Etta cackled gleefully. "Not the Lord, child. He ain't the Lord. He's rich as milord, master, and your master was called Lord Tilden when he was home in England."

Brianna and Alicia exchanged glances and silent chuckles. The perception the Negroes had of visitors from faraway places was sometimes bizarre.

Marguerite's voice drifted happily through the doors and they could hear her delighted laughter. Then she was calling them from the kitchen. "Brianna. Alicia. Come and meet an old friend."

The two looked at each other, smiling at their appearance and shrugging to do her bidding. Alicia was untying her apron as she walked into the foyer of the house and smiled as she noticed that Preston and Wesley had turned out for this visitor.

And then her feet refused to move another step as her eyes found his face.

"Two of my daughters, Lord Seavers," Marguerite was saying. "Brianna, Preston's wife, and Alicia, our very own . . ."

She couldn't move. Her eyes became round and astonished and a certain dizziness seemed to envelope her. As her arm went out in the direction of the wall, she saw him match her astonished look as he moved quickly toward her. He did not have a chance to reach her before she began to swoon, but as a swirling started to overtake her, she was in his firm grasp.

Geoffrey Seavers knelt beside her and held her head off the floor. He lifted her in his arms while Etta bustled through the kitchen doors. "The poor lass has been standin' in that hot kitchen too long, bless her. This country's hot as a red cinder when first ye come; it took me years to stop fainting with the heat. You get that poor lass t'bed."

"Well," Geoffrey said with a shrug, "if you'll show me the way, I already have the situation in hand."

"Let me," Wesley offered.

"I assure you, Lord Tilden, I don't mind at all." He smiled into Alicia's eyes. "It's hardly a burden."

"I'm all right," Alicia protested. "I can manage the stairs."

Etta was out in front of them, working her wide frame up the stairs, chattering her worries as she went. "You be careful how you handle this lass, son. She's mighty precious stock in this house."

Geoffrey made for the stairs as quickly as he could so that no other man would take his burden away from him, though he was followed up the stairs by both Marguerite and Brianna, worried frowns marking their previously happy faces.

"Still light as a feather," he whispered.

Alicia pursed her lips and looked away from his face.

"Perhaps a trifle heavier," he observed under his breath.

Alicia's eyes narrowed and she glared at him, but she could not deny that the feel of his arms holding her off the ground was as delightful as it was unsettling. He set her gently on her bed and stood up to look down at her, his eyes aglow and a smile on his handsome face.

"Do you feel all right?" he asked.

"I feel just fine," she snapped. "Thank you for your services, my lord," she managed with something of a sneer.

Geoffrey found himself moved out of the way as Etta and Marguerite fussed around the bed, Alicia trying to avoid their fluttering hands and insisting she was perfectly all right.

Wesley and Preston were at the doorway of Alicia's room and she could hear their voices. "We don't always welcome our guests in this manner, Geoffrey, but in this household anything can happen."

"I'll admit, sir, that I seldom find a woman in my arms before I've been properly introduced," Seavers laughed.

Properly introduced, indeed, Alicia thought with malice. The nerve of him to come *here*. For what? To taunt her the more? Or had he *now* changed his mind? Well, it would do no good, she would have none of him. He was out of her life, as she was out of his.

"Well, you might want to try some of my brandy, now that you've earned it," Wesley invited Seavers.

"I would indeed, my lord, but if that is what you Virginians consider hard labor, I'll be settling here sooner than I expected."

"And a welcome addition you would be, son," Wesley said, dropping an arm around his shoulders and leading him downstairs.

Alicia fell back into the pillows, fighting the urge to scream. How dare the pirate come here to unsettle her new life! How dare Preston allow it! How dare her family actually *approve* of him! Her heart pounded with fury that he would presume so much.

And in another place in her heart, a place she would not acknowledge, there was a mellow song rising: he had come *here*.

seventeen

*I*t was not in the least unusual for Geoffrey Seavers to be in no hurry to leave the Tildens' fine accommodations; many visiting merchants and sea captains stayed on and on. But the situation put Alicia in dour spirits. Only Preston and she knew the intimate details of how Geoffrey had affected her life. And she could not think objectively when he was about.

In the morning, she waited to descend to the dining room until she suspected breakfast was finished. And her efforts to maintain an attitude of cheerfulness and joy were doubled, for she didn't want to draw any attention whatever to her upset over Geoffrey. She greeted her mother in the kitchen with a kiss on her cheek. "Good morning, madam," she cooed.

"I trust you're well rested by now," said Marguerite, smiling.

"I've become lazy," Alicia said apologetically.

"Rest while you can, dear. I imagine your responsibilities will triple in years to come — as mine have."

"Oh, madam, I could help you more. Please, what would you have me do for you this morning?"

271

"Alicia," her mother sighed. "I don't mean that I need your help. I mean that when you find yourself with as many to care for as I have, your days of lolling abed will be over." She touched Alicia's soft, ivory cheek. "I'm glad that you can be a little lazy. I think you deserve it."

"I'm lazy only because you spoil me."

"Well, I haven't been able to for years. And I won't be able to spoil you for long. You've grown up without me. Now, go sit down and let Etta bring you something to eat."

Alicia happily took her seat in the lonely dining room and waited for the housekeeper to bring her tea and fruit. She smiled brightly at Etta's appearance; the housekeeper kept a grim expression on her face in the best of times, and Alicia had become fond of it.

"Ah, you're better," she observed. "You work in the morning and do a little less in the afternoon. This heat gets better after the crops are brought in."

"It was difficult for you, wasn't it Etta?"

"It's all new, t'be sure. But don't you fret, you're strong and healthy." Etta stuck a chubby finger under Alicia's chin and looked into her eyes. "Aye, you're healthy. You'll be fine, once you get used to it."

"How long have you been here?"

"How long have the Tildens been here?" she countered.

Alicia shrugged. She didn't quite remember when her family first sailed for America.

"I've been here just as long. Lord Tilden bought my papers just about the time his first grandson was due to be born. I barely got a proper meal before someone was havin' a baby. Missus talked mostly 'bout you when she held her first grandchild. Aye, a long time ago."

"But you're not indentured anymore," Alicia remarked. "Why haven't you gone back to England?"

"Lass, there's no more England for me. My family is all gone and this is my family now. No, all I remember of England is Newgate, and I've no need to see that again."

"Etta, was it horrible?" Alicia asked, remembering that her worst fear throughout the ordeal with Geoffrey had been imprisonment.

"Aye, it was grim. A foul nest. And I'd have been dead but for Lord Tilden. They planned to hang me."

"For what?" Alicia heard herself ask.

"God's bones, has no one told you about old Etta? They said I killed my husband!"

Alicia let her mouth drop open as she stared at Etta. She was large and muscular and had a stern, gruff appearance. She looked as though she could have strangled a man her own size. "But you didn't," Alicia insisted.

"Should have," Etta said, shaking out a napkin and placing it on Alicia's lap for her. "He was a worthless old mutt."

"No more horror stories, Etta," Marguerite's voice came. She entered the dining room with a cup of tea in her hand and sat at the table opposite Alicia. Etta mumbled something and went back to the kitchen.

"She didn't," Alicia said to her mother.

Marguerite simply smiled and sighed. "I think Etta could defend herself or someone she loves by killing. But, no, I don't think she did. I truthfully don't care. She's a good woman."

Alicia nodded and began to spoon the berries and cream into her mouth.

"What plans do you have for your day?" Marguerite asked.

"Nothing, madam. I can do whatever you need done."

"I have no chores for you, darling. But if you want the carriage for a drive, I can arrange it. Or is someone coming to call?"

"No one, to my knowledge, madam."

Marguerite's eyes became sad. "Is there a reason why you won't call me Mother?"

"No, madam, I — I'm sorry, Mother. I still feel a bit like a guest here."

"You needn't. This is your home now. We are family."

"Thank you, Mother," she said solicitously.

"I think maybe the troubles with your father are smoothed over for now, Alicia. You were a trifle hard on him. He thinks only of your best interests."

"I know that," she said quietly. "I'm sorry."

"Is Bryson coming to call this week?"

Alicia sighed. "I've been hard on all of you," she said. "I should give Bryson more understanding."

"Not unless he is what you truly want, Alicia. Unlike your father, I do not consider your marriage of the greatest concern right now. But your father —"

"He only wants what's best."

"No, that's not the whole of it, dear. He doesn't understand that there was more to your life than we know about. He doesn't understand that there are things you have to forget about England before you can settle yourself to a new life in Virginia."

Alicia moved the berries to her mouth more slowly. There was indeed a great deal to forget, to undo, before she could consider romances — marriage. She wondered if she ever could.

She smiled at her mother, appreciative of the understanding, and put her spoon down to take a sip from her tea. She drank a little and replaced her cup, stretching her back and sighing.

"When do you expect your child will be born, Alicia?" Marguerite asked.

Alicia's head snapped up in surprise and she stared at her mother with something akin to horror.

"I delivered six of my own children and have watched the grandchildren coming for several years. You *are* with child, aren't you, dear?"

Alicia could not speak, but a tear gathered on her lashes and she simply shrugged at her mother, watching her through blurred vision.

"Do you want to tell me about it?" Marguerite asked.

Alicia dropped her head and looked down. Tell her mother that she was part of a bargain with Lord Seavers to gain a dowry she had no right to? That she'd lain with him, though it was not part of their agreement, and that there was nothing for her now but emptiness and pain?

"You don't have to confide in me, Alicia. It's your affair."

She looked up from her lap. "I've brought disgrace to your household. I can leave you and —"

"No, darling, I am not disgraced. And if you leave me now, my pain would triple what I felt fifteen years ago."

"But, madam, what am I to do?"

"Is there a man you would name responsible?"

Alicia shook her head. "I'm not unaware of the father, madam, but . . ."

"I see. Well there is a dowry and —"

"I'm sure he would be *most* grateful for that," Alicia said bitterly, sniffing back her tears.

"Alicia, I would not allow your marriage to a cruel and selfish man. If you do not love him, then the subject is closed. He won't marry you. But I trust you will remember that love and passion are not always one and the same; willingness to provide for you and protect you can be a man's greatest display of love."

"I *do* believe that, madam. I do."

"Then you will know what to do, Alicia. I have no fear."

But Alicia simply shook her head and let the tears flow. She didn't have the vaguest idea what she should do: confront Seavers and let him inherit *again* through marriage; carry on the courtship with Bryson and let him carry Seavers's debt; or simply bear her own disgrace and birth the child without naming a father.

"Alicia," her mother was saying, "it seems urgent, but it is not." She looked up at her mother. "You are already caught; a little while longer won't matter much."

She nodded piteously, not sure whether offending her family with less than virtuous behavior, or her own dilemma, burdened her the more.

"You needn't make a decision yet."

"But madam, I —"

"You have time, Alicia, and I mean for you to use it. Do nothing until you have thought this over. I can assure you, I am the only one to notice."

Marguerite rose from her seat and moved to Alicia's side of the table, bending to place a kiss on her brow. "I think even you refused to notice until now."

"I had hoped it was not so," Alicia murmured.

"I know, darling. And I promise you, you are not the first maiden to be thusly burdened."

Marguerite left the dining room as quietly as she'd come, leaving behind only her wisdom and understanding. And as Alicia thought about her mother's words, she could not say that she'd been criticized or reprimanded. But no matter how understanding her mother had been, she strongly doubted her father would be as sympathetic. She vowed to let very little time pass before coming to some decision.

And at this point, she preferred a life with Bryson to allowing Geoffrey to stumble upon another rich dowry.

Alicia spent the day in deep thought, coming to no conclusions at all. Etta brought her a cool drink in the afternoon and sat down on the veranda beside her, something Etta almost never did.

"That fancy Lord What's-his-name been askin' after you .lass. He's waitin' to know how yer doin' now and I told him you're a strong woman; no need for him to fret 'n fear."

Alicia did not respond, hoping to discourage the discussion.

"That's one fancy lord, that What's-his-name —"

"Lord Seavers, Etta."

"Aye, Seavers. He's thinkin' about stayin' on a long time, he is. He's got his land here and —"

"His land is *here?*" Alicia said.

"Aye, as he tells it. That boy's thinkin' is mightly like all these Tilden men: he's thinkin' ships 'n' fields and women." Etta laughed at herself. "I think he's mighty interested in you."

Alicia stood up abruptly and brushed at her skirts. "And why should that surprise anyone, Etta? I'm sure one of the first things he heard about was the new Tilden woman with the dowry."

Etta simply cackled. "That dowry talk gettin' in the way of your eyes, lass?"

"No, but it gets in the way of everyone else's!" Alicia huffed, stepping down off the porch and starting to walk at a brisk pace. She moved quickly, cursing under her breath. Seavers only compounded her delicate problems. She turned once to see Etta finish her drink and go back into the house, back to her chores. And Alicia kept walking, trying to clear her head.

The wooded areas around the Tilden house reminded her of the land around the inn, the place she would dodge to, to keep out of sight when Armand thought of additional chores. And now she entered the wooded path to keep from having any more discussions about Seavers, marriage, and other such confusing topics. After she'd passed a little time plucking wildflowers and enjoying the trees, she was ready to face the house again, but as she would have approached it, she spied Geoffrey and Preston just rounding the corner to go inside. They saw her at exactly the same time and stopped to stare at her for a moment.

Alicia tugged her shawl tighter around her shoulders and turned on her heel, heading back toward the river. But too late, for Preston called to her.

I will not turn, she silently vowed, taking longer strides. I will *not.*

She heard his footfalls as he came up behind her, and she also heard that he came alone, a fact that heightened her rage. And then she felt his hand on her arm to halt her, and she turned with a curse on her lips.

"Unhand me, you —"

"You shouldn't be this far from the house alone, darling," Preston said. "Come on, I'll take you back."

"I thought you were —"

"I know." He nodded toward the house and Alicia saw that Geoffrey stood on the veranda talking with Marguerite. "Don't you think you should talk to him?"

"Not if I can avoid it," she muttered.

"He's come to see you, of course," Preston said.

"And why did you *let* him? You knew I wished only to be free of him! Why didn't you tell him to go away?"

Preston grabbed her by the arms and looked down into her eyes. "He is a friend of this family, not just me. And his land is just upriver: land he was granted by the king for his bravery in battle. If he chooses to stay in Virginia, in this house for the next year, he will be made welcome, Alicia."

"And so that bloody pirate and thief can be coddled by this whole family, while his only intention is to make me miserable."

Preston nodded. "Unless, of course, you wish to tell your parents what the scoundrel has done to you."

"Oh, certainly," she snapped, crossing her arms over her chest and turning with a pout.

"I feel certain they'd come to your colors."

"What do you imagine I could have done to him?" she asked tartly. "Could I have him gelded?"

Preston laughed heartily, draped an arm around her shoulders, and started her back toward the house. "More likely Father will insist he marry you. Legitimately, that is."

"Does he mean to make a great deal of trouble for me?" she asked her brother.

"I would guess," Preston said and shrugged.

"Well, what am I to do? I can't *tell* them. And I can't make him leave. And I can't abide being in the same *country* with him!"

"You *could* tell them, if it comes to that."

"But I don't want to! I like it the way it is; my past a private and forgotten affair and the future all left to my will."

"So be it," Preston said, walking.

She stopped suddenly and looked up at him, horror in her eyes. "Preston, *he* won't tell them, will he?"

"I think he is less proud of the entire affair than you are. No, I don't believe he'll tell them." Alicia turned with a sigh of relief and continued back with Preston, deciding she couldn't avoid passing Geoffrey from time to time. "But I tell you true: he's come here to see you."

"Well, now he's seen me, he can go," she said stiffly, walking up the road to the veranda. As she climbed the last step, Geoffrey bowed briefly before her. She nodded and attempted to pass.

"You're looking a good deal better, madam," he said.

"Thank you, sir," she said.

"I'm a little disappointed," he said, unabashed that her own mother was standing right beside him. Alicia looked at him in awe.

"Disappointed?"

"Aye. I had my heart set on being present should you swoon again."

Alicia pursed her lips. "I assure you, my lord, I shan't swoon again. I'll trust my own legs to get me where I'm bound." And with that, she went into the house, her steps quick and sure.

The taverns at the wharves in Virginia were not unlike the ones in London, but perhaps just a little less crowded and a good deal newer and rougher in design. But like the ones in London, they were commonly visited by every sailor in port and every prostitute in the vicinity, and they were good places to gather information about people in the colony.

A tall, handsome, dark-haired man spent the better part of an afternoon in such a tavern, talking to various people, including the proprietor. He was a merchant from England who had booked passage to Virginia to investigate the trade. He called himself Samuel Tyler. And he asked after some of the people who monopolized the shipping trade.

"I've heard a great deal about the Tilden family," he said. "I've been told they have a fleet of merchant ships that now number twenty."

"At least that, friend. At the very least," the innkeeper told him. "They might be the richest folk here, and if not, damn close to it."

"All from shipping, no doubt."

"They own a couple hundred Negroes and run a decent farm as well. And they breed like rabbits; two grandchildren a year at least. Give 'em twenty years and they'll own the coast."

Tyler picked up his ale and pondered the mug. "A good many children, you say?"

"Five. Sons."

Tyler nodded and drank.

"Make that to be six — their daughter's just come home from England. Been there since she was a baby, they say." The innkeeper leaned closer. "They say she was their lost baby, but won't say where she's been since."

Tyler raised a brow and looked at the proprietor. "What difference?"

"There's talk." The innkeeper leaned closer. "The minute she turned up, old Tilden put a big dowry on the lass, like he's trying to cover up for what she's been. Folks around here are decent and God fearin' and don't much like the fuss over this girl, like she's some kind of returned angel. By the looks of her, she's been schooled real good.

Real knowin' around the men, and this is a decent, God fearin' city."

Tyler looked around the tavern. The clientele was average for such a place: bawdy, reckless types, drinking too much, looking for illicit and temporary love, fighting whenever they were moved to. He looked back at the man he shared his conversation with. "Of course it is."

"Argh," the man scoffed. "What a man does in port don't make no difference, but the folks that *live* here hold themselves as decent, God fearin' types. And their children as well."

"Well," Tyler said, "I'm certain the Tildens are grateful to have their daughter home, whatever her circumstances before she was returned to them."

"I'd say so, if they lie for her, treat her like gold, and show her off to the whole of this country. They been havin' parties for the lass, takin' her t'church, lettin' her court —"

"Court?" he asked.

Again the man scowled. "The men around here seem to forget the other women. They want a piece of that Tilden company. I got me a daughter t'get married and I been watchin' her all my life. I *know* she's decent and clean. But the Tildens don't care a hoot for decency. They show her off like she's some queen come callin'. I say it's a dirty shame."

"You do?"

The man studied Tyler closely. "But I won't be sayin' that to any Tilden, you can be sure. And if anyone says I did, I'll swear it's a lie."

Tyler laughed. "They give you a bit of business here, eh?"

"A good bit, an' I'll learn to hold my tongue around strangers for the keepin' of it."

"Not to worry, sir. I won't be passing your gossip along. It's safe with me."

"I thought the Tildens to be good folk; honest and decent. I just can't cotton to lyin' about their dealings.

They're passin' her off fast as they can, an' it ain't honest. No matter to me, what they do, but just the same..."

"Never mind, I know what you mean. But, good sir, you must understand how a man and woman feel when their lost child's come home at last."

"Aye," he acquiesced.

"Then a part of you understands their position, I'm sure."

"I never said the Tildens were a bad bunch, Mr. Tyler. I just said it don't sit well with me that they pass the girl off as decent when they won't say a word about where she's been all these years. They could clean up the gossip, but they don't think they have to, see. Because they're Tildens."

"Certainly, sir," he replied.

But as he sipped at his ale an appreciative smile grew on his lips, for the proprietor had said a great deal more than he even realized. So, Preston Tilden did bring her here as his lost sister, and the family accepted her as readily and faithfully as Charles had accepted her as Charlotte Bellamy. How refreshing he found the news.

Then, he wondered, who *is* the wench, in all truth? He had lain with her when she was a serving wench, danced with her in the king's court, and would see her next as the daughter of a wealthy plantation lord.

England had not been saddened to see him go. His brother, the only family member to have held on to any money and title worth mentioning, would not help him any further. He accused him, as did Seavers, of killing his betrothed for her lack of inheritance. And King Charles had cast off his information in an angry and impatient move. Perry'd been told by every power he hoped would support him to push off and find his fortune some other way than through them.

His resources were low. There was no rich bride available for him to marry; no land grant and bonus for efforts in battle, because he had never fought; no bribes had come, since he had virtually no political power; and there was no trade he knew save courtly etiquette.

I wonder, he thought, how much Lord Tilden values his daughter's life? A thousand pounds? Ten . . . ?

A dinner table that took a year and seven months to finish and could seat thirty people was Wesley Tilden's pride and joy. He'd worked as hard on the table as he had on the house, all in the hours that he was not farming or shipping or sailing one of his own vessels. He still found it hard to lay abed after six in the morning. And he still beamed with joy when his family and guests sat around that table for the evening meal.

It was here that Alicia faced her greatest trials these days. Not only was she self-conscious about her condition, but Bryson continued to be a regular guest, and now Geoffrey Seavers occupied a space at the long table.

She tried to avoid Geoffrey's eyes during the meal, but almost every time she looked up, she found him staring at her. When Wesley Tilden put down his fork for the last time, she sighed with relief. She could finally leave the table.

"Would you like me to walk with you outside, Alicia?" Bryson asked.

"Thank you, Bryson," she replied quietly. "I think not. I feel like being alone."

He shrugged off his disappointment and joined the men in the study. She joined the women, who tended the young, nursing them or tucking them in, while the men sampled Wesley's brews and tobacco, the latter of which Alicia found stank horribly and watered the eyes.

Alicia had no one to tuck in and soon became bored with her needlework. She was too restless to sleep, too anxious to sit, and too confused to talk. She excused herself from the sitting room early, fetched her shawl from her room, and stepped out into the night.

The stars seemed closer to the ground in Virginia. They were brighter. The air was clearer, of that much she was certain. But however clear, cool, fragrant, and jeweled the night, it did nothing to help her understand the complexity of her situation.

"It does refresh," Geoffrey's voice said behind her. She whirled, looked at him, and made to pass him.

"Alicia, don't go. I'll keep following you until you talk to me."

"There is nothing we need to discuss."

He reached into his pocket and withdrew the necklace. She remembered it instantly and felt her heart jump when she saw it again. "You left this behind," he said.

"I didn't feel I had a right to it, sir. It belongs to the Bellamys." She tried again to pass him.

"No, Alicia, I am not ready for you to leave," he said, holding her arm.

"If you force me to scream, I promise you my father will come down hard on you."

"You won't scream, love, just because I touch you."

"Don't be too sure, Geoffrey, I —"

"If you force me to, I will explain my interest in your child."

Alicia stared at him, shocked.

"It's true, isn't it? You carry our child."

Alicia let out an exasperated gasp. That she was one of the last to realize her condition seemed absolutely ridiculous. But nonetheless, her mother and now Geoffrey had apparently guessed the situation.

He chuckled a little. "You're just a tiny bit fuller than when you left me. And your eyes just a bit brighter, I think. I'm willing to stand responsible."

"Why would you do that?" she asked in all sincerity. "Why would you convict yourself of your thievery, your lies . . ."

"Because you are my wife and you carry my child."

"No," she said stiffly. "No, my lord, I am an actress who was paid handsomely to play the part of your wife. And the child I carry may not be yours."

He grabbed her arms and pulled her close, his green eyes angry and his jaw tensed. His hand slid to her belly. "Do you hate me so much that you would slander yourself? Alicia, I have come to make things *right!*"

"Too late," she breathed. "Again, my lord, you have come too late."

"Tell me that what you feel for me has changed," he said, his voice hoarse and quiet.

Tears came to her eyes and she ground her teeth in frustration. She did not want to be hurt or angry. She wanted him to matter so little that she felt nothing when she faced him.

"Has what you feel for me *changed?*" she asked him. "You told me to go where I would; you would see the bargain through and be done. Has that changed?" she asked, stressing every word carefully.

"I could not bear to lose you."

"Truly," she said, a tear coursing its way down her cheek. "Or did you perhaps see yet another dowry waiting for your ardent pursuit?"

"Alicia, no . . ."

"And with another wedding, another dowry, you can perhaps build twenty ships: a fleet that would rival even the Tildens'."

"Your love is all I sailed here to find," he whispered. "Only your love, Alicia." And his mouth came down on hers, overwhelming her with the familiar taste and texture that sent her mind reeling with excitement. A sob escaped when he released her.

"My love, Lord Seavers? I offered you that long ago, but you would not take it."

"I was a fool."

"And is it a coincidence that your love and my family name have come all at the same time?"

"Damn the family, it is you I want!"

"Never! I would never be sure! I will marry someday, Lord Seavers, and perhaps the lucky man will marry my purse, but at least I will be sure what he wants. With you it could always be more lies, more bargains."

"You are mine, Alicia, whether you give credence to that or not. You will not marry another while I have breath in my body."

"You cannot stop me!" she said with bravado.

"I can! And one day soon I will taste that sweet flesh again!"

Her hand came out of nowhere and struck his cheek, a ringing slap that left her palm red and sore and his cheek embarrassingly pink. He grabbed her again, again crushing her to him, his arms pressing her tightly against him as his mouth sought hers, devouring her, tasting her sweet freshness.

And he was above her, looking through her with those green eyes, the eyes she could not forget, the eyes that haunted her every dream, every memory.

"This battle wears on too long, Alicia," he said.

"You know how to fight with fire and swords, Geoffrey. I know how to fight in this kind of war."

"I will not give you up."

"You will have to one day, my lord. I belong to no man."

"You are mine!"

"I am *my own!*"

He released her gently and let her collect herself. She did not let it show that her knees threatened to give way and spill her on the ground.

"Aye, my love, you are your own. But I will not cease until you promise to share your life with me."

"Then you will exhaust yourself, my lord, and become too tired to seek your next fortune."

She turned and walked hastily toward the house, her shoes clicking on the veranda as she crossed to the door. Just inside, she paused to look at her reddened palm and a slow smile crossed her lips. Without further pause she climbed the stairs.

Preston stood just outside the study, from which poured smoke and loud male voices. The next to enter was Geoffrey, his pace somewhat less hurried than Alicia's had been. Preston gave a nod and took a drink from the glass he held.

"Do you have another one of those?" Geoffrey asked.

"Aye, but you'd better take it in your room." Geoffrey's perplexed look caused Preston to laugh softly. "Your cheek, my lord, bears the mark of my sister's hand."

Geoffrey smiled in embarrassment. "If there is as much passion in her yielding, it will have been worth it."

eighteen

*G*eoffrey returned to the garden with his drink. He touched the cheek that Alicia had slapped, but it did not pain him now. And he recounted her words, their argument, giving more credit to what Alicia was made of than he had before.

He knew much of her history — enough at least to draw some conclusions. She had been owned all her life; indentured to this family or that, though there were no papers of sale or indenture. She had to earn her meals in some way or another, whether working in a tavern or playing the part of Lady Seavers. Here had come the first opportunity in her life to be a member of her natural family, and owe only love in return for being fed.

Perhaps she had earned the right to fight him. He had, after all, been one of the many to use her to his own ends. And he had reinforced her fear to trust, with his love words and passion in the night and detachment in the morning light. He had taught her how to mistrust him.

He roamed the grounds of the manor in the darkness of night, musing over a bush, leaning against a tree. The brandy had warmed his heart and cooled his head, and now he held an empty glass. The house was darkened and quiet when he considered it time for him to be asleep. He climbed the stairs to his own room and paused briefly before Alicia's door.

And then he was looking down at her with a light feeling in his chest. Her hair was spread on her pillow, her dark, sooty lashes resting peacefully on her cheek. He had been robbed of the right to look at her loveliness: first by his own stupidity and later because her family protected her from him, not knowing they protected her from her own husband.

He could not resist the urge to reach out and touch the silken skin, and he gently brushed her cheek with his finger. Ah, you are everything I dreamed a woman could be, my Alicia, he thought passionately. Beauty, wit, charm, and devotion. And how you fight! Such pride and fire! And when that stands beside a man, it makes success and good fortune. Only a fool would cast it aside and not appreciate its worth.

You think I've come for another handsome dowry, my love, but you are wrong. I've come to claim you and to keep you safe. I will build you a mansion and slipper your feet in silver. And for that I will work — harder than you've ever seen a man work. I will not need food when you satisfy the hunger that's grown in me with your lips. And I will not need wine, for just to look at you makes me grow dizzy with desire. Alicia, how can you deny that I love you. . . .

As his mind rambled over his words of devotion, she sighed softly and turned, throwing her covers partially off. He smiled to himself as he thought how angry she would be to know that in her sleep she exposed herself to his view, the thin material of her nightdress covering her body inadequately. He imagined her beauty ever increasing as she grew with child.

He reached down gently to cover her and quietly stole out of her room. Sleep is impossible, he thought, when all I have dreamt of for months is to hold her close, feel her resting safely beside me. . . .

When the sun rose, Alicia's eyes opened slowly. She smiled again, at the visions and dreams that had danced through her head all through the night. She sat up and stretched lazily, throwing her legs over the edge of her bed, and her eyes spotted a glass on her dressing table. She frowned as she looked at it and moved to pick it up. She wrinkled her nose at the sharp smell of Wesley's spirits inside the glass.

She didn't have to wonder long at how the thing came to be there; neither Preston nor her father would steal into her room while she slept.

She knew the hour to be long after the men had breakfasted and left for their duties, for the house below her was quiet and still. On her way to breakfast alone, she passed the closed study doors and she could hear Geoffrey's voice from within.

"The letters do not convict him, but call for his return to England under guard, where he will be tried and very likely hanged. It will not fill the need for vengeance in me, but it will serve as best as can be expected at this late date."

"And where do you go?" Preston's voice asked.

"It would not be considered unusual to see me about the wharves, do you think? After all, my ships will put in to port whenever their repairs are complete and a crew can be found. Plague wiped out most of my crew."

"Then you think to find him here? I can't imagine him putting himself within a thousand miles of either of us again."

"The last that was heard was that he booked passage out of England to the Colonies when even his brother would not support him. I intend to find him. Rodney waits near the wharves now, in watch."

"Anything to report on my sister's mood?" Preston asked.

Alicia crept closer, nearly pressing her ear to the door.

"You saw the mark yourself. She does not come gently to heel."

Alicia felt her face burn with anger. To heel! How dare the blackguard!

"Did you tell her what you've done?"

"I told her I've come to make things right, but she will not hear me. She's every right to hate me, but I can't let this drag on too long." He cleared his throat. "There are a dozen good reasons why we must end this trouble between us and settle ourselves to a more stable life — marriage."

"My parents have a handsome dowry set aside for her."

She could hear Geoffrey's laugh from outside the door and she was enraged. She considered bursting through the study doors, but even that would not satisfy her anger. *The idea of my dowry is amusing, eh, Lord Seavers? she thought. I suppose you think it is very nearly yours. Well, we shall see about that!* And she fled from the hall to the dining room.

"The dowry will take care of the heavy fine I am to pay immediately," Geoffrey said with some humor. "When I would have expected the king to have me drawn and quartered, he offered to let me buy off his anger."

"A reasonable conclusion," Preston said. "Especially since your death or imprisonment will not fill his purse."

"Ah, but the truth feels good," Geoffrey said. "All those months that I struggled with the lies wore on me. I could not even see how I loved Alicia, the pain of betrayal stung so deep."

"I wish you had told me from the beginning."

"Lies cause a man to lose faith in everything, my friend. It fairly gnarled up my soul. But that is past and now I've a criminal to catch and a woman to seduce. Wish me well."

"Tread gently, rogue," Preston chuckled. "She may well scar you before you are able to reach her heart."

Rodney Prentiss leased a small and quite inadequate room in the business district near the wharves. He asked around among the sailing men to see if anyone had information regarding Culver Perry, lately known as Lord Perry in England. Nothing turned up. His description fit many: tall, blue-eyed, ruggedly handsome, and most usually dressed in finery. Aside from the clothing, he was every other man on the street: no marks, strange affectations, or mannerisms. An accent fresh from London was not noticeable here; the grand majority of settlers were from England. Rodney had nothing to report when Geoffrey arrived.

"We will continue to look, ask, and make ourselves available to anyone who thinks they might have seen him."

"And the letters?" Rodney asked.

"I've given them to Randolph Hussley, His Majesty's guard, judge, and captain here. They're in safekeeping. And they cannot be stolen from me."

"Can they be bought?" Rodney asked.

"I think not, as the papers relate the incidents to the Tilden family. When I have the chance, I shall thank Alicia from the bottom of my heart for turning out to be a Tilden."

Rodney laughed under his breath. "And is the lady in good keeping?"

"I am only sorry you must stay here, my good man. She's looking good and your old eyes will feel new when you're able to see her again."

"Aye, and how did she receive you?"

Geoffrey immediately rubbed the cheek that had been slapped. "She will fight me every step of the way."

Rodney's ruddy old face broke into a bright smile. It made his heart glad to know the lass had lost none of her determination as she suffered the changes in her life. "Aye, she'll have none of you."

"You needn't be so damned pleased about it. I'll find the way to court her, mark me."

"Aye, you'll court. You'll earn this one or come up empty."

"I fail to remember what I did to you to cause this lack of sympathy you have for me. You love it best when I'm punished."

"Never that, lad. I admit I gain a fair amount of pleasure when the lass will not give in to your every whim, but she does not punish. She only assures you of the worth of what you fight for."

Geoffrey thought for a moment and, with a nod, conceded. Aye, she was worth all he'd been through. But he could not let her test him much further. He had made up his mind: he would let her have it her way for a while, but time was short. There was building and birthing to be done. And always the chance he would be called home to England to stand by his charges.

"Let's get on the streets, man, and see what we can find. I can't stay here long, I've got to talk to a man about a bride."

"No need for you here, lad, if the Tilden home is where you need to be."

"I'll see to this first. I'd rather have something firm to tell Lord Tilden before I return. I'd like to have an idea where that bastard Perry is hiding."

The town produced nothing. Geoffrey found it as impossible to get answers as Rodney had. By the end of the second day, Geoffrey had nearly concluded that Perry had not made it to Virginia after all, but sought some other haven. With Rodney's blessing, he returned to the Tilden manor.

Wesley Tilden could be found in his study, going over the accounts, a complicated mass of figures resulting from harvest and preparations for winter. The Tildens did a good deal less sailing in the colder months, and storage, contracts for spring trading, and buying for the next planting made his days wild where his accounts were concerned. He was usually pleased to see Geoffrey, but this time he did not greet the young man with much warmth.

Geoffrey eyed the rolling pages, ink splotches, and look of frustration on the elder Tilden's face.

"It appears, my lord, that even with five sons you could use an extra hand here."

"It is perhaps because of my sons I need a hand. They produce for me, true, but they produce a business that is impossible to understand."

Geoffrey laughed. "But would you scoff at more ships and another manager, my lord?"

"I have no lordship here, Geoffrey. Relax on your titles a bit. I am a farmer and merchant."

"Your lordship is firmly accepted here, sir. As to my proposal: more goods, more ships, more land . . ."

"If you're looking to buy into the shipping, lad, I gave my promise to your father before he died that if a new life had to be started, our families would unite whenever there was need. I can give you a decent figure."

"I have letters of marque from His Majesty and my ships are available to England for her wars, but I am free to operate my trade as I will. I would gladly align my vessels with yours, but I don't wish to buy into the family. I plan to build here, close enough to your family to be a part of it."

"Sounds to me as if you are looking for adoption, not partnership."

"In a manner, sir. Your daughter." He chose his words carefully. "I think she is the perfect woman to stand at my side as my wife."

Wesley Tilden cleared his throat and moved around to the opposite side of the desk; this was a friendship turned business. He admired and respected young Seavers, but Alicia fought him the harder the more he tried to help her. Something greater than caution possessed him.

"You love her?"

Geoffrey looked down and shuffled his feet, feeling no older than fourteen. "Aye," he said.

"How do you know?" Wesley insisted.

"I know," Geoffrey insisted, not looking up at the older man. "I have loved her for a very long time."

"I wouldn't consider less than a fortnight a very long time, son. Not under the best of circumstances. And from what I may judge, my daughter has not glanced your —"

"Sir, I admit that I was well acquainted with Alicia in London, the details of our — ah — friendship are rather — that is, very hard to explain."

What Geoffrey faced now was certainly an angry scowl.

"If you will try, I'm certain you can do some explaining."

Geoffrey rubbed the back of his neck uncomfortably, then turned and meandered about the small room. "My lord," he attempted, "I — ah, damn, this is difficult. I truly cannot divulge the details, but I can assure you that while I was acquainted with Alicia in London, I treated her with the utmost respect and caution. If you ask Preston to bear this out, he will attest. If you can trust me for a while longer, I must see some personal matters settled before I can confide the intimate details of what I feel for your daughter."

Geoffrey looked at the glowering man's suspicious eyes and flinched slightly.

"My lord, I have, all my life, been truthful with you. I know your wish to protect your daughter is paramount, but I assure you, my intention is the same. I love her. And I believe she loves me, though it is certain she will fight me."

"And why, Lord Seavers, will Alicia fight you?" Wesley asked very slowly.

Geoffrey took a breath, bolstering himself. "Because, my lord, I was not gentle with her feelings. War was calling, my ships were leaving port, and I treated her ill. I was not there when she needed me. It is difficult for her to let me make things right."

Wesley's expression did not soften. However much he admired the lad, he would not see his daughter hurt.

"The Tildens are, all of us, a prideful and stubborn people. Alicia has already proven she is made of the same stuff. You may not be able to change her mind."

Geoffrey straightened himself with determination. "I will change her mind, my lord. I love her." He had learned, today, that saying that aloud felt amazingly good. "Can you accept me as her husband?"

"I will have to have her word on it, that is all I can say."

"It would help considerably if you were in favor of the idea."

Wesley found laughter on his lips. "You would like a sponsor, eh, lad?"

"It wouldn't hurt, my lord.

Wesley could hardly suppress the smirk. He had not foreseen how enjoyable it would be to interview a prospective son-in-law. "And you have ships? Land? A title?" Geoffrey nodded to each question asked. "All debts are settled and there is no trouble with the law?"

Geoffrey felt tension build. "There are a few loose ends, my lord. Minor, I assure you."

"And what are your expectations of dower goods?"

"None, sir. I am interested in Alicia, not her dowry."

"I have a substantial one that I look forward to giving her as her wedding gift, should she desire marriage. How do you feel about that?"

"I have some money and a debt that waits for me in England. If her dowry is even meager, I can pay my debt and build a house for her and will her my land. She will have security all of her days."

"Then she would control her dower purse?"

"Of a certain, without your asking."

"You are a very accommodating groom, Lord Seavers. I wonder what my daughter has done to make you so eager."

"It was during a time when I was never so determined in anything as to keep free of bonds and promises, that Alicia touched my heart. I have been like a man crippled since she left London with no word. Now I've found her, I won't let her slip away again."

Wesley thought for a moment and looked up at Seavers again. "Tread carefully while you are here, Geoffrey. If your presence does my daughter ill, I will have you moved from this house."

"Aye, sir."

"And remember, Seavers, that this once my approval will not help you. If Alicia chooses another husband, my will rests on her choice." He cleared his throat. He was a man too successful in all his endeavors to admit that in this he had no control. He feared Alicia's flight from his family.

"She will not, my lord. As I taught her not to trust me, I can teach her to trust me anew."

Again Wesley frowned. "In deference to my close kinship with your deceased family and your friendship with my son, I will allow this nonsense about the *details* of your friendship with my daughter to remain private — for now. But should I ever learn that you — "

"I swear, my lord, my foolishness in the way I treated Alicia can all be rectified if I am given half a chance to win her heart."

Wesley grunted. "Preston dotes upon the lass. I suppose he wouldn't allow you in this house if you had acted improperly."

Geoffrey felt his pulse quicken and hoped the older gentleman would not notice. He was worried that his truthfulness on the matter of their marriage might only force Wesley to support him — endorse a marriage — but that was not what he wanted. He wanted her to come to him of her own free will. "Aye, sir," he said.

"Remember my warning, Seavers. Take care with your treatment of my daughter."

"I will take the greatest care, sir."

Wesley sat behind his desk again and Geoffrey made a brief, stilted bow and left the room. Just outside the study doors he paused and breathed a sigh of relief. He thought it would be best if he could quickly straighten things out: before Wesley Tilden learned the details of his bargain with his wife and had him horsewhipped.

So, she wants to be courted, he thought. And her father's warning lies over my head at my every word and movement. Alicia, I pray you work out your anger quickly. Before the leaves turn with autumn our dilemma may become... obvious.

On a sunny morning, as Alicia sat on the veranda paring apples so that Etta could make a special pie, Geoffrey approached and bowed. "Madam, I would deem it an honor if you would walk with me for a while this morning."

"Another time, Lord Seavers. I have a busy morning ahead," she said briskly, picking up her pans of apples and peels and entering the house. She went straight to the kitchen.

At dinner that night Geoffrey leaned across the table and addressed Alicia. "Alicia, I beg a private moment of your time. Would you take a ride in the carriage with me in the morning?"

She looked around at the faces, all turned toward her as they waited for her answer. "What is it you wish to discuss with me, Lord Seavers?" she asked coolly.

Geoffrey's jaw tensed. "Alicia," he said quietly, "must I play my court in public?"

"I apologize, Lord Seavers. I did not mean to mislead you. I am not interested in courtship now."

He tried to keep his embarrassment from showing. The other family members began to eat again, except for Wesley, who sat frowning at Alicia. When she looked at him no words needed to be said; she knew he approved of Geoffrey and disapproved of her reluctance toward marriage.

"May I be excused, sir?" she asked.

Wesley Tilden nodded and Alicia left a silent table.

On a rainy evening, when one of the first fires of the fall was built in the sitting room, Geoffrey approached her again. "Alicia, a word, I beg. May I speak to you for a moment?"

"I beg to decline, Lord Seavers. I tire easily these days and was just about to go up to my room."

"I would have you set aside some time for me, Alicia. At your convenience, of course," he said, his voice terse and strained.

Though there was no one else in the sitting room at the moment, Alicia decided against a confrontation. "Perhaps, Lord Seavers. I shall certainly tell you when I have the time. Good night."

She rose and walked slowly to the sitting room doors, her stride even and consciously unhurried, since she knew that as she walked, he was watching her back in near fury. When she closed the sitting room doors behind her, she leaned against them and smiled.

"I don't like what you're doing," Preston said.

She looked up at him in surprise. "Whatever do you mean, Preston?"

"I don't like this game you're playing with Geoffrey. It is dishonest and cruel."

"And did he treat me with honesty and kindness?" she asked in a whisper.

Preston leaned closer. "If it is vengeance you carry, tell me when you think it will be spent so that I can advise the man to humiliate himself no more."

"When I am satisfied that he no longer uses me!" she

snapped, her voice cautiously low and her eyes darting about to make sure no one was around to hear them.

"Will you satisfy yourself by refusing to speak to him? By running from his presence and keeping armies of family about you so that he may not speak his mind? Will your hostility be spent and your heart satisfied before *his* child is born?"

Alicia's eyes blazed. "I see. How many are left that are still unaware of my problem? Has he told the entire family?"

"As far as I know, I am the only person here with whom Geoffrey shares confidences — and he divulged that information only that I might understand the urgency of another problem. One that I seek to help him solve."

Alicia stood tall, her chin lifted indignantly. "He neglected to mention, Preston, that I need only one husband to help me solve my problem, and I think there are other men here attracted enough to my dowry to do me the honor. Lord Seavers is not the only man asking."

"Take care, Alicia. You can buy more with tenderness than you can with hatred."

The sitting room doors opened and Geoffrey stood there looking at them.

"Leave her alone, Preston. Let her have this her way. I will wait."

Alicia looked at him in wonder. Preston slowly withdrew from them and went down the foyer in another direction. For a long moment Alicia stared at Geoffrey, and then, picking up her skirts, fled toward the stairs, tears glistening in her eyes as she went.

"I will wait, love. . . ." Geoffrey said softly.

The sight of Bryson's carriage approaching the house surprised Alicia, but she met him on the porch with a smile of welcome on her lips. She found herself almost wishing that Geoffrey was nearby to see for himself that other attractive men were interested in her, but she had not seen him about the house since morning.

"Bryson, what a pleasant — "

"I imagine I should have sent a request to see you, Alicia, but I feel this is rather urgent. I need to speak to you alone."

"Certainly, Bryson," she said, bewildered by his brusque manner and terse words. It was unlike him to be any less than cautious in how he spoke to her. He was usually deferential and apologetic.

"Can we walk?" he asked.

"I suppose. What troubles you so?"

"It is my own impatience, Alicia, and my desire to protect you."

"Protect me? From what?"

"From anything in life that would injure you. I've asked your father's permission to have you as my wife, and he leaves the matter to your discretion. I don't understand his decision at all."

"I thing perhaps he trusts my judgment," she said, knowing that was not the truth. He was extremely angry with her reluctance to do something to insure her future; she knew Wesley wanted her married and settled.

"That may be, but I think we should be married at once."

"Oh, you do?"

"I do. Before people begin to speak of you unkindly."

"Why would they do that?" she asked. For a moment her greatest fear was that the whole of Virginia was aware of her condition.

"You have long since reached the age when a woman marries, and people wonder at your reluctance. I have made it well known that I desire marriage with you, yet have been unable to gain your acceptance of the idea." He stopped and grabbed her by the arms and turned her to face him. "Alicia, you know I want to marry you."

"Yes, Bryson. I know."

"And now that Seavers chap is living under the same roof with you, and some say you're interested in him."

Alicia thought for a moment. She had been openly impatient with Geoffrey, publicly unkind, and less than decorous. "I don't see how anyone could think that."

"Never mind, I know you're not — "

"You do?" she asked. "How could you know that?"

Bryson sighed, visibly annoyed that his romantic schemes were not unfolding as quickly as he'd hoped. "The point, Alicia, is that so little is known about your past, and your family is so silent on the subject, that people are apt to talk. It is jealousy, I assure you, but the best relief is a quick and suitable marriage, and I am willing to give you that."

How strange, she thought, how many dire things can be cured with marriage. She had a basket of ills that would all disappear by simply repeating the vows of matrimony. "And you are not concerned about my past?" she asked.

"I am prepared to accept you in whatever condition you are in."

"Condition?" she asked, her eyes sparkling. Perhaps the whole of Virginia *did* know about her pregnancy.

"It does not matter to me if you are not a virgin."

"Did it occur to you to ask?"

"No. Ah, it seems unimportant now."

Alicia thought for a moment and her eyes narrowed slightly. "Tell me, Bryson, how will you support me?"

"I have a fine house, Alicia, and the possibility of even greater financial success. You have no need to worry about your future."

"You have an interest in milling, haven't you?"

"Aye, and that project should be among the first things to get underway."

"I imagine my dowry would help immensely."

"I won't have you think your dowry is the most important thing in my consideration. I am very attracted to you."

Alicia sighed audibly. "Yes, I imagine you are."

"You don't believe me?" he asked, stopping their stroll again.

Alicia paused too, looking earnestly into Bryson's face. She suspected he was being honest with her. She thought perhaps he really did love her, but he wouldn't mind the financial boost her dowry would bring, either. No one would. It would aid Bryson's success as it would aid Geoffrey's or any other man's.

"How do you suppose a maid can be assured that the man she chooses to wed truly loves her?" she asked.

"Alicia, I don't intend to take you to a far-off land where you are without the benefits of your family. You have five brothers and a father. Would I ask for your hand in marriage and move you to a house a few miles away, if it were my intention to abuse you?"

"I suppose not . . ." she mused.

"Of course, I wouldn't. And for that matter, what more could I do to convince you that my love for you is . . ."

But Alicia didn't hear the rest. Her mind was elsewhere. Since coming to America, Geoffrey had tried as carefully and at least as loudly to convince her that he loved her. But her anger was so powerful she could not hear him. The hurt she felt at his rejection in England would not abate enough for her to ask herself the most important question: *whom do I love?*

"Bryson," she said suddenly, looking up at him, "kiss me."

He stared at her in shock for a moment, then looked around the yard to see who might be watching. Alicia wrinkled her nose as she noticed his worry over spectators. She had a feeling Geoffrey would be carrying her to the nearest grassy bed, his wanting was so intense.

Satisfied that they were alone, Bryson carefully encircled her waist and pulled her near, his lips moving over hers with delicate intent. She put her hands on his shoulders and pulled him nearer still, but nothing moved in her. There was simply no passion in their kiss. He released her and sighed with absolute pleasure.

Alicia sighed as well, but it was at the difficulty of the task before her. "I'm sorry, Bryson. It is impossible for me to marry you."

"Impossible?" he questioned, aghast.

"Impossible."

He looked completely crushed. "Alicia, you could learn to love me if you — "

And then it came to her as naturally as if it had always been there, the answer simply waiting for the question. "It is impossible, Bryson, because I am already married." And she picked up her skirts and started back in the direction of the house. She smiled as she went. Of course, she was married. She had perhaps been using another name, but the vows had come out of her mouth, her heart. It would need legal attention — perhaps a second ceremony using the proper names — but these were mere details! Somehow it would be corrected.

"Married to whom?" he insisted at her back.

"Lord Seavers."

"But you don't love him!" Bryson blustered.

Alicia stopped suddenly and Bryson nearly trampled her. When he had stopped himself and backed up a space, she looked at him as if he were a complete fool. "But of course I love him, Bryson. He's come all the way to America to find me again."

"Why didn't you tell me?" he demanded, his face twisted into an angry pout that made him look more like a four-year-old than a grown man.

Now that she had blurted it out, she wasn't sure why she'd let so much agony stand between her peace of mind and the truth. "I don't know," she said as she contemplated the question. "I suppose I've been very foolish." She shrugged and smiled. "Well, I'm sorry for you if you're hurt, Bryson. I told you I didn't think you should count on so much from me. Good day." And she was in the house, leaving the badly disappointed and deflated Bryson to gather up his mettle and take himself to find another bride.

She wanted to rush to her mother and father and allay their worries, but she quickly reconsidered. She decided it would be best for everyone if she talked to Geoffrey first and they both delivered the news. Perhaps between the two of them it would not be necessary to tell tales of bargains, treasons, and lies. Perhaps her family would be satisfied to know that she had married, conceived, and, during a bitter falling out, left her husband to seek out her family.

If they love me, she thought, they will allow —

And then a deeper feeling of ease grew in her chest. It did not really matter whether they accepted her story. She loved Geoffrey . . . and her place was with him, raising their child. And that was where she would be.

Alicia waited on the veranda for the men to return from their various duties. Wesley was the first to come home. But at dinner, Preston and Geoffrey were still absent. Throughout the evening she cocked an ear toward the front of the house, hoping to hear them when they returned, but the hour grew late and her spirits sank, for they still did not return.

Her mother was still stitching at her needlework when Alicia smothered a yawn. "You don't usually stay up so late," Marguerite observed.

"I've been waiting — " she started. She sighed. "I've been waiting for Lord Seavers to return. I wanted to speak to him."

Marguerite laughed softly. "Well, you might just as well get some rest: they're spending the night in Hampton, I'm sure. Preston wouldn't venture home if his arrival would be so late."

"Are you sure, madam?"

"Quite sure."

"Why did they go to Hampton today?" she wondered aloud.

"I couldn't say. Some business of Lord Seavers's that had them both very excited when they left. Preston said he didn't know how long it would take."

Alicia sighed again. "Perhaps his ships are finally in port," she said, recalling the conversation she had overheard. And then, she thought, those damn ships come between us more than any other thing.

nineteen

*I*t pays to talk about," Rodney explained to the two young lords who accompanied him. Their shoes clattered on the planks as they set a brisk pace to a tavern Rodney was telling them about. "The keeper isn't sure, but the man he talked with not long ago sounds very much like Culver Perry."

"Does he know where the man stays?" Geoffrey asked.

"Hasn't any idea, lad, but he's asked about the Tilden family. I think that's reason enough to be suspicious."

"Everyone asks about the Tildens," Preston put in. "We own more ships than anyone else. We do more trade than anyone in Virginia. Any visiting merchant would ask about us, as our dinner table proves. There are more guests than family for Etta to serve on some occasions."

Rodney stopped short and Preston halted with him. "But, lad, have you talked to a merchant from England by the name of Samuel Tyler?"

"I have not, but my father may have."

"And what is your father's routine? To speak with them at the wharves and leave them to an inn?"

"No, it is not," Preston acknowledged, taking off at a brisk pace once again. In that, Rodney was definitely right. Wesley would not have left any merchant to ponder their business without offering dinner and perhaps a decent bed. If this man Tyler had asked after the Tildens and did not make contact with any of them, it could be suspicious.

The innkeeper was a bit at odds when the three men burst upon him with no pause for social amenities. They were anxious and full of questions.

"Hold," the man begged. "Why do you look for this man? What's he done?"

"Murder," Geoffrey put in. "Twice. Both times women who had no defense. Now, quickly, tell us what he asked of you."

"He asked about the Tilden family, sir, that's all."

"The number of ships?" Preston asked.

"Aye," the man confirmed. "And the family, the wealth, children born to Lord Tilden."

"And he claimed to be a merchant?"

"Aye."

"From England?"

"Aye."

"What goods does he bring? What does he want to buy?"

The man thought for a moment, his finger picking at his chin. "I guess he never said."

"So we have a merchant to buy and sell, but we know not what. He asks about the Tilden family, but does not make contact for trade. Was there anything about him you remember clearly that sets him apart from any other man?"

"No," the man said. "He seemed a friendly sort. But there was the ring . . ."

"What ring?" Geoffrey asked.

"Wore a handsome ring, he did. A blue stone in the center and a letter, I think. I don't read so I don't know —"

"A signet ring," Geoffrey said to Preston. "And how

many merchants have a crest they wear on their finger? I think we've got him, if we can find him."

"Didn't seem the sort of chap who'd murder a woman. Truth is, he seemed to have a great respect for women. He defended your sister, Mr. Tilden."

All eyes turned back to the innkeeper.

"Defended her? How?"

"Beggin' your pardon, sir, he didn't seem to see anything wrong about her being fussed over, and the dowry and all, when she's been out of the country and her parents' home all these years and all."

Geoffrey turned and looked at Preston, his eyes alive with fire and hatred. He walked past the other two men and out onto the street. There he stopped.

"Well, he thinks he's found her, that's clear," Geoffrey said: "I don't know what he thinks that will get him, but I think if we stay close to Alicia we may find our man."

"Rodney, find the local magistrate and inform him of what's happening. You stay here and keep a close eye out for our friend."

"Preston, we'll return to your father's house immediately, and whether or not Alicia is ready to hear me and consider my protection, she shall have it. I'm going to tell your father today what's taken place over the Bellamy inheritance and how Alicia came to be my wife."

"That should take his supply of good liquor down a quart."

Geoffrey shrugged. "If the king can forgive my transgressions, Wesley Tilden can. And you can thank your friend Prentiss for telling me where Alicia went and who she turned out to be. I only hope Alicia is as civil as the king was. He seemed to understand my plight — enough so to levy a respectable fine against me and legitimate the marriage. But he's none too happy with the corpse that was buried at Bellerose, and has a special distaste for a man who would murder women."

"I suppose if you can corner Alicia just long enough to tell her — "

"Tell her that she has no legal right to choose any husband other than the one the king endorses. She is my legal wife. And she will accept that now. Her play at fighting me will no longer interfere with her safety. The wait is over."

"I'm for getting home," Preston said. "I don't like learning what I've learned and having Alicia there without our protection."

Geoffrey clapped a hand on Preston's shoulder. "She will have me at her side from now on, day and night, whether she likes it or not. The lass has had her way about this long enough."

The afternoon sun grew hotter and the days shorter. Busy black maids polished the Tilden home from top to bottom; the men in the fields loaded bails of tobacco and cotton onto carts to be stored or sold at the end of the harvest.

Marguerite had gone early in the morning to a neighbor's house where a baby was being born. Brianna sat in the sitting room stitching away at monograms on Preston's handkerchiefs, a chore Alicia hoped would never be expected of her, for she was far too restless for stitchery. Etta fluttered through every room, overseeing the maids at work. The men of the family were all either at the wharves, in the fields, or busily watching the warehousing of their goods.

Alicia sat with Brianna for a time, growing tired of that quickly. Then she followed Etta from room to room, but there were no little chores she could do; no vegetables to pare, no dough to knead, and no one to talk to.

She sat on the veranda with a fan, mulling over in her mind what she would say to Geoffrey when he returned. She wanted to fight him, but she wanted to yield. In truth, she wished to be his wife.

There are some things that cannot be changed, she thought. The fact that I love him will never change, and if he can leave behind our problems, so can I. And that this is his child cannot be denied any longer, for the sake of us all.

A rider came up the long drive that led to the main road and the river, and Alicia watched him come closer. Not many traveled by horseback in the spring and summer, but now the river was lower and the barges slower. A small black boy at the edge of the veranda saw the rider and jumped up to do his chore of ringing the bell to announce to the household that company had come.

As he drew in on the house, Alicia began to rise slowly. The brim of his hat partially covered his face, but her worst fears were realized as she recognized Culver Perry.

He tied up his horse and dismounted, taking his hat off and stepping up onto the porch. He bowed briefly before her. "You're looking as beautiful as ever, Alicia," he said suavely, his white teeth gleaming.

Etta was on the porch instantly, like a mother lion protecting her cubs. When the master and mistress were out, this was *her* house. "Sir," she greeted, "who do ye call upon?"

"Samuel Tyler," he said, again bowing briefly before her and smiling very easily. "I've come from England, where it was my pleasure to make the acquaintance of Miss Tilden. I promised her I would visit when I had the opportunity to come to Virginia, and it was much sooner than I dared hope."

Etta looked at Alicia sharply. "Do you know this man, mum?"

Alicia struggled to maintain some sense of calm. She knew Perry's antics well, and it was safe to assume he had come all this way for the purpose of blackmail. If she could pretend to satisfy him until Geoffrey returned, he would know what to do.

"Yes, Etta. He is an old friend."

"Would you have me stay here with you, lass?" Etta asked.

Alicia laughed softly, her attempt at taking the situation lightly not convincing to the old woman at all. "Of course not, Etta. Go about your work."

Etta looked the man over one more time and then huffed back into the house. She stuck her head out and called to the little boy on the edge of the porch. "Boy, come here. I have some chores for you."

The little boy looked perplexed, for ringing the bell was his chore, but he obediently rose and went into the house. Etta grabbed him by the neck and dragged him nearly to the other end of the house, through the hall, dining room, and kitchen to the back door. "Boy, you go and find your master. You tell him to come quickly; tell him there's a mite o' trouble at the house."

"Somebody sick, Etta?"

"Quick, now! And don't dally as ye go, you hear me? Be quick and spare yerself a lashin'."

Etta crept back to the front of the house and stood just inside the door, but she could not make out their conversation, for both spoke quietly.

"What do you want of me now, Lord Perry?" Alicia asked brittlely.

"I'm just the curious sort, madam. You've inched your way into so many inheritances that I wonder who taught you to act?"

"This is my family, sir, in all truth."

Perry laughed loudly. "I imagine it was a simple move for you, what with Tilden hanging about Seavers's ships all day and spending his free time with you. When you heard he was looking for his lost sister, why, you could be she."

Alicia stiffened slightly, but would not defend her legitimacy to him.

"And the great Tilden family knows what you've done, of course. . . ."

"They don't seem to care what my past has been."

"They know that you cheated the king out of an inheritance by lying and pretending to be Charlotte Bellamy."

"They do not ask me."

He looked over the length of her, his eyes glittering with mischief. "It occurred to me long ago that I could use someone like you, but that was before I learned that Seavers still broods over you."

Alicia allowed a small superior smile. "He is here, Lord Perry," she informed him.

Perry was taken aback by the news. In all his questioning, he had not thought to ask after Seavers. He assumed Alicia had been abandoned when her job was done. It was the way he would have handled it. "Here? In the house?"

"Ah — yes," she stumbled.

Perry smirked and raised one brow. "It amazes me, Alicia, how divine you are at lying on the one hand, and perfectly miserable on the other."

"Tell me what you want, Culver," she said, her voice steely.

"Tyler, madam. Samuel Tyler. I, too, have adopted a new identity. So tell me, Alicia, what will you pay me to hold silent on your clever scheme with Seavers?"

She watched him closely and reminded herself to hold him at bay until she could ask Geoffrey what to do about him.

"What do you want? I haven't much money."

Perry laughed loudly. "You have an entire fortune under you! But for now, dear Alicia, I would only request that you walk with me for a time and tell me how you've come to acquire so much."

"I don't want to go with you."

"Now, now, dear, let's do be friends. I can earn my living either way: by keeping your secret from your 'family,' or by keeping their secret from the king. Whichever, when it's out, you'll be in trouble."

Alicia tried to look bored, but within, her heart pounded ferociously. "Your secrets didn't get much attention in London."

"Ah, but that was London! These good people are not soured and jaded with simple gossip. They already wonder loudly at your lack of a husband. The Tildens will be hard pressed to maintain their glory in Virginia once the truth is known about where their daughter's been and what she's been about."

She stared in silence, and slowly it occurred to her that this might be the man Geoffrey was looking for. She struggled to remember a part of the conversation she had overheard in the study. *"The letters do not convict him, but call for his return to England, where he will be tried and very likely hanged. . . ."*

"Charlotte Bellamy," she started, feeling weak. "Where is she now?"

"Died of the plague, poor lass."

"Plague?"

"Aye. I paid handsomely to have her carted away with the other corpses. Our Charlotte went off on a cart of the dead with no name."

"You murdered her!"

"How hardened you've become, Alicia," he said, scanning the area with his eyes. "Come along, I want to move away from the house."

"And Andrea, your betrothed. You killed her as well!"

Her voice had risen considerably, fear growing wild within her, but on the last word, the door to the house opened and Etta stepped onto the porch.

Perry looked between the two women and he took a step closer to Alicia. "Lay one hand to the lass, blackguard, and you'll live to regret it — if you live," Etta threatened.

314

Ignoring the housekeeper, Perry's hand came out and grabbed Alicia around the wrist, pulling her down the steps toward his horse. Etta was close on his trail. She threw herself between them, her large, muscular arms pushing and struggling with Perry, doing all she could to prevent him from holding Alicia. Perry let his fist fly and the old woman went sprawling into the dust.

Alicia took up the fight, her hands flailing wildly at his face and chest. If he thought to grab her around the waist and carry her away on his horse, he was biting off more than he could chew, for her punching hands, his grunts, and her screams made it impossible to grab any part of her.

Alicia fought so desperately that she did not hear the pounding of horses' hooves, and it was not until Perry jerked his head in the direction of the approaching horses that she turned to notice Geoffrey and Preston coming down the road in a cloud of dust.

Perry looked at her in contempt. "Bitch," he growled, flinging her away from him.

He mounted his horse and was trying to ride away from his pursuers, when Wesley Tilden came riding around the corner of the great house, a look of fury etched in his weathered face. His thick white mane rode the wind, and he wielded a huge stick. He had seen Alicia struggle to escape the man on horseback, and needed to know no more.

He brought himself up alongside Perry with ease and struck hard. One devastating thump knocked Perry off his horse and threw him to the ground. His animal escaped, but Perry did not. He lay either unconscious or dead, his face in the dust.

Wesley looked toward the porch and saw Alicia helping Etta to her feet, brushing her off. Neither appeared to be hurt, so he dismounted to examine the man he had just felled. Just as he rolled him over, Geoffrey and Preston arrived and jumped off their horses.

"Who is this bastard?" Wesley demanded.

"You don't recognize him, Father? Culver Perry is his name."

"Perry? Lord Perry?"

"The earl is his brother, this man no longer has lordship. He was betrothed to Andrea, just prior to her death."

"I have papers calling for his imprisonment, sir. If you'll have him tied I'll see him taken away." Geoffrey did not stay a moment longer to discuss or explain the situation, but bolted to where Alicia stood.

"What the hell was he doing with my daughter?" Wesley demanded.

Preston sighed and took off his hat, striking it against his thigh to beat off the dust. "I think he would have taken her and demanded ransom, Father. But I'm not sure if he would have called for money from you or Geoffrey. It's a very long story."

A low moan came from Perry and he rolled his head, leaving a little trail of blood on the dirt. Wesley looked over toward the porch and saw Geoffrey run up to Alicia, grab her by the arms, and talk to her in some rapid, intense fashion, the substance of which he could not hear or guess.

Geoffrey assured himself that Alicia was not hurt, though tears of pure fright coursed down her cheeks.

"It's over, Alicia. You are my wife and will be under my care from now on."

"Geoffrey, he'll tell them everything," she sobbed. "He killed Charlotte, he killed your sister, and before he is through he will —"

"Hush, Alicia, it's *over*. Before I came here I told the king the truth: I rode to Salisbury, where the court had moved from Hampton, to confess and accept punishment. Charles has fined me and given me documents to legitimate our marriage. My marriage to Alicia Tilden."

Her wide eyes watched him carefully as he spoke.

"It is over, Alicia. Culver Perry cannot hurt us and he will be punished in England for his crimes."

"Legitimated our marriage?" she asked quietly.

Geoffrey nodded and smiled. "I couldn't let you go. I couldn't live apart from you another day . . . and that decision was made long before I knew who you actually were."

"But Geoffrey," she said, "you didn't *ask* me."

Geoffrey threw back his head and laughed loudly, sweeping her up in his arms and carrying her up the steps, across the veranda, and into the house.

When Wesley Tilden saw from a considerable distance his daughter being swept away a second time, he left the unconscious Perry where he lay and took long strides in the direction of the house.

"Father," Preston attempted, trying to halt him, but failing.

Wesley stomped on, cursing under his breath and still holding his large stick. When he reached the veranda, he found himself staring into Etta's eyes, her arms folded across her chest and her expression commanding. "If you want to come inside this house, milord, you'll have to come through me."

"What the hell's going on here?" he demanded.

"From what they just said, plenty. And none of it your concern, milord."

Wesley turned and looked at Preston, who wore a look of frustration and confusion himself. All he could do was nod.

"But she won't give him the time of day!" Wesley insisted.

Preston shrugged and gave his father a lame, apologetic smile. "In all actuality, Father, they are married and expecting a child."

He looked at his youngest son with a scowl on his face. "I want the story now, and it better be good!"

Preston laughed a bit uncomfortably, knowing he'd been left to do all the explaining. "It's good, sir. Let's go in the study and get a drink while Etta gets some men to tie and hold Perry."

Brick and timber were stacked on the land that had been given by grant to Geoffrey Seavers, but building in earnest would wait until the warmth of spring. In a house that seemed to expand to accommodate the family faster than ever, Seavers stacked his belongings beside his wife's It pained him not at all to live under another man's roof for now, provided he could enjoy the luxury of holding his wife in his arms again.

When other members of the Tilden family spent their evenings in the study testing Wesley's stock, or in the sitting room with the children, Geoffrey found his pleasure in closing the door to Alicia's room and relishing the comfort of her presence.

"I will build you a house bigger than this," he told her often. "I regret that it will not be ready before the child arrives."

She laughed lightly and encircled his neck with her arms. "For a long time I searched for a way to tell you that a cabin in the wood was all I needed for eternal happiness, if I could only be there with you. Whatever you build, only promise you'll share it with me."

His hand caressed her swelling middle. The child within her grew rapidly. It seemed as though the moment they could lay their troubled past aside, Alicia blossomed with their child. "I had hoped for a son, *chérie*, and now I think perhaps I would favor a daughter: one with your devil's locks and bright eyes. Ah, but she'd be hell to protect from the men!"

She tilted her head to kiss him. "Even when I thought I hated you, Geoffrey, I longed to hold our child in my arms. I confess I was frightened of bearing a child without a hus-

318

band, but in my heart I was glad our love proved fruitful."

"Whether it be a young lord or lady . . ." he soothed.

"And what name shall we choose?" she asked sleepily, basking in the warmth of his arms.

His lips brushed her brow, the question far from his mind. "I love you," he whispered.

"Whatever the name," she said softly, "let's be very certain she needs only one for her lifetime."

"Only one," he promised her.